STRIPPED BARE

Susan Mac Nicol

Though two years past, Matthew Langer is still getting over the death of a loved one. He's steered clear of serious relationships, but when he meets the irascible, dirty mouthed and tempestuous Shane Templar that decision has never been harder. Shane is sexy, warm and funny, and Matthew finds himself trying like hell not to fall for him. Especially when Shane, with his quick wit and hacking skills, is quick to stand up for justice and avenge wrongs. Then Shane strikes at the wrong target, and Matthew realises just how far he's already fallen. At the threat of losing for good yet another man who has broken through his armour, Matthew finds his heart stripped bare. He must face the demons of his soul or a future without love.

STRIPPED BARE

Susan Mac Nicol

www.BOROUGHSPUBLISHINGGROUP.com

STRIPPED BARE

Digital edition created by Maureen Cutajar
www.gopublished.com

ISBN 978-1941260111

Acknowledgments

I have to thank these individuals for their part in bringing this book to fruition—in no particular order of importance, I promise you:

John Trevillian, for his part in being my beta reader and self-professed 'cultural liaison' in the world of the gay man and sense-checking my sex scenes as well as offering invaluable advice on the story.

Gabriele Gandlau, for translating my English phrases to German.

Kindle Alexander, J T Cheyanne and John Trevillian for reading the story and giving me wonderful quotes for the cover and quotes page. Ladies and gentleman, you rock.

Jill Limber for her tireless efforts in editing and guiding me to be a better writer. It was Jill's first foray into the world of the gay male romance and she asked some rather 'intimate' questions in her desire to understand some of the plot. We had a few giggles.

Contents

All Tied Up with Nowhere to Go

Shane Templar watched the man standing by the bed. Shane had no idea how he'd gotten himself into this situation, but he had to admit that this wasn't the first time. He'd thought he was cleverer than he used to be. He went through a mental checklist as he ticked off the items that had led him into the predicament he now faced.

Male ✓
Gay ✓
Intelligent ✓
Streetwise ✓
Pretty smoking hot ✓
Experienced escort ✓
Pushover X

No fucking way.

So, with that all established in his head, he wondered how in hell *he* was the one with his five-ten frame tied spread-eagled to a bed in the middle of a client's very luxurious hotel room in central London while said client, David Debussy, a regular, jerked off in front of him.

Shane's brain felt woolly, and he knew he'd been slipped something. He cursed at his lack of observation and awareness. He never made mistakes like this. *Never.*

Shane had met Debussy, as requested, at the five-star Baglione Hotel in Kensington and escorted the man through an interminably boring dinner for stockbrokers. But while the dinner had made him consider slitting his own throat, the man beside him had made it almost bearable. Shane enjoyed being with David. He'd partnered the man close to half a dozen times over the last year, very much as a companion only.

Not once during the previous "engagements," as Shane's exclusive escort agency, Carrington Knights, called them, had it turned into anything more than a quick kiss goodbye on the lips and a promise of another date soon. Shane had often left his engagements with David with a raging hard-on and had to make his way to the exclusive gay club in the middle of the West End. At Essence, Shane could usually find someone to alleviate his situation.

David was in his mid-twenties, a few years younger than Shane. He was charming, with deep russet hair, a physique like a Greek god, a backside that made Shane's fantasies take free reign, and wealth from a trust fund his mother left him that made Konrad Feldman look like a pauper. He also had a domineering father who tried to rule David with an iron fist.

Debussy was intelligent, attentive, and as sexy as hell.

At the end of this evening, David had suggested Shane join him for a drink in his room. Shane had agreed. He had a firm policy about sleeping with his clients. Contrary to popular belief, he didn't fuck them all. He was choosy about whom he let take him home. He had to like the person, feel comfortable with them, and they had to make him horny. But after the second glass of champagne and a lot of hot and heavy kissing and crotch banging, he remembered nothing more. Until now.

Shane pulled at the cords that bound his wrists and ankles to the posts of a four-poster bed. There was no way he was getting out of the bindings any time soon. His naked body was splayed out on a luxurious Matelasse bed spread. The fierce erection that had sprung up when he and David were making out earlier had flagged.

He groaned, hoping to distract the man sitting on the corner of the bed close to him, frantically stroking his dick and looking as if he was going to let loose at any minute. The man's eyes stared at him with a look of sheer greed, darting from Shane's hairy chest to the blond line of hair that ran down to his groin. Shane thought gloomily that at the moment there wasn't much to see. He blamed it on whatever drug he'd been given.

"Erm, David? Honestly, you didn't have to go all this trouble to jack off. I would have done it for you, you know that. Maybe if you took these ties off me, I could finish the job? Hand or mouth, I don't mind either way. If you want to top, that's fine with me too. I mean, I'm not even that hard either, so maybe we can work on that. Give you something more to look at." He grinned through gritted teeth. There was no way Shane was getting the bastard off but it didn't hurt to let him think that. He was more likely to punch the sly bugger in the nose. He disliked being made a fool of.

David moaned but didn't stop what he was doing. "God, Shane, you are just perfect any way, you know that? You have got the most incredibly sexy body. Not buff but really toned." His plummy accent, which earlier had been very seductive to Shane's ears, was now an irritating high-class whine in Shane's brain. "I'm sorry I had to slip you something and tie you up, but I prefer you that way. "

Shane wondered if David had done this before and what the reaction had been from other men. He planned to make an example of the fact that it wasn't the "done thing" in his book just as soon as David cut him loose.

"I really wanted you tonight, Shane. I liked undressing you while you slept, and then splaying you out like that for me to see." The man shivered in ecstasy and Shane could see he was close to climaxing. "That's what gets me off. I mean, I paid for you, right? So I should get what I want. The customer's always right, correct?"

Who the fuck did this guy think he was, treating him like a piece of meat? He might have paid for the evening, but that didn't give the bastard any right to do this to him.

"I didn't think you'd mind."

The whining increased, adding to the slow burn of fury that ebbed and waned through Shane's chest. He gritted his teeth, needing to talk the other man into letting him go, not blasting him with a tirade of salty swear words Shane had learned from his fisherman grandfather. He had a rather profane mouth as a result.

"David, you look pretty close to eruption, so why don't you let me go and I can help you with that? You like the look of my arse? Well, if you let me up, you can have it. It's all yours."

David moved closer to Shane, still tugging himself madly. David's gasps grew more strident and louder as his body began to jerk uncontrollably. Shane closed his eyes in resignation. It was too late. The hot, wet, acrid-smelling ejaculate shot all over his stomach and groin as David directed it over him and shouted out in release.

Shane was bathed in white spurts of semen that shot across his lower belly like silly string, warming his flesh and leaving sticky snail trails. It wasn't the first time he'd been bathed in the stuff, but it was the first time it had been done without his permission or willing participation. He opened his eyes to see David smiling at him.

"God, Shane, that was incredible," David blabbered, missing Shane's narrowed eyes and complete lack of humour as he bobbed around on the bed like a kid at Christmas. "Let me get those bonds off you. Hold on and I'll untie you."

A distinct sense of relief flooded Shane's body that he wasn't closeted with a psycho about to carve him up or rape him. He knew he'd been lucky tonight and that made him all the more mad. He didn't like taking risks like this one.

Shane watched as the other man fiddled with the ankle restraints, and when he'd freed Shane's legs, David moved up over Shane's body to untie his wrists.

He was oblivious to the stillness of Shane's body and the tensing of his muscles as he waited to be set free.

As soon as he unties that first one, I am going to fucking deck him right across his pretty face and beat the shit out of him.

A sense of satisfaction ran through Shane's body as he planned his revenge. Just as David was about to untie his wrist, a mobile rang. Shane looked over at the antique escritoire where the noise was coming from.

"Untie me first, David. Then you can answer it."

"That's my dad's ring tone," the other man said, a look of abject fear on his face. "I have to answer it now. He wouldn't call if it wasn't important."

He darted off the bed. Shane groaned in exasperation. He was starting to feel cold, the sticky stuff on his stomach was irritating him and he wanted nothing more than a shower and to get home.

David picked up his phone and when he spoke, Shane could hear no trace of the usually confident man he'd been partnered with on and off over the past year.

"Dad? I'm sorry I took so long to answer. What can I do for you?"

Shane shook his head in disbelief. *The phone had only rung twice for God's sake! How quickly was the bugger expected to answer it?*

Shane moved his legs, trying to get the ache out of them after being bound. He desperately needed to pee. He watched in concern as David sank naked to the floor, his face going white, the phone still pressed to his ear.

"Dad, honest, that one isn't my account. It's Lewis'. I really don't know what happened. You can't blame me for this one." His voice faltered and he closed his eyes with a look of complete misery. "I understand," he whispered. "I'm sorry, Dad. I'll be home soon and we can talk about it. I—" He cut his words off, moved the mobile away from his ear, and stared at it.

Shane imagined "Dad" had hung up in his mid-sentence. "David, for God's sake can you let me loose? I really need a piss."

David stood up, stumbled over to the bed and leaned over, his fingers struggling at the ties. His flaccid dick dangled in front of Shane's face and Shane turned his face aside lest he get hit.

Shane's desire to punch David had dissipated at the man's obvious state of distress.

I'll have it out with him later, let him know how I feel.

Finally the restraints were off and Shane sat up, rubbing his wrists and watching David sit trembling on the bed, his naked body goose pimpled as he wrapped his arms around his knees.

Shane sighed. *Christ, I'm not even going to get the satisfaction I deserve at this rate. The man is a bloody mess.*

He stood up, padded butt naked over to the wall-to-wall cupboard and opened the doors. As he'd expected, there were extra blankets and a rather snazzy duvet. He pulled out the duvet, taking it back to the other man. He wrapped it around David's naked shoulders. David looked up at him, his face stark.

"Thank you," he whispered. Shane nodded and made his way to the bathroom, his bladder near to bursting.

After he'd relieved himself he came out to find David still sitting almost comatose on the bed.

Shane looked around for his clothes and found them neatly folded on the tapestry armchair. He got dressed, deciding he'd shower at home. It was no real hardship having drying semen all over. He'd experienced worse.

He moved over to the bed, sitting cross-legged next to David and reached over to flick a lock of stray, sweaty hair back from the man's waxen face so he could see his eyes.

"So," Shane said. "What's the matter? Why has your father put a bug up your arse?"

David's eyes were dark shadows in a pale face. He shrugged. "My dad lost a whole load of money. He blames me."

Shane frowned. "Was it your fault –some stock broking decision you made?"

David shook his head. "No. It wasn't my account. It was my brother, Lewis'."

Shane looked at him, perplexed. "Then how come it's your fault?"

"Because Lewis blamed *me*. He told Dad he was acting on my advice." David fell silent. Shane's teeth ground together as he tried to temper his frustration at being drip-fed morsels of information like a baby bird in a nest.

"And *did* you tell your esteemed brother Lewis what to do?"

David again shook his head. His hands were still twisting at the cover around his shoulders and he closed his eyes and lay down on the bed, his whole attitude one of defeat and resignation.

Despite his earlier ire, Shane's heart went out to the man. He lay down behind him, his one hand trailing through David's hair as he tried to get the full story. Shane thought it was just as well there was a thick duvet between them because the man in front of him was definitely starting to make him horny. The smell of sex still pervaded the air and David's hair smelt of sandalwood. He cleared his throat.

"David. For God's sake, please tell me the full story. I'm dying here. Why does your dad think it was your fault?"

David rolled over to face him. Shane caught his breath at the sight of his amazing hazel eyes filling with tears.

"Because whatever Lewis tells him, he'll believe!" he spat out. "Lewis is straight. He likes women. I'm the fag son so in Dad's eyes; I'll never amount to anything. It's always my fault. Ever since Mum died, he's been worse." Tears trickled down David's tanned cheeks. Shane reached down and brushed them off with his thumb. His earlier irritation had vanished, although he'd make his displeasure known at some stage.

"Christ, David, then just tell him it wasn't you that lost the money. Tell him it was your bloody brother."

The other man shook his head. "Dad will never believe me and Lewis will just cover his arse anyway. He always has." He picked at the coverlet. "Lewis and I have never been the best of brothers. He's too like Dad." He smiled. A twisted grimace marred his handsome features. "It was better when my mother was alive, but now she's gone, I seem to be the odd one out."

"And why are you so scared?" Shane asked. "What will your dad do to you anyway?"

David gazed at Shane, his eyes full of pain. "It doesn't matter," he said. "I need to get up and go home, face the music." He reached one soft hand to Shane's face and kissed his lips.

Shane reached for him, but David pulled away. "As much as I'd like that, I need to get going. I'm going to be late enough as it is."

He rolled away from Shane and got off the bed, letting the duvet drop as he hunted around the bedroom for his clothes. Shane's breath caught at the sight of the man, his taut backside with a slight tan line, his broad shoulders and the firm stomach. Not to mention what he had between his legs. Shane felt a pang of regret. The evening had not turned out the way he'd planned. He watched as David got dressed.

"David, exactly what will happen when you get home?" Shane couldn't let it lie there. The man was terrified of something. He could see it in the trembling of his hands and the set cast of his face. "You're bloody shaking, for God's sake. Will your dad hurt you?"

"Let it go, Shane." David's voice was implacable. "Don't ask me that. I promise you I'll be all right." But his voice didn't sound sure. Shame moved off the bed, walking over to the other man who was now fully dressed and looking around for something.

"Where the hell are my bloody keys?" David muttered. "I know I had them here somewhere."

Shane moved a tray that had the champagne on it, and pulled out the set of Porsche keys lurking underneath.

David smiled. "Thanks, Shane." He picked up his grey jacket, strung it over his shoulder, and walked back to the bed. "I'll be in touch about getting together again. I'm sorry it all went tits up. I'll make it up to you soon, I promise."

He reached out, pulled Shane's head towards his and took his lips in a desperate kiss. Shane leaned in, his hands pulling David toward him, and for a while they kissed, tongues meeting each other's and hands caressing at anything they could find. The fact he'd been roofied and jerked off over was escaping Shane.

Finally, David pulled away, his lips rosy from kissing, his eyes haunted. "I have to go. Bye, Shane."

He turned and walked to the door, leaving Shane with both a raging hard-on and a sick feeling in his stomach. He watched the door close behind the other man and then sank onto the side of the bed, running a hand across his face.

Shit, this had to be one of the worst nights he'd ever had. And he'd had a few. This one was less to do with anything crazy or kinky and more to do with the sense of foreboding that things were about to go very wrong.

Family Trials

Matthew Langer sighed as he pinched the bridge of his nose and leaned back in his chair. He stretched his six foot two frame, raising his arms above his head and yawning. His body was tired, his muscles cramped from sitting reading legal documents all afternoon.

Time to go to bed.

He straightened all the papers on his desk into neat, square piles and smiled. Sam had always said Matthew's tidiness had driven him crazy, as well as his constant need to have everything under control. But they'd managed to compromise. Matthew would ignore the piles of clothing on the floor at the side of Sam's bed each night. Sam would in turn appreciate the fact that the bathroom towels had to be rightly aligned on the rails and would do his best to keep them that way.

Matthew looked at his watch. Ten p.m. The time piece was his pride and joy, an Emporia Armani that Sam had bought Matthew for his twenty-eighth birthday two years ago just weeks before Sam had—no, best not go there.

Matthew had been trying to shut the thoughts out all day. Today would have been Sam's thirty-second birthday. It was the reason he'd been closeted in his study upstairs, ignoring the world outside and throwing himself into the dry tomes of the family affairs of his employer, Walter Debussy.

Matthew switched off the goose head light, plunging the room into darkness. He moved away from his desk, picking up his mobile, and walked out onto the landing, dimly lit by wall sconces.

Thank God the day was nearly over.

He dreaded the eighteenth of August. It was a mix of sweet and sour emotions. The sweet remembrance of Sam's face when he blew out his birthday candles and the feel of his warm mouth when he kissed Matthew a thank you for his present. It was the warmth of his knowing smile and his strong arms when they celebrated his birthday by making love in the ornate four-poster bed in their bedroom. The same bedroom Matthew was headed to now. The sour was the simple fact that Sam was no longer around to enjoy the evening as they used to. He gazed unseeingly out into the quiet Chelsea street below. The neighbourhood was still. No dog walkers or late-night revellers walked past. It was one of the reasons he and Sam had bought the three-bedroom, two-storey brownstone. It was in a cul de sac in a quiet residential neighbourhood, not far from the Fulham Broadway tube station.

His phone rang and he smiled. He knew who it was before he glanced at the caller ID. A look of tenderness crossed his face as he answered it.

"Rach? Hi, big sister. How are things in Tokyo?"

Rachel Langer was a fashion model who travelled all over the world on fashion shoots. Matthew knew she was in Tokyo at the moment for a hectic swimwear shoot.

"Matt? How are you, little brother?" Rachel's slightly Americanised voice echoed down the phone. She spent a lot of time in the States and had a tendency to pick up the accent. She was also the only one in the family to call him Matt, preferring the more American version of his name.

"I'm doing okay, thanks, sweetie." Matthew knew why she was calling. She'd rung him on Sam's birthday for the last two years.

"Bullshit. I bet you buried yourself with work. I know you so well."

"So I was working. You know it takes my mind off things."

Rachel's voice was sympathetic. "I know, Matt. It's a bad day for you. It's why I like to call you before you go to bed and cry yourself to sleep."

Matthew flushed. "Rachel, come on. You don't know that's what happens."

Her sigh was audible. "Oh no? So you don't do that then?"

Matthew scowled at his mobile.

His sister sighed again. "Matt, honey, how's the love life doing?"

Matthew rolled his eyes. This was the question she asked him every time she spoke to him. "How's the love life, have you found a man, are you having regular sex so you don't explode?" He'd cringed the last time his older sister had asked him that question and he hoped like hell she wasn't going to ask him again tonight.

"I'm too busy working for the Debussy family to have a love life. Walter keeps me busy."

Rachel's snort echoed down the line. "That bloody twat?" Rachel might be Americanised but she'd spent enough time in the UK to still use the vernacular. "You're still working for him? Honestly Matthew, surely you can find a job where your boss isn't a prick like that man. I don't know how you stomach him. He always looks down his nose at you because you're gay."

Matthew felt a prickle of annoyance. "You know why Walter and I put up with each other. For me it's a *very* well-paid job, and I work from home so I don't see him all that often. For him, he doesn't have an 'outsider' coming in and prying into his financial affairs. I know everything about his business from working with Dad, so he's comfortable with me. Having a gay lawyer is obviously the lesser of the two evils."

Matthew had been subjected to the occasional snide remark or eye roll when Walter was about, but he was used to that attitude from some people.

Rachel sniffed. "The man is a nasty prat. He treats David like crap."

Matthew sighed. He knew exactly. David was his best friend. "Like I said, I know his business and I do my job well." He huffed, wanting to change the subject. "I'm not a model like you, getting paid shitloads of money to take my clothes off and have men ogle you."

"But you could, sweetie," Rachel said, ignoring the acid tone of his voice. "You know that Klaus would just love to see that fine backside of yours in swimming trunks showing off your package."

Matthew blushed pink. "Christ, Rachel, leave my "package" out of this. And Klaus is nothing but a bloody lecher who's been trying to get into my pants since I was sixteen and of legal age."

Klaus Brandenberg was Rachel's manager, a bisexual man with an innate sense of picking models who were meant to be stars. He'd built Rachel from a willowy and beautiful seventeen-year-old into the sought-after model she was today. He'd had his eye on doing the same to Matthew, but that had not been a path Matthew wanted to follow.

Matthew had given modelling a go once with Klaus, when he was eighteen, just to shut his mother and Rachel up. He hadn't liked it at all. He didn't like being told what to do, pose this way, walk this way, wear this, turn this way, stick that cock of yours out so those men who want to ogle you can see it.

And Klaus had been grabby and had no idea of personal boundaries. Matthew's backside could attest to that, having had Klaus' groin pushed into it at every opportunity the man could find.

His sister giggled. "Klaus is rich, not bad looking, swings both ways and just adores you. You could do worse."

"Hmm. Thanks but no thanks."

Rachel sighed. "I think you made the right choice. Modelling is absolute chaos and everything's spontaneous. You wouldn't last a day in my world. And oh my God, sharing a dressing room with a bunch of other models would take that OCD of yours and make you into a gibbering idiot."

Matthew frowned. "I do not have OCD, Rach. I just like things in their place."

"Uh-huh. You call it what you want, little brother." Her voice softened. "Anyway, I have to go. It's six a.m. here and we're on our way to some mountain or other to do a photo shoot. Matthew, darling, let loose. Find a man and have some fun. I know you loved Sam, sweetie, but it's time to let go."

Matthew kept quiet. Rachel sighed. "Go to bed. Have your cry and think of Sam. Give him a kiss from me."

Matthew's throat choked up. "I will. Night, Rach. Thanks for the call. I love you."

"I love you too, little brother. Sweet dreams."

The phone went dead. Matthew shook off the feelings that threatened to overwhelm him and entered his bedroom. That was another thing. It was no longer "theirs." Now it was just his alone. He'd never get used to that. Before, they'd had plans for a family.

He stripped out of his dark blue jeans and casual tee shirt. He was already barefoot, loving the feel of the cool wooden floors in the house in the mid-summer heat.

Matthew wandered into the en-suite bathroom and performed his nightly routine without variation. He brushed his teeth first and then washed his face. Finally he made his way to the bed, sliding in between the cool cotton sheets. He looked lingeringly over at the empty space beside him, his eyes pricking with tears.

"Happy birthday, Sam, sweetheart," he whispered. His throat clogged up and Matthew celebrated Sam's birthday alone and in tears.

He was dreaming of a dragonfly. He had no bloody idea why but his dream consisted of a very irritating and constant buzz as a large, iridescent green-winged insect flew around his head incessantly. He raised a hand to swat it away but just couldn't seem to shut it up.

"Bugger off, you poxy thing," he muttered. "Leave me alone. I'm trying to sleep."

But the dragonfly didn't listen, and in a sudden temper, he lashed out at the insect. His hand collided with something solid, sending a jolt of pain down his right arm. He opened his eyes in panic, only to realise the dragonfly was his mobile on vibrate and he'd just knocked over the bedside lamp. The lamp had knocked over his tumbler which now lay on its side, dripping water onto the polished wooden floors.

He cursed and sat up, the sheet falling to his waist as he picked up his phone. The time showed 3:00 a.m. His heart sank when he saw who it was. It could only be bad news when his employer Walter Debussy called him at this time of night.

"Walter? Is something wrong?"

"Matty, I need you down at the hospital. Chelsea and West. It's David. He's been hurt and I think I might need some help."

Matthew, worried about David, ignored his annoyance at the man's use of the pet name Sam had used as he swung his legs out of bed.

"What's wrong with David, Walter? Was he in an accident?" he demanded as he pulled on his boxers and a pair of jeans one handed. He couldn't manage his shirt so he switched his mobile to speakerphone and put it down on his bedside table.

Walter's tinny vice reverberated in the quiet of his bedroom. "No, not an accident, Matty. Just get down here, will you, as soon as you can. I'll be in A and E."

"Walter, how badly is he hurt—"

The phone went dead. Matthew cursed again.

This didn't sound good. He might be the Debussy family lawyer, but he had no idea what he would be able to offer Walter down at the hospital. What the hell was going on down there?

His stomach clenched when he thought of David being hurt. He and DD had known each other since Matthew's father had become the family lawyer when they were boys. Matthew finished dressing, gave his short, thick black hair a cursory brush and picked up his car keys. He was fortunate enough to have a parking space in the street, another reason he and Sam had bought this place. It cost him a small fortune, but it was a small price to pay for having the privilege. He locked the door behind him and made his way down to his car, a deep blue Audi A3 cabriolet and his pride and joy. Matthew climbed in and settled himself in the driver's seat. He heaved a great sigh. He wasn't looking forward to whatever was waiting for him at the hospital.

When he arrived at the hospital about fifteen minutes later, Matthew strode into the A and E to see a rotund but elegantly dressed Walter Debussy pacing the floor like a caged tiger. His face brightened when he saw Matthew.

"Matty, good of you to come. Come over here, sit down."

Once again Matthew ignored the diminutive of his name. He felt a prickle of ire at the fact Walter knew that had been Sam's special name for him and now, especially at this particular time of year, it seemed cruel to be calling him by the name his dead husband had affectionately used. Matthew had a feeling in his bones that it was a definite ploy to unsettle him, but now was not the time to be petty.

"How is David, Walter?" Matthew asked as the older man led him over to a quiet, unoccupied corner of the waiting area. "What the hell happened?"

Walter glanced around. Matthew's spidery senses went on high alert. This didn't smell good at all.

"David was hurt during a fight and he suffered a rather nasty head injury." Walter's voice was quiet. He stared directly into Matthew's eyes. There was no guile in them, but Matthew knew instinctively that David's injury had something to do with Walter. It wouldn't be the first time, although David always had an excuse to hand about how his black eye or his bruised chin had been sustained.

"Exactly what kind of fight and with whom, Walter?" Matthew's voice was deceptively quiet.

The older man shrugged. "Someone attacked him just outside the gate to the house while he waited for the gate to open. They pulled him out of the car and beat him. We think someone pushed him and he hit his head against the brick pillar. Roy saw what was happening and called an ambulance. They brought my son here and here we are."

Roy Parsons was Walter's factotum, his shadow, who would do anything for Walter. Matthew despised the man. The feeling was mutual. Roy was one of *the* most homophobic individuals Matthew had ever met. He lived with the Debussy family in a small cottage on the premises. Walter held him in high regard. Matthew had no idea why. Roy was an extremely unlikable man.

"Did Roy recognize David's attacker?"

Debussy gave a shrug of distaste and shook his head. "Probably some queer boyfriend that he got involved with who decided to try and be a man for a change. My son should pick his friends with more care."

Matthew's hackles rose. Walter detested the fact his younger son was gay, as if it were a slur to his fatherhood. David's mother had kept Walter in check, but with her passing, Walter's contempt of his son's lifestyle had gotten worse.

The whole story sounded concocted and far too easy. Matthew had a feeling that it was a complete lie. He stared at Walter. The other man met his eyes with a slight smile. Walter knew it would be hard to disprove. David would never have the guts to speak out against his domineering father. Matthew loved David but he knew his friend's limitations.

"And where was Lewis when all this...action...occurred?" By his tone, Matthew knew Walter would be very aware that he hadn't believed a word he'd said.

"Lewis was in the study upstairs trying to fix a mess David had made and regain control of a lot of money my younger son lost through sheer stupidity. I think David was out with one of his man friends," Walter sneered, his nostrils twitching in disgust. "But when I called and told him to get home, of course, he came."

Matthew nodded. "Did Lewis see this fracas at the gatehouse?"

Walter looked annoyed. "No, Matthew, he didn't. I've told you what happened and of course, Roy will tell you the same thing."

Of course he will. But at least they were back to his full name.

"I still don't know what I'm doing here," he said. "Why do you need me down here other than as support for David?"

Walter waved a hand in exasperation. "I need you to control this situation for me. You're good at all the legal stuff, and if truth be told, a lot of the publicity stuff as well. I don't want this getting all blown out of proportion. I've already seen one nosy reporter lurking around with his fucking camera. I need you to do damage control for me. Keep things under wraps so it doesn't get sensationalised."

The lawyer's blood boiled at the arrogant matter-of-fact manner in which Walter Debussy appeared to expect Matthew to make his self-inflicted troubles go away. But before he could retort, a rather harried-looking doctor appeared at Walter's side.

"Mr. Debussy? Doctor Waite. Your son is resting comfortably. We managed to stop the bleeding from the head injury and put some stitches in. He's got quite a few cuts and bruises and a cracked rib from the beating he took."

Matthew's blood ran cold at the full extent of David's injuries. Walter had nothing on his face but a complete expression of concern for his son. Matthew felt a burning anger that the man could outwardly show such concern yet inside be so uncaring about his son.

" Of course, until he wakes up we won't know if the injury to his head has aftereffects, so we'll just have to wait and see. But if you want to go and see him, I'll show you to his room."

Walter smiled. "Thank you, Dr. Waite. I appreciate everything you've done for my boy." He turned to Matthew.

"Matthew, you wait here while I go to see David. I doubt I'll be too long; then we can discuss things further. Roy should be here any moment to take me home. I'll be no good waiting here with David whilst he's sleeping."

Matthew watched with narrowed eyes as the older man followed the doctor.

He's not sleeping, you tosser, he's bloody unconscious from a blow to the head that I think you or that prick Roy gave him!

He was distracted from his thoughts as he heard a loud noise at the entrance. Matthew watched curiously as a man came flying into the waiting area. The man moved over to the reception desk. The whole waiting room could hear his rambling words, delivered in a voice reminiscent of Richard Armitage, one of Matthew's favourite actors. It went well with his persona. He was dressed in a very expensive and dapper grey business suit and had an air of panache that, despite his concern, seemed to ooze off him like he was born to the good life. He'd obviously been running. He was slightly out of breath and there was the sheen of sweat on his face. His dark blonde hair fell over his forehead in loose swathes.

"You had a friend of mine brought in earlier," the man said. "His name is David Debussy. Is he all right? Can I see him?"

Matthew's next thought was, *God he has a sexy voice,* followed by a certain sense of envy. *From the way he was carrying on, this man is a good friend of David's. David is a very lucky man.*

He could see the receptionist trying to explain to the man that David was in recovery and only family were able to see him. The more she explained, the more the man got agitated.

"You don't understand. I could have fucking stopped him. I knew something was wrong when I couldn't get hold of him. I shouldn't have let him go back home to his fucking father-"

Matthew's ears pricked up at that last sentence even as he winced at the foul language coming out of the younger man's mouth in a public waiting room full of sick people. Matthew wasn't averse to bad language when used in private or in the bedroom, but frowned on it in public. There was just no need to subject everyone else in earshot to profanity.

If Matthew was being employed to do damage control, he'd better bloody do it before this man made any more rather inflammatory statements.

He glided over to the reception window, seeing the young woman's look of relief as he tapped the agitated man on the shoulder. The man turned, and Matthew was pierced by the most incredible blue gaze he'd ever seen. The man's eyes were clear, bright lapis lazuli blue, and at the moment, angry and frustrated. He blinked, seeming taken aback at seeing Matthew standing behind him. A strange expression flitted over his face and then he scowled.

"Yes?" he growled. "I'm having a bloody conversation here; can you wait your turn?"

He turned back to the receptionist and Matthew sighed.

"I'm the Debussy family lawyer. I think I might be able to help you, Mister...?" He raised a quizzical eyebrow at the man who'd now turned back and was watching him suspiciously.

"Templar. Shane Templar." His face tensed. "Lawyer? Are you here to try and clean up after the old bugger then? Shove it all under the fucking carpet?"

Matthew took hold of the man's arm, smiled at the receptionist and pulled Shane over to the corner of the waiting room. The man's muscles tensed under his jacket, and Matthew braced for a possible punch.

"Leave me the fuck alone," Shane hissed, wrenching his arm out of Matthew's hold. "I don't remember agreeing that you could touch me."

"Mr. Templar, if you want any chance of seeing David, then I suggest you get me *on* your side, not alienate me." Matthew's voice was hard and uncompromising. It was the tone he used when he was in full lawyer mode. "David is unconscious but he's being looked after."

At the words, the other man's body relaxed. His eyes closed and Matthew was struck by how long and dark the man's lashes were. Then that blue laser stare was back on Matthew's face.

"What happened to him?"

Matthew crossed both sets of fingers on his hands as unobtrusively as possible. Better toe the party line until he knew what this young man knew about this evening's events.

"He was assaulted by someone as he drove in to his home. He hit his head, and that's why we're all here."

The one thing he hadn't been expecting was the explosive laugh that came from Shane. A very nice mouth in a square jaw,

Matthew noted distractedly. Full, well-shaped lips, white teeth in a mouth currently twisted into a wolfish snarl. He certainly had a *je ne sais quoi* for Matthew.

"Don't fucking give me that bullshit. I know his old man had something to do with it. David was bloody petrified when he left me earlier. And I fucking let him go."

Matthew closed his eyes. "Do you think you could tone down the swearing?" he asked as he opened them again. The other man looked at him in disbelief. "This is a hospital waiting room, there are children here, and I don't think it's doing anyone any good."

Shane looked around, seeing the wide-eyed stares of the few boys and girls. He looked shamefaced.

"I get your point," he said between gritted teeth. "I'll see what I can do. But don't try feed me any more crap." He looked uncomfortable at swearing again and gave a guilty glance at the watching children. "Something was wrong earlier on, and I just knew something bad was going to happen."

"Who called you to let you know?" Matthew asked. "As far as I know it was only family and the Debussy assistant that knew about this. How did you get the news?" He used Roy's formal title loosely as "assistant."

Shane's face became guarded. "I called his mobile and he didn't answer. I wanted to see if he got home okay because when he left me he seemed out of sorts. So I called the house instead, and one of the ladies there told me he'd been taken to hospital." He frowned. "She sounded pretty tense and I thought something really bad had happened. She wouldn't tell me where or why and then put the bloody phone down on me!" His face grew angry. "I knew he'd probably be brought here. It's closest to his home."

"Did David give you the house telephone number then? It's unlisted and they tend to be very careful about who they give it to. David's gotten into trouble before about giving it out to a boyfriend. I would have thought he'd be more careful about doing it again." Matthew watched Shane's face. He had a feeling once again he wasn't being told the truth.

What the hell was wrong with everyone tonight? Was it national Liar's Day or something?

"Why does it matter whether he did or didn't?" the other man expostulated. "What's with all the fu—questions? Jesus, I feel like I'm being interrogated by the Gestapo! And I'm not his boyfriend." He ran a hand through his wavy hair and Matthew watched, mesmerised at the action. He was uncomfortably aware that he was finding this man very attractive indeed. He cleared his throat.

"Let's move into one of those empty visitor rooms over there. We can talk more privately there without wondering whether you're going to let something loose."

He strode over to the small room, hoping that Shane would follow. He entered the room and stood looking out into the darkness beyond. Seconds later he heard Shane come in. Matthew spun around. The man stood, leaning against the door, his slim frame outlined against the light of the A and E waiting room. Matthew could appreciate him more now. His broad shoulders filled his suit to perfection, tapering down to lean hips and long legs. He looked wiry and lean. Matthew could see the faint glint of golden chest hair at the opening to his shirt.

The lawyer's stomach lurched, and the turmoil in his groin was growing. He cleared his throat. "Can you tell me what you and David were doing earlier to make you think he was upset or in danger?"

Shane's suddenly sly smile and lascivious look caught him off guard.

"What we were doing? He had me tied down to a bed and was jerking off over me." His taunting words went straight to

Matthew's groin, the images being conjured up enough to make his cock strain against the front of his trousers. He had a feeling it was exactly what the other man was trying to do.

Shane glanced down at Matthew's groin and grinned. "Well, well, look at that," he said. "And here was me thinking you were so self-contained and controlled, Mr. Lawyer Man. Being so officious and all." He moved closer and Matthew could smell the definite scent of some oriental fragrance mixed in with what was definitely sex. The man reeked of it. Matthew's nostrils flared.

"Unfortunately, I didn't get a chance to shower afterward, as David was upset and I was trying to calm him down. Then I got distracted." Shane's eyes watched Matthew's throat as he swallowed. "So I think I might smell rather rank." His fingers lightly brushed Matthew's hand, and it was as if a live cattle prod had suddenly been shoved at him.

Matthew growled and moved away. "Thank you for sharing that with me. Yes, I'm gay too. So now we've joined the ranks of the exalted brotherhood together, can we get back to this all being about David?"

The two men glared at each other for a moment and then Matthew heard the voice of Walter Debussy at the door.

"Matthew? You look as if you're squaring up in a bloody cock fighting ring, man. Stand down before I have to get the hose out for you two." His words sounded jovial but Matthew knew Walter well enough to hear the nastiness behind them. His words had been well chosen. "Who is this man anyway?" He moved into the room.

His dark eyes assessed Shane and found him wanting as he turned to the man standing behind him. Roy Parsons was ex-military, about five foot five, powerfully built with a wiry strength that belied his size. His brown eyes were focused on Matthew and Shane with a look of sheer disgust on his face. Matthew hadn't seen him arrive, but then he'd been busy trying to control the rogue Shane.

"Roy, if this man is one of my fag son's filthy lovers, find out what the hell he wants and sort it. Then meet me outside. I'm going for a smoke. Don't be long."

He turned back to Matthew. "Matthew, call me later so we can talk about how to handle all this. The police have already got wind of the whole thing. How, I don't bloody know. Bastards. No doubt we'll have to sort out the story. Better still, come over for lunch about twelve. That should give you enough time to have a cold shower and get your head around what we need to do."

"No." Matthew's quiet word caused all three men to look at him in surprise. Shane's eyes narrowed.

"What do you mean, 'no?' You're my lawyer. You'll do as you're told." Walter's tone would brook no argument, and he turned to leave.

Matthew shook his head. "I won't be helping you do anything on this, Walter. I want no part of whatever it is you and Roy are trying to keep a lid on. Your son is lying in there in a hospital bed, after having been beaten, with a head injury that may affect him when he wakes up. I'm not happy with the story you told me. I'm not going to be party to anything you want to tell the world. You and Roy are on your own."

Walter's face was puce, his jaw set and his dark eyes narrowed. "Matthew, I pay your bloody salary and keep you in that bloody silly car you like so much and that house you have. Of course you'll do what I want."

"No, I bloody won't." Matthew's voice grew heated but he knew he needed to keep his temper in check in the hospital. He was also aware just how precarious his job situation was becoming in defying Walter this way. He felt sick, but he had his principles, and there was no bloody way he was giving them up on this issue.

"You don't need me. I'm sure you have enough people in your legal team to help you cover this up. What I'm saying is that I won't be one of them."

Fists clenched, Matthew saw Shane looking at him with a glimmer of respect on his face. Walter took a slight step toward Matthew and the lawyer saw Shane do the same, almost putting himself in between him and the approaching man.

It seemed he had a protector. Matthew felt warmth at the thought.

"I don't need a bloody lawyer that won't do what I tell them to, Matthew. Have you considered that option, you stupid man? And tell this cocky little sod to get out of my way. Christ, it's like a bloody plague. You're everywhere." Walter's voice was a snarl. Matthew's hands unclenched even as he realised with a pang that he was now probably going to be jobless.

"What do you mean by that, Walter? Could you be talking about *homosexuals*?" Matthew's voice was tight as he emphasized the word. "I always knew you were a homophobic bastard but I'd never appreciated just how much until tonight. You really have a bug up your arse about us, don't you?"

Roy growled and moved across the room like a panther. "Rather apt choice of words, Matthew. We're not the ones who have things up our arses."

Matthew went still at Roy's contemptuous tone, his slow temper rising. Shane stepped forward, his face white as he squared up to Roy.

"You're a fucking nasty piece of work, aren't you?" the blond man spat at Roy. Roy smiled.

"I'd be careful if I were you, little cocksucker," Roy drawled to Shane. "One wrong move and I'll break your fucking arm." He waved a languid hand. Matthew could see the streaks of blood across his knuckles and took a deep breath. It looked like Roy might have done Walter's dirty work for him.

But this was going nowhere fast.

Matthew suspected Roy didn't make idle threats. "Roy, there'll be no need for that. Shane is a friend of David's and he was worried about him, so he called the house. That's all. I think we should all take a step back and look at things."

He was about to give up the best job he'd ever had. God only knew what he'd do next.

"Walter, I'm sorry. You've given me no choice. I quit. Find yourself another lawyer. I cannot continue working for you. To be honest, I don't know why you've put up with me for so long." He heard the bitterness in his voice and the lump in his throat.

The dislike on Walter's face tore right through to Matthew's heart. He might not have liked Walter all that much, but he'd thought they'd had a better relationship that what was now unfolding.

"You bloody well know why, Matthew. Your father made sure of that."

Matthew was puzzled about Walter's words. "What are you talking about? What should I know? How was my father involved in this?"

Walter shook his head and sneered, but oddly his eyes gleamed with a sudden relief. Roy chuckled, his predatory gaze on Shane, who was standing looking ready to pounce like a cat on an unsuspecting bird–the bird being Roy. The dislike between the two men was palpable.

"Don't play the bloody innocent with me. You know exactly why I've put up with you over the past three years since your father died."

"Put up with me?" Matthew's voice rose. "I've worked my backside off for you, Walter. Believe me, I've earned every bloody penny you've ever paid me. But I draw the line at cover-ups where I believe you, or more likely, this piece of shit from the look of his hand." He gestured to Roy. "Beat your own son senseless and then expect me to help you protect yourself. And I've no bloody idea what the hell you're talking about as far as the thing with my dad is concerned." His voice broke.

He hated the emotions building up inside. He wasn't good with emotion.

Walter was looking at him knowingly. "You really don't know about it, do you?" he said, almost to himself. "All these bloody years and I was worried about nothing." His voice was almost wondrous, his face relieved. He turned to face Shane. "How in the hell did you know David was down here anyway? Who told you? And how did you get my home number?" His face turned rosy with anger.

Matthew noted he didn't contradict his accusation about letting Roy beat his son.

Shane regarded Walter, a sneer on his face. "There's this fag club I go to in the city. I was in one of the toilets the other day and lo and behold on the back of the door was your name and number. It said you sucked dick really well, so I wrote it down in case I needed it. But now I've met you there's no way you're going anywhere near my dick." He shot out a quick, hungry grin. "But I bet he'd like you to blow him." He motioned at Roy.

The other man went white, his eyes murderous, and he regarded Shane with a deadly gaze. Matthew closed his eyes in dread at Shane's snark, even as he wanted to snigger out loud at the man's quick wit. Undoubtedly he just made things worse.

Roy stepped forward, his face full of hate, his hands balling into fists that had already done violence that night.

Shane inched closer to Roy in defiance and Matthew could sense the suppressed violence in the man.

Much as Matthew would like to do the same thing, this was neither the time nor the place. Walter's face was thunderous, his lips white, and he was probably a minute away from punching Shane himself.

Matthew moved forward swiftly and pulled Shane to one side, stepping in front of him as he faced his soon-to-be ex-employer. "Walter, this is a hospital. We don't need another beating victim. That would shoot your little story all to hell. Just leave it alone."

Walter glared at him, but his face said he knew. He couldn't afford a scene if he wanted to play out his own version of the truth.

"Luckily I'm a gentleman," he blustered. "So I'll let that comment pass me by. I also don't want to soil my hands with your blood. God knows what I could catch. But you are a little shit, aren't you, pretty boy." He was looking at Shane with utter dislike.

Shane growled beside him. "You're just a damned bully, Debussy," he snarled. "David was petrified earlier to go home. Now I know why, you bastard."

Roy moved forward toward Shane, his hands balled into fists. He hocked up a wad of phlegm and spat it on Shane's shoes.

Shane's face whitened and Matthew grabbed his arm. It took all Matthew's strength to hold him back. "Leave it, Shane. He's not worth it."

Roy smiled like a shark. "Your little pretty toy-boy fuck, is he, Matthew? You want to watch him. He's a real little slag."

Matthew wanted nothing more than to punch the smirk off Roy's face himself, but that wouldn't help the situation. He was still struggling to hold Shane back, the violence in the man's body simply oozing the promise of the pleasure of pain to Walter's factotum.

Walter shook his head, looking amused by all the male testosterone in the air. "Just because you've both had your cock up my son's arse doesn't mean you know him or me. David deserves everything he gets. He's nothing but a bloody disappointment and a deviant. If I could cut off his trust fund I would." He scowled at Matthew. "But your bloody father made sure I couldn't do that easily, didn't he, not without a very good reason or me getting into trouble with the law. He had it all sewn up tight like a virgin's pussy. But everything can be broken with the right motivation." He smirked. "I have a couple of aces up my sleeve, and I think I might just play them soon."

The terms and conditions of David's specific trust fund from his mother were tightly controlled. Matthew had wondered about it when he'd taken it over after his father died. Now he knew why. His father had been trying to protect David's inheritance from his father's homophobic hatred. But what the hell else was going on with Matthew's dad and Walter's seeming hold on Matthew was a mystery.

"And my son will never tell. He's still a Debussy. His first loyalty is to me and the family."

This much Matthew knew to be true. A sense of despair washed over his body.

Walter waved an airy hand. "Fine, Matthew. Go out and find yourself another job if you can. I release you of your duties. Roy will be in touch about what needs handing over. I'll get a final salary cheque paid into your account. Then we can call it quits. I can find myself a real heterosexual lawyer. And Roy, we'll need another maid or housekeeper, too. When you get home, check the telephone recording system and find out who spilled the beans to the little fairy here about my son. They obviously disregarded all the warnings we gave them to tell no one anything about it."

Shane drew a deep breath, no doubt realising he'd just gotten someone fired. Matthew closed his eyes at the gloating tone of Walter's voice. Walter had just managed to make him feel almost dirty about his sexuality, a feeling he hadn't felt in many years. A warm, strong hand laid itself on his arm. Shane stood beside him, his eyes sympathetic.

"Matthew, come on. Let's get out of here. This bastard doesn't deserve any more of our time, and David is in good hands here in the hospital. We can figure out what to do about all this later." He reached up a hand and caressed Matthew's hair. "It's late and you look exhausted. Let's go. Come on." He ignored the look of revulsion the other two men gave them as he took Matthew's hand. Matthew followed him, unresisting, out of the waiting room into the cool and still-busy waiting room.

Getting to know you…maybe

Shane tugged Matthew outside onto the wide concrete steps of the hospital. The air was warm, almost balmy, and the street was busy but not crowded. He glanced at Matthew anxiously. The other man had started off all confident and feisty, but Walter Debussy's harsh words had left their mark on him.

When Shane had turned and looked up into Matthew's incredible deep grey eyes as he stood behind him at the reception desk, he'd lost his breath. Matthew was unconventionally a beautiful man, a few inches taller than Shane. He also had an air of authority and composure that really appealed to him. All of these emotions had surged through his body the minute he'd seen the man. He'd been trying not to let his tongue hang out ever since.

As they stood on the pavement, Shane looked at his watch. It was close to 5 a.m.

He looked at the man now standing beside him. "Matthew? Are you all right? You were really impressive back there, telling that tosser where to get off. I'm glad you did that. I thought you might be inclined to protect that sod, seeing as he's your boss."

Matthew gazed at him. "*Was* my boss." He laughed harshly. "My friend's in hospital, I've just lost my job and I found out that my employer is even more of a rabid gay hater that even I thought. Other than that, I suppose I'm doing okay."

Shane could hear the hurt in the words. He reached out and touched Matthew's face. He wasn't normally that forward with touching strangers but something about this man just brought out the protector in him.

The man flinched. Shane drew back, hoping he hadn't overstepped the mark. "How does a man with your sexual proclivities get to work for a slimy homophobe like Debussy?" he asked.

"I took over from my dad when he died," Matthew said. "It seemed to work for both of us until now. He's never been that obvious about it before."

"I don't know how you could have worked for that bastard," Shane said, his hands waving in agitation. "And that other bloke is a complete arsehole."

Matthew frowned. "I don't disagree on Roy. But beggars can't be choosers. It was a good job. Walter left me alone as long as I did what he needed to sort out his trust funds and financial affairs. We managed to tolerate each other."

Shane nodded. "Sounds like a match made in heaven." He ignored Matthew's scowl. "Do you have a car nearby to get you home?"

Matthew nodded. "Yes, it's in the hospital car park. I suppose I should get home and get some sleep. I'll need to start looking for another job later today, I suppose." He stared unseeingly out across the car park then turned to look at Shane. "How about you? Do you need a lift home? How did you get here anyway? It looked like you'd been running when you came in."

Shane nodded. "I had. I heard the news and the tubes had stopped running. There were no taxis, so I legged it from the Baglione. It's no big deal. I've run longer distances." He'd grimaced as he remembered he'd left his treasured laptop, called Bushwhacker, back in the safe. He'd have to go back and fetch him.

"Were you at the hotel with David?" Matthew asked. "I know he was staying there tonight. I thought you said he wasn't your boyfriend."

Shane looked at Matthew. "I'm not. I was his escort for the evening."

"I see." In those words, Shane thought he sensed judgement and he scowled, his back up.

"I'm not a fucking prostitute. I'm an escort. I don't sleep with all my clients, only if I choose too. So don't take that tone with me."

Matthew looked taken aback by his sudden vitriolic outburst. "Jesus, Shane, don't have a hissy fit. I'm sorry if I sounded off, I wasn't judging you. It's just been a rough morning, that's all. I'm bloody tired." He shifted and rubbed the back of his neck. "You don't have to explain yourself."

Shane felt guilty. "Sorry. I suppose I misread you. I get fed up when people think I do nothing more than shove my arse in the air for anyone." He grinned. "I suppose I should explain my earlier comment about David jacking off all over me then? In case you get the wrong idea?"

He saw Matthew's wince and chuckled. "He's a bit of a kinky bastard it turns out. He likes to roofie his dates. Then he likes to tie them up on the bed and jerk off. It started out fairly promisingly. I'd already decided I wouldn't mind fucking him, but then he slipped me something and the next thing I knew I was covered in come."

"Hell, Shane, don't mince your words, will you?" Matthew's mouth twisted in both amusement and possibly distaste. "Thanks for that very graphic picture in my mind. I had no idea David was that way inclined. And I've known him since we were teenagers." He frowned. "You have a real potty mouth, don't you? Does swearing come naturally to you or is something you've cultivated?"

Shane felt nonplussed. A prejudice against swearing seemed to be a thing with this man.

"My grandfather was a fisherman," he muttered sulkily. "I used to go out on the boats with him and he swore like a trooper. I suppose it's a habit I've picked up on."

"Not a good one either. I've never quite understood why people feel the need to use profanity for everything. There are times and places for it." Matthew's tone was wry.

Shane felt as if he'd just been told off by his teacher. He looked at Matthew in disbelief. "Christ, you sound like my father might—if he were still around. You're only, what, early thirties?"

"Thirty," said Matthew. "I obviously look older than I am."

Shane was embarrassed. "Hey, I didn't mean you looked older. You just seem it. I think it's that whole 'control freak' thing you have going on. I think you look just great anyway." He grinned, feeling mischievous. "And that broken nose is very sexy. So is the whole designer stubble thing you have going on around your chin. Makes you look manly and rugged."

Matthew raised an eyebrow, a gesture Shane found very sexy. His trousers felt tight all of a sudden.

"Control freak? Is that what you see when you look at me?" Matthew asked. Shane noticed he'd sidestepped the comments about his appearance.

Shane smiled slightly. "That and a really hot body. And I love your accent. It's different." His attempt at flirting seemed to pay off as Matthew's face flushed even under the olive complexion of his skin. He ran a hand through his think, dark sable-coloured hair and Shane watched, mesmerised.

"I think this conversation just ended." Matthew reached into his trouser pocket and took out a bunch of keys. "I need to go home, get some sleep. Can I drop you off, save you running anywhere?"

Shane nodded. "You can swing by the Baglione so I can pick up Bushwhacker. Then I'll catch some shut-eye there—seeing as David paid for the room already—and then go home later today."

"Bushwhacker?" Matthew looked perplexed. "Is that a dog?"

Shane grinned. "My trusty laptop. It's a tool of my trade as an IT security consultant." He used the term people were used to, not wanting to explain right now that he was actually a very qualified and notorious hacker. It was also how he'd managed to track down David's home number. "I don't go anywhere without him."

"Him? Your bloody laptop has a gender *and* a name?" Matthew sounded flabbergasted.

Shane chuckled. "Careful, Matthew, language, mate. You've given *me* the lecture, best get your own house in order." He winked at the other man. "By the way, you know my full name but I'm damned if I know yours. What is it?"

"Matthew Langer."

Shane looked at him. "Is that a German surname? That must be the accent I can hear in your voice."

The lawyer nodded. "Yes it is. I was born in Dresden, and I spend a lot of time there."

Shane cocked an eyebrow at Matthew. "The English version would be 'Longer' if I remember my school German at all. Does that apply to anything else other than your surname, Mr. Langer?" He was getting a second wind despite the time and the fact he hadn't slept. Matthew sighed and shook his head, moving out across to the parking lot. But Shane got the distinct impression he didn't mind the flirting. He followed the man, taking time to admire his firm backside as he walked. *The man is definitely a bit of an enigma*, he thought. *One I wouldn't mind getting to know better.*

In the car Shane buckled up and sat back for the short ride to his hotel. He gazed around the car. It was immaculate, looking in almost showroom condition. Matthew started the engine and drove off. His hands were large, with long fingers and well-groomed nails. For the first time Shane noticed the thin gold band around his left ring finger. His heart lurched.

So the man was in a committed relationship. That was something he hadn't considered.

"This car of yours looks as if it doesn't get out much," he remarked as he fiddled with the knobs and fixtures in the car. Matthew glanced at him.

"I don't have the need to use it often, other than the occasional trip. Most of business has been in and round London. But I like having the option to have my own wheels."

He changed gears expertly as he navigated the traffic. The roads were quiet since it was still so early. Rush hour hadn't yet begun. "Do you have a car, Shane?"

Shane laughed. "God, no. I find the three T's do me just fine: tube, train, and taxi. I live in St. James's so I'm pretty central anyway. Where do you live?"

"I have a house in Chelsea." Shane noticed Matthew gave nothing more away than what he was asked. He'd have to fish deeper, in a direct way—the only way he knew how.

"How does your husband feel about you being called out at all hours of the night to deal with that bastard Debussy?" He watched Matthew's face. He wasn't prepared for the look of sheer pain that made a fleeting appearance.

"I don't have a husband." Matthew's tone was curt.

Shane felt uncomfortable. "Oh, I'm sorry. I saw your ring and thought…" his voice trailed off as Matthew's incredible eyes caught his. He saw a flicker of raw grief in them and wanted to cut his tongue out.

"I'll shut up now," he muttered and sat back in the seat, watching the lights spin by and the cornucopia of activity that was

London in the early hours of the morning come to life. Matthew drove in silence along the relatively quiet London streets.

"What are we going to do about David?" Shane blurted the words out suddenly, anxious to cut the uncomfortable silence. Matthew looked over at him with a slight trace of amusement.

"That didn't last long, did it?" he said drily. But he smiled, and Shane thought he might have been forgiven for his earlier prying. The other man sighed.

"I'll go see him tomorrow, see how he is. *If* I can get in. Walter might have given the nurses instructions to keep me away from him. But I'll try." He swung into the valet parking areas outside the Baglione Hotel.

"I want to go with you." Shane opened the car door and got out. He leaned down and flicked a card onto the passenger seat. "Here's my card. Give me a call before you head out tomorrow and we'll go together. Strength in numbers and all that." He looked at Matthew. "Have you got a business card?" he asked hopefully. "Just in case I hear anything first, I can call you."

Matthew smiled and reached into his jacket pocket. He took out a small white card. "My mobile number's on there. If you hear anything at all about David between now and tomorrow, let me know."

Matthew looked at Shane's card. "Carrington Knights? I could never afford to book one of their escorts. Pretty high class from what I hear." He grinned, his face transforming into something that Shane thought might one day break his heart. "I guess I'm lucky to have one free of charge by my side."

Matthew's teasing tone made Shane's dick stir in his trousers, where it had been on high alert ever since meeting the man. He'd have to do something about that when he got into the hotel bedroom. The friction and tight throbbing was unbearable. He swallowed, thinking about what he was going to do with himself while thinking of this man. "Are you flirting with me, Mr. Langer? Because if you are, I like it."

He held Matthew's gaze and the two men stared at each other for a moment. There was a definite current of electricity and Matthew's eyes darkened as his lips parted, as if he was about to say something. Then the strident tones of a car horn bought them back to their senses and ruined the moment.

"Oi, you tosser!" came the exasperated shout from the taxi parked behind the Audi. "Get a bloody move on, will you?"

"I guess that's your cue to move then," Shane chuckled as he closed the door. He watched as Matthew looked back at the street, gunned the engine, and disappeared back out into the traffic.

Aftermath

Matthew got home close to six in the morning, and the first thing he did was go for a shower. He felt drained, both physically and emotionally over David, and dealing with the rather turbulent Shane Templar had taken the last of it out of him. He was dealing with him not only as a friend of David's and a mutual enemy of Walter Debussy, but also as a man he was very attracted to. Matthew didn't give himself lightly. He'd never been one for sleeping around, or being with a different man each week. Well, not unless you counted his total meltdown when Sam died and he'd also lost—he quickly checked himself.

No point in dwelling on *that*. That way only bought back deep, dark memories and a crushing sense of failure.

He'd had a couple of short-lived relationships, trying to assuage the ache of Sam's loss, but they'd fizzled out as soon as soon as the other men realised he still hadn't gotten over Sam. Now he found the occasional solace in one-night stands at the clubs when the pressure was on, or like he was going to do now, relieving the tension himself in his shower or in his bed.

He started the shower, shed his clothes and stepped under the hot, needle-like onslaught that washed over his aching shoulders. He turned his face up to the water, catching the droplets with his tongue, feeling the stress and strain of the evening soaking out of his face.

His left hand stroked his cock, slowly at first, then faster. His hand was slick with water as he increased both the pressure and the speed. He groaned, the sensations building up quickly. *It won't take long*, he thought as he took a deep, shuddering breath. He'd been aroused the whole time he'd been with Shane, the man's intense blue stare and obvious concern for him a real turn-on. Just the man's touch on his skin had been enough to make him hard. It was a long time since anyone had seemed to care about Matthew that way. Not since Sam.

He closed his eyes as his imminent orgasm took over his thoughts, his mind conjuring up pictures of the naked Shane tied up on David's hotel bed, and with a strangled gasp, he came, hot fluid arching up onto the shower wall, covering his hands with sticky semen that quickly washed down the drain.

He leaned his forehead against the cool tiles, his chest heaving. *God, that had been intense.* Matthew felt less stressed but still not completely satisfied. He felt almost cheated. He wanted the real thing. But that wasn't going to happen. He should never have given the man his business card. Getting emotionally involved with someone now was not in the cards. It hurt too much when it all fell apart.

Back in David's paid-for hotel room, Shane was doing much the same thing but with a lot more vigour. He was lying gasping on his back on top of a large bath towel spread on the Matelasse bedspread, the warm air from the open window caressing his naked skin, as he rode his dick with strong, sharp bursts of speed, the image of a naked Matthew Langer bending over in front of him, his tight backside inviting and ready to be fucked foremost in his mind.

"Christ al-fucking-mighty," he moaned as all the muscles in his legs and backside tensed. Digging in his heels, his body lifted an inch from the bed as he climaxed, long jets of white fluid streaming over his hand and stomach, which clenched in pleasure at the sensations in his groin. He landed back on the bed, panting as he let his dick go, and his body relaxed on the bed. His chest was heaving with the exertion. He stared up at the ceiling in disbelief.

Hell, how had this man managed to do this to him?

Shane prided himself on his self-control, but tonight he just hadn't been able to last more than five minutes.

He'd gone to the reception desk, picked up Bushwhacker and just made it into his hotel room before taking another pee, ripping his clothes off and falling naked onto the bed. He had, however, had the foresight to rip a towel off the rail to protect the bedspread. He didn't think it fair that the housekeepers had to deal with his jissom all over their expensive duvet. Then he'd let rip and five minutes later he'd erupted like Old Faithful. Shane felt better. He needed a shower before climbing under the covers. He ponged like a well-worn rent boy. Tomorrow he'd need to test the waters, see if the flirting they'd started came to anything else. He was rather looking forward to that.

His phone rang later that day around one. He was already up, showered and dressed, and ready to leave to go home.

Matthew's voice was strained. "Walter has made us *persona non grata*, I'm afraid. He's given explicit instructions to let neither of us in, and he's even got a personal bodyguard outside David's room. So I'm afraid we won't be seeing him any time soon. One good thing though: He's regained consciousness and seems fine. That's all I could get out of the nurse."

Shane was relieved his friend was okay but disappointed that he wouldn't be seeing Matthew today. "At least he's all right. I suppose that's it then. We'll have to wait until he's out and about to make contact with him." He hesitated. "How are you? Did you manage to get a decent sleep?"

The lawyer sighed. "I slept enough. I need to spend this afternoon looking for another job. I'll have some time as Walter still owes me quite a bit of money, but it won't last long." He stopped. "Sorry, that's probably more information than you needed. It's my problem, not yours."

"Are you always this self-sufficient?" Shane asked. "I don't mind if you share things."

The line was quiet. "We don't know each other that well," was the soft reply. "I'm used to managing things on my own. But thanks anyway."

Yes you are, and that's half your problem, mate.

Shane took the plunge. "Do you want to get together for a beer or something sometime? I know a great little Dutch pub in Soho with a bit of atmosphere."

Again there was silence. Shane stared at his mobile in frustration, wishing he could reach through and shake the man's self-sustaining attitude out of him.

"I don't think that's a good idea. I'm going to be pretty busy finding work and getting things sorted out." Matthew sighed. "I've never been unemployed before. It's a bit of a novelty and a bit scary. So I need to focus."

Shane felt a pang of disappointment. "Oh, okay. Well, you have my number. If you change your mind give me a call."

"I'll do that. Thanks for this morning and stay safe, Shane. Be seeing you." The line went dead. Shane glared at his phone.

Well, that was a bloody total loss. That had so not gone the way he wanted. He kicked the bed leg sulkily. Now what was he supposed to do? He glared around the hotel room as he puffed his cheeks out in a sigh. He supposed he'd better be getting off to his own home. He was already an hour overdue on his check-out time, and they'd be kicking him out sooner or later. He gathered up his belongings, packed Bushwhacker into his case, and slung his computer satchel over his shoulder. When he got home he thought he'd do a bit of digging on Mr. Matthew Langer. See what made him tick.

Despite his usual respect for corporate companies and their systems, leaving them alone for the most part, Shane didn't apply the same philosophy to people. He had an unfortunate tendency to disregard it when it came to them. He believed it was his God-given right to use the talents he had to pry into people's affairs. After all, the internet was nothing more than a huge data dump of information, and he was an expert at mining it. It was knowing where to look that was the key. Shane smiled in satisfaction as he left the hotel to walk back to his flat.

Two hours later Shane took a sip of his red wine and leaned back in his office chair. His eyes were gritty and tired from staring at his computer screen. He frowned at the images in front of him, populating his screen like wall tiles.

He'd managed to find out quite a bit about the man, to the extent that he now had his very own folder on his computer. Nothing earth-shattering, but at least it gave him a clue as to who he might be beneath the controlled exterior. Matthew Langer was indeed thirty years old, born in Dresden, Germany on May third.

Hmm, a Taurus. That explained a lot. Cool, calm and collected. And bloody stubborn, he imagined.

Shane had an affinity for the "science" of star signs, himself being a Gemini. His birthday was on the eighth of June. He'd already done a quick search to see what the blurbs said about them being compatible. It wasn't very encouraging. Earth plus Air tended to make dust, apparently.

Matthew was the son of a German banker—his mother, Greta—and Erich Langer, a solicitor, now deceased. Greta worked for a branch of the Dresdner Bank in Dresden, where she lived, having moved back there after Erich's death. Matthew had stayed in London. He had an older sister, Rachel, a fashion model, who seemed to travel a lot. She was a real stunner too, a lot like her brother, only a feminine version. She had the same grey eyes and hair colour.

Matthew was on no social networking sites that Shane could find, which didn't surprise him given the man's control issues. He had a Gmail account, named, logically, like the man himself, mdlanger@gmail.com. Shane had found out Matthew's middle name was Dominik. Shane rather liked that, thinking it was unusual. Other than the usual legal sites and professional associations, he didn't seem to have any particular hobbies or interests. He wasn't a member of the local Gaymen society, or a dom at a BDSM club (something Shane was disappointed in, that would *so* have suited the man, especially one with a middle name like Dominik), or even involved in anything charitable that the hacker could find. Matthew was indeed a bit of a dark horse. But at least he wasn't a member of the local cross-dressing society, the arty drag queen scene or, thank the saints, involved with any specific religion. Shane was an atheist and wasn't one to suffer religious fools gladly. "Live and let live" was his motto as long as people didn't try to convince him of their side. The man might be a God-fearing Christian or C of E member, but there was nothing evident in the ether indicating anything extreme. That would have put Shane off straight away despite the look of the man's rear end and his incredible eyes.

He looked at the pictures dotted on his screen. They showed Matthew in various poses and shots, all taken at charity dinners and business events, mainly for Debussy Enterprises. Some showed him talking to other businessmen, while in others he stood to one side as others basked in their moment of photographic glory. But the one thing that had intrigued him was a picture of Matthew standing closely next to an older man, their hands almost touching, their heads bowed together in what looked like true affection. The other man was taller than Matthew, with a slim build, a mane of dark deep red hair and a winning smile. The caption simply said;

Matthew Langer, lawyer to Walter Debussy, and Sam Cartwright, local entrepreneur at the recent Debussy "Children's Day" Charity Gala event. The date stamp was April 2009.

He felt a slight twinge of jealousy at the way the other man was staring at Matthew.

"Who are you, then?" he murmured. "Mr. Sam Cartwright, I certainly need to find out what your role in the delicious Mr. Langer's life is."

Half an hour later he wished he hadn't been so curious. The one story that he'd uncovered was deeply personal and even Shane felt a sense of shame at delving into the man's personal background. Sam Cartwright had been Matthew's husband. He'd been two years older than Matthew. They'd been married under a civil partnership in 2007.

In May 2010, just a couple of weeks after Matthew's twenty-eighth birthday, Sam had been driving home from his office late at night. A truck had jackknifed and hit his car. Sam had died instantly in a mangle of metal and blood. It had been a quick, merciful death according to the pathology reports that Shane had managed to access.

Merciful for Sam, but not for Matthew. Shane closed his laptop, feeling sick.

He'd seen the flash of pain in Matthew's eyes when he'd asked him about his husband. Obviously he still wasn't over his lover's death. Shane wasn't sure *he* would be, after three years together with the same man as a husband and who knew how long before that. And violent death was always the worst. No chance to say goodbye. From what he'd found on the net, Matthew's father had died three years ago of a heart attack as well. So the man had lost two close family members.

This is crap. I have the hots for a man with a few demons of his own and who's still probably in love with the man he lost. Go figure. I find one I really like and wouldn't mind a relationship with and he's already taken.

He scowled as he stood, up, prowling around his flat in his sweatpants.

I'll probably never even see the guy again.

New Beginnings

Matthew glanced around his new office on his first day at work and heaved a sigh of relief. The last week had been a nightmare as he'd filled in form after form online applying for jobs. Finally he'd heard via a friend from university that a small law firm in the city was hiring. He'd taken the plunge and called them direct and was glad he had. He and his new boss, Bartholomew Maxwell, had gotten on like a house on fire in the interview and found they had much of the same interests and ethics. Bartholomew, never to be called Bart, as he'd warned Matthew with a glint in his eyes, had hired him there and then as another one of his General Counsels. Matthew had been on cloud nine when he'd gotten the offer and promised his new employer he wouldn't be sorry.

Now he had his very own small office overlooking the financial district in London and the promise of a pay cheque at the end of the month, even if it was less than he was used to. He'd make it work.

He smiled as Julia Francis, the office manager, came into his office with a wide grin. He quite liked her and they had hit it off straight away. She was in her early forties, a dark-haired, rounded, buxom woman with an endearing personality and, apparently, a rod of steel in her back. She kept the office ticking over, acting as a general manager, and Bartholomew seemed to hold her in high regard. Her clear blue eyes regarded him now, her expression warm.

"Matthew, you're settling in? I know the office isn't very big, but at least it will afford you some privacy and a place to store those mountains of paper your wonderful boss is going to give you." Her tone was wry. "Before you know it we won't be able to see you behind the desk. I might have to send out a search party to look for you."

Matthew chuckled. "I'm looking forward to getting stuck in. Don't worry, it won't be the first time I've had to be physically extricated from a mountain of paperwork."

She laughed. "I'm glad to hear it." Her face grew more serious. "I've been meaning to ask you. How is your friend, the one who was in the hospital? David, was it?"

Matthew felt touched she'd even remembered the story from his interview.

"He's a lot better, thanks for asking."

He'd called the hospital and found out that David was out of hospital and back home. He hadn't yet managed to make contact with him. He suspected Walter had put the fear of God into him not to speak to Matthew.

As he said the words, a sudden thought of Shane popped into his mind. He wondered if Shane had seen David yet, perhaps even escorted him anywhere. Just the thought of that sent a slight surge of jealousy through his body. The idea of the two of them getting into each other was just too much.

He'd tried very hard to put Shane out of his mind but he had to confess, he wasn't making a very good job of it. He still jerked off in his lonely moments to the thought of Shane tied up on a bed, those amazing blue eyes looking up into his, the thought of those very kissable lips moaning under his assault....

He became aware Julia was looking at him. "Everything all right, Matthew? For a moment there you zoned out on me."

He shook his head. "Everything's fine. I was just thinking of David."

She nodded. "It's tough when a friend gets hurt. From what you told me, you two seemed very close." Her face coloured. "Is he, you know, a boyfriend or something?" She clapped a well-manicured hand to her mouth. "Sorry, Matthew, that's really none of my business. I shouldn't have asked."

"Or something." Matthew grinned at her mortified expression. "We've been friends since we were fourteen. And don't worry; I'm not offended. Believe me, I could do worse than David. Rich, handsome and a pretty good conversationalist. Just not my type."

No, his type was about five-ten, dirty blonde hair, an even dirtier mouth, blue eyes and a cheeky demeanour that threw him every time the man opened his mouth. He didn't even know how old Shane was. Probably in his mid-twenties. Too young, really. He needed someone more his own age or older. Someone like Sam.

Julia smiled. "Well, the man that gets you will be a very lucky one. You've already broken a few female hearts here when they heard you weren't available." She chuckled. "I understand they had a bit of a lucky draw going on as to who might get to bring you your first cup of coffee and get to chat you up with a view to a bonk." She pretended a horrified expression. "Oops, did I really say that aloud? You won't have me up for sexual harassment, will you?"

Matthew laughed, a sound he hadn't heard from himself lately. "I think I might like it here. No standing on ceremony. Always a very admirable trait." The pair smiled at each other comfortably.

"If you need anything, you let me know. My door is always open and you can come to me with anything." Julia smiled and disappeared. Matthew sat down in his office chair, feeling a huge sense of relief. He thought this might just work out fine.

That night as he left work he decided he'd trawl the clubs and see if he could locate David at any of his usual haunts. Matthew needed to find out how he was and what had actually happened that night before the hospital. He worried that David might be in even more danger than he realised.

Matthew went home and changed into his club clothes: his black, ass-hugging jeans, a striped black and wine silky long-sleeved shirt and a favourite black sweater with buttons in the front. He took a good look at himself in the mirror and sighed. He may as well do this in style. Maybe he could even get lucky tonight. He'd been feeling the stress of being celibate for the last few weeks, and he needed some human company. His hands were getting tired doing all the dirty work. At least there might be some benefit to running around looking for David.

He went to three of David's preferred clubs before finding him at an exclusive venue in Soho called Essence. Essence was one that Matthew hadn't been to before but he knew David liked it. He paid the exorbitant entrance fee and walked in, struggling his way through the crowds on the dance floor to the bar at the back of the club. He was starting to get fed up. It was costing him a small fortune getting into the places and it was money he could ill afford. He *had* been hit on half a dozen times, had his arse groped and endured myriad looks of lust, combined with hair flicking, lascivious winks, and lip licks.

Despite all the action he was offered, he still hadn't been ready to make a move with anyone. He told himself he wanted to find David first before he got his rocks off. Matthew wasn't keen on the nightclubs, but they were a necessary evil when you didn't want emotional ties.

The nightclubs had been Sam's forte. He'd loved dancing with Matthew to the music, but the slow ones had been Matthew's favourites. The memory of Sam groping his backside and the feel of his crotch against his own made him smile as he stood sipping his gin and tonic at the bar, his eyes scouring the room for any sight of David.

He found him in a corner booth, obviously enjoying himself as it looked like his tongue was stuck halfway down some guy's throat. Matthew unpeeled himself from the bar and once again fought his way through the dancing couples on the floor. He ran the gauntlet with his drink held high, and found himself at the table occupied by David and his partner. Matthew coughed loudly and David opened his eyes, looking up at him. For a moment there was a flicker of uncertainty in his eyes at seeing Matthew, but then he uncinched himself from his partner and stood up. He still looked pale and moved slowly as if he was still in pain, but overall he looked a lot better.

"Matty! God, fancy seeing you here. I didn't think this was your kind of scene." David was the only other person in the world that Matthew didn't mind using the name. It had been David's name for him ever since he could remember. The two men embraced and as they drew apart, the man David had been asphyxiating turned around.

Matthew's eyes were riveted by the clear bright blue gaze as Shane faced him. The lawyer's heart jumped and he felt his hands clench at his sides. Shane regarded him steadily. David waved a hand and leaned in to talk into Matthew's ear. The music was fairly loud and he had to concentrate to hear what David was saying.

"You two know each other, don't you? You met at the hospital, Shane tells me. Thanks for coming to that debacle, Matty. I'm so sorry you and Dad had a falling out. You know what he's like. He can be a real bugger. I'm sorry you lost your job, Matty. But I'm fine now, all better."

"Shane." Matthew nodded at the other man. "Good to see you again." His body was flushed with heat, desire and annoyance in equal parts.

"Matthew." Shane shifted over on the bench and waved as he spoke loudly over the noise. "Sit down. I'm with David on this one. I never figured you for the club scene."

Matthew sat down in the booth on Shane's left and David sat on the other side of him. His temper was rising. He leaned over and spoke at full volume into Shane's ear. "I was looking for David. I've been all over bloody London trying to find him."

He scowled as he leaned over to speak to David. "I wanted to see how you were, DD, seeing as you haven't been returning my calls this past week or so. I see you were both very busy."

His pointed tone was directed at both the fact that David had ignored him and the fact that he was here with Matthew's very own wet dream. Matthew couldn't say why he felt so aggrieved or such a sense of possessiveness for a man he hardly knew. Shane had declared an interest but he'd fobbed him off.

He had no right to feel the sheer jealousy he'd had seeing them kissing. Shane looked incredible; his broad shoulders snug in a thin white tight-fitting polo neck jumper. His blond hair was tousled, probably from where David had been running his hands through it and his lips were swollen from kisses. He looked delectable and Matthew couldn't stand it. He stood up abruptly, slamming his glass down on the table top. He shouted over the sound of the blaring music.

"Actually, I can see you're both all right, so I'll leave you two alone."

David reached a hand out and started to speak as Shane eyed Matthew cautiously.

Matthew knew he sounded like a petulant child but he couldn't help himself. He waved a hand airily, not caring if they could hear him or not, just wanting to get the words out.

"Get back to what you were doing, enjoying yourselves. Don't choke on each other's tongues." He turned heel and hot-footed it through the club to the exit.

Outside, he stood in the cooling night air, trying to calm himself down. Matthew had a temper, but it didn't often come to the fore. At the moment he really wanted to punch someone or something. The bouncer eyed him warily and shifted on his feet as if in warning. Matthew nodded at him in camaraderie. The last thing he wanted was to be manhandled by a man who looked as if he fought gorillas in his spare time.

"What the fuck was all that about? Poor David has no clue what the hell just happened. I said I'd come out and talk to you." Shane's angry tones jolted him out of his thoughts and he turned to see his glowering face behind him. Shane was tense, his body language aggressive as he stood close to Matthew, who glared back at him.

"Would it have killed you to call me and let me know he was okay? You've obviously been seeing him, and I haven't even been able to get hold of him for ten bloody days. For all I knew his dad could have beaten him up again and he was back in hospital."

Shane's gaze was frosty. "Firstly, this is the first time I've seen him. He's only been out of the hospital a few days. Secondly, he told me he *had* called you and given you an update. He said you were fine with it. He obviously lied. Thirdly, what the hell? You don't bloody own me *or* him and you've no right to be so bloody rude to either of us."

Matthew raised an eyebrow. "Are you with him tonight as a paid escort, or a free date?"

He knew even as he said the words that he'd gone too far. To be honest, he was ashamed at the words even as they left his mouth.

Shane's face went white as he stepped forward.

For a moment, Matthew thought he was about to be smacked across the jaw. Instead, he found himself being pushed against the wall, Shane's greedy lips finding his in a kiss that made him rock hard. Matthew couldn't help himself. His lips parted involuntarily as Shane's hungry tongue crept into his mouth, meeting his own as his body pressed against Matthew's in sheer carnality. Matthew tasted whisky, mint and pure sex.

The younger man knew how to kiss. His lips were demanding and warm and his tongue definitely knew what it wanted.

All sense of anything rational left him as the other man's hips pushed against his. Matthew lost all breath in his body feeling Shane's raging erection against his own. He groaned and gripped Shane's blonde hair as he ground his mouth against the other man's in a frenzy of sheer need and want.

Shane's hands were on his backside, gripping him fiercely, pulling their two bodies together.

Christ, he's a great kisser. He must be total dynamite in bed. God, I want this man.

The thoughts were fleeting. Matthew found himself being released and the incredible sensations in his body were relieved somewhat as Shane pulled away.

The other man's face was dark, his eyes stormy. His lower face was reddened from the roughness of Matthew's chin, from the stubble that grew around his mouth. Shane's voice was fierce when he spoke. "Is that what you wanted, Matthew? It certainly felt like you did." He reached down and brushed Matthew's groin.

Matthew gasped.

"I'd say you want me. Why the hell are you so uptight about it? Be honest with yourself."

Matthew couldn't quite find his voice. He took a deep breath trying to calm down the emotions surging in his chest.

Shane watched him and then shrugged. His voice sounded disappointed when he next spoke. "Fine, then. You've had your chance. Twice. So don't bloody well think I owe you anything." He turned to walk back into the club.

"Shane, wait." Matthew didn't recognise his own voice. It was husky, needy, and not in control. "I'm sorry. That last comment was a cheap shot. You didn't deserve it."

Shane stood, his eyes watchful.

Matthew tried to formulate his words. "I'm not good at not being able to control situations. Sam used to tell me I was a control freak too." He realised he'd invoked Sam's name and saw Shane's eyes narrow. One day he'd have to explain who Sam was. "Yes, I'm attracted to you, a lot. I've never had that experience before, so intense. I suppose I don't really know what to do with it. And you're younger than I'm used to."

Shane raised his eyebrows. "Really? You don't know what to do with it? How long did you say you'd been a gay man?" His eyes glinted but there was a trace of amusement in them now. "And I'm twenty-eight, Matthew. Only a couple of years younger than you, old timer."

Matthew scowled. "You know what I mean. Don't be such a bloody smart-alec." But he was surprised and glad at the similarities in their ages. The man looked much younger.

"Tut tut. Language, Mr. Langer."

The way Shane said his name sounded so dirty. Matthew swallowed. Shane moved away from the door, back to him. His hand reached out and he ran it through Matthew's hair, his fingers gentle. Matthew closed his eyes at the sensation. It had been a long time since anyone had touched him with such tenderness.

"You are so bloody uptight and controlled," Shane whispered into Matthew's ear. His breath was warm, the fragrance of whiskey on his breath intoxicating.

Matthew was aware he was standing on a London street in front of a gay bar with a man seducing him but he couldn't care less at this junction. His whole body was on fire, and his cock felt so huge in his jeans he was surprised he hadn't burst the zipper.

Shane continued whispering. "I would love to break that control. See you beg, hear you say my name as you beg me to fuck you. Watch you let loose and just be yourself. Oops, sorry, I didn't mean to swear. You can cane me later."

Shane's suggestive tone made Matthew's legs wobbly. He managed to squeak out a few words. "I told you, there's a time and a place for using words like those. In private, I have no problem. Christ, Shane, please kiss me again." He felt Shane shiver at his words but he didn't argue.

His mouth found Matthew's again, softer this time, his tongue warm and probing. Matthew slid his hands around Shane's waist, as Shane ran his hands behind Matthew's head, his fingers entwined in his hair. Finally they pulled apart, both taking deep gulps of air to be able to breathe again.

"I've wanted to do this since I met you," Shane whispered. "You taste and feel even better than I thought. God, we need to take this somewhere. I'm going to explode if we stand here. Have you got your car nearby?"

Matthew shook his head, his mouth trailing down Shane's jaw line causing the other man to shudder in his arms. "No. I came by tube. We can go to a hotel if you like. But we need to get a taxi because I'm not bloody running anywhere."

Shane grinned as his hands brushed the front of Matthew's trousers. The lawyer groaned as the other man gave a wicked chuckle that made his skin tingle.

"My place is close. St. James's. I'll get us a taxi. But I don't want to be responsible for making some poor taxi driver suffer unmentionable trauma, so you'll have to behave yourself in the cab. Let me go inside and tell David."

"Won't he be upset? I mean, you were with him…"

Shane shook his head. "No, he'll be fine. He had his sights set on some poor Asian lad inside who won't know what's hit him. The kiss you saw us in was just an opportunistic one on his part. He still owed me an apology for roofying me and tying me up. I made it clear it wasn't something he should be doing to anyone. So he decided to make it a kiss. He knew I was waiting—" He cut his words off. "Stay here. Don't go anywhere." He gave Matthew one last fierce kiss and disappeared inside.

Matthew leant back against the wall for support.

The bouncer rolled his eyes and Matthew grinned. He felt like a teenager again, necking outside a nightclub. It felt good. Shane's words about him losing control still echoed in his ears. He had no doubt that if any man could make him do that, it was Shane Templar. Shane, who wanted to fuck him until he begged for mercy. Matthew trembled at that thought. God, it had been a while. He was pretty versatile, not minding bottoming or topping but the thought of Shane inside him made him feel faint with sheer hunger. He wondered what Shane had been about to say when he'd stopped. Waiting for what? Waiting for him? The thought made him giddy. Shane appeared in front of him a wide smile on his face.

"Right, David says well done. The taxi should be here any minute." He leaned back against the wall beside Matthew with an air of nonchalance. "You look incredible, by the way." Shane's soft voice breathed into his ear. "I love that shirt on you. Of course, I'd love that shirt off you more. I intend doing that myself though. Undressing you, I mean. I love opening presents." His body was close to Matthew's, his hip touching his as they stood.

"Hell, Shane, give it a rest unless you want me to come right here." Matthew's breathing was ragged. "I think we should stay apart until we get to your place. Or else I won't be able to control myself."

Shane's eyes were black and his breathing uneven.

Matthew felt a sense of power at being able to turn the man on like this. He decided to turn the tables and assert some control himself. "I hope you have loads of condoms and lube at your place. I have the feeling we're going to need it."

He laughed as he saw Shane swallow and close his eyes. The taxi pulled up and the two men got into the back. Matthew was careful not to sit too close, remembering Shane's words about not traumatising the taxi driver.

He's probably seen it all anyway, Matthew thought. *I doubt there's much a London cabbie hasn't seen, let alone two guys making out in the back of his cab.* But if he started now he wouldn't be able to stop.

Getting to know him

The trip to St. James's took less than ten minutes, which in Shane's opinion was nine and a half minutes longer than he wanted to wait. He wanted to pounce on this man, rip those well-fitting clothes off and pound into him until both of them were completely spent.

When he'd seen Matthew standing there beside the table in the club, his first reaction had been visceral. His dick had leapt to attention and his stomach had clenched. He'd thought the lawyer had felt the same way from the hungry look in his eyes.

Then Matthew had got all hoity-toity and left and Shane had been left wondering what the hell had just happened.

David had looked at him. "Go after him," he'd said with a wave of his hand.

So Shane had. And now they sat together in the back of the taxi, itching to launch themselves at each other but having to wait. He couldn't bear it.

He needed something to take his mind off what he really wanted to do. "So," Shane said. "What do you think of the weather?"

Matthew's mouth twitched. "The weather?" He seemed to be controlling a laugh.

Shane flapped a hand in the air. "Well, they say all this global warming is causing havoc with the environment. Rainstorms, blizzards and shit like that. I wondered if you had an opinion."

Matthew cocked an eyebrow in that sexy way he had and Shane nearly came. "Well, I'm no expert, but I think that shit like that happens and it's just Mother Nature's way of redressing the balance."

The two men looked at each other then burst into gales of loud laughter that had the taxi driver shaking his head.

Matthew wiped tears from his eyes. "Hell, Shane, you say the damnedest things at the damnedest times."

Shane shrugged. "What can I say? It's a gift. I had to say something to break the tension. It's driving me crazy." Despite his resolve to stay away from Matthew until they got to his place, he moved his hand up Matthew's leg, stroking his knee. Matthew's body tensed and strained as he pressed back against the seat.

"Not fair," he said between clenched teeth. "We said—"

"Hmm, I know. But I think this taxi driver might have seen it all, so." His lips curled in a wolfish smile. "I thought I'd test the merchandise. Have a taster, so to speak." He licked his lips, watching Matthew's pupils dilate and his breathing quicken. Shane's sly glance at the lawyer's groin and his lip-licking was having the required effect.

"Don't you bloody dare. You cannot give me a blow job in the back of a taxi."

"Why not?" Shane regarded him with a lazy stare. "He won't see anything." He jerked a finger at the driver. "And if he does, all he'll be worried about anyway is not getting come all over his seat. So if I swallow it all, he won't have that problem."

Matthew was squirming now, and Shane was having fun. He'd no intention of doing what he threatened. They probably *would* get arrested for lewd conduct, but seeing Matthew's total meltdown was such a turn-on.

He'd said he wanted to break the man's control issues, and he seemed to be doing that. But he was also driving himself nuts. He wasn't sure how long he could hold out. He leaned back in the corner of the cab and heard Matthew's sigh of relief.

Or was that disappointment?

"Fine. I'll behave myself." He grinned in the darkness.

Matthew spoke, his voice still ragged. "I wanted to ask you. What did David say about that night? Does he still insist it was a mugging?"

Shane nodded. "Yes. He won't tell the truth, whatever that was. He's petrified of his dad. You should have seen him before he left me. The man was scared stiff. But he'll never talk out against his dad or tell us who did it to him."

No doubt it had been his father and that twat Roy Parsons. Their luck was about to change for the worse, Shane thought in satisfaction.

After the affair and insults at the hospital, Shane had made it his mission to find out everything he could about Walter Debussy and Roy Parsons. After days of exhaustive hacking and a caffeine rush that had almost made him sick, his late-night/early-morning vigils had yielded gold. He'd managed to track down a personal bank account Walter Debussy kept in the Channel Islands. The account held a considerable sum of money, more than Shane had ever seen in his lifetime. Shane intended "misappropriating" some of it. Walter Debussy didn't know it, but the princely sum of five million pounds was about to disappear from his account into another one that Shane had set up in the Caymans. It had taken some careful planning and time, but it was now set up in a dummy name.

The money was intended for David, if something should ever go wrong and his father cut him off somehow. It was the one thing that worried David and gave him sleepless nights. He thought he'd be nothing without his money, despite what Shane told him to the contrary. The transfer was due to take place in a few days' time.

Matthew sighed. "I hope David will be all right with him. I also hope there isn't any next time." He frowned. "How did you manage to track him down anyway? He's been avoiding me like the plague. I trawled the clubs looking for him." His tone was aggrieved.

Shane shrugged as he smiled. He wasn't about to tell Matthew that he'd hacked into David's phone and seen a text message saying he'd be at Essence.

"Coincidence. I spend a fair bit of time at Essence myself. David just happened to be there." He leaned over and trailed his hand down Matthew's jaw line. The other man shivered perceptibly. Shane grinned.

"How's the job hunting going?" he murmured. "Have you managed to find anything yet?"

Matthew nodded. "I'm working as senior counsel for this law firm in Bank Street. Maxwell, Smith and Jordan? I don't know if you've heard of them."

Shane shook his head as Matthew continued.

"My boss, Bartholomew Maxwell, is a real peach; very old school." He smiled. "He doesn't like Walter either. Called him a despicable man. It's a nice enough office as well, not too big. I think I'll enjoy it there."

"I'm glad you got sorted with a job. That's great news." Shane was genuinely pleased. He imagined not having a job would be very high on this man's list of "things that made him nervous" in not having the control he so obviously needed in his life.

Shane's hand stilled its journey up Matthew's thigh, and the other man breathed a sigh of relief as Shane turned to look out of the window. "This is our stop."

The taxi pulled over to the kerb, and Shane leaned in and paid him. The two men got out of the taxi, which sped down the quiet, residential street. Shane gestured at his apartment building, a large, dark brick structure on a tree-lined street in St. James's, an affluent area of the city. The river ran in front of the building, and the whole ambience was one of wealth and opulence.

"Welcome to Shane's World. Come on. Let's get upstairs. I'm so horny I should be two rhinos." They walked through the glass doors into the spacious, plant-filled lobby.

Matthew spluttered with laughter at the other man's words. "Now that's one I haven't heard before."

Shane glanced at him. "Oh, I'm sure there's a lot more you haven't heard before that you'll hear tonight, including my screams of delight." He grinned as Matthew followed him over to the lift. He'd seen the man swallow and clench his hands.

"Does this lift have cameras in it?" the other man murmured.

Shane nodded. "Sorry, yes, they do. So no hanky-panky in there if that's what you were thinking of doing."

Matthew murmured a reply. "Pity. I like mirrors. There's something about watching someone's face in them when they're up close and personal that's such a turn on."

Now it was Shane's turn to swallow. The lift opened and the two men stepped in. The doors closed and both men heaved a deep breath. Their eyes met, gunmetal grey and sapphire blue. But they stayed where they were, knowing if they got to close to each other it would be all over. The lift seemed to take an interminable time to reach the fifth floor. Finally the doors opened and they stepped out. Shane led the way down the dimly lit corridor, to a door at the far end of the hallway. He reached into his trouser pocket, removing a set of keys. He unlocked the door. He'd only just walked in and was about to switch on the light for the entrance when he heard a low growl behind him. He felt himself being smacked against the wall, his face flat against the cool surface.

"You are the biggest bloody tease I've ever met." Matthew's voice was deep, husky. Shane was pulled around to face the other man. "You have driven me fucking crazy all the way here."

"Jesus, Matthew, language!" Shane gasped with a laugh, even as his shirt was pulled out of his jeans and the other man's hands started unbuttoning it.

"We're in private, no one to hear, so bad language is fine. Especially with a bad boy like you."

Shane could hardly believe this was the same man he'd just sat next to in the taxi. He was just aching with the need to have him. He toed his shoes off urgently as Matthew finished his unbuttoning and slid his shirt off his shoulders onto the floor. Matthew's hands were on his jeans zipper, slowly easing it down. Shane's hips pushed forwards in reflex, his dick straining with a need to be free. His own fingers stroked down Matthew's arms, feeling the strong muscle play beneath his fingers, the silk of his shirt a complete aphrodisiac like the man himself.

Matthew slid his hands into Shane's waistband and pushed his trousers down his legs. He crouched, sliding them down to his ankles. Shane felt his warm breath on his erection as he stood up. Matthew beckoned with an imperious gesture for Shane to step out of them. Shane wasn't sure when the tables had been turned and he'd gone from aggressor to subordinate, but he wasn't going to argue. He stepped out of his trousers and boxers and stood, completely nude, in front of a still-fully dressed Matthew. Both of them were breathing heavily, and Shane's dick was standing out in front of his body, already leaking and just throbbing with pure lust.

"You are simply exquisite." Matthew's tone was reverent, as his eyes caressed every inch of Shane's body. "You have a body like an athlete." He ran his hands over Shane's flat stomach, his eyes wide. Shane's breath was ragged. He felt as if he'd just run home from the club. His heart was pounding, the heaviness in his groin unbearable.

Matthew stopped touching him and lifted his arms above his head. "You wanted to undress me. Do it then. Quickly, because I really want you to fuck me."

Shane needed no further urging. He lifted Matthew's shirt above his head, gasping at the sight of the man's flat, firm stomach and hairy chest, his arms strong lengths of sinew and muscle. Matthew stood stock still, his eyes holding Shane's. Shane unzipped the tight black jeans and pulled them down over Matthew's lean hips. His eyes widened when he saw Matthew had no underwear on. His erection sprung free, in much the same state as Shane's—swollen, engorged, and leaking. Shane even thought it might be bigger than his. His own twitched at the thought of that inside him. Although tonight, it was definitely his turn to top.

The lawyer smiled. "I was planning on getting lucky tonight," he murmured. "I always find going commando makes things easier." He leaned forward as his jeans fell to the floor. He stepped out of them. "Of course, I didn't realise I'd be *this* lucky." The sheer tone of desire in his voice was the final straw for Shane, and he pulled Matthew to him, his mouth violating his, voracious and hungry. His passion was returned; their bodies snapped together like they were made to fit. Groaning sounds filled the apartment until Shane pulled his mouth away long enough to gasp, "Come through to the bedroom. Let's get out the bloody hallway."

He took Matthew's hand and led him across the wide entrance hall with its high walls and artworks decorating the spare space, through the enormous lounge into the dimly lit corridor and down to his bedroom at the front of the apartment. He'd left a bedroom light on. The glow warmed the room, casting shadows on the ceiling and walls.

Matthew gasped in awe when he saw the bedroom. "Wow, Shane. This is incredible. This whole bedroom is the size of the ground floor for my house. You must make a lot of money as an escort. And that view is amazing."

Shane wasn't going to enlighten him yet on how he made his money or where it had come from. His father had been an unwilling beneficiary toward his current state of wealth. But that was a story for another time.

"Shut the fuck up about the decor and just get on the bloody bed," he growled. Matthew obliged. He lay on his back on the duvet, a golden-and-bronze-coloured quilt, watching through smoky eyes as Shane lay next to him.

"Christ, you are so beautiful." Shane's fingers caressed Matthew's stomach, his shoulders, his hips, as the man hissed in pleasure at his touch. "When I first saw you, that was the first thing I thought. Such a beautiful man." He leaned over and his mouth trailed across the other man's abdomen, his tongue tracing the ridges of muscle, finally heading down lower to his hips and the curve where his hips met his groin.

Matthew moaned, his hips thrusting up, his hands clenching the duvet.

"And now I get to taste you at last." Shane's mouth closed around Matthew's erection and the man uttered a deep cry, pushing himself deeper into Shane's mouth. Shane moved his mouth up and down the shaft, his tongue licking and circling all the sensitive areas he could find. He knew what he liked when someone was sucking him off, so he imagined Matthew would appreciate the same treatment.

He swirled his tongue around the tip, piercing the opening and causing Matthew to make small noises like a kitten mewling. His hand cupped Matthew's balls, squeezing gently, and the kitten noises grew louder. It was a complete turn-on hearing the man lose it.

Shane sucked and prodded and twirled and lathered and there was a great sense of satisfaction when he realised the man in his mouth was completely undone.

"God, Shay, that is so good, don't stop. I'm not going to last much longer. It's been too long since I was with anyone like this."

Matthew's new name for him spurred Shane on. Men had used it before but he had never enjoyed it as much as from this man's lips. He sucked, feeling Matthew pushing at the back of his throat as he took him deeper. The kitten sounds had turned more into lion roars by now as Matthew bucked and tossed on the bedspread, his hips punching upwards as he thrust himself in and out of Shane's mouth, his hands twisting feverishly on the bed spread.

Shane teased him unmercifully, driving him to the brink then bringing him down. It had been a while since he'd had such a willing and incredibly responsive participant like the delectable Matthew Langer. Finally Shane felt the man swell and throb in his mouth and Matthew gave a great growl as he came, his semen spilling out in hot spurts into Shane's mouth and down his throat. He swallowed it as it erupted, loving the taste of this man and the tang of the fluid in his mouth.

Matthew's body jerked like a puppet on the end of a couple of strings. Shane looked up at him as he moved up over his body, his hand caressing his skin, causing Matthew to shiver.

The man's eyes were unfocused and dazed.

Shane found his lips and thrust his tongue into his mouth, feeling him sigh as he returned the kiss.

"Can you taste yourself, Matty?" he whispered, wanting to have a special name too. "I loved how you tasted. So bloody good. And now it's my turn." He reached over and opened the bedside drawer, taking out the condom and the lube he kept in there. Matthew's eyes darkened at the sight, his pupils dilating with the knowledge of what was to come. His breathing quickened as Shane opened the condom packet.

"Your choice, Matty. Which way do you want to do this? I don't mind either way."

"I want to see you when you come," Matthew said. "I need to watch your face."

Shane nodded as he knelt in front, as the other man spread his legs wide for him, bringing his legs up towards his shoulders. "As long as I get to be inside you, I don't care," he whispered.

"Shane." Matthew's voice was quiet. "It's been a while since I did this. I'm out of practice."

Shane leaned down and kissed him. "I'll be gentle, I promise. At least to start with. I'll get you there. Trust me."

He rolled the condom on. Then he took the lube and squirted a liberal amount onto his fingers and applied a thick layer to Matthew's entrance. His fingers gently rubbed the lube into the crack and Matthew hissed at the cold between his cheeks.

"Stop being such a baby," Shane chuckled. "I'll soon warm you up. Or rather my dick will."

Gently he rubbed the opening, his finger slowly slipping inside, stretching the other man. Matthew hadn't been wrong. He was very tight, but Shane knew he'd get him where he needed him to go. He rotated his finger gently around, hearing the man's gasps at the sensations.

"Everything all right, Matty?" He hoped the answer was yes because he had no intention of stopping.

"Yes, Christ, it's fine. Just keep doing that. I'd forgotten how good it feels." Matthew's voice was strangled. His hands were once again gripping the bedspread.

Shane was gratified to note that once again Matthew's dick was gaining traction and starting to harden as he manipulated the man's opening. He inserted another finger, rolling it around, then as he felt the muscle start to give way, another finger until he had a squirming Matthew just where he wanted him. He decided to spice things up a bit, so he moved around inside until he found the sensitive spot he was looking for and pressed hard.

Matthew almost levitated off the bed with a fierce yowl, and Shane couldn't help a small wicked chuckle.

"Hell, Shay, do that again. Christ, I *had* forgotten how good that felt, no word of a lie." Matthew panted in short gasps, and Shane obliged him, loving the sound of a man close to the edge. He was pretty close himself, having controlled himself so far, but he wasn't going to last much longer.

His dick felt like it was going to split in two and ask each other to dinner. He moved up over Matthew. The sweating face of the man looking up at him, his grey eyes trusting and full of want, was all he needed.

"Ready, Matty?" The other man nodded and Shane pushed inside him gently. Matthew gasped and pushed back, urging Shane on. Shane held back, not wanting to go too fast when what he really wanted to ram himself full tilt into Matthew's tight passage. He pushed deeper, his neck muscles straining with the effort to control his depth. He withdrew and slid in again, deeper this time.

"Shay, just do it already! Stop pussyfooting around. Fuck me, for Christ's sake!" Matthew's agonised voice spurred Shane on. He pushed himself into the other man, hearing his shout of both pain and pleasure as he buried himself up to the hilt in the man beneath him. His balls slapped against the man's backside as he thrust in and out.

Matthew's hands grasped his hips, pulling him deeper and deeper inside. The incredible feelings as Matthew's muscles closed around him flooded his body, his groin. He felt his backside prickling with sensitivity as the other man's fingers dug into his flesh.

Shane moved the angle of his body to spear Matthew and hit his sensitive spot.

He grinned as Matthew yelped and jerked, nearly driving him through the roof.

Matthew's strangled voice sent shivers down Shane's spine. "Do *that* again, too. Don't bloody stop, you animal. You *are* good at this, aren't you?"

Shane gave Matthew a wicked smile and moved himself as directed. Matthew was powerless to speak, his hands clutching Shane, his eyes dazed. The two men grunted in unison as they moved as one. Time seemed to stop; there were only the sounds of heavy sighs, moans, and pants and the slap of flash against flesh.

Shane thought no one watching them would believe they'd just met. They just fit together so well.

Shane was ready to explode. The man beneath him was groaning uncontrollably, the sound turning Shane on more than he could bear. He looked down at Matthew to see those wonderful eyes staring up at him with an unfathomable expression whilst Matthew stroked himself.

It was the last straw. Shane felt his orgasm building and the tightness that was Matthew constrict around him causing an unbearable pressure. He cried out as he climaxed, his ejaculate flooding the condom, as his body trembled and racked with spasms in the final throes of his orgasm.

He heard Matthew gasp and felt warmth flood his stomach. He looked down to find Matthew had come too, his warm semen showering Shane, leaving white trails of come down both their bodies.

"Hell, Matty, that's not bloody fair," he gasped. "You've come twice now. You owe me one." He collapsed on top of his partner, his mouth finding the other man's. As they kissed, he felt a sense of belonging he'd not felt in a long time. This man was something special, he knew it. He wanted more than one night with him.

"Shay? You're bloody heavy. Do you think you can get off me now?" Matthew's muffled voice echoed in his ear and he chuckled, withdrawing slowly from the man and lying back on the bed.

"Sorry, but I was pretty comfortable." He rolled to his side to face Matthew, who was watching him with a strange expression. He wasn't quite sure whether it was a good or bad one.

"What is it? Did I hurt you?" He leaned over and brushed a strand of dark hair from Matthew's face. The other man shook his head.

"No," he said. "You didn't hurt me. That was incredible though. Thanks for trying to take it slow. But I liked the rougher bit better." He pushed Shane onto his back and looked at him critically. "Men seem to make a habit of coming all over you, don't they?"

The semen was already drying on Shane's stomach, but as he watched, Matthew leaned over and started to lick him with his tongue, like a cat cleaning its partner.

Shane had never seen anything so erotic in his life and certainly no one had ever cleaned him with their tongue before. He held his breath as Matthew licked the semen off his body, his mouth warm and wet. Shane finally needed to breathe, and he took a great gulp of air as he watched the man finish licking up all his own bodily fluids. Matthew crawled back up to Shane and kissed him, and Shane sighed in pleasure at tasting him on his mouth. Perhaps in a while they could go another round.

"That was different," he murmured in between kisses. "You're quite the enigma, Mr. Langer. Who taught you that little trick? I like it."

Matthew stiffened and rolled away. He lay, tensed on the bed, staring up at the ceiling. Matthew didn't answer, but Shane saw his quick glance at the gold wedding band on his finger. The room was deathly silent, the atmosphere heavy. Finally, after the quiet got too much to bear, Shane sat up, puzzled.

"Matty, what's wrong? What did I say?"

A look passed over Matthew's face and he sat up suddenly, his back muscles rigid. "Nothing. I need to get home, Shane."

No more 'Shay,' no more teasing or erotic tricks, just a curt comment that sucked all the air out of Shane's lungs.

He moved over to Matthew, kneeling behind him as his hands touched Matthew's shoulders. The man flinched.

Shane kept his hands where they were. "Matty, talk to me, damn it. What just happened?"

Matthew stood up, shaking Shane's hands off him and walking through to the en-suite bathroom. He closed the door behind him and Shane heard the sound of him peeing. He waited until the man came out then eyed him carefully.

"I at least thought you might stay over, Matthew. I didn't figure you for the 'wham bam thank you ma'am' type." His voice was steady but it sounded hurt, even to him.

Matthew sighed. "I'm sorry, Shane, but I think I should go. This was fun, but let's not make a big deal of it. I need to go get my clothes and get dressed." He walked out of the bedroom, leaving Shane staring open-mouthed at the sudden lack of Matthew in the room.

"Screw this for a bloody lark," he snarled. He grabbed a robe from his bedroom door, shrugged his shoulders into it and went out to find Matthew. The man was bending down to pick up his jeans. Shane let rip and slapped the man's bare behind with a fierce *thwack*. Matthew jumped a foot in the air and turned around, his eyes blazing.

"What the hell was that for? Jesus, that stung, you bastard."

"For being a son of a bitch. What the hell is wrong with you? We have a great night then you go and turn into the Hulk and tell me not to make a big deal of it. By just wanting you to stay over, that's a big deal?" Shane stood in front of Matthew as he dressed. Matthew didn't answer.

"Is this because of Sam?" Shane hadn't meant to mention the man's name. He winced as he realised what he'd just done. He couldn't let the man know he'd been investigating him.

Matthew's face went white, his lips thinned, and he glared at Shane. "How do you know about Sam?" he hissed.

Shane fidgeted but saved his bacon by remembering an earlier comment. "You mentioned his name back at the night club earlier. I saw the wedding band. I just put two and two together."

"Sam is none of your bloody business," snarled Matthew as he pulled on his sweater. "I appreciate the evening, Shane, but it's over now."

"You've had your itch scratched; now you can go back to being the control freak?" Shane spat. "Fine, run away then. You seem to be good at that."

Matthew drew himself up and moved over to Shane, the extra couple of inches of height giving him a commanding presence. "And what the hell is that supposed to mean? What the hell do you know about me?"

Shane pressed his lips together, refusing to be intimidated. He didn't want things to go from bad to worse.

Matthew looked at him. "You don't know anything about me."

Shane wanted to tell him he did but he knew that would be suicide. "You run away when things get emotional," he said. "You did it at the club, and you're doing it now. It's easier to turn tail and pretend things didn't happen and that people don't make you feel things, rather than accept them and deal with it."

Matthew laughed harshly. "An escort and a psychologist," he said. "You could charge double rates for that, Shane. In fact—"

He took out his wallet and counted out a bunch of notes which he placed on the hall table. Shane watched the gesture in disbelief, feeling sick to his stomach.

"There. Now I've paid the price. I don't know what you normally charge but three hundred should do it. If not, send me a bill."

Shane clenched his fists at his side, not wanting Matthew to see how much that gesture had hurt. "That's the second time you've done that to me. Get the fuck out of my home, Matthew," he said, his voice seething with anger. "Before I punch you." He picked up the money and went to the front door, throwing it out into the corridor to drift like coloured leaves onto the polished flooring in the hallway. "Get the fuck out."

Matthew was breathing heavily and looked as if he wanted to say something but he left. Shane slammed the door behind him and leaned against it, his hands shaking.

God, that man was such a bastard. Such a mixed-up son of a bitch. Why the hell had he ever gotten involved with him? Well, it wouldn't be happening again, that was for sure. The man was a complete emotional wreck, and life was too short to be with someone like that.

With a heavy heart, Shane made his way back to his bedroom. He opened the French doors and stood gazing out over the London skyline.

Regret, Remorse and Make-Up Sex

Matthew left Shane's flat, took the lift down and soon found himself on the street. He started walking back toward his home in Chelsea. It was a couple of miles, but the walk would do him good. He could get rid of all the frustrations and guilt he was carrying.

How the hell could he do something like that to Shane?

He could still see the hurt in the man's eyes as he'd put the money down on the table. He'd truly thought he'd get decked.

Even in that Shane had been the better man. Matthew felt a shame in his soul the likes of which he'd never felt before. He stopped, considering whether to go back and apologise. He decided things were too raw. Better to wait until both of them were less emotional. Matthew stood against the railing on the river bank, staring out across the water at the twinkling lights of the other side. He'd had the best night he'd had in a long time. He'd got laid by a man who had taken his needs into consideration, he'd had the best couple of orgasms he could remember, and then he'd treated another human being like dog shit.

He wanted this whole thing to stay superficial, non-committal. And somewhere deeper he knew it might not end up being that way with this man.

When Shane had asked the innocent question about the licking thing, memories had come flooding back. Sam had introduced him to that. Matthew had always found it intensely satisfying and a real turn-on. He'd wanted to do the same thing for Shane, something he'd never done with any man except Sam before. He had no idea why he felt this strongly about Shane Templar, just that he did.

He'd glimpsed his wedding ring on his finger and realised that he hadn't taken it off. He was studious about removing his wedding ring before he went with another man. It was disloyal to Sam's memory to wear it and screw someone else. But tonight, in the heat of the moment, and his overwhelming lust for another man, he'd forgotten. Seeing it still on his finger, knowing he'd just performed that most intimate act with Shane, a man he barely knew had driven him temporarily insane. That was the only excuse he had because Shane sure as hell didn't deserve what he'd been given at the end.

Matthew passed a trembling hand over his eyes and continued his walk. He'd have to contact Shane and try to talk to him tomorrow. If Shane would talk to him. He had his doubts. But he'd have to try. He couldn't let things lie as they were.

Matthew reached into his pocket and fingered the money he'd picked up from the corridor outside the flat. His felt his face flush. He'd treated the man like a common prostitute. He could never forgive himself for that. He wasn't sure Shane would either. Emotion had got the better of him once again and cemented the fact he really needed to be in control.

The following morning Matthew waded through various legal briefs and documents, his mind not focusing on his work.

Finally he heaved a sigh, sat back in his chair and picked up his mobile. The card Shane had given him sat on his desk, and he picked it up, looking at the front. He'd put this off long enough. Time to make the call he was dreading. He dialled the mobile number on the card and waited. The phone rang –once, twice, three times. Just as he felt a slight surge of relief that Shane wasn't going to answer, the ringing stopped.

"Shane Templar." Just the voice of the man was enough to send Matthew's hormones raging with the memories of what they'd done last night.

"Shane, it's Matthew. I wanted—"

"Fuck off." The phone went dead. Matthew stared at it in despair. *That* hadn't gone well. He closed his eyes and ran a hand through his hair. He stared unseeingly at the business card still clenched in his hand.

"Matthew, are you all right?" Julia's concerned voice cut through his thoughts. He looked up, managing a smile.

"Hmm? Yes, fine thanks." He tucked the card under a legal brief in a quick motion.

"You don't look fine." Julia walked in and sat down on the visitors' chair on the other side of the desk. "You look like a man who got no sleep and who just found out his dog has died. Want to talk about it?"

Her blue eyes regarded him appraisingly. She waited, not giving up. Finally he relented. Perhaps it might help to talk about it to someone. Not the details, just the principle.

"I did a bad thing last night. I insulted someone who didn't deserve it and hurt them and now they won't even talk to me so I can apologise. And I need to tell him I'm sorry that I was a complete bastard."

"Then go find him." Julia said softly. "It's nearly lunchtime. Take the time and go and see him. Don't let it fester. The longer you leave it, the further away the problem becomes, and you end up never resolving it. Take it from someone who knows."

Matthew shook his head. "He won't see me. I doubt I'll even get past his front door."

"Try." Julia stood up. "Just try, Matthew." She smiled and left his office.

He stared after her. Half an hour later, he found himself standing outside Shane's front door, his heart hammering in his chest and a sick feeling in his stomach. Before he could lose his nerve, he rang the buzzer. He heard a muffled acknowledgement from inside and then the door opened.

Shane stared out at him, no look of welcome on his face. He was dressed in a pair of grey chinos, with a form-fitting red sweatshirt that clung to his body. The sleeves were rolled up, and Matthew could see the fine hairs on his forearms. Arms that had held him close last night.

Shane glared at Matthew. "What the fuck are you doing here?" He scowled. "No matter; you won't be staying."

He made to close the door and Matthew threw caution to the wind and put his size-eleven foot in the doorway. "Shane, we need to talk."

Shane snarled. "Get your bloody clodhopper out of the way before I break it. You made your point very eloquently last night. We have nothing else to say to each other."

Matthew heard the words, but he also saw the flicker of vulnerability in Shane's eyes. "I'm not leaving," he said. "I need to apologise to you for being such a bastard last night. Please, Shane. Please let me in."

He watched the play of emotions across Shane's face: anger, hurt, and frustration, then finally a grudging acceptance that he wasn't going to get rid of Matthew so easily. He made a curt gesture with his hand and motioned to Matthew to come in. Once inside he shut the door and turned to him, his face grim.

"Say what you have to say. I have work to do. *Real* work, not man-fucking." His voice was harsh.

Matthew flinched. Time for the speech he'd been rehearsing since he'd been kicked out last night. "You were right about me. I don't do emotions easily; I never have. And it's been worse since Sam died." He swallowed as Shane watched him intently. "Sam was my husband. He died two years ago in a road traffic accident."

Shane's eyes flickered as he folded his arms in front of his chest. He looked impenetrable, but Matthew had to try and explain to him why he'd been such an arsehole last night. "We were together for six years before he died." Matthew took a deep breath. "He was my world. We met at a lawyer's conference in Atlanta in the U.S. in 2004. Sam lived there for a long time although he was British by birth. One thing led to another and we started a long distance relationship. It was hard for the first six months. Then he decided he couldn't bear being away from me and to move back to the U.K. so we could be together permanently." Matthew smiled as he remembered Sam's insistence that he was going "crazy being away from his honey" and needed to be with him. His warm American drawl had been one of the first things that had attracted Matthew to Sam in the first place.

Shane shifted in the entrance, uncrossing his arms, his body watchful. He still said nothing, just focused on Matthew's face with that blue gaze that seemed to spear his soul.

"We moved in together in the house in Chelsea I still own, and we got married in 2007." He swallowed, remembering the ceremony in his birth town of Dresden, a ceremony filled with family and relatives, joyous and warm, his parents so accepting of their new son-in-law. They'd adored Sam just as he had.

His voice caught at his next words. "Then on the eighteenth of May two years ago, Sam was driving home late from work." The date was seared on his memory like a cancer. "We were supposed to be at a family dinner. My folks had come over to visit and we had some really good news for them we wanted to announce. He'd been called in by his boss and asked to work late on an important case. Sam was a criminal attorney. He was used to having to do things at a drop of a hat. So we all stayed at our place to wait for him. On his way home a truck jackknifed and—" Matthew swallowed, feeling the grief well up in him, "It hit his car head on.

He was killed instantly." His throat closed up and Shane shifted. He moved towards Matthew and placed a hand on his arm.

"Matthew, come and sit down." He pulled the other man towards the lounge, indicating for him to sit down on the soft brown couch that seemed to fill the room.

Matthew sat down, his body numb. Shane sat at the opposite end, his body language not as aggressive as it had been but still wary.

Matthew looked down at his shaking hands. "I had to identify his body. He was pretty messed up." Matthew's voice tightened. "My dad took me and we did it together."

Shane shifted closer. His eyes were softer now, the gaze not as piercing as it had been. Matthew took a deep, shuddering breath. "I went to pieces. I started drinking. I drank so much I slept around. I didn't even care if they used protection or not. It was like I had a death wish. I thought about it." His voice went quieter. "Dying, I mean. But that would have killed my folks." He had more to tell but he wasn't ready yet to tell Shane the whole story. That was too raw and this was all still too new.

Shane reached out a warm hand and took Matthew's cold one. His earlier touchiness had certainly disappeared. "God, you'd lost someone, Matthew. Someone you loved. You were allowed to go off the rails although I'd never advocate killing yourself. And you pulled yourself back from the brink. You're here now, aren't you?"

Matthew had already said more than he'd intended, but Shane was so easy to talk to. He didn't want this to become more emotional that it was. "I'm so sorry I was such a prick," he managed to say at last. "Last night I saw Sam's wedding ring still on my finger after we fucked and it just all came flooding back. I normally take it off, but I forgot. It just made me crazy. I—I like you, Shane. I want to see more of you. But I'm just not ready to make it anything more than just sex and two men sharing each other's company. If you can live with that, maybe we can strike a deal."

Shane stared into Matthew's red rimmed eyes. "I'm happy to take it slowly and see where it goes." He smiled. "But I am an impatient bastard. When I find something I like, I tend to want to get it. So be warned."

He leaned forward and kissed Matthew, his impatient, hungry tongue seeking out Matthew's own. Matthew loved the taste of him, the unique taste of mint, coffee and just Shane.

Suddenly the loud tones of Muse's "Supremacy" shattered the quiet of the apartment. Shane grimaced as he detached his lips from Matthew's and stood up. "Mobile," he explained at Matthew's puzzled look. "Work beckons." He moved over to the kitchen top and picked up his mobile. "Shane Templar. Afternoon, Kade. What can I do for Moonshine Inc. today?"

Matthew saw Shane's brow furrow in concentration as he listened.

"I can take a look for you. It sounds to me like users need to upgrade to the latest version so that it takes care of the security issue. That software is bloody wide open from the sounds of it. The last thing you want is that level of vulnerability. Send me the links and I'll take a look. No problem. Cheers, Kade."

He finished his conversation and looked at Matthew.

"Sorry about that. Now where were we?"

Matthew frowned. "That sounded pretty impressive. I don't even know what you do for a living other than the escorting. I know you said your laptop was your trusty tool but what exactly does that mean?"

Shane looked wary. "I do consultations for companies."

"What kind of consultations?"

"I help them with their security arrangements."

Matthew thought Shane was being extremely cagey with his job details. "Again, what exactly is it that you do?"

Shane sighed. "I suppose you'd know it better as hacking. I help people find the flaws in their online security and shut the loop holes." He looked at Matthew as if expecting him to ask a question.

"So you're a hacker? Do you have a Certified Ethical Hacker— a CEH certificate?" Matthew felt a glimmer of satisfaction at Shane's surprised expression.

"Yes, I do, amongst other things. You know about this stuff then? I help companies find the flaws in their security systems." He grinned. "The first question people normally ask me is can I hack into their bank and put money in their account, change their University scores or whether aliens do actually exist in the CIA database. It gets boring." He smirked. "Even if I can do all those things. But I hate to tell you, there are no bloody aliens out there." He smiled. "I've been doing this since I was a kid, found I had a talent for it and did a whole load of courses and certifications." He shrugged. "It's a good living doing something I love."

Matthew chuckled and nodded. Now that he'd shared some of his burden about Sam, he felt a lot more relaxed. "Sam had a case once which hinged around criminal activity in hacking. We used to talk about it. He was helping prosecute a young man who was a cracker, who'd gained access to a major bank group and defrauded them of over three million pounds. I learnt quite a bit about it then. I helped him research it." He looked at Shane. "Are you good at it then?"

Shane smiled, looking as if the fact Matthew knew something about what he did was quite a turn-on. "Yup, I'm one of the best, baby. *Backdoor* at your service. Bushwhacker and I are legends in there." He waved toward his laptop.

Matthew almost swallowed his tongue. "*Backdoor?*" he gasped. "Really, that's your online name?"

Shane grinned. "You know it. A bit of the old double entendre. Backdoor as in going through a system arse about tits and of course," he winked cheekily, "there's the other bit as well."

Matthew chuckled. "God, you are incorrigible. I thought I'd heard everything when I learnt about your bloody computer and the fact he had a name. I'm going to have my hands full with you, aren't I?"

Shane leaned forward and trailed his lips across Matthew's. He looked pleased at Matthew's words, a faint smile on his face.

"I'm counting on it. In *so* many ways, Mr. Langer."

Matthew groaned. Five minutes later after some fairly intense lip activity and lots of nuzzling Matthew was feeling much better. God knows how he was going to make it back to the office without poking everyone on the tube with his raging hard-on, but he'd have to manage it.

"I really need to get back to work," he said as he lay cuddled against Shane's side. "I called and told them I'd work later to make up for the time. But I don't want to take advantage of them. I really like working there."

Shane kissed the top of his head. "Fine. You go back and do your lawyerly stuff. Maybe we can get together on the weekend and really get to know each other better." He stroked Matthew's cheek softly. "But before you go…"

"Shane, what the hell are you doing?" Matthew gasped as Shane's hands reached inside his now miraculously open trousers and grasped him firmly.

"Make-up sex," he said huskily as he bent over Matthew's lap. "Always the best kind. I can't have you going back to your prissy law firm with something like this. It would be such a bloody waste."

Shane stood at the window and watched as Matthew made his way across the busy street to the tube to return to work. The raging emptiness inside Shane that had been there since last night had been immediately assuaged by the sight of the other man standing, pale and looking like shit, on his doorstep. The earlier phone call had simply caught Shane at a bad time. He'd been feeling pretty miffed about the whole sorry event of last night. But seeing the man in person, knowing that he'd got guts to do that for him, knock on his door not knowing what to expect—that had been different.

He'd liked the fact that Matthew thought he was "going to have his hands full with him." In his book that implied a longer-term relationship than he'd thought Matthew had wanted.

Shane had always been a nurturer. His mother had used to say that if Shane saw something broken he'd want to fix it. Unfortunately, that seemed to extend to humans as well. And Matthew Langer, sexy, tortured, and great tasting, was someone he wanted to repair. Shane had sent Matthew on his way after relieving his pressure with a quick blow job. Matthew had promised to call him tonight after work. Perhaps there might be a chance of a get-together. It was Friday night after all. And the weekend ahead sounded promising.

They'd agreed on the use of the word "friend" for each other in public. Matthew had not been keen on using the word "boyfriend" as Shane suggested, saying it was too personal and too soon. He hadn't liked "partner" either, saying that inferred a long-term relationship. As they were lovers in the physical sense of the word, Matthew hadn't objected to using that one—in fact had seemed fairly proud of it.

Shane had gotten frustrated at the man's anal tendency to have everything labelled properly. He'd sarcastically suggested "fuck-buddy" at which Matthew had scowled and shaken his head. Grudgingly Shane agreed 'friend' would have to do the trick. But privately he'd decided he'd use whatever word he liked to describe his relationship with Matthew if he was out of earshot. Starting with boyfriend. He'd never liked the word partner anyway. That was for business.

He sat down to check on the progress of his five million pound transfer and smiled in satisfaction. All on track. That sleazy Walter Debussy wouldn't know what hit him on Monday morning when banking opened. And that little weasel Roy Parsons was in for a nasty surprise too, even sooner than that. Shane had managed to plant a computer virus on his mobile phone, one that would download gay porn from various websites and send the pictures out to people in his phone book. The man would have a lot of explaining to do. Shane knew he was taking a chance with the whole gay thing being the trigger, but he'd covered his tracks well. Neither Roy nor Walter knew about his online talents, so he figured he'd get away with it—for a while anyway. He snickered.

"You're about to become a gay porn superstar, you little motherfucker. That will teach you to threaten me and my new boyfriend."

Thinking about it made him extremely horny, so he thought he'd take a shower and perhaps alleviate some of his own stress in there. He put the lid down on Bushwhacker, gave him a soft, loving caress and made his way to the bathroom, whistling. Today hadn't turned out so badly after all.

All hell breaks loose

Sunday morning Matthew sat gingerly at the breakfast table in Shane's flat. He was dressed in a pair of sweats, his backside tender as Shane had pounded away at it most of the weekend. However, he'd promised Matthew that it was his turn next to have Shane's. Matthew was looking forward to that. He watched as Shane moved around the kitchen making breakfast. The man appeared to be quite a good cook. Matthew wasn't bad, but if he could get away with not doing it, he would.

Shane's grey sweatpants hung loosely on his lean hips, the top of his arse just visible above the waistband. Matthew could have looked at it all day. He dragged his eyes away to find Shane's eyes fixed on his.

"Finished looking at my arse now?" he teased. "I promise you it's yours next time. I've been hogging yours enough, so I think it only fair."

Matthew felt a thrill of excitement at the thought.

Shane carried two plates with very well-turned omelettes and two slices of toast to the table. He sat down and the two men started to tuck into breakfast.

Shane smiled at him. "I wanted to ask what happened to your nose. It has this crooked thing going on with it."

Matthew shrugged. "I used to play hockey when I was at school. One of the guys lost control of his stick and whacked me across the nose with it. It was broken and they fixed it, but it was never the same." He frowned. "Why, do you think it looks strange? My sister's always telling me to have it fixed, but I've never really seen the need. She's a model so looks to her are important."

Shane shook his head. "It's cute."

Matthew scowled. That was a term he hadn't been called often before. He wasn't sure he liked it.

Shane grinned. "It gives you this air of being a reprobate. I like it. Tough and manly." Matthew felt better at that remark.

The soft rich voice of Michael Bublé drifted through the kitchen as they ate. Matthew was quite a fan of the man's music himself. It seemed that was another thing he and Shane had in common. He wondered if Shane had the same man-crush on Mr. Bublé that Matthew had, but that was one fantasy he wasn't sharing.

"What made you want to become a hacker?" asked Matthew. "It's not the usual thing a boy decides he wants to be when he grows up, is it?"

Shane shrugged. "I was a bit of a know-it-all at school, and I seemed to drift into computer science. One thing led to another and I found I had a real aptitude for being able to spot things in computer programming that other people couldn't see. It became a bit of a passion. I studied it in my spare time, found a mentor online who taught me a lot, and it just grew from there."

"What did your folks feel about that?" asked Matthew. "Did they understand what you were doing?"

Shane's face darkened. "They just thought I was a geek. I don't think my dad had any idea what I did. Then things fell apart when they found out I was gay."

Matthew stared at him. He'd come out when he was fifteen to his mother and father and they'd been nothing but supportive. He'd had his share of troubles growing up but at least his family had understood.

"What happened?"

Shane shifted uncomfortably on the kitchen stool. "It wasn't a case of talking about it, more showing..." His voice tailed off.

"My dad walked in on me doing the next-door neighbour's son. I had my dick up his arse at the time and like I said, my dad didn't take it too well." He gave a curt laugh. "Dad had an image to maintain with his fancy oil business and his money. It didn't include a gay son."

Matthew's mouth dropped open. "God, that must have been awkward. What a way to find out." His voice held a slight trace of amusement. Shane frowned.

"Yeah, well, he kicked me out of the house. Told me to pack my stuff and piss off along with some other choice phrases," he said bitterly.

"And did you?" Matthew asked. "Piss off, I mean."

Shane nodded. "I packed my bags, kissed my mom and left. I've never been back. I still see my mother though. We meet every now and then and Skype, do the whole birthday card and Mother's Day thing but I won't go back home. I don't want to see my dad." He looked down at the table. "I haven't seen him since I was seventeen."

"Seventeen? How the hell did you cope, leaving home so young? Where did you go?"

Shane looked evasive. "I had a place to stay in London for a while."

Matthew looked at him. "You're not telling me something, Shay. What are you holding back?"

Shane flushed. "God, you are so nosy. I told you. There's not much more to tell. Can we drop the whole subject please?" He seemed annoyed at Matthew's questioning. Matthew suddenly felt the penny drop and had to know the answer. "You said your dad had an oil business."

Shane fidgeted, looking uneasy. Matthew thought he regretted saying anything at all about his family from the look on his face.

"Is your father Ray Templar, the oil mogul? Templar Oil and Gas?"

The younger man scowled. "Yes."

For the umpteenth time since meeting this man. Matthew's jaw dropped. Templar Oil and Gas were one of the foremost oil and gas companies in Britain, owning a string of wells all across the world.

"Christ, Shane, he's a multimillionaire! And you have nothing more to do with him?"

Shane scowled. "No. I don't. His choice, not mine. I haven't spoken to him in eleven years, and I don't intend ever doing so. So if you think I'm the meal ticket out of your lawyerly life, think again." His whole easygoing demeanour had changed instantly with the talk of his father.

"That was uncalled for," said Matthew, his temper rising. "I'm not here because I thought you had bloody money."

Shane quirked an eyebrow at him. "No, you're here because you like the look of my arse. And I don't like talking about my father."

Matthew leaned forward, still a little annoyed at Shane's last comment. "But you still see your mother? Have you ever wondered whether your dad might regret what he said? Tried to contact him maybe?" Matthew had adored his own father and he couldn't imagine never having had him in his life.

"No." Shane said. "I haven't wanted to talk to him. Can we leave this conversation alone now?" He stood up and walked over to the sink, his back taut with tension.

"Where did you go when you left home?" Matthew's voice was quiet.

Perhaps leaving Shane's father out of the conversation might get things back on track. Shane definitely had a bug up his arse about that subject.

Shane turned to look at him, his eyes distant. "I got on a train and went to London to find someone I thought might help. A man called Michael who I'd met when I went to a Gay Pride March when I was sixteen. He was a lot older than me but we hit it off, and he gave me his number and told me if I was ever in trouble to call. Mikey was happy to take me in, give me somewhere to stay while I got settled."

Matthew looked into Shane's blue eyes. "How much older than you was he?"

Shane looked at him, frost in his eyes. "What does that matter? And what the hell's with the first degree anyway?"

Matthew stared at him. "Sorry. I just wondered that's all. Making conversation, getting to know you."

Shane messed about in the sink, his back to Matthew. Matthew kept quiet, not wanting to make things worse.

Shane spun around. "If I answer your questions do I get to ask some of my own to you?" His voice was challenging.

Matthew felt his face tighten. "It depends on the questions."

Shane huffed, his eyes dark. "I thought that would be the answer." He glared at Matthew but relented. "Mikey was eighteen years older than me. And before you ask, Mr. Nosy Parker, yes, we were lovers."

Matthew was taken aback. "Hell, Shane, you were just seventeen years old. That seems a little opportunistic of him."

Shane glared at him. "It was either that or live on the bloody streets, Matthew. I had plans to get some money but I needed a base of operations to work from so I could get the funding I needed. I'm sorry that relationship doesn't fit in your neatly ordered and controlled world." His tone was biting and Matthew's temper flared again.

God, had he just found another tender spot from Shane's past?

"Hell, Shay, you can be such a brat. I wasn't judging you, more wondering about a man a lot older than you taking advantage of a young, lost teenager." He felt irked at Shane's comment about his "neat and orderly" world.

So he liked order in his life. Was that such a bad thing?

Shane raised a sardonic eyebrow. "I can assure you he didn't take advantage of me, Matthew. In fact, it was the other way around. I seduced him into fucking me. I was a very persuasive brat." His words were harsh as he stared at Matthew.

Matthew wondered in confusion how a few nights of sheer heaven could have turned into this ugly spat so soon. He'd obviously found Shane's Achilles' heel.

Shane watched his face. "Mikey had always had a soft spot for me. It was no hardship getting him to take me to bed. I knew then I'd at least have a place to stay until I sorted out my money situation." He snorted explosively. "And please don't tell me like others have that I had 'daddy' issues. I can assure you there was nothing 'daddy-like' about the things Mikey and I used to get up to."

Matthew stood up and took his plate over to the sink. He turned to face Shane, whose face was set. "I'm going to shower." Matthew said. "It looks like we've touched on a couple of subjects you don't want to talk about, so it's best that I disappear now before I put my foot in it anymore. Let you simmer down a little. Thanks for breakfast."

As he headed toward the bedroom he heard Shane clattering the plates again in the sink. He went to the en-suite and started the shower. Matthew's stomach was clenched tight, and he had an ache in his chest that the warm water did nothing to diminish.

God, the man was infuriating. He was usually so easygoing, but it looked like he had his own demons just like anyone else.

Matthew liked being with Shane, but if this was what he had to look forward to, he wasn't so sure he wanted it anymore. Things could get very complicated. Fifteen minutes later he was clean, dressed, and ready to go home. He picked up his jacket from the bed, his wallet from the bedside table and left the bedroom. He found Shane standing gazing out at the river, his eyes fixed on some point beyond the horizon.

Hell, the man still did things to him even though he was a complete pain in the arse. He was simply the sexiest man Matthew had ever seen.

"I'm going now," Matthew said as Shane continued to stare out the window. "I'm sorry if I touched a nerve asking the things I did. I was trying to get to know you a little better. Call me if you want to talk or anything any time soon."

He took a deep breath and left the flat.

Shane heard the front door close and he leaned his forehead against the cool glass of the window. He closed his eyes in despair.

Shane Templar, you can be such an idiot. One mention of your dickhead father and Mikey and you're all neurotic and growly. You should have just told him to stay away from the topic. But no, you felt you needed to share. You just want to please that bloody man, don't you?

He moved away from the window, making his way to the shower. He could still smell Matthew in his bedroom, the scent of his body and his maleness on his bed sheets. Shane sat down on the bed and buried his face in his hands.

You are such a prick, Templar. At least the man left you an out to call him, surprisingly enough seeing as how we're talking about Matthew Langer. Beautiful man but oh, so bloody reserved and controlled. You're bloody lucky he didn't just say goodbye now and get you out of his life, given that he wants uncomplicated.

Shane heaved a great sigh as he stood up to shower. Perhaps after he'd washed and dressed, had another cup of coffee and spent some time on Bushwhacker, he'd have his head straight and he'd give Matthew a call. Explain a little more about why he hated talking about his father and the memories it invoked. And the thing with Mikey that had been so complicated.

Mikey had been the first man to really break his heart.

Shane managed to last until after lunch before making the phone call to Matthew. He'd considering texting him but he needed to hear his voice.

Hell, I've got it bad, he thought, as he listened to the phone ringing on the other side. I'm like that bloody seventeen-year-old teenager all over again, waiting for Mikey to come home.

"Matthew Langer."

"Matty. It's me." Shane waited for a reaction.

"I know. Caller ID. What's up?" Matthew's voice was wary.

Shane swallowed, his nerves getting the better of him. "I wanted to say I was sorry. About this morning. I'd like to maybe get together again and start the day over." He took a deep breath, waiting for Matthew's response. There was silence on the other end.

"Matthew? You there?"

"I'm here." Matthew's quiet voice sounded tired. "I'm not sure this is such a good idea, Shane. We seem to rub each other the wrong way a lot. Maybe it's just not meant to be."

Shane's heart lurched in fear and he resorted to his usual foil for situations like these— levity. "Matty, we definitely rub each other in the way we're supposed to, I promise you. Please don't give up on us."

Matthew sighed. "Shay, I don't want to give up. I'm just conscious we both have skeletons in our closets. I'm damned if I know which ones of yours not to take out."

"We can get to know each other and learn which ones we can leave in, which ones we can live with and which ones we can share. I want to share some of them with you, but I'd like to do it face to face."

There was silence then a long sigh. "What do you have in mind?"

"My place, I guess, around eight? We can talk and see what happens from there." Shane held his breath waiting for Matthew's answer.

"Fine. I'll see you at eight. Listen, I need to go. I'm meeting a friend in a little while. See you later."

The line went dead and Shane disconnected the call and laid his mobile on the dining room table. At least Matthew was coming over. That was a good start.

Matthew arrived at eight p.m., casually dressed in chinos and a tailored shirt and as punctual as ever. Shane motioned him inside.

God, this man looked good in whatever he wore. He wore clothes like a fashion model, with his broad shoulders, lean hips and long legs and an arse that made Shane want to bite it—again. Shane's mouth watered at the prospect of getting up close and personal with said backside again. He had to play his cards right tonight.

"Drink, Matty?"

Matthew nodded. "I'll have a beer, Shane. I had a whiskey earlier with a friend of mine and a beer would chase it nicely."

"Oh? What friend would that be?" As he fiddled getting the drinks, Shane pretended he wasn't worried.

"A female friend. Julia from the office. I've told you about her." Matthew smiled slightly. "She's quite a character. She gives as good as she gets and she calls a spade a spade. You'd like her." He grinned. "She doesn't put up with any nonsense from me, I can tell you. At work or outside the office."

Shane felt a sense of relief course through his body. "Yeah, I remember her. She sounds cool. I'd like to meet her one day. Compare Matthew notes." He heard Matthew chuckle and felt a sense of relief that perhaps things would be all right. Shane passed the beer to Matthew and sat down beside him on the couch. They were both silent as they drank from the bottles.

Finally Matthew spoke. "Has the bitch left the building then?"

His voice was even, with a tinge of something Shane thought might have been amusement. Shane felt his face flush. "She's on holiday, at least. Christ, Matty, I'm sorry. It's just when things turn to talk about my dad and Mikey, I tend to get all agitated."

"I noticed," Matthew remarked drily. "I definitely hit a sore spot this morning. And I thought we were doing so well."

Shane shifted on the couch. "About my dad. I need to tell you something about the day I left."

Matthew nodded, his eyes watching Shane's face intently.

Shane took a deep breath. "When my dad came into my room, without knocking and found me with my dick embedded halfway in Dean's backside, he went crazy. He hit me so hard I went flying across the room. He kicked Dean out, and then he told me he was disgusted that his son was a faggot, a queer, and he didn't want such an abomination in his house. He looked as if he wanted to kill me."

He took a shuddering breath at the memory of his father's anger and disgust. "I told him I couldn't help what I was, that I'd known for nearly two years, but been too afraid to say anything. I didn't know how my parents would deal with it. My dad wasn't an out-and-out homophobe, but he had his views. Believe me, they were black and white that night. I'd never heard him so mad." His voice trembled.

Shane had thought he was over the hate some people felt for men who loved other men. His voice trailed off.

Matthew leaned forward and stroked his thumb across his hand, his eyes focused on Shane. "Go on," he prompted. "You need to talk about this."

Shane closed his eyes then opened them to see Matthew's grey ones boring into his, encouraging him. "I said I couldn't live without being who I was, and he told me then I needed to leave. So I packed a few things, went down and kissed my mum and left. My mother was in such a state, I was worried she'd have another fit if she got upset."

He met Matthew's puzzled look. "Mum's suffered from epilepsy since she was a child but it was under control. I told her I was leaving for a while, that I'd be back. But I had no intention of ever going back. I was seventeen, Matty. And he threw me out for being gay. I went to Mikey's. He got me a job as a barman in a dubious gay bar in the centre of London." Shane hoped his next words might lighten the atmosphere. "I had to wear a bloody cowboy outfit, for God's sake." He waited for the reaction.

Matthew laughed.

Shane grinned. "I knew that would get your interest. Maybe we should try it one night."

Matthew reached over and pulled Shane into his arms. "We should *definitely* try it one night," he agreed as he stuck his tongue in Shane's ear, causing Shane's dick to rise towards the ceiling.

Matthew was obviously very into the cowboy story. "Matty, I'm trying to be serious," he chuckled.

"Oh, I'm serious," his lover murmured as he nibbled Shane's ear. "Serious about getting you in just leather chaps and a cowboy hat. God, I want to come just thinking about it."

"Matty, can I finish my bloody story before you fuck me senseless in your head, please?"

Matthew sighed and stopped his teasing. "Fine. Carry on, Billy the Kid."

Shane nestled into Matthew with a low laugh. "I stayed with Mikey for about six months. In that time I managed to make enough to buy some better laptop equipment and make myself some money. Once I had that, I could afford to move out. I bought this place when I turned eighteen. Mikey and I saw each other seriously for a while, but it finally tapered off." He shrugged. "He went to Spain on some cruise line and that was it. Probably found some cute Spaniard. He called me and told me he wasn't coming back."

He remembered how hurt he'd been by Mikey's casual disappearance. He'd been Shane's first real love. Shane blamed his father for this first heartbreak too. If he hadn't kicked him out, he'd never have gotten involved with Mikey to the extent he had and not had his heart broken in the process. It might be a twisted logic, but it made perfect sense to Shane.

"You cared for him a lot. I can hear it in your voice. The wanker. How could anyone give you up?" Matthew's voice was fierce. Shane raised his lover's hand to his lips and kissed the knuckles.

"I was a needy eighteen-year-old kid. He got tired of it, I guess. I threw myself into work, learned more about my craft, studied, went to night classes. I just wanted to forget about him. I kept in touch with my mother, seeing her every now and then outside of the house. She told me my father was getting over things and that he wanted to speak to me." His voice fell quiet. "But she didn't see his face when he hit me. She didn't hear the disgust in his voice. My own father couldn't bear the sight of me."

Matthew leaned forward and cradled Shane's face in his hands. "He was an arsehole," he said roughly. "You didn't deserve that, babe, and I can see how it would upset you now to dredge it all up."

He kissed Shane and Shane fell into the kiss like a drowning man being given an oxygen mask. This was what he wanted— Matty's lips on his, his hands on his body and his closeness. Telling Matthew had been a good idea.

Matthew pulled away, leaving Shane bereft and extremely horny. He hoped that was going to get sorted soon.

Matthew laughed. "This is one heck of a relationship we've started, Shay, saying sorry to each other all the time. We're like a couple of bitches." His lover smiled to take the sting out of his words. He waved a hand around the very trendy St. James's apartment. "So this is all paid for by your hacking and escorting talents? You must be very good at what you do." He grinned. "I can vouch for the one but not the other."

Shane fidgeted and saw Matthew regarding him with narrowed eyes. Shane flushed again. His boyfriend seemed to be becoming adept at spotting his tells.

Matthew stroked his chin. "I'm thinking the answer to that one is a no then? So how did you pay for all this luxury and that sexy clothing I love so much?"

Shane mumbled something under his breath.

Matthew cocked his head in query. "Sorry, I didn't catch that. You must have had something in your mouth and it wasn't me."

"I stole it, all right? I hacked into my dad's offshore accounts and took enough money to set myself up. The bastard had more than enough and he could spare it."

Matthew didn't look very surprised at that admission. "I see. Well. I expected some dodgy admission, but this one's a doozy. How much did you steal? So I know how much proceeds of crime I might have to defend you for if anyone ever tries to arrest you."

Shane was scornful. "They won't find me. My dad's computer system was filled with holes, seriously flawed. I bet a kindergarten kid could have gotten in—"

"How much, Shane?"

There was a long pause. "Three million pounds." Shane scowled. "A lot less than I wanted to take, but I knew if I took any more he'd definitely never stop looking for the culprit. Three mill to him was chump change."

At the look of incredulity on Matthew's face Shane chuckled, reached out and pushed Matthew's jaw closed. "You look like a bloody goldfish trying to take in air, Matty. Not very fetching."

"Three million fucking pounds?" Matthew's voice was disbelieving.

Shane nodded, a small smile forming on his lips. "Uh-huh. So you, my friend, are bonking your very own millionaire. And your language is becoming atrocious, Langer. You want to watch that."

Now that the admission was out in the open, Shane was enjoying the reaction it had caused in his still gobsmacked lover. He waved a hand at the flat around them.

"I paid cash for this place. The rest of the money is in its own offshore account earning me interest. No one raised an eyebrow. They tried to find the money. I watched them scurrying about like ants for about six months after I took it. But they never found anything. They didn't suspect it was me because of course, I was just the queer son with no discernible talents other than sticking my dick where it didn't belong." His voice grew bitter. "And my dad's never bothered to find me, never come looking. He didn't care much I suppose."

He reached out and tousled Matthew's hair, who was still staring at him.

"I can't believe this," the lawyer said dazedly. "Shane, you stole a fortune of money from your own father?"

"Oh get over it, Matty. The man is a prick." Shane picked up an apple from the bowl on the coffee table and crunched into it. Juice dribbled down his chin and he wiped it absently. "My dad has probably made more than that in the past week. He's still out there taking over the world. He's in Russia at the moment, tomorrow, Asia, the next day, the moon."

He glanced at Matthew. "I have investments. I live well but I'm not crazy with it, or I'd have a bloody Ferrari. But honestly, it's more for my old age than anything. I have a couple of places I support with funding, like the shelter on Knights Street for the rent boys and a couple of the abuse homes for battered men and women. But I'm pretty good with it actually. I don't want to go crazy and get any alarm bells ringing. Someone somewhere might still be looking for it. I know it's been a while but I still like to be cautious."

He stood and leaned into Matthew, planting a kiss on top of his head. "Now you know what I got up to." He grinned. "It's getting late, lover and I fancy a shower. Give me a minute and you can join me if you like." He winked wickedly and disappeared, leaving Matthew still sitting on the couch looking as if the sky had fallen. Shane hoped he wouldn't be too long following him into the bathroom. He had a problem that really needed resolving.

Monday morning Matthew was sitting in his office, reading over some documents. He was still shell-shocked recalling the conversation of yesterday and wondering what the hell he'd gotten himself into with a millionaire who thought he could just take what he wanted. He'd also noticed that in their last conversation Shane had seemed to be very au fait with his father's movements and wondered what that was all about. Was Shane still taking the man's money or was he simply curious about his father and keeping tabs on him?

He was glad Shane had shared his story. Matthew couldn't imagine the pain and hurt he must have gone through having his own father kick him out because of his sexuality. Matthew had encountered problems with his being gay before, but at least he'd always had his family to back him up. His mobile rang. He picked it up. "Matthew Langer."

"You little bastard." The words spat venomously down the phone made the lawyer sit up in shock.

"Walter? What the hell? What's your bloody problem?"

"What did you do, you little fag? Where the hell is my money?" For a moment, Matthew imagined this was Shane's father calling him about his three million missing pounds. He gave himself a mental shake as he spoke curtly into the phone. "Walter, what the hell are you talking about? How the hell do I know what you did with your bloody money?"

"I've had five million pounds disappear out of a private offshore account that only you and your father knew about. The Channel Islands one. Seeing as how your father is deceased, that leaves me with one option. You. So perhaps you'd like to tell me what the hell you've done with my money!" The man's voice grew louder and uglier with every spoken syllable.

Matthew's heart sank. He thought he might know who had taken his ex-employer's money. He was sexy and blonde with a distinct lack of ethics. "I don't know anything about your missing money. Don't blame me because you can't manage it."

"Matthew, I'm warning you. Don't fuck with me. You were the only one other than Roy who knew about this account. The bank is investigating and they will find out what happened, I promise you."

"Well, perhaps you should ask Roy," Matthew said, his voice tight. "Originally you said only my father and me knew about it. Now good old Roy also knew it was there. Who else, Walter? The butcher, the baker, the candlestick maker? It had nothing to do with me, so leave me the hell alone." He disconnected the call and leaned back in his chair, closing his eyes in despair.

"Shane, what the hell have you done, you arsehole?" He dialled his lover's number, scowling when it went to voicemail. He left a terse message.

"Shane, I've just had a call from Walter Debussy asking me if I had anything to with some missing money. Please tell me you had nothing to do with that. Call me back."

He rang off and sat and stared at his computer screen for a while, his mind racing. His mobile rang. It was Shane. He picked it up quickly.

"Shane? You got my message?"

"Hello to you too." Shane didn't sound all that worried, and Matthew started to feel relieved. Perhaps he was barking up the wrong tree after all.

"Sorry, I'm rather uptight this side. Walter called me accusing me of doing something with his money. It's gone missing and I was one of only a couple of people that knew about this account. He thinks I may have had something to do with it."

"So money goes missing from some rich guy's account and all of a sudden I'm your number one suspect?" Shane's voice was even.

Matthew started to feel uncomfortable. "I know you have the means to take his money, and you certainly had the motivation after the way he treated you at the hospital. I just wanted to make sure you didn't have anything to do with this whole thing."

There was silence. Then, "No, I didn't. It was nothing to do with me. If he's lost money, it's through his own carelessness, or a bank error." Shane sounded out of sorts.

"Shay, I'm sorry I had to ask. It's just—"

"Never mind. Look, I'll talk to you later, all right? I'm in the middle of something and I need to get it finished. I'll call you." Shane rang off.

Matthew sighed. He hoped this wasn't yet another time he'd have to apologise to his new buddy.

Back home Shane was storming round his study, his face black with anger—anger at himself.

Christ, had he just dropped Matty in it?

He'd had no idea when he took that money that there was any way Matthew could possibly have been connected with that bank account. Now Walter Debussy thought he might have been involved and there was no way he was letting that be laid at Matty's door.

No bloody way.

He slammed his fist on the desk. He'd have to move the money back somehow. He'd have to create a record that looked like a clerical error or something the bank had done. It wouldn't be the first time he'd engineered such a thing. He'd have to move quickly though. He had no doubt they'd be investigating Walter's missing money. The quicker these things were done the less likely they were to be noticed and scrutinised, especially if it went back in quick enough.

Shane ran a hand through his hair and sat down at his desk, hitting the keyboard in a series of fast strokes, totally focused on the task hand, his fingers flying as he moved the money back into Walter Debussy's account.

It took him an hour, but finally he thought he might have sorted it. He watched as the screen scrolled and the flickering images flashed, and he heaved a sigh of satisfaction as the balance on Walter's account increased by five million pounds. Walter might think it was a coincidence that the money was back in his account just after speaking to Matthew, but he could do nothing about that.

Hopefully the trail he'd left would be noticed as simply being the clerical error he'd created. Let the bank explain it if they could. They'd probably be satisfied that the money was back and one of their biggest customers was happy.

"Sorry, David, old son," he muttered to himself. "You just lost your nest egg. Better that than have my new boyfriend arrested. I can't have anything happen to him. He's been through enough."

Agreeing the boundaries

Matthew arrived at Shane's place around eight with a bottle of wine in one hand and a good bottle of whiskey in the other after Shane texted him to come for dinner. Relieved that Shane wasn't upset about Matthew's questions earlier concerning the event with Walter, their relationship appeared to be back on track.

He knocked and waited for the door to open. When it did, his legs nearly gave way. Shane was dressed in the sexiest little black number he'd ever seen. Smooth black chinos tapered down his legs to his ankles. He was barefoot. A tight-fitting, long-sleeved black silk shirt, half opened, left a broad expanse of pale chest with a smattering of blond hair on show. Matthew knew that hair extended all the way down. His dark blond hair was mussed up and still wet and his very kissable lips smiled such a warm welcome that Matthew was instantly smitten once again by Shane's utter sexiness.

"Matty, come on in. And close your mouth. We'll do that a bit later, I promise."

He chuckled, the sound making Matthew's groin throb and he found himself so hard he could barely walk.

Shane apparently noticed because his eyes glinted. "Calm down. You think this is for you?" He gestured casually at his outfit as his boyfriend followed him into the kitchen. "I got offered such a good deal on a Carrington engagement later with some rich Arab Sheikh that it was too good to turn down."

Matthew's temper flared at the thought of someone else with Shane. His body stilled as Shane continued.

"Apparently he loves slim blond men in black and he likes to—
"

Matthew could take it no longer. He slammed down the bottles of wine and whiskey onto the counter top and gripped Shane, pushing him against the wall with a fierceness that made their bodies slam together. He saw Shane's sly smile, felt his rising excitement in the hard press of his erection against Matthew's hips.

"You had better *not* be going out later dressed like that to meet some rich client," he said through gritted teeth. "I have my limits, Shay. And you've just reached them." He took Shane's mouth in a hard kiss, his cock pushing against him. Shane moaned into his mouth, his breath warm and his tongue as eager as his hands that stroked down the front of Matthew's trousers, caressing the hardness he found there.

"Matty, I was joking, honest," he laughed between rough kisses. His skin was already starting to feel tender from the bristle on Matthew's chin and top lip. "Christ, you're like my own personal sandpaper. Easy, tiger."

Matthew drew back, breathing hard, his eyes dark and unfocused. He felt such a sense of possession that it was hard to relinquish his hold on the man standing in front of him with swollen lips and eyes that looked like cool, clear pools of azure water.

"This is all for you, Matty," Shane whispered as his lips nuzzled Matthew's ear. "Only for you. Now can we get back to other social niceties so we can at least eat first before we get onto more of the good stuff?"

Reluctantly Matthew pulled away and walked unsteadily around the centre island of the kitchen, craving a drink to calm his nerves.

"There's a word for men like you," he said huskily as he uncorked the wine.

Shane grinned wickedly. "Really? And what would that be then?" Matthew ignored him as he poured two glasses of wine and passed one to Shane.

"Ta. That looks good. Spent more than a fiver on this one then, did you?" He moved deftly out of the way of Matthew's slap to his arm and dodged around the island to the other side.

"God, you are very physical tonight. I'm looking forward to that later." He sipped his wine and moved over to the stove. He busied himself with sorting out whatever was on the top—it smelt deliciously like fish—as Matthew watched him. He took a deep breath, not wanting to spoil the mood but needing to speak to Shane.

"Walter Debussy had some woman who said she was his PA call me." He took a large gulp of wine and then another one.

Shane continued messing about at the stove. "Oh yes? I thought that douche bag Roy was his PA. What did she have to say?"

"That it seemed there had been some glitch with the bank and Walter's money had been found safe and sound."

Shane turned and threw him a dazzling smile. "See, I told you. The bank cocked up. I'm glad it got sorted. I didn't like the idea that they thought you had anything to do with it."

Matthew sighed. "As long as he's got his bloody money back I don't really care." He gulped his wine. He hadn't eaten at all today, and it was giving him a bit of a buzz.

Shane looked at him in amusement. "Let me fill that up for you." He took Matthew's glass and topped him up. Matthew smiled his thanks.

"Right, I think we can eat. Poached salmon with lemon butter sauce, baby potatoes, mange touts and my personal favourite, asparagus spears."

Matthew's mouth watered. "God, that sounds good. You'll make some man a good wife one day." They grinned at each other as Shane dished up, and soon they were eating heartily whilst telling each other about their day. Finally they both sat back, stuffed with good food and probably more wine than was safe for a weeknight. Matthew had the feeling he might have a bit of a headache in the morning.

Shane stood up. "Come on, into the lounge. Time to kick off your shoes and get comfy on the couch. Maybe there's a decent movie on we can watch. Leave the dishes. I'll sort them out later. That's what dishwashers are for."

Matthew didn't listen but instead busied himself packing the dishwasher while Shane watched him in resignation. Matthew smiled at the look he got. "You cooked. I clean. Fair's fair. Can't have the little woman doing all the housework." He chuckled as Shane reached out and cuffed the side of his head.

Once the kitchen was clear, he wandered over to the couch. He flopped down on it, kicking off his shoes, and his socks followed soon after. He wiggled his toes, loving the sense of freedom in having nothing on his feet and settled back with a satisfied smile. Shane leapt onto the couch, sitting cross-legged next to him. Matthew made a small noise, closing his eyes at the feel of Shane's hand running through his hair.

"You're like a cat, you know that? You and your cat noises," chuckled his lover.

Matthew opened one eye indignantly. "I am not. When do I make cat noises?"

Shane leaned in, his lips brushing Matthew's ear. "Well, when I was sucking you off the other night, you definitely made little baby cat noises. And then when you came, you roared like a bloody lion." He laughed in delight at the flush that crept over Matthew's face. He glared at Shane.

"And then there's the cat-like licking…" Shane watched his face and Matthew thought Shane was testing the waters. He smiled and leaned over, running his tongue along Shane's jaw line.

"I like licking you," he whispered. "You taste good." He licked his way down to Shane's mouth and kissed him, his lover's lips soft and yielding beneath his. The pair drew apart and Shane snuggled in under Matthew's arm.

"You drive the remote. Find something we can watch until our supper settles."

Both of them liked horror movies. *28 Days Later* was showing, and they settled into watch Cillian Murphy wander aimlessly through the streets of a zombie-strewn London.

They were halfway through the movie when Shane's hand was rubbing Matthew's thigh as he watched the film.

Matthew had one thing he needed to discuss. It had been on his mind since the weekend, but he'd thought it was too soon to broach the subject then. But perhaps now might be a more amenable time especially given Shane's earlier comment about the Arab Sheikh.

"Shay?"

"Hmm?" Shane's hand was getting higher and Matthew was finding it difficult to concentrate on Cillian being pursued by dead, flesh-eating zombies.

"I know you said you were joking earlier about going out later, but *are* you intending still doing the escort work while we see each other?" His voice was quiet and he saw Shane sit up and look at him. He met the blue gaze with a level stare and forged ahead.

"I know you said you didn't sleep with your clients unless you really wanted to, but I'm not sure I could live with that in any way. I know this is early days but I'm not a player, Shane. If I start seeing a guy, it's one at a time, no matter what the nature of the relationship is. I'd expect the same from the person I'm seeing. That may sound unfair, but it's the only way I can do it."

Shane smiled. "I don't really need the money. I did it mostly so I could touch hot guys and get blow jobs. If you're going to meet those needs—*often*," he emphasized with a wicked grin, "I don't really need anyone else." He leaned forward to tickle Matthew's ear with his tongue. "As long as you're man enough to keep me happy in that arena, I guess I could give it up for you. Maybe one day I might even get to see where you live. It would be nice to see you on your own turf for a change."

Matthew felt uncomfortable. Taking Shane home to the house he'd shared with Sam wasn't on his dance card anytime soon. That implied a level of commitment he wasn't ready to give.

"I don't expect you to give up the escorting," he murmured. "Just stick to the escort servicing and nothing else. At least until we figure out what we want from each other."

"I know what I want from you," Shane whispered in Matthew's ear, causing him to squirm in sheer tortured pleasure. "I want you to suck me off. Then I want you to fuck me."

"Christ, Shay," Matthew groaned. "I was trying to have a serious conversation here. You can't say things like that and expect me to stay bloody sane."

Shane bit the lobe of his ear, causing Matthew to take a deep breath. "Of course," he murmured, "me screwing other men might teach me a few things I can bring home and show you."

His words were cut off as Matthew's face darkened. He grasped Shane's face in his hands.

God, this man drove him crazy.

"If we are to continue this, we *are* exclusive in the sex thing," he growled. "I'm not having anyone else put their bloody hands all over you. You're mine. I'm not into sharing."

Shane laughed, a deep, sexy sound that had Matthew's groin in knots. "So we agree. I'm officially all yours." He grinned, brushing his hand across the front of Matthew's groin whose cock was already standing up waving and saying hello.

"Are you sure?" Matthew growled. "You're not going to swap me for some Arab Sheikh?"

Shane kissed him more tenderly. "Yes, Matty. You have me." His kiss grew deeper and more urgent. "And you are *having* me too. Right now."

He moved over onto Matthew's lap, straddling him, his backside grinding into Matthew's groin, as Shane leaned down and took his mouth in a kiss that was full of both passion and sheer possession. Matthew felt himself harden, felt Shane's erection pressing against his stomach. Both of them groaned, tongues twining and darting like fish in a pond.

"Hell, we have too many clothes on," gasped Shane. "We need to get them off. I need you, Matty. I've been waiting all bloody day to feel you inside me."

In one fluid movement, he pulled his shirt over his head. Matthew took in the sight of his lean torso and stomach.

Shane reached for Matthew. Matthew lifted his arms as his shirt was taken off and flung onto the floor behind the couch. Shane's eyes darkened, his face greedy as he ran his hand over the lawyer's shoulders, down his chest, sliding silkily across the muscles of his stomach. He leaned forward and sucked Matthew's nipples, one then the other, taking the hard nubs between his teeth and sucking and biting them until Matthew could take no more. He was ready to explode.

"Shay, I need to feel you. Get your trousers off. Then get back here."

Shane grinned and stood up lithely, unzipping his trousers and letting them fall to the floor. His cock jutted out, proud and swollen, inviting Matthew to lean forward, pull his hips toward him and take it in his mouth. Shane hissed, his hands digging deep into the other man's hair as his groin curved into the fit of Matthew's hungry mouth. Matthew took him deep, his lips tightening and sucking as his tongue swirled around the tip.

"Jesus," Shane was gasping as his hands pushed Matthew's head down, his hips thrusting into the other man's mouth with an uncontrollable urgency. "Keep doing that."

Matthew knew he had a pretty good knack at giving blow jobs. He enjoyed the taste of having another man in his mouth, of feeling him squirm and curse as he sucked the life out of him.

He raised his eyes to Shane's as he watched his face, sheer bliss etched across his features.

In turn, Shane watched himself going in and out of Matthew's mouth. "I am not going to last much longer if you keep doing that," Shane's husky whisper only served to inflame Matthew more, and he increased his efforts.

To his credit, Shane lasted a fairly long time. Finally he swore and grunted as his hands dug tighter into Matthew's hair, pulling. Matthew felt Shane's thigh muscles tighten and strain as he gave a loud, uncontrollable curse, jerking forward as he climaxed. The hot, acrid fluid ran down Matthew's throat. Matthew took everything he could get and when he was done, he lifted his mouth from Shane's spent member and stood up, unzipping his trousers and letting them fall. He sat back down on the couch, his hands already stroking himself in anticipation as he motioned to Shane, who was still standing, spent and trembling, watching him with unfocused eyes.

"I need to be inside you. Sit on my lap and let me get you ready." He reached over to the side table where the lube and condoms were waiting. Shane straddled Matthew again, the warm feeling of his skin against his own and the smell of sex making

Matthew faint with hunger. Matthew ripped open the condom and rolled it down. He poured lube into his hands and stroked his condom-covered cock, then slid his finger into Shane's eager entrance.

The other man hissed and arched his back as Matthew fingered him, gently stretching and opening him up. Matthew knew it wouldn't take long to get him where he wanted. But Shane had other ideas.

"Fucking enough already," Shane grunted as he positioned himself over Matthew. "It's time to let rip." He grinned wolfishly as he impaled himself, hissing in pleasure as he took him deep inside. Matthew pushed upwards, his hands firmly on Shane's hips as he pushed the man down on him, desperate to feel every inch of himself inside the other man. The two watched each other's eyes as they moved together, Shane lifting himself then going back down, gasping every time he did so, until there was only the sound of flesh slapping flesh, grunts and sighs and the wet noise of open-mouthed kisses.

Shane's warm skin, the sweat on his face, the look of tenderness in his eyes as he moved on top of him made Matthew's chest swell with feeling. An amazing sense of well-being flooded his senses and made him feel whole again.

"God, you feel incredible," Matthew panted as Shane tightened around him in practised and well-timed movements. His voice trembled as Shane spread his legs wider either side of Matthew and leaned back, forcing Matthew deeper and at a different angle, his hands gripping Matthew's shoulders, holding on for dear life.

The sensations grew even more intense and though Shane had already come once, Matthew could see his lover coming to life once again. He reached down and grasped him, feeling Shane jerk wildly with the sensation of being touched again. "Stroke me, just like that, make me come again. You owe me one, remember?"

Matthew chuckled as his fingers moved up and down Shane's shaft with practiced fingers, coaxing his lover on. "You're just bloody greedy," he grunted as his groin began to flood with heat and there was a rising sensation that said he was about to come.

His head reared back against the couch as he closed his eyes, giving way to the explosions inside him that felt like mini volcanoes erupting. He growled and thrust his hips up toward Shane, who leaned forward and kissed him with a wet, hot mouth. Matthew's growl grew louder. He thought the top of his head might explode with the pressure.

He felt the hot release of his own fluids shooting into the condom like jets from a water cannon. His body jerked and spasmed uncontrollably.

Shane collapsed against his chest as he came too, warm splashes of fluids reaching Matthew's stomach and chest, matting in his chest hair. The two men lay sandwiched together by semen, chests heaving as their bodies recovered from the intensity of their lovemaking.

"Now that felt good," murmured Shane as he sat up, and Matthew twitched as his sensitive cock moved inside Shane. "Having you inside me was a very fine idea. I'm glad we both go both ways." He kissed Matthew, his mouth sweaty and warm.

Shane shifted off Matthew. Matthew grimaced and removed the condom. He wiped his chest and stomach with tissues on hand on the table beside the couch and tossed them aside. He pulled Shane into him and they lay together for a while, Shane curled against Matthew's shoulder like a contented puppy.

Matthew wondered what the hell was happening here. It was all moving along far too quickly, having this brash, sexy, tender and caring man lying in his arms, feeling as if he belonged there. He wasn't ready for the feelings that overwhelmed him. This was supposed to be about sex and nothing more. It was all very disconcerting. He needed to focus on something else.

"Shay?"

"Hmmm?"

Matthew could tell the other man was almost asleep. "We need to try and see David again. I spoke to him last week and he sounded lost. We text every now and then but I'm still worried about him."

Shane shifted and looked up at Matthew, his eyes soft. "You know that won't be easy. He's been told to keep away from us both, and he's not going to disobey his dad. You know how much he controls him."

Matthew sighed and kissed the top of Shane's head. "I know. It's just...we used to be such good friends." He heard the wistfulness in his voice and knew Shane had heard it too when he reached up a hand and caressed Matthew's cheek.

"Can I ask you something?" Shane's voice was unsure.

Matthew looked at him carefully. "You can always ask, babe."

"Have you and David ever been an item?"

Matthew gazed at Shane in horror. "Good God, no! Whatever made you think of that?"

Shane shrugged. "The way you talk about him. You're very fond of him, and I just wondered."

Matthew ran a hand through his hair in agitation. "David and I are like brothers. We've known each other since we were kids. I've never even thought of him in that way. And he's way more into you than me. I'll have to watch him on that score." He frowned. "Having said that, what about you and David? You partnered him a few times. Did you ever do the horizontal or vertical mambo with him?" He felt a pang of jealousy even as he asked the question.

Shane spluttered with laughter. "God, you have a quaint way of putting things." He leaned forward and kissed Matthew hungrily.

"Let me put it in Shane language. I have never fucked David. Other than having his come all over me, that's as close as we ever got to bedroom action."

Matthew grinned and leaned over to draw Shane to him. "Good. Glad to hear that. David's my best friend, so knowing you two didn't screw each other is a good thing."

Matthew sighed. "I don't feel as close to him as I used to, though. We were really tight, but now Walter has driven this wedge between us. It's like a part of my life has ended and I don't know how to get it back."

"That part of your life may have ended, Matty, but this one's just beginning." He took Matthew's hand and laid it on his own warm chest. Matthew swallowed at the gesture, feeling Shane's heartbeat beneath his palm.

Something was definitely developing here, despite Matthew's best intentions. He felt scared at the thought.

It's all about the money

Two weeks of great sex and getting to know Shane later, Matthew was still enjoying it all. He found his relationship with Shane getting better every time the two men were together. Shane was an incredible lover—warm, funny and mischievous. And nothing seemed to faze him. He knew how to make Matthew's world rock when he went down on his knees to take Matthew in his mouth or made love to him in a variety of positions Matthew had never even dreamt were possible. He was caring and easygoing for the most part as long as Matthew stayed away from the topic of his father.

Shane had met his part of the bargain. He'd told his escort agency, Carrington Knights, that their "Templar Knight," as they slyly called him, was no longer available. They'd been pissed off, as he was one of the most popular they had. Matthew could believe that.

One afternoon Matthew managed to get an afternoon off and decided to surprise Shane at his flat. Armed with a bottle of wine, he drove over to Shane's place. He knew Shane didn't lock his door when he was working.

Matthew found the door open as usual and he snuck in quietly. He heard Shane muttering to himself in the kitchen, probably fortifying himself with strong coffee. Soft strains of what Matthew recognised as the jazz tones of Jamie Cullum floated through the room.

Matthew walked into the living area and laid the bottle of wine down on the dining room table. Bushwhacker was sitting idly on the table. The familiar page of Bradford Bank and Investments winked out at him from Bushwhacker's glowing screen. Matthew grew curious. That was the bank that Water Debussy used for his offshore accounts.

He peered closer at the screen and lost his breath.

The page detailed the transactions for Debussy Inc in the Channel Islands. Matthew could see the whole account detail and history, detail he was very familiar with in his previous role as the Debussy family lawyer. He felt a heat rise up through his stomach to his chest as he pondered the significance of what he was seeing.

"Matthew, what are you doing here?" Shane's wary tones echoed behind him. Matthew turned, his mind racing. Shane stood with his coffee cup cradled in his hands. He was dressed casually in cut-off jeans and a loose, white tee shirt. He was barefoot as usual and his hair was tousled and mussed.

"Surprising you, it seems." Matthew glared at Shane's noncommittal face. "Why are you in there on the bank account for Debussy Inc, Shane? I thought you told me you had nothing to do with that whole missing money saga. Now I come and find out you're accessing an account that only he and I and a couple of others apparently knew about."

Shane moved closer and put the laptop lid down. He laid his coffee cup on the table and glanced over at Matthew.

"I was checking something out." He didn't even try and hide what he was doing. He'd been caught red-handed and his voice was flat when he spoke. "I keep an eye on that account. You never know when David might need money. After the last incident I like to keep close to what's going on."

Matthew's voice was icy when he next spoke. "*Did* you take that five million pounds from Walter's account the day he called me about it going missing?"

Shane regarded him then nodded.

Matthew closed his eyes and counted to five. "You lied to me," Matthew said, an iron grip seizing his chest. The sickness in his gullet grew stronger.

Shane looked at him in exasperation. "Matty, I originally took it for a reason. If Walter ever went too far or excommunicated David, at least he'd still have some money. The man deserves it after all he's been through."

"You bloody *lied* to me," Matthew repeated, hearing a roaring in his ears as blood rushed and rose in anger.

Shane glared at him, his own face growing darker. "Yes, I fucking lied to you. I took the money after the fracas at the hospital. Then I learnt you knew about the account. I couldn't let Walter hound you. I made it look like a clerical error. I didn't want you to get into trouble or have to say you knew anything about it if I was found out. Plausible deniability and all that crap."

Matthew felt ill at the way the conversation was going. The day had gone from envisaging an afternoon of romance and good sex with his lover to a full-blown argument. "Christ, Shane, you can't just do stuff like this."

Shane laughed harshly as he walked around the table and picked up his coffee cup. He drank it, looking over the rim at Matthew. "It must be nice to live in your world, Matty. All clean and neat and ordered. Everything in its place. My world isn't quite like that. I have talents. I use them to help people."

"You steal money, Shane. No matter which way you look at it, you're a thief."

Shane's face flushed and he slammed his coffee cup down on the polished table. "I am not a fucking common thief. I resent that." His expression darkened. "You just walk in here and interfere in my business and *I'm* the bad guy? You'd never have known about anything if that laptop had been closed before you snuck in here." He slammed the table top with a flat hand, his face ugly. "And if it hadn't been for the fact that I found out you *were* involved, that money would still be sitting in an offshore account and David would now have it waiting just in case." He stopped, breathing heavily. "So get over it, Matthew. Stop that holier-than-thou fucking shit and climb down off that bloody high horse."

"I didn't sneak in." Matthew said. "I wanted to surprise you. I bought wine." He gestured toward the wine on the table. "I thought we could have a nice afternoon here. I was wrong, obviously." He was feeling more and more out of his depth.

Shane snorted. "Yes, it's always here at my place isn't it? Mr. 'I'm so bloody closed off I can't even let my lover come to my house.' When are you going to let me in, Matthew? We fuck, we have fun, we talk occasionally, and yet you never take me to your home. If we're talking about vices and things we don't like, what about that one then?"

"Why is it such a big thing for you to come to my house?" Matthew exclaimed. "Isn't it enough that we're together, no matter where we are?"

Shane looked at him in pity. "No, that's not what it's all about, Matty. It's about you opening up a little to me. About you taking that bloody wedding ring off your finger and me being able to call you my boyfriend instead of always not knowing what to call you. Oh sorry, my 'friend.' That's what we agreed, isn't it?" His voice grew edgier. "I'm not asking for a declaration of bloody affection or anything, just a reasonable expectation of being one half of whatever this relationship is that we have."

"I made it clear when we started that I didn't want to get too involved," Matthew shot back. He saw the flinch on Shane's face. Matthew knew once again he was being a bastard. Shane seemed to bring out the best and the worst in him.

"Yes. You've made that abundantly clear." Shane's voice was cold. "But perhaps we need to re-evaluate that based on what's happened here tonight. You don't approve of what I do. You called me a thief. Well, maybe I am, technically, but you know what? At least I try and make things better instead of shutting people out and living in the past like you do, trying to control every emotion you have."

Matthew stared at him, his gut clenching. "You know why-"

Shane cut him off with a wave of an impatient hand. "Yes, I know, Matty. And I deeply regret what happened to you. But it was a long time ago. And to be honest, which is something I have to tell you're not, especially with yourself, I think you are starting to care for me. You just don't want to admit it."

Matthew went cold. He took a deep breath.

Shane regarded him with eyes that were suddenly kinder. His voice was saddened and trembled a little. "Matty, maybe we need some space. I'm not going to stop being who I am and neither are you. And if we can't meet halfway then maybe this whole relationship thing is a bad idea. We've only known each other a little more than a month but we see each other nearly every day and spend the weekends together. Maybe it's too much."

Matthew didn't know what to say. The thought of not seeing Shane was the scariest thing he could think of at the moment, but perhaps it made sense to take a timeout. He nodded. "That could be an idea."

Shane gave a rueful sigh.

When he didn't speak, Matthew said, "Maybe some time to think things over would be a good idea." He turned to leave.

Shane nodded and made no move to stop him.

"Just be careful with that thing, Shay." Matthew indicated to Bushwhacker. "Don't go getting too clever and causing trouble for yourself. I don't want to have to be the one to bail you out of jail."

Shane stayed silent as Matthew made his way to the door and disappeared into the corridor.

Two days later Shane checked his phone for about the fiftieth time. He sighed. Still no message from Matthew. He kicked the side of his desk moodily and gazed at the computer screen flickering in front of him. His extremely unselfish plan to give Matthew time to get over his anger appeared to have backfired on him. He hadn't wanted to make that offer knowing what the man was like, but Shane had thought it was what he needed, and of course Matthew had accepted with alacrity.

"He hasn't called or texted, Bushie," he muttered to his laptop. "The bastard is really such an arsehole. He is so fucked up." His hands drummed impatiently on the desktop as he regarded his computer. "It's driving me bloody crazy not seeing him. What do you think I should do?" He sighed again. "Am I going to be the one making the first bloody move to get us back together? Because you know I'm not too proud to do that." He scowled at that thought. "He's a stubborn shit, is what he is."

He felt better at getting all his insults about Matthew out in the open even if the man wasn't there to hear them. He picked up his mobile and deliberated.

To text or not to text? Call voice to voice? What the hell was going to bring Matthew back to him?

Shane had had time to think about things whilst they'd been apart. He knew he tended to interfere, but he'd had David's best interests at heart. Walter didn't deserve any bloody consideration after what he'd done. Shane believed in poetic justice and retribution and he wasn't going to change anytime soon. He'd never knowingly hurt or destroy anyone - well, maybe a little but only if they deserved it. And the thing with Matthew's house—it pissed him off royally, but it *had* only been a month. Matthew had also been clear he hadn't wanted to get too committed too soon, and Shane, stupid bastard that he was, had accepted that. Shane's face darkened as he thought about his options. Finally he gave a deep sigh and picked up his phone. He texted a message to Matthew.

This is getting bloody boring. Are we going to talk anytime soon? I miss you. S x

Shane risked the kiss at the end. He wasn't too proud to beg where Matthew was concerned. He waited impatiently for a return text. He was still waiting two hours later when he went to bed at midnight, pissed and royally pissed off.

The following morning around seven, Shane woke to the sound of his phone chanting its customised message of 'Message received, all hands on dick!' over and over again until he managed to find it lying somewhere in between the bed covers. He'd been holding it when he'd fallen asleep, waiting for Matthew to text back. He checked the screen.

Sorry, I was out. Only saw your message now. Maybe we can get together to talk. Tell me when's suitable. M.

Shane swore. "Shit! He was bloody out? Where the hell was he? Getting his bloody rocks off at the club maybe? Matthew, you tosser." He threw the phone down on the bed and went to shower. By the time he'd finished he was feeling less stressed and sat on the bed with his towel wrapped around his waist. He picked up his phone and shot back a quick, to-the-point message.

What are you doing lunchtime? Come over for one o'clock? My place of course. S

He was still feeling miffed and didn't think Matthew deserved another kiss, and the snarky comment about his place was just— well, it was just the way he wanted to make a point.

One is fine. See you then. At your place. Of course. M

Shane smiled at the last few typical sardonic Matthew words. He then proceeded to be on tenterhooks the whole morning. He managed to occupy himself with a new job he'd taken on, but his mind was not in the game.

Shane made sure he dressed to kill. He wanted Matthew to see what he'd been missing. He pulled on his tightest, ass-hugging blue jeans, his favourite pec- and ab-outlining shirt, a pale blue, long-sleeved silky shirt that hugged his slim body and was easy to get off. No buttons. He decided against wearing underwear and shoes. He liked the feel of the floor beneath his feet and if things went the way he wanted them to, it was one fewer thing to get off in his haste to have Matthew's body. It had been too bloody long since he'd had Matthew's lips and body against him, and he was feeling the pinch.

When the doorbell rang at one on the dot, Shane was there to answer it. He'd been pacing the lounge, waiting for Matthew to arrive, and he had a knot in his stomach the size of the Shard.

He opened the door. Matthew stood there, looking pale and tired. Shane's heart melted at the sight of his man looking so vulnerable. He wanted to reach over and pull Matthew into his arms, but he didn't think that would go down too well.

"Shane." Matthew nodded, looking apprehensive. Shane gestured inside.

"Come in, Matty. I'll get us a drink."

He turned and made his way to the kitchen, as Matthew closed the door and followed him.

God, Matthew looked incredible, even with that tired look. His black chinos clung to his legs as if they'd been moulded to him, and the deep khaki formal shirt that he wore effortlessly, half-unbuttoned, looking as if he'd just casually thrown it on, suited his shoulders and colouring perfectly. He looked like a coffee-coloured muffin ready to eat.

Shane's groin was already heating up and the other man had barely been inside his home a few minutes. He busied himself pouring each of them a whiskey then took them to the lounge and set them down on the centre table. Sitting down, he patted the couch next to him.

"Sir down, Matty. How have you been the last couple of days?"

Matthew sat down next to Shane, regarding him with appraising grey eyes. "I've been okay, thanks. Work's been busy, so I've been getting home late."

Shane nodded. "I hear you. I have a job for the London Eye at the moment, re-designing some of their security and protocols for their systems. It's proving a bit of a challenge, but I'll get there."

"I'm sure you will." Matthew leaned forward and picked up his drink, taking a sip. Shane watched his lips touch the glass, saw the stubble on his chin and felt faint with hunger to have those lips on his dick, like it used to be. Said member twitched in his pants and he tried to ignore it.

Give me a break, you horny little bastard. We're supposed to be talking, not fucking. Not yet anyway.

"Been anywhere exciting? Your text said you'd been out." Shane sipped his whiskey, waiting to see what Matthew would say. Matthew nodded.

"Bartholomew and I were at one of those interminable legal gatherings last night which seemed to go on forever. Speech after bloody speech." He frowned. "I honestly don't know how people manage to spout off about so much crap. I thought it would never be over."

Shane sighed in relief.

So the man had been at a business dinner with his boss. That was a good sign.

There was a small silence. Then Matthew took a deep breath. He laid his glass down on the table and with one fierce movement he reached out and pulled Shane toward him. Shane went willingly, not quite knowing what was coming, but happy to go with the flow. Matthew had his hands all over him and Shane realised that was all that mattered.

Matthew's lips took Shane's in a savage kiss that made his balls ache and his dick spring to an immediate salute. He kissed Matthew back, his tongue slicking against the other man's, and he smiled into Matthew's mouth as he heard his deep groan.

"Christ, babe, I missed you. I know it was only two bloody days but I wanted you so badly. I was so glad when you sent that text. I don't think I could have lasted much longer." Matthew's voice was husky as his lips claimed Shane's again.

You could have sent the first text, you bloody control freak. If I hadn't, how much longer might this have taken?

Shane's thoughts disappeared into a void as Matthew pushed him back against the couch, fumbling with his jeans zipper.

"Jeez, Matty," Shane chuckled as the other man's frantic hands unzipped him. His dick reared up, rampantly ready for whatever was coming. Hopefully him. "At least buy me bloody dinner—" his words were cut off with a strangled moan.

Matthew dropped to his knees on the floor and his warm and hungry mouth wrapped around Shane's dick like a starving man, his lips and tongue causing all manner of mayhem in Shane's body.

"Oh my God," Shane moaned as he arched his back against the couch. "I missed this, I really did…"

He felt Matthew's low laugh against his skin as he pushed down deeper onto Shane. Shane's hands tangled themselves in Matthew's thick hair as he gripped and forced himself deeper into his lover's mouth. The heat, the pressure, the soft wet licking and swirling tongue—it all felt so right. Matthew stopped what he was doing and looked up at Shane, his pupils black and blown, his mouth wet with Shane's fluids.

"Your turn to do me next, Shay. Just like this. Then later, I'm going to fuck you into the mattress. That's the plan, baby. Now just sit back and relax while I make you come so hard you'll feel it for a week."

The words were enough to make Shane hyperventilate as his backside clenched against the couch. Matthew returned to his cock and annihilated the last of Shane's sanity. With a loud gasp, he came, liquid passion spilling into the warm mouth around his dick and he gave a loud cry of release and sheer joy. He thought he might well be feeling that sensation for the next week.

Panting, he relaxed back against the seat, as Matthew stood up. He moved over Shane, finding his mouth again, bringing the taste of semen and musk.

"Now it's your turn," Matthew growled when released Shane's mouth, which felt bruised and tender from the ferocity of his lover's kiss.

Matthew stood up, dropping his chinos and silk boxers to the floor. Shane's eyes roved greedily over the erection that jutted out and he needed no further instructions. He pulled Matthew down onto the couch, onto his back. He knelt in between Matthew's legs, watching his face as he kissed his stomach, his pelvis, nipped at his hips and buried his face in Matthew's groin. He nuzzled at the wiry curls there, feeling them brush his cheeks.

He heard Matthew's heated and impatient, "Christ, Shane, get a move on. Did you forget the whole 'your mouth, my cock' thing?"

"Patience, Matty," Shane chuckled as he licked the tip that promised him so much pleasure. "You can be so bloody bossy. I'll get there, I promise."

And get there they did. By the time Shane had finished with Matthew, the man was a mewling mess on the couch, his body trembling, his skin hot and sweaty and the taste of come in Shane's mouth like fine wine. He collapsed against Matthew, both of them still with their shirts on, naked below the waist, sprawled together in an entanglement of limbs as Shane brushed wet, sweaty hair from Matthew's eyes.

"I take it we're not fighting anymore?" he teased as his fingers trailed across his partner's hard stomach. Matthew shifted to look at him, his eyes darkened, his mouth swollen.

"I never wanted to fight with you, Shay. I had time to think. Maybe I overreacted somewhat. I know what you do is important and you'd never hurt anyone." His hand reached out and traced the contours of Shane's lips, his touch soft and warm.

If Shane had been a cat he would have purred. "But you can be bloody scary, the things you can do. I guess I never know where they'd stop."

Shane shifted against Matthew's warm body, his arm draping over his chest as he kissed his lover's nipples. "I know my boundaries. Matty. Most of the time anyway." His chuckle against Matthew's skin caused the other man to break into goose bumps. "I can promise you I'll never do anything to knowingly hurt you or anyone else. That's the only promise I can make. You need to take me as I am, the same as I have to with you. My sexy control freak."

Matthew's hand stroked Shane's hair. "I missed you so much these last couple of days. I promise you, I'm trying to let you in. I've let you see more of me than anyone ever has since Sam died. Can you live with that?"

Shane nodded drowsily. "Uh huh. As long as it means I get to be here with you, like this, I suppose I can put up with the fact your house is off bounds and I'm in a relationship with a man who has to have his towels lined up just so."

Matthew laughed at that. "You noticed that, huh?"

Shane nodded. "You change stuff in my flat, Matty. I now find my tins all facing outward, the toothpaste cap is always screwed on and there are endless neat, squared-off piles of papers everywhere. Yes, Matty, these are things one tends to notice."

"Did you notice anything else?" Matthew whispered lazily as his hands caressed Shane's backside and he slowly ran his fingers in between Shane's taut arse cheeks. Shane sucked in a breath at that languid touch.

"You're a horny bastard." Shane's voice held the trace of a laugh. Matthew chuckled against Shane's ear.

"You got that right. I think it's time for the bed. I seem to recall I made you a promise to fuck you right through it and I think that time has arrived."

Shane could only nod as Matthew heaved himself off the couch, grabbed Shane's hand and led him toward the bedroom. Shane just knew he was in for a rough time.

German sex talk and old friends

Shane opened one eye and smiled at the sight of his boyfriend's face only inches from his own. Matthew slept on his side, his lashes long and curling against his toned skin, his mouth slightly open. He was snoring. Shane kissed his own fingers and then reached out and gently touched them to his lover's lips.

The man looked adorable when he slept, but then, the way Shane was so smitten, he would look adorable doing anything. He'd never felt such a connection so soon to a man before. It had only been eight weeks together and already he felt like he'd known him forever.

The last few weeks of getting to know Matthew had been some of the best he'd ever had. His last boyfriend, Cole, whom he'd been with a year before they parted company eighteen months ago, had been someone he'd thought would last. Then Shane had found out his boyfriend had been bonking some young cute thing over at Essence, and he'd totally lost it. Committed relationships were meant to be monogamous in Shane's opinion, if they were ever to have any chance of working. He didn't subscribe to playing the field when you had someone you really cared for. It was why he'd agreed to Matthew's conditions so easily. Shane started escorting after he'd kicked Cole out. He'd started it as a dare, found he enjoyed the variety. He grinned as he watched Matthew sleeping. Thank God he had or else he'd have never met the man he was falling hard for.

He would have to fight damn hard for Matthew. The man's shell was a tough one to crack. The only thing that rankled with him, other than the bloody wedding ring still being on Matthew's finger, was the fact he still hadn't been invited to Matthew's house. He knew he'd agreed to let Matty have space, but this was starting to piss him off. Shane may well have to push the issue soon. He knew that this relationship, if one could call it that, was very weighted in Matthew's favour. The man was an emotional wreck, not wanting to feel anything in case he got hurt again. But Shane had a plan to change that, gradually. He could be patient. Within reason.

Matthew wrinkled his nose, opened his eyes and blinked blearily. "I thought I felt someone watching me," he said huskily and then yawned. "Are you stalking me even when I sleep?"

Shane leaned forward and kissed his cheek. "Not stalking. Admiring."

Matthew chuckled and rolled onto his back, his eyes dark and warm as he looked at his boyfriend. Shane was please that they'd finally officially graduated to the title. He felt like he'd been to University and come away with an honorary degree.

"And just how long exactly have you been admiring me?"

Shane's mouth found Matthew's as his tongue trailed a soft lick across the other man's lower lip. "Long enough to know I really want to get up close and personal with the item in question."

He reached down under the covers, finding his lover's morning woody, softly stroking it.

Matthew shivered and he closed his eyes. Shane smiled. Some mornings this was all it took. The two of them, warm and sleepy, skin against skin, mouth against mouth and a mutual need that was slow and tender. A dance of bodies and sweat, of heat and rushing tides of feelings that ebbed and flowed like washes of gentle waves on the shoreline. Both men were adept at it, at slow, languorous movements and touches that drove the other crazy and over the edge.

This morning was no different. Soon the two men were gasping, fingers clutching, mouths seeking and hearts beating together in a rhythm that was like a well-played symphony, notes of pure emotion combined with the clashing cymbals of mutual pleasure.

Shane laid back, his skin slick with sweat. Matthew uncoupled himself from the other man's body and lay back on the pillows, his breath ragged, his face flushed with exertion. "Hell, Shay, I love morning sex with you," he panted, as he tried to get his breathing back to normal. "I get woken up, I get violated, I come like a steam train and then we shower and the whole thing starts all over all again. What is this magic you do so well, Templar?"

Shane laughed. "No magic, Langer. Just a really good motivation. You have no bloody idea how sexy you are. My pure, beautiful sexy Matthew. You make it too easy."

Matthew reached up and caressed Shane's jaw line. "I knew the first time I saw you I wanted your body. I think we owe David a magnum of champers for bringing us together."

Matthew's face shadowed and he sat up, pushing the pillows against the wall and leaning back. "Talking of David, I need to give him a call today. The last time we spoke, a couple of weeks ago, he sounded really down. He was going away on some business trip for a week. I need to talk to him again, see everything is okay." He scowled. "That prick of a father of his is really driving him hard. And that twat brother of his, Lewis, is really making life difficult for him too."

Shane chuckled. "Have you heard yourself lately? You swear like a trooper. I am a bad influence on you, aren't I?"

Matthew reached over and stroked his fingers down Shane's collarbone, causing the other man to shiver. "In every way possible," he drawled. He reached across a lazy hand to the bedside table to check the time on his mobile. He jumped as if an electric prod had been shoved up his backside.

"Christ, Shane, it's bloody late. I'm due at work in an hour. What the hell am I thinking?"

He leapt out of bed, giving Shane a very good view of his tight backside and the slight bruise marks on his rear where Shane had dug his fingers tightly. Shane felt a sense of satisfaction at marking his man. Matthew scurried through to the bathroom and the younger man heard the shower start.

Shane grinned and slid out of bed, making his way to the bathroom. Matthew was already late, so another little diversion would hardly be a problem. He scowled when he found the bathroom door locked. He heard Matthew's satisfied chuckle at hearing the door handle turn.

"Shay, I knew I couldn't trust you to keep your hands off me. Temptation, baby. I wasn't putting it in your way. You'll just have to make do with what you had earlier."

Shane frowned sulkily and moved away, getting back into bed. "Fine. Be like that. I might have to withhold my wares next time you feel like them."

He heard the other man's snort of laughter. "That'll be the day. I just have to bat my eyelashes and you're mine. You can't hold out against my considerable charms."

Shane scowled, knowing Matthew was right. "Stop being so bloody full of yourself," he muttered at the bathroom door. But he smiled. The sudden familiar Black Keys melody blared across the room and Shane picked up Matthew's mobile. His eyebrows lifted when he saw who it was. He got out of bed, padded naked across the room and knocked on the bathroom door.

"Matty? Your mobile's ringing. It says 'Mutter' on the caller ID. I remember enough school German to know it must be your mother. Do you want to take this?"

The bathroom door flew open and Matthew came out, nude, wet and still with soap in his hair, as he reached for the phone. He looked worried.

"I only spoke to her last week. I hope nothing's wrong with her or my sister." His face was worried as he answered the phone. Shane took the opportunity to ogle him as he stood there.

"*Mutter? Ich bin's Matthias. Ist alles in Ordnung?*"

The soft, Germanic tones sent a thrill to Shane's groin and gave him an instant boner. He knew Matthew was fluent in his home language but he'd never heard him speak it before. It was a complete turn-on, including hearing him call himself 'Matthias,' which he imagined was the German version of Matthew.

His lover's eyes flicked down to Shane's groin and he choked back a laugh as he turned and continued his conversation.

Shane watched Matthew's taut backside, gleaming with water and slightly red from the heat of the shower, and contemplated pounding the other man's arse when the conversation was over. But Matthew obviously realized Shane's intentions as he gave his lover a sly smile and continued his conversation, going back into the bathroom and locking the door behind him.

Shane scowled as he heard the muted sounds of the conversation from outside, the German Matthew was speaking still causing his groin to heat and his dick to turn to cement.

"You think you're so bloody clever, don't you." Shane muttered as he got back into bed and covered himself with the duvet. If Matty wasn't going to take advantage of the erection he currently sprouted, he'd have to sort it out himself later.

Twenty minutes later he was on his own, the day his to command. Matthew had point blank refused any more morning sexual activity, as he was already late for work. He'd told Shane everything was fine at home, his mother just needed to let him know his uncle Berndt would be in the UK soon. His mother was sending her son a present via him. As he kissed him goodbye, ducking and diving from Shane's grasping hands, Matthew had wickedly whispered something in German in his ear, causing Shane to squirm in sheer pleasure at what he assumed was his lover's deliberately whispered sex assault.

"Das must Du leider ohne mich tun." Shane had a good memory, and as soon as Matthew had left he'd turned to Babylon for translation. He'd scowled when he thought he'd found out it what it meant.

"You'll have to take care of it by yourself."

He was busy on Bushwhacker when his mobile rang later that day. His face brightened when he heard who it was.

"Timmy, you dog! It's been months since you called. Where the hell have you been?"

His friend's deep, baritone voice echoed down the phone. "Shanester, I have been in South Africa visiting the family. I got back a few days ago. I thought we should catch up." The melodic African tone of Timmy's voice had always sent shivers down Shane's spine. He thought idly that he seemed to have a sexual attraction to men speaking in other languages or accents. Timothy Zwane was a well-built, six-foot-four Zulu man from South Africa. They'd met at a national hacking conference just after Shane had left Cole. The pitch-black, handsome, regal Zulu with the wide smile and great shoulders had immediately attracted Shane's interest. Timmy had felt much the same about the brash blond with an attitude.

They'd had a brief, passionate affair which had ceased when Timmy had gone back to his home country for a family funeral. Their affair had been mostly around sex and not been anything serious. Both of them had moved on but remained firm friends.

Shane grinned. "I'd love to catch up. But won't that boyfriend of yours get a little jealous? He's never really taken to me."

Timmy chuckled. "Sifiso was just wary of you, Shane. You know he is a very traditional man and the fact I was boning a white man never sat well with him, even though you and I were over before I met him." He laughed. "And what he doesn't know will not hurt him anyway. He is still in South Africa with his family. He will only be back in a week's time." Timmy's voice was hopeful. "I am in London for a while. I thought perhaps we could get together tonight if you're not busy?" He chuckled. "Just for a chat and a drink."

Shane contemplated the idea. He wanted to see Timmy and better still, he wanted to introduce Matthew to a really good friend. "I guess you could come over here to my place about seven. Then I can introduce you to my significant other. I'd love you two to meet. Maybe we hit a club or something together afterwards?"

"You have a new lover?" Timmy sounded wickedly satisfied. "I thought you were still doing the whole escort thing?"

"Nope, I gave that up when I met Matty. You'll realise why when you meet him."

"Well, I am suitably impressed. You sound very serious about this man."

Shane laughed. "I am serious about him. He's trying not to get serious about me but I think he's fighting a losing battle. You know how persuasive I can be." He chuckled. "Just please do me a favour and tone down our past relationship. No need to go into too much detail other than we used to screw each senseless for a short time. He has a bit of a jealous streak in him."

"I see. Then I shall not tell him about the time we snuck into the Museum of National History and made our own boners rattle—"

"No, Timmy, you won't be fucking telling that story to Matty." Shane cut him off as he remembered that night of sheer debauchery under the spotlights at the dinosaur museum after they'd hacked into the security system and disabled it temporarily. They'd only just had time before the guard did his round to finish their rather interactive session as they leaned against the huge dinosaur skeleton whilst Timmy drove in and out of him like a piston engine. It had been a night to remember.

Timmy chuckled. "I shall try and keep my sense of decorum intact with your new lover. It will, of course, depend on how much whiskey I have to drink later. I will see you at your place around seven. I look forward to it." He rang off. Shane grinned as he put his phone down. He was looking forward to the two men meeting tonight. It would make for some interesting conversation.

More trouble in paradise

Matthew sat back in his chair and sighed. The legal briefings he'd started that morning were finished, and Bartholomew would be pleased. Matthew had made it to work twenty minutes late. He grinned. He couldn't believe his boyfriend got so turned on by him speaking German. Shane had made him promise to teach him some of the more risqué words that he could use when they were in bed. He quite liked that idea. Just whispering to Shane this morning had made the man swoon. It was something that could come in handy when he wanted Shane to let rip.

He looked at the files on his desk and sighed. It wasn't that anyone clock-watched at Maxwell, Smith and Jordan, and God knows Matthew put in enough late hours to make up any tardiness. It was just that he was the new kid on the block, and he found himself wanting to impress the calm, professional and admirable man that was Bartholomew Maxwell. In some way, he reminded Matthew of his father. Steady, dependable, straight as a die in the truest sense of the word. An iron fist in a velvet glove. Nothing like Walter Debussy. Matthew still thanked his lucky stars each day for getting out of his clutches. His phone rang as he stood up to go take the completed briefs to Julia. He saw who it was and smiled.

"David? This is a surprise. I was only talking about you this morning to Shay. How are you?"

"I'm downstairs, Matty. Can you tell the desk to let me in? I need to speak to you." David sounded harried and stressed.

Matthew's instinct for pending trouble kicked in. "Of course you can come up. But what the hell's going on? Has your father—"

"Matty, not here. I'll tell you when I see you. Here's the concierge." He'd handed his mobile over to the reception desk and Matthew confirmed that David Debussy could indeed come up to the fourth floor.

He walked over the lift to wait for his friend. A few minutes later, the lift doors opened and David stepped out. Matthew gasped. The man was pale, his normal tanned skin white and waxen and his cheeks drawn. Under one eye it was black and swollen and he had a large, deep gash on his lip. He looked like a man who'd gone to hell and back.

Matthew took his arm and led him into the one of the quiet conference rooms.

"Jesus, DD, you look terrible. What the hell happened to you?"

"Thanks, Matty, that's encouraging." David scowled. "You know how to make a man feel better, don't you?" He wandered restlessly over to the window, looking out at the street below, his hands fidgeting nervously beside his body. Matthew came up behind him and laid a warm hand on his arm, turning him to face him.

"Please tell me what's going on." His quiet tone seemed to settle the other man, who swallowed and stared at his friend with eyes filled with trepidation and something else—it almost looked like shame. David took a deep breath.

"I should have listened to you and Shane last time. I shouldn't have let my father control me like he did, after he let Roy smack me around last time." His voice faltered. Matthew gazed at him in horror.

"He watched while Roy beat you up? For God's sake, why did you let them get away with it? Especially that little prick, Roy."

His tone was venomous and he wanted to punch the smaller man until his knuckles hurt.

"It all got a bit out of hand, Matty. I know I've stuck with the story; it seemed the best thing to do. I didn't want to make my dad madder at me." He stared at Matthew. His face was stark. "But it's gone too far now; I can't take it anymore—" His voice broke and Matthew watched as the man fell apart. He reached for David, pulling his friend closer, rubbing his back as the other man sobbed. Matthew had a lump in his throat as well.

"What the hell did they do to you?"

He saw the conference door open. Julia came in, stopping suddenly as she saw the two men together. She shook her head in apology and went out, quietly closing the door behind her. Matthew could hear her telling someone outside that the room was in use and no one was to disturb the occupants.

He made a mental note to thank her later and try to explain why he was at work with a sobbing man in his arms.

"My dad thinks I can get over being gay, Matty," David whispered. His hands twisted in Matthew's shirt, now wet with tears. "But you know it's not like that. My dad and Roy thought they could get someone to try and change me, to make me heterosexual." He spat the words out. "He wanted me to go out with a woman he knew, someone he said could show me what it was like to be a real man. I told him I didn't want that, I was quite happy. I told him," his voice faltered, "that it was about time he accepted who I was and how I chose to live my life." His dark eyes looked at Matthew, the pain in them only too real. "He went ape shit. He hit me across the mouth then told Roy to carry on and teach me a lesson." David stepped back from Matthew and turned to stare out of the window. "Then he walked out of the room and that little bastard beat the crap out of me. When he turned around to look back at Matthew, his eyes were blank. "I called my father afterwards from my room, screamed at him, told him he was a bastard. Do you know what he said?"

Matthew just shook his head. David needed to get all this out.

"He said I should have done what he wanted, that I should have tried to see what real sex was like. That I should be grateful he cared about me enough to try and help me. Then he told me to come home and get to work. He had some business dinner he wanted me to attend. I told him to fuck off and I haven't been home or spoken to him since Friday."

David drew a ragged breath. "He cancelled all my credit cards, had my bank account frozen somehow and left me with nothing. He's even got the trust fund put on hold."

Matthew shook his head. "He can't do that, DD. My father made sure he couldn't do that. He's breaking the law if he tries to mess with those funds. I'll see what I can do to get it released, but it will take a while."

"Leave it alone, Matty." David's voice was resigned, defeated. "Dad said, and I quote, 'If Matthew tries to stop me, tell him I'll drag him through the mud and the two of you will never hold your heads up in this city again.'"

Matthew wondered how he was going to make this right without harming either of them unduly. There had to be a bloody way to fight Walter.

David nodded. "And you know he'll do it, Matty. He'll make us both out to be some perverted gay couple that sacrifices babies and neither of us will be able to fight him. I'm not dragging you into this bloody mess. You've been hurt enough by my father." He gave a twisted smile. "I'll have to find a way of making an honest living instead of relying on a trust fund."

There was silence as both men considered the situation they found themselves in.

"All the time Roy was hitting me, he was telling me it served me right for what I'd done to him a few weeks ago." He frowned, perplexed. "I had no idea what he was talking about. He said that would teach me to put shit on his phone about gay boys. Apparently there was some porn material that got sent to everyone in his address book that was pretty disgusting. He was so mad about it."

Matthew felt a prickle of fear ice down his spine at the words. "You didn't have anything to do with it then?" he asked.

"God, no. I wouldn't have a clue where to even start doing something like that. Way above my intelligence. I'm not very au fait with technology and shit like that."

Matthew knew someone who was very familiar with "shit like that," and he closed his eyes in trepidation. He wondered whether David knew what Shane did for a living besides escorting. The recent argument he and Shane had had about his hacking activities reared its ugly head. But this would have all happened before they'd fought that battle.

"Are you still staying at the hotel?" he asked. David shook his head.

"I had to check out. I paid until today. No credit card." He grinned faintly. "I knew you and Shane were spending the weekend together and I didn't want to disturb your fun."

"Christ, you should have called me, not done this all on your own." Matthew shook his head and reached over to his jacket pocket. He took out a bunch of keys. He clipped one off and handed it to David.

"Get your stuff and go over to my place. You can stay with me until we get this all settled. I have enough room to put up with you for a while. I will get you your money back, DD. One way or another. Your mother left you that trust fund, not your dad. He has no right over any of it." His voice was fierce.

David smiled gratefully. "Thanks, Matty. But I don't have any stuff. It's all back home and I'm damned if I'm going back there."

Matthew sighed. "Feel free to check out my wardrobe. We'll find out how to get your stuff later. Now you need to go. My boss must be wondering what the hell he's got himself into employing me. I'm going straight to Shane's after this, so I'll be home much later."

"If at all," David said with a wink.

Matthew grinned. "No, I'll be home. I have work in the morning and I need to get my routine sorted. Shane made me late for work this morning anyway with his shenanigans."

David smiled wistfully. "You two are hitting it off, aren't you? You seem to care for him."

Matthew shook his head, feeling a thrill of unease down his spine. "I've just got a boyfriend. A bed buddy."

David stared at him. "You keep telling yourself that. I've seen you two together, remember? I see how you look at him." He reached out a hand to cuff Matthew's jaw line lightly. "It's no sin to get involved again with someone. Sam would have wanted that. And you need to take a chance with your heart."

He left Matthew breathless with this parting shot.

"I'll get out of your hair, then. Let you get back to the job before you get fired. Thanks Matty. I appreciate this." He kissed Matthew's cheek and let himself out of the office. Matthew heard him murmur to someone as he left. He was still reeling from his friend's comments.

"What the hell," he muttered to himself as he gazed out of the window. "We *are* just bed buddies. A boyfriend is just a bloody title anyway." Even to him he didn't sound convincing. He turned as Julia came in, her face concerned.

"Matthew? Is your friend all right?"

"Julia, I'm so sorry. David was in a bit of a state. I needed to give him the keys to get back to my place. I know the workplace isn't a place to sort out personal issues. I'll go and see Bartholomew and apologise too. It won't happen again, I promise."

Julia had been trying to get a word in. She reached over and placed her fingers on his lips in exasperation. "God, Matthew, give it a rest! It's fine. Hell, you hardly leave here before seven every night. I think we can allow you the occasional personal issue during working hours. I simply want to know if everything's okay."

Matthew nodded. "There are a few things we need to sort out. I may need Bartholomew's advice on a trust issue. But at least David is out of his father's house now and he'll be safer. He can stay with me for a while."

Julia nodded. "I'm glad to hear it. You're a good friend." She turned to go and then hesitated. "Would you like to go out again for a drink together sometime, maybe one evening after work?"

Matthew was touched. He enjoyed Julia's company. She was a good listener. "I'd like that. Perhaps one night next week we can go down to Coolio's. They're supposed to have a great Tequila Sunrise."

She smiled. "Good. I look forward to it." She turned and left the office. Matthew ran a hand through his hair as he sat down at his desk to tackle the next set of legal briefs. It was going to be a long afternoon.

Meeting the Zulu

Matthew got to Shane's about eight p.m. He was tired, feeling fractious and not in the best of moods. He'd been trying to figure a way to have David's trust fund released. Walter had gotten his new lawyer, Gordon Brett, a real sleazeball in the industry, to find a loophole that allowed him to take control for forty-eight hours pending a full application to have it signed over to him. How he'd managed to do that Matthew had no idea but he had the feeling that the fact the judge in the case was a good friend of his had something to do with it.

He let himself into Shane's flat using the key he'd been given, and stopped short at the sight of a very large, handsome black man towering over Shane, looking very at home. Shane turned as he came in and smiled a warm welcoming smile that made Matthew's heart skip a beat. Shane looked incredible, his dark blue jeans low on his hips, his tight, wine-coloured tee shirt outlining his chest and the broad line of his shoulders. As usual, he was barefoot. Shane hated wearing shoes if he didn't have to. It was a trait they had in common.

"Matty. You're late, babe. Let me introduce you to Timmy. He's an old friend of mine, popped by for a visit."

Matthew nodded. "Timmy. Good to meet you." The two men shook hands and even Matthew had to look up at the man.

Timmy grinned, showing white teeth. "I have heard a lot about you, Matthew. You must be special indeed to have Shane so in a spin. He is enamoured with you." His glance was admiring. "I can see why he likes you so much."

Matthew felt uncomfortable, and even Shane seemed nervous at Timmy's side. "Tim, that's enough. You're going to scare Matty away. He's rather relationship-phobic."

Matthew frowned at these words. He was beginning to feel like everyone thought they knew him better than he did.

"Drink, Matty? What do you fancy?" Shane made his way into the open-plan kitchen.

"I'll have a glass of red wine, please. Make it a large one." Matthew sat down on the kitchen stool at the island and nodded his thanks to Shane as he passed him his drink. Timmy sat down with what looked a large shot of whiskey in his glass.

"So, Timmy, where do you know Shane from?" Matthew glanced at the two men. Shane sat down beside him with his glass of red wine. He looked uncomfortable; something Matthew wasn't used to seeing in the other man.

"Actually, Matty, we were together for three months about a year ago. I was escorting at the time. We met when I took on an engagement with Timmy at a hacking conference, and we had a bit of a relationship."

Matthew felt a surge of sheer jealousy at the fact that this man, this dark, smooth and very imposing man had been intimate with Shane.

Shane was watching his face anxiously.

Matthew nodded. "Oh. I see. " He took a sip of his wine, feeling the turmoil in his stomach.

Shane grinned in relief. "The cool, calm and collected Mr. Matthew Langer, ladies and gentlemen. Nothing fazes him."

Matthew scowled as Shane got off his stool and came over to run a hand through his hair and place a hard kiss on his lips. "You're the only one for me, Matty. Timmy here has his own boyfriend now, Sifiso, a rich git from the Cameroon or something. I think he might even be a prince."

Timmy chuckled but didn't confirm Shane's theory. Matthew was mollified by the kiss. "So what do you do for a living, Timmy?"

"The same as Shane. I work with software companies and sort out their security. But I'm afraid I'm nowhere in this man's league. My man Backdoor is total legend and one of the most sought-after hackers in the industry."

Matthew felt a swell of pride. "I know he has talents, but I don't profess to know too much about what he does."

Except he manages to piss people off royally and steal money from them. I need to talk to him about that later. I'm sure he's the one who messed with Roy's phone. Shane will be mortified when he hears it got David into trouble. After *I tell him about what happened to David and that he's staying with me. That might not go down too well either.*

Timmy was leaning back with a wide grin on his face. "Oh, he has talents all right. My man Shane has an IQ of 145. That makes him truly gifted."

Matthew stared at Shane in awe, noting his face turn pink at the attention. "Lover, is that right? I'm bonking a genius?"

Shane shook his head. "I'm not a bloody genius, you idiot. I just have an ability for certain things, that's all. IQ tests aren't a great barometer of intelligence." He reached over and ran his hand down the stubble on Matthew's chin. Matthew almost purred. Timmy laughed softly and shook his head.

"My God. You two are like an old married couple." He regarded them affectionately, then frowned as he looked down and saw the ring on Matthew's finger. He looked at Shane in sheer confusion. "Is there something you're not telling me, Shanester?"

Matthew stiffened.

Shane stood up, uneasily glancing at Matthew, then back at Timmy, who sat there wide eyed. "No, that's not *our* ring, Timmy. Um, it's a long story and we don't need to go into it now."

His friend narrowed his eyes. "I never thought you would go out with a married man, Shane. That was always something you said you would never do." His glance at Matthew was less friendly than it had been before.

Matthew felt the rising ire in his chest at the man's sudden change of attitude. "I'm not married now," he said curtly. "I was and I just haven't taken the ring off yet."

"That seems unfair on Shane," said Timmy, his nostrils flaring.

Shane tried to change the subject. "I think it's time for another drink, don't you? Anyone for a margarita?"

Matthew regarded Timmy with a level stare. He knew the other man only had Shane's best interests at heart, but he didn't want to share his story with a man who was still a complete stranger.

"Like Shane said, it's a long story. And Shane is fine with it. So I suppose you should be too. But I appreciate the concern you have for him."

Timmy stared at him for a moment appraisingly and then nodded. "You are right. It is none of my business what your personal circumstances are. I apologise for questioning you. Shane, I will certainly have one of your famous margaritas."

Shane gave a sigh of relief and went to sort out the drinks. The ring topic over, they settled back into more of a conversation, although Matthew could see Timmy was still wary of him. But his comments had hit home. Matthew looked down at his ring. He supposed it *was* unfair to Shane. But then Matthew had been clear that he didn't want a relationship. As long as the ring was there it was a reminder to Matthew that he wasn't free to give his heart. The problem was, he was starting to doubt his commitment to that as well. Seeing Shane standing there next to a man he'd had feelings for and looking so sexy had made Matthew's hackles rise and his jealous green beast roar inside. He would have decked the man, bigger or not, if he'd found him with a hand on his lover. He squirmed at his thoughts and took a large slug of his wine.

"Did you manage to speak to David today like you said you would?"

Matthew realised Shane was speaking to him and he looked up. "Hmm? Yes, David came by the office today. That arsehole Roy beat him up again, and David's left the house. He says he's had enough. But Walter has frozen all the money he has, even the trust account. I need to see what I can do tomorrow to get it opened again."

Timmy whistled. "Shane has told me this story. This young man's father seems like a real nasty piece of work."

Shane went still. Matthew could see the rise and fall of his chest under his shirt and see his hands clenched tightly at his sides.

His eyes were glacial. "They beat him up again and his father shut off his trust account?"

Matthew nodded. "I'm going to speak to my boss tomorrow about it. He's an expert on this sort of thing and I'm hoping he can help." He finished his wine and stood up to pour another glass, taking a deep breath. "David's at my place at the moment. I gave him my key and told him to stay for a while until we can get things sorted."

Shane moved around the side of the island. "David's at your place? With a key? Wow, what a lucky man. As you know *I* haven't even seen your place yet." Shane's voice was biting. Matthew sighed. "He had nowhere to go, and besides, David's been there many times before. It's no big deal, Shay. I—"

With one sweep of his hand, Shane sent his wine glass crashing across the top of the island, to fly into space and smash to the floor on the other side. Matthew stood up in sheer panic, as did Timmy.

"Hell, Shay, honey, take it easy," exclaimed Matthew as he hurried over to Shane's side. The man's face was twisted in frustration. "No need to go crazy."

"Well, no need apart from the fact he gets to be inside your bloody house and you won't even take me there and the fact his father is a vicious, bullying wanker who thinks he can get away with anything." Shane's breath was deep, his face rosy. He moved over to the cupboard, pulled out a dustpan and brush and started angrily started sweeping up the glass shards.

Timmy looked uncomfortable at being caught up in the middle of this particular conversation.

"Why the hell did David get beaten this time? Did he mince too bloody much for Walter?" Shane's angry tones echoed through the kitchen as he swept.

Matthew shook his head. "He was trying to get him to go out with a woman. David refused. And Roy was upset because of some gay porn he'd had sent from his phone. I imagine you had something to do with that, Shane?" Matthew gave a deep sigh. "Another consequence of your actions, Shane. He thought David had something to do with it and he beat the shit out of him for it."

Shane went grey. "Roy blamed David for that? Is that why he was beaten?"

Matthew shook his head. "No. You can't be blamed for all of that. David had the hell knocked out of him because he refused to go on a booty call with some woman his father picked out for him. He told his father to bugger off. But it didn't help that Roy didn't like the pretty-boy pictures you sent to all his bloody friends using his number and took it out on the only gay man he could readily get his hands on." He couldn't help the angry tone of his voice.

Timmy stood up suddenly. "I think I should leave now and let you two talk this over." He picked up his coat which was slung over the back of his stool. "I shall call you tomorrow, Shanester. It was lovely meeting you, Matthew. I shall see myself out. You two carry on. You obviously have some issues to address and I think it will be better that I'm not here."

Shane nodded and leaned in and hugged Timmy. "Yeah. I'll speak to you tomorrow. Sorry about this."

Timmy smiled, white teeth flashing. "No problem, my friend. Try not to kill each other." He waved and departed.

Shane turned to Matthew and passed an unsteady hand over his eyes. "Jesus. I fucked up badly. How the hell could Roy think it was David? He doesn't have a bloody clue about that stuff."

Matthew regarded him in sympathy. "Shane, you can't keep messing with people just because you can. Where the hell does it stop?" He walked over to the couch and sat down, weary to the bone. He closed his eyes and laid his head back against the couch. The couch seat dipped as Shane sat down next to him. He smelt the distinct woodsy aftershave of Shane's cologne and felt the heat of his body as he leaned toward him.

There was warm breath in his ear as Shane whispered, "God, I'm sorry, Matty. I didn't know David would pay the piper for that trick. I have to speak to him, tell him I'm sorry. I'll go see him tomorrow."

Matthew said nothing. He sat there, letting the hectic events of the day seep into the tiredness that was his body and mind. His head was stuffy, crammed with thoughts and emotions.

Shane stroked the top of his hand. "I'm sorry I didn't tell you about that. But we didn't know each other that well then."

Matthew opened his eyes and looked at the other man. "You can't just go in there—" he waved at Bushwhacker sitting on the lounge table, "—and do what you want. It's pretty scary just how easy you seem to make it happen. God, I'd hate to see what you'd do if I pissed you off somehow."

Shane stiffened beside him and he pulled back from Matthew. "I'd never do that to you, Matty, no matter what happens. How can you say something like that?" He sounded hurt, and Matthew reached up and caressed his cheek.

"You're a one-man wrecking crew, Shay. And you're impulsive. I appreciate you'd never intentionally do anything, but in the heat of the moment, who knows?" He grinned wryly. "I could end up being shipped off to Siberia, or suddenly be dead and not know it." He laughed to take the seriousness out of his words. "Hell, how do I know you don't already have your own Matthew Langer file in there, waiting for some secret code to be triggered that deletes me from the world if we ever part ways?"

Shane shifted and Matthew looked at him in dread. "You don't have a file in there on me, do you? Please tell me you don't." Matthew was a very private individual and the thought of someone knowing more about him that he chose to reveal was abhorrent to him.

Shane looked at him, his eyes steady. "No, I don't have a secret file. Why would I need a bunch of online stuff when I've got the real thing sitting in front of me?"

His warm lips pressed against Matthew's and for a while there was no more talking. Finally they came up for air.

Matthew took a deep breath. "Shay, about the house. I'm sorry it's such a thing with me. I know I'm a prick but you knew that when you took me on. I promise I'm working on my issues about that. Just be patient with me."

Shane regarded him then shrugged. "Whatever." But Matthew could still see the hurt in his eyes. "You made it clear when we started this…relationship…what it was all about. Sex, no strings, nothing too personal. You wear your wedding ring; you keep me away from your home. I'm just the available fuck buddy."

"You are *not* just my fuck buddy," Matthew growled.

Shane raised an eyebrow. "Oh? No? Then what am I, Matthew?" Shane's voice was even.

"You're *not* just my fuck buddy," Matthew whispered, closing his eyes. "I don't know what you are yet."

The words hung in the air. He realised he might just have uttered the first words indicating Shane was more to him than he wanted him to be. The thought was both exhilarating and frightening. He didn't want to dwell on it right now.

Shane seemed to realise this was a small breakthrough as a small smile played across his lips. He settled into Matthew, leaning into his shoulder, passing his hand across his chest as he leaned in. "You called me honey just now," Shane murmured in his ear.

Matthew felt the slow lick of a tongue along his ear lobe. He shivered but stayed where he was. "I like the sound of it." The lick got deeper, causing havoc in his groin despite his earlier frustration.

"Did I? Must have been a slip of the tongue."

Shane laughed throatily, causing Matthew's hard-on to strain at his trousers. "No Matty, I think this is what would be classed as a slip of the tongue."

Shane's warm, hard mouth took Matthew's and true to promise, his wet, insistent tongue forged its way inside, teasing his lips, tasting like wine and uniquely of Shane.

Matthew groaned and grasped the other man's hair, winding his fingers through it, grinding his mouth against Shane's in a frenzy of passion. He pushed Shane back against the couch, covering his body, groins pushing together as they grappled.

Shane's eyes were unfocused, beautiful, his lips swollen with the roughness of their kisses. His chin was slightly red from where Matthew's stubble had rubbed against it. Matthew licked the reddened skin slowly, from Shane's chin up the jaw line as his hand rubbed Shane's groin, feeling the hardness still growing and hearing his man's groans of deep satisfaction.

"You *are* my lover, Shane," he whispered, feeling a sense of release as he said the words. "My sexy, annoying, amazing man." He kissed Shane passionately. "*Mein Liebhaber,*" he whispered.

Shane heaved a deep shuddering satisfied sigh at this declaration as he reached down to stroke Matthew. "God, Matty, let's get our clothes off. I need to feel you inside me. Badly." Shane's voice was husky as he fumbled with his jeans.

Matthew nodded, standing up and lifting his shirt over his head.

"You are so beautiful." Shane's words were reverent. "I never get tired of seeing you like that. You have an incredible body." He reached for his tee shirt, ripping it off in one fluid movement, then lifting his backside to undo his jeans and push them off, along with his boxers.

Matthew watched him lay back naked on the couch and lost his breath. Shane's body was lean and naturally sculptured. His chest was smooth, his groin pale blonde with his cock rearing, red and swollen, sticky with fluid. Matthew though he had never seen a sexier sight than this man lying bare before him. He dropped his chinos, enjoying the sense of freedom being naked gave him, as his cock lurched out of confinement and sprang proudly free.

Shane's eyes were predatory, greedy. "I want that," he whispered as Matthew pulled him to his feet.

"Bedroom," Matthew commanded. "Much more comfortable there."

It was just as well Shane's bedroom was warm as he and Matthew hardly ever seemed to make it under the covers until it was time to go to sleep. The two men made their way there and Shane climbed onto the bed, lying wantonly back against the pillows, on display, and Matthew thought he was going to burst at the sight. He clambered onto the bed beside the other man, slowly rubbing the palm of his hand across Shane's stomach, up to his chest, pinching the nipples until they were hard.

Shane huffed, small sharp breaths that told Matthew just how turned on he was. Shane's lithe body felt so good under Matthew's hands, hot and sweaty. Matthew could never get enough. Slowly, seductively, Matthew explored with his mouth and hands, as his lover squirmed and moaned beneath him. He kissed light feather trails down Shane's chest, licking the sweat off as he made his way up and down.

His tongue found Shane's belly button, burrowing deep as his lover groaned.

"Matty, there's no bloody gold in there, babe. As much as I love all the exploration, I have something that I'd rather you focused on between my legs."

Matthew chuckled at the tone of need in Shane's voice. He finally let his hand travel down to Shane's cock and gripped it.

Shane gave a gulp of breath, his pupils already dilated. Matthew began to stroke his shaft, slow movements from base to head, hard, tight then slower and looser, until Shane was squirming in his hand, his thigh muscles tensed against the bed. His hands gripped the bedspread. Matthew's own cock felt impossibly large as if his skin was being stretched by an alien being just clamouring to get out.

"Matty, just keep going, keep up that hard stroke." Shane's groans of pleasure and his small pants of breath were turning Matthew on even more.

"You taste so good," he whispered to Shane as he bit his neck, ran his tongue along his jaw line and nipped the skin of his shoulders causing Shane to hiss in both pain and pleasure.

He took Shane's lips in a voracious kiss, pressing their sweating bodies together as he increased the pressure on Shane's straining erection.

Shane gave a loud muffled shout against Matthew's lips, his body spasming off the bed as thick trails of semen jetted out, coating Matthew's hand and chest. Breathing ragged, he collapsed back against the pillows.

"On your knees," Matthew whispered. Shane heaved another shuddering breath and turned over, getting on his hands and knees. Matthew caressed his flanks gently, kissing his buttocks, trailing his tongue along the smooth, taut skin. He reached over to the bedside table for the ever-present lube and condom. Shane watched him over his shoulder, his eyes darkened with desire, his lips slightly parted.

Matthew thought he'd go mad if he didn't take his man right now. He put the condom on and applied a liberal dose of lube and squeezed more onto his fingers. "Ready, babe? I need to get you nice and ready so I can just slide this inside you and make you scream."

Shane snorted. "You have a very inflated opinion of your skills with your dick, don't you? Give it your best shot. No messing around."

He gasped as Matthew inserted his finger, stretching him, moving deeper, past the ring of muscle which tightened around his finger. Shane groaned, his arms straining with keeping his body up.

"Matty, I'm fine. Just do it, please."

His throaty entreaty made Matthew take a deep breath as he gripped Shane's hips and slid inside. He gasped at the feeling of having Shane around him, muscles tightening as the man groaned. Matthew withdrew and plunged in again, watching himself as he slid and out of his lover. It was the most erotic sight he'd ever seen.

Shane held his breath as his lover moved in and out of his channel with hard, fast strokes, causing his groin to throb, his body to flush with heat and his skin to prickle. He was getting hard again. This felt so right, Matthew's strong, firm body behind him, his warm hands on his rump, his dick moving in and out of him as if they were made to fit together. He could hear his lover's harsh breaths, feel the growing excitement in his body as his fingers gripped him and his balls slapped against Shane's backside. As much as Shane loved being inside Matthew, he loved the other man taking him more.

The words Matty had uttered earlier about not knowing what Shane was to him had lifted his spirits, made him feel that there was something developing in this relationship.

Shane already knew he was falling in love with Matthew. He'd known from the moment they'd first met that this man could be someone special. He also knew that the sooner he deleted the folder he had on his lover on Bushwhacker, the better. He felt guilty for lying, but it was easy enough to make sure all the stuff he had on Matthew disappeared.

A groan escaped his lips as Matthew pumped harder, deeper, his rising excitement evident in every thrust into Shane's tight and willing channel.

He felt his lover's orgasm long before he heard it, as Matthew swelled and throbbed inside him, then roared in triumph, his body jerking with the force of his climax.

Shane felt his own dick swell at the sheer exuberance and enjoyment of his lover's final spasms. Matthew collapsed across Shane's back, as Shane's arms gave way and he sank flat to the bed, Matthew on top of him, still embedded deeply. He loved the feeling but he could hardly breathe. Matthew, a slab of skin and muscle, probably weighed at least one hundred and eighty pounds. But he was enjoying the closeness of his lover's body too much to ask him to move. He was able to breathe until Matthew relaxed on top.

Shane needed air. "Matty, you need to move," he managed to gasp. "I love us like this but I'm really battling here."

Matthew sighed and lightly brushed the nape of his neck with his warm lips. "You are so bloody needy. Now you want air as well as great sex?"

Shane felt his lover's lips form a grin against his skin as Matthew disengaged himself and rolled over to his side, discarding the condom and pulling Shane toward him snuggling into his back.

"Is that better?" He murmured. Shane pushed back against him, wigging his backside deliberately against his lover's member. At Matthew's hiss of breath against his back, Shane grinned.

"It would be even better if you could take care of something for me." He took Matthew's hand and moved it down to his groin, where his now-firm dick jutted out.

"Christ, you are a greedy little bastard, aren't you? Where the hell did that come from?" Matthew's hand indulgently caressed Shane's erection with nimble fingers, causing him to push back into Matthew, feeling his lover twitch against the crease of his backside.

Matthew heaved a loud, long, suffering sigh as he shifted, pulling Shane over so he was on his back. "I have a better idea," he murmured as his warm mouth trailed down Shane's stomach, his tongue slowly licking the ridges of muscle, down to his hips and down to where Shane wanted him most.

Discoveries and Need

David Debussy looked around at the empty lounge. He'd let himself into Matthew's house, taken a shower, found some suitable fresh clothes in Matthew's closet and made himself something to eat. He'd proceeded to mooch around, flicking through TV channels, watching bits of programmes with a lack of interest whilst his mind race with thoughts of how he'd like to tie Roy Parsons up and beat him with a heavy metal bar. The thought of making the man bloody and bruised gave him a distinct thrill which surprised him. He was generally not a violent person.

Earlier he'd wandered around the house, noting with approval the new artwork on the wall. Matthew was painting again. Not many people knew his friend loved watercolour painting. Matthew was good at it too. He specialised in creating landscapes and people's portraits from photos he took when he was out and about. It had been a while since he'd done any, citing a lack of time to David. But David had known he'd lost his creative spark when Sam died.

It was almost eleven thirty and Matthew wasn't home yet. He grinned. The man was probably being screwed to within an inch of his life by Shane. He didn't know which one was luckier. They were both very sexy and cute men. He wondered idly if they'd be into a threesome. The thought made him hard and he stopped thinking about that rather delectable idea before it made him even harder.

A noise at the door had him padding to the entrance in a pair of Matthew's socks. Matthew was just coming in the door. He looked tired and David smirked as he saw the faint bruise marks on his neck, love bites that were evident because Matthew's shirt wasn't buttoned like it usually was. He also noticed with a sly smile that his friend looked like a man who had indeed been royally screwed.

"Good evening, Matty?" he enquired with a grin.

Matthew smiled as he put his car keys on the side table. "I see you settled in and managed to find my good stuff to wear," he said wryly. "That's my Ralph Lauren sweatshirt and my Versace jeans. Couldn't find the old stuff then?"

David had the grace to look shame faced. "Er, I just pulled these out willy-nilly. But they fit well."

Matthew nodded drily. "I see. Well, they look very good on you." He moved over to the minibar in the corner of the lounge and poured himself a large whiskey. He took a sip, savouring the taste, kicked off his shoes and sat down in the armchair with a sigh of relief. David sat on the couch. "I'm glad you came home. I thought maybe you'd stay over at Shane's."

His friend shook his head. "As tempting as it was, I needed to get home and get some sleep. I have a board meeting in the morning and I didn't want to look as if I'd been dragged through a hedge backward." He chuckled. "If Shane had his way, I'd be screwed every which way possible and thrown out of the bed just in time to have a shower and perhaps put some clothes on in the morning. And Shane can be very persuasive. So I thought I'd better leave while the going was good. I'll finish this drink and then it's into bed."

David smiled. "I'm so glad to see the two of you getting on so well. And you're painting again. I love the new one of the Birdkeeper's House in St. James's. It's stunning."

Matthew smiled, obviously pleased David liked his artwork. "Yes, I did that a few months ago. It felt good to get back in the saddle."

"I agree. It's about time you got over Sam."

Matthew stood up abruptly, a scowl on his face. "Yes, well, that's not a subject for tonight."

David read between the lines and knew Matthew meant it wasn't good any time, not just now. He sighed. "Shane has been very good for you. I've never seen you more relaxed. And he adores you." He frowned. "And when are you going to take off your wedding ring? Don't you think—"

"DD." Matthews voice was soft but dangerous. "Stop blabbering. It's late, and I'm not in the mood for that discussion."

"You're never in the mood for 'that discussion,'" David said. "Have you even invited Shane around to your house yet?" Matthew regarded him with a tight mouth. "I know you don't like bringing your boyfriends here because this was yours and Sam's place, but you're going to have to do it sooner or later."

"Jesus, if I wanted a therapy session I'd have booked one with someone a damn sight more experienced than you." Matthew's voice was harsh. "Can you please just give it a rest?" He drained his drink as David watched him. "I'm going to bed. You're hopefully settled in the spare room. I hope you sleep well enough. Tomorrow I'll speak to my boss, see what we can do about getting that trust fund of yours available again."

David shrugged, seeing that he was not going to get anywhere. "Fine with me." He frowned. "Actually, you probably have all the original papers your dad used when he set up the fund with my mother. You might want to look them out. If I remember he made a lot of notes about the fund and how it needed to be set up for best effect. You might find those helpful if you still have them."

Matthew frowned. "I do recall that. Any documents would come in handy. I think I got a box of stuff when Dad died but I can't for the life of me remember what the hell I did with it."

Energised by the thought there might be something in there that could help him sort out David's problem, he disappeared into the small study off the lounge. David sighed. Matthew had an obsession about completing something when he got a bee in his bonnet. This meant that he wouldn't rest until he found what he was looking for. He decided he'd had enough of today and made his way to bed.

In the study, Matthew was muttering to himself and opening every cupboard and drawer in search of the elusive box of "stuff" he'd received when Erich had died. He remembered a small box of documents and assorted items that he'd always meant to look through but always put off for another day. As he opened the sideboard and pulled out some old Christmas ornaments and a pile of old newspaper clippings for God knows what, he exclaimed in triumph at seeing the box he wanted at the back of the cupboard. He reached in and drew it out, pushing all the other stuff back in and closing the cupboard.

"Eureka," he muttered. He sat down at his desk and adjusted the gooseneck lamp. He'd just see what was in here, give it a quick run-over then he supposed he'd better get into bed.

An hour later he was still sorting through the papers. He picked up a DVD lying at the bottom of the box and flipped it over with a frown. There was some writing on the one side. "Mona's Attack." Matthew was puzzled.

Mona's Attack? What the hell was that all about?

The name Mona sounded vaguely familiar. He slid the DVD into his player, switched on the small screen LCD TV and sat back to watch. There were no opening credits or sound, just a grainy picture of what looked like a rather swanky bedroom. The angle seemed to be played from a high spot in the corner of the room. Matthew guessed it was a hidden camera, placed in an air vent or perhaps the top of a picture. The room had plenty of artwork on the walls.

Matthew leaned forward. A door opened and a woman came in, tall and beautiful, with long red hair and a low-cut top displaying two rather large, perky breasts. Matthew thought she looked familiar.

A man followed her, a stout figure, stumbling and lurching, looking very drunk. Matthew's stomach lurched as he recognized Walter Debussy, who reached out and grabbed the woman, jerking her towards him roughly as he kissed her.

Christ, whoever she was, she certainly wasn't Linda, Walter's late wife!

He peered at the date stamp in the lower left corner. It was dated 10 October 2009, the day before his father's death. Matthew had a premonition of dread and his blood ran cold as he focused on the events playing out on the small screen.

Walter was getting rougher with the woman, his hands pawing at her breasts. She was trying to calm him down. It seemed to work. She turned to the bed as she got undressed. Walter had pulled off his shirt, his hands fumbling with his trousers.

The woman turned to face him in her scanty underwear. Matthew gasped when he saw the bulge at the woman's crotch. Now he remembered where he'd seen her before. Mona Casales, a.k.a. Manuel Casales, was a transsexual his father had helped with a child custody battle.

Walter went still, then moved toward the woman swiftly. Mona stepped back, her hand raised in front of her. She seemed to be pleading with Walter. From what he could see, Walter had not been aware the woman he'd just kissed was actually a man. Given Walter's homophobic tendencies, Matthew held his breath, knowing the scene would certainly get ugly.

Walter must indeed have been very drunk to get this far along in the game. Matthew heaved a gasp of horror as Walter struck Mona in the face with a great deal of force. The blow propelled her backwards onto the floor.

Matthew glanced back at his study door, to make sure David wasn't standing there. Walter might be a total bastard, but he was still David's father. Matthew breathed a sigh of relief before turning back to watch the drama on his TV.

His fists were clenched in impotent fury as the man laid into the woman now lying on the floor, kicking her savagely. Mona tried to crawl away. Walter continued to lash out. He kicked her full in the face, causing her head to snap back. Then he reached down and pulled her to her feet roughly, holding her up with one hand and pummelling her face with the other, his face twisted in sheer rage.

The attack on Mona seemed to go on for ages but when Matthew drew a breath and looked at the video display only five minutes had passed. Walter was getting dressed now, putting his shirt back on, gesticulating wildly at Mona, battered and curled up in a foetal position on the bed. Her face wet with blood, she looked badly hurt.

Walter finished dressing and approached the bed. Mona cowered back. He reached down and twisted her hair in his hands, pulling her upward. He delivered another vicious slap to her cheek and her head flew to the side. Then, his rage seemly spent, he let her go and turned to walk out of the door without a second glance.

Matthew felt sick to his stomach at the acts of violence and a surging fury that Walter could do this and get away with it.

How could his father not have done something about it, given the evidence he had in his possession? That thought made him feel even sicker.

He switched off the DVD player, removed the disc and was about to place it back in the box when he saw a stamped envelope at the bottom of the box with his name and address on it. His father had obviously intended posting it to him. He reached for it with a trembling hand, and opened the envelope. It contained a sheet of paper with his father's distinctive handwriting and another DVD. He could almost hear his father's soft Teutonic accent as he read.

Matthias,

Son, I intend convincing Mona to go to the police with this evidence and lay a charge against Walter. Mona told me about the video recordings she made for her clients and I went and retrieved it. I have contacted Walter and told him I know about this incident. As you can imagine he is not a happy man, but I have to do the right thing. I also told Walter that I had made a copy of the video and intend sending it to you. Put it in a safe place. This is our little bit of extra insurance, Matty. I do not think I have put you in any danger, and it will all be over soon anyway

Your loving father, Erich Langer.

Emotion welled up inside Matthew. His father was speaking to him from beyond the grave. He felt the slow burn of tears at the back of his eyes and his throat closed up, his chest tightening in sheer grief at his father's voice in his head.

He wondered what had happened to Mona. If she'd laid a charge surely Matthew would have known about it.

He took a deep, shuddering breath and lifted his mobile from the desk with a shaking hand, dialling a number.

It rang three times before Shane's sleepy voice answered. "Matty? Are you okay?"

Matthew felt a wave of relief at hearing Shane's voice. "Shay, can you come over to my place? I know it's late—" Matthew's voice choked up and he closed his eyes in sheer weariness.

"Matty, of course. Are you okay, baby? You sound upset."

"I need you," Matthew whispered. "Please get here as soon as you can." He gave Shane the address.

There was a quiet pause. "I'm on my way."

The call was disconnected and Matthew leaned back in his desk chair, closing his eyes and struggling to breathe evenly and get his feelings to subside. He sat back and tried to clear his mind, listening to the faint street sounds outside. It was almost one thirty in the morning and he was bone tired.

The ringing of his mobile on the desk woke him up. He started, feeling disoriented as the phone buzzed and played "Gold on the Ceiling" by the Black Keys. It was Shane. He picked up, wincing at the muscles in his back protesting at the way he'd been dozing in his chair.

"Shane?"

"Do you mind opening the bloody door?" Shane's voice held a trace of irritation. He also sounded out of breath. "I've been knocking, as I didn't want to use the doorbell and wake David up. I imagined he was sleeping."

"Christ, of course. Hang on a minute." Matthew cut the call and moved out to the hallway. He could see the outline of someone out there and he unlocked the door. Shane stood there, sweaty, hair mussed, in a track suit and running shoes. Matthew's heart fell.

"Shane, you didn't run all the way here did you?" He stood aside to let the other man in. Shane stepped into the hallway, out of breath.

"Matty, it was one thirty in the morning when you called. No car, no taxis, no tubes. How else was I going to get here?"

Matthew felt this was quite a surreal conversation. The man standing in front of him was a multimillionaire and could have bought his own taxi firm to be at his beck and call, yet he still ran when he needed to get somewhere in a hurry. It was a testament to Shane's complete lack of desire to material things and wealth that made him all the more special. Matthew closed the door.

"I'm sorry, I didn't think. I shouldn't have called you."

Shane leaned over and pulled Matthew into his arms, his strength and warmth making Matthew feel at ease.

"Babe, you call me all upset and say you need me. I would have run twice the distance just to get here for you, to hear you say that." He cupped Matthew's face in his hands and kissed him on the lips. "Now tell me what's wrong."

Matthew drew him into the dimly lit lounge and filled Shane on in everything he'd found out since opening the cardboard box his father had left him.

"My father died before he could mail this to me," he said as Shane watched him in sympathy. "The letter is dated the day before his death." His face shadowed. "It seems a bit of a coincidence that he had a heart attack around the same time. Perhaps the stress of all this had something to do with it. I think this is what Walter was talking about when he thought I had something on him."

Matthew drew a deep breath when he explained who Mona was. "As Manuel, he had a daughter with a woman who was trying to keep the child away from him due to his, according to her, 'perverted sexual deviance.' He was undergoing medical treatment to change his gender. But Manuel had been a good father. Dad was never one to judge someone on their sexual proclivities." He smiled in fondness. "I'm a case in point. Dad met Manuel via one of the shelters and learned about his problem with his daughter. He helped build a case where at least the man could have visitation rights. I met him as Mona a few times at Dad's office. She was a high-class call girl from what I recall."

Shane made the occasional comment but otherwise simply listened to what his lover was telling him. When Matthew was finally spent, he sat back on the couch with a wide yawn.

"I just needed to tell you all this, Shay. Seeing my father's writing, hearing his voice in my head as I read his letter—I wanted you here with me."

Shane kissed him. "I'm glad you called me." He rubbed his thumb across his lover's hand. "That's one helluva story. But it clears up that little mystery of what Walter thought you had over him and confirms what a bloody bastard he is." He looked at his boyfriend. "It's too late now to do anything for Mona. But you can do something for David."

"What do you mean?" Matthew yawned again, feeling his eyes closing.

"You can use this against him and tell that prick Debussy that unless he reinstates David's funds, you'll give the video footage to the police, go the newspapers, tell the TV stations. He has no choice but to do what you tell him."

Matthew opened his eyes. "God, I wouldn't want you as an enemy. You always cut straight to the marrow, don't you? Maybe we can talk about it in the morning. For now, I just want to go to bed. I have a bloody board meeting in six hours and I look and feel like shit." He stood up and stretched. Shane remained where he was, looking unsure what to do. He looked around the lounge.

"You have a lovely home here, Matty. I assume the man in the pictures is Sam?" His face was non-committal.

Matthew could see the faint pulse in his throat and the shadow in his eyes and felt a surge of guilt. He hadn't even thought about what Shane might see when he got here. The house was still full of his late husband.

"Yes, it's Sam. I'm sorry. I didn't think about all of this," he waved a hand around the room. "I didn't mean to make you uncomfortable. I just wanted to see you. In hindsight it was a crap idea."

His boyfriend shook his head. "It's okay. I know it was a spur of the moment thing." He stood up. "I don't want to run all the way home so would it be all right if I stayed here on the couch? Or in a spare bedroom, if you have another one. I don't want to share with David. The man might rape me while I sleep." He grinned.

"No. No couch and no spare room." Matthew's voice was firm, but he was quaking inside at what he was about to do.

Shane's eyes narrowed. "Fine. I'll suppose I'll start walking then." His voice was tight.

Matthew drew a deep breath and reached out a hand and took his lover's. "Don't be an idiot. You sleep with me, in my bedroom." He felt a shift inside at his own words, at the impact of them.

He'd never had another man in his house since Sam died, let alone his bed. But this felt right. This was a man who'd just run two miles in the early morning just to be with him. He hadn't even known the reason why, just that Matthew needed him. A man who was quite prepared not to cause a scene and walk two miles home just to placate him and give him "space." He didn't know what he'd done to deserve such sacrifice, and he was humbled by it. The least he could do was invite him into his bed. Matthew desperately wanted to feel Shane close to him tonight.

Shane took a deep breath and stared at him with his incredible eyes. "Are you sure, Matty? I wasn't going to presume anything—"

Matthew nodded. "I'm sure. Come on, lover, follow me. And there'll be no hanky-panky tonight, get it? I need some sleep and I don't need your incredible attractions distracting me."

Shane followed Matthew out of the room. "I hear you. But I can't promise anything. Once I get close to you, you know that's it for me. I'm toast."

Matthew could hear the grin in his lover's voice. "I mean it. Please leave me alone or I'll be a total wreck at the board meeting."

Shane chortled. "That's the first time I've ever had a man beg me to leave him alone. The first time we met, you begged me to kiss you, remember?"

"I remember," Matthew smiled at the memory of that scorching kiss as he reached the bedroom and pushed open the door. He paused as the reality of the moment hit him. He was finally having another man share the bed he had last slept in with Sam. Then he pushed past his trepidation and waved at the space. "Bed, bathroom over there in the corner. I sleep on the right side. I'm going to brush my teeth. I have a spare toothbrush if you want it. I'll leave it out for you." He disappeared into the bathroom.

Shane sat down on the bed, feeling awkward. He hadn't missed the hesitation when Matthew had entered the bedroom.

Much like the man himself, the space was tidy, organised and muted. Nothing flamboyant like his. He noticed the lovely watercolour paintings hanging on the wall, one of St. James's Park and another one of Sam, delicately rendered in pale cream and beige tones, with touches of red for the hair. The man's eyes stared out at him, brown eyes direct and warm. Shane swallowed. This was going to be difficult. Even if Matthew had been amenable to a bit of 'hanky-panky', Shane wasn't sure he'd have wanted to, being observed by those eyes.

The bed was king-sized, always a good sign, with a metal headboard that made Shane wonder whether any bondage games had ever taken place here. His groin throbbed at the mere thought of Matthew tied to those metal railings, his for the taking. He knew if he ever got the chance, he'd do it in a heartbeat. Or vice versa, which made him even hornier. But without Sam's likeness watching him.

The bedspread itself was a muted mix of cream, russet and brown, warm and soft. In the corner, mounted on the wall were a TV and a DVD player. The sideboard was heavy and wooden, with ornate brass knobs, a selection of aftershaves, and other personal effects scattered across the top. On each of the bedside tables was a lamp, a tall, oriental effect with a deep rusty shade, one of which was switched on, casting a dim light across the walls.

He knew Matthew inviting him in here was an enormous breakthrough. He'd never expected this. He'd thought the best he'd get away with was bunking down on the couch.

In truth, he had no idea how the man was coping with it. He was probably a basket case in the bathroom, regretting his offer. But there was nowhere Shane would rather be. Matthew had said he needed him. Those alone were words he'd been waiting to hear. He sighed as he waited for his turn in the bathroom. He'd known instinctively that going in there to share the space with Matthew in an act as intimate as brushing their teeth together wouldn't be a good idea. Best wait till Matty came out.

In the bathroom, Matthew leaned his forehead against the cool mirror. He'd known what he was doing inviting Shane to stay over, but it still made his stomach churn and his heart beat faster. Seeing Shane there in his bedroom had brought on the anxiety.

He finished brushing his teeth, rinsed his face with water and took a deep breath. Thank God Shane hadn't come in while he was in here. That action would have been too intimate to bear. It would have reminded him of the times Sam and he had fought laughingly for control of the bathroom sink, shoving each other back and forward until it had turned into caresses and kisses and finally making love in the shower.

"You need to do this," he muttered to himself as he gazed back at the tortured soul in the mirror. "You *can* do this. Shane deserves that much."

He walked out of the bathroom to see Shane sitting on the left side of the bed. Sam's side. He swallowed and slipped out of his trousers and underwear, reaching for a pair of jogging bottoms and pulling them on.

Shane cleared his throat. "Finished in there, then?" He indicated to the bathroom and Matthew nodded. Shane stood up and disappeared into the small room.

Matthew pulled back the covers and got into bed, leaning back against the headboard as he waited for Shane to come out. His eyes fell on his wedding ring. His breath caught. He didn't want to share this bed with another man while still wearing his ring. It didn't feel right. He stared at it for a minute, then he pulled it off his finger and opened the bedside drawer, placing it reverently inside. He closed the drawer and lay back in bed.

Five minutes later, he heard the toilet flush, the water run and the sound of Shane brushing his teeth. It had been a long time since those familiar sounds of another man had echoed in this bedroom. A few minutes later Shane came out, still dressed. He pulled his sweatshirt off and Matthew's cock twitched in appreciation at his lover's body. Shane stripped to just his boxer shorts and crawled into the bed beside Matthew. He lay back against the pillows, his body already relaxing. Matthew switched off the bedside light, plunging the room into darkness.

"Are you sure you're all right with this, Matty?" Shane's quiet voice split the quiet of the room. "I know this must be hard for you."

Matthew's throat tightened. "It's a challenge but I'll be fine. Just settle in, and let's get some sleep." He slid down under the duvet, pulling the covers up to his waist as he turned on his right side, facing away from Shane.

"Can I at least snuggle?" came the voice from behind him as a hundred and sixty pounds of warm man moved closer to him.

"As long as you promise to behave yourself. I need to sleep. If I feel anything of yours anywhere near my nether-regions or my arse, I shall do you harm." He smiled as Shane draped an arm across his stomach and burrowed in.

"Aye, aye, sir. I'll be on my best behaviour. Of course I can't guarantee I won't do anything to you when you're asleep. I've always had this recurring fantasy about giving a man a blow job when he's sleeping and then he wakes up and is so horny that he just turns me over and—"

"Shane." Matthews voice was husky, his groin on fire with his lover's nearness and his masculine scent. "Shut the hell up and go to sleep."

There was a warm chuckle as Shane did as he was told.

Morning After

The following morning, Matthew woke up at six and laid watching Shane sleep. His blond hair was tousled and Matthew reached out a hand and smoothed it gently off his face, caressing the warm cheek. Shane sighed, his breath ghosting Matthew's cheek, but he didn't wake up.

Matthew smiled softly at the sight even as he felt a sense of peace flood his body. The world was still there. The universe hadn't cracked open and dragged him into a deep hole, and Sam's ghost hadn't appeared like the Ghost of Christmas Past to censure him. He'd had a man in his bed for the first time since Sam had died and he had to admit that it felt good.

He looked over at Sam's smiling face on his wall. He blew him a kiss.

"You'd like him," he whispered, and the tears didn't sting his eyes as they had done every night he'd lain awake in this room grieving for his dead husband.

Matthew slid quietly out of bed and went to take a shower. He tidied up his stubble, wrapped a towel around his waist and went into the bedroom to get dressed.

Shane was awake, artfully sitting up with the duvet pushed down below his hips, his morning erection poking out of the top of his boxer shorts. He grinned at Matthew.

Matthew ignored him even as his cock leapt to attention under the towel. He busied himself getting dressed.

Shane sighed, his disappointment evident. Matthew hid a smile. It was taking all his self-control not to jump on the man in the bed, but he needed to get to work.

Shane gestured to the picture of Sam. "It's a great picture. Beautifully rendered. I notice you have quite a few watercolours around the walls. Whoever the artist is, he or she is very good." Shane's voice was soft.

Matthew swallowed. "I'm the artist."

Shane sat up, his eyes wide. "You painted them? You have quite a talent. I had no idea you were so creative."

Matthew shrugged as he pulled on trousers and a shirt. "I like painting. There's a small room at the back of the house that I use as a studio." He felt a twinge of sorrow at remembering what it had originally been going to be used for. "I generally paint from photographs." He pulled on socks and slipped his feet into his shoes, stood up and looked around for his wallet, spying it on his dresser.

He reached into the cupboard and took out a suit jacket that matched the trousers and slipped the wallet into the jacket pocket.

"You really are a dark horse. Any other secret hobbies I should know about? Anything else personal you want to share with me?" Shane's voice was nonchalant but Matthew sensed a slight annoyance in it. The atmosphere had gotten chilly all of a sudden.

"No, that's my only hobby. Not my vice, though. That would be you." He grinned, hoping to lighten the sudden darker mood his lover seemed to have fallen into. Shane leaned back moodily, pulling the duvet up to his waist. There was a sudden movement at the door and David appeared, bleary-eyed, hair sticking up, dressed in just a pair of Matthew's boxers. His face brightened when he saw Shane lying in the bed.

"Shane! God, it's good to see you here. I had no idea Matty had relented and invited you over, the awkward sod." He bounced over onto the bed like a puppy, kissing Shane on the lips, his hand snaking out to cup his cheek as he did so. Matthew watched, his eyes narrowing. The man was far too intimate with Shane for his liking. He seemed to have no boundaries.

"DD, I'd prefer you didn't paw my boyfriend, thanks. Go find your own." His words were mild but his tone was acidic. Shane tried to disentangle himself from the other man's fawning affection even as he smiled at Matthew's words.

"Christ, get off me, you idiot." Shane pushed him away as David withdrew with a pout, looking at Matthew.

"Jeez, Matty, no need to get all alpha male with me. I was just saying good morning."

"Looking as if you're going to stick your tongue in his mouth is not my idea of a good morning greeting," Matthew murmured.

Shane winked at him, his bad mood appearing to have evaporated. "I like you being all alpha male, Matty. Feel free to do it anytime you like."

Matthew's mouth twitched. "I need to get off to work." He looked at Shane warningly. "We'll talk about that stuff we discussed last night later. Maybe we can figure out what we do with it."

"What stuff?" asked David as he sat cross legged on the bed next to Shane.

Matthew shook his head. "Personal stuff between me and Shane." He walked around to the bed and leaned down to kiss his lover, who sighed in satisfaction and pulled Matthew down for a harder kiss. David watched them with a smile.

"I can't believe the two of you are together, here. I'm glad for you both."

Matthew pulled free of Shane's grasp and straightened up. "Right. I'll see you tonight, DD. Try stay away from the best stuff in my wardrobe. We need to go and get *your* stuff and figure out what we do next. Shay, I'll call you later."

He disappeared out of the bedroom. Both men heard the front door slam. David looked at Shane with a lascivious expression.

"Well. This is a turn up for the books. I never thought I'd see the day. Do you know what a milestone this is for Matthew? Being in his house, sharing his bed?"

Shane felt a warmth sweep through his body. "Oh yes, I know what this means. He said he needed me, David. And he was definitely jealous about you jumping on the bed like that. I think I might be getting to him." He reached out a hand and touched the bruise under David's eyes with tender fingers.

"God, he really planted one on you, didn't he? And you look like a sexy bruiser with your split lip." It reminded him he needed to apologise to David for the planting of the gay porn virus on Roy's phone. He opened his mouth to do so but was distracted by David bouncing on the bed like a young child.

"Did you notice anything else?" David was rubbing his hands in glee.

Shane sighed in exasperation. He'd apologise once David got this out of his system. The man was like a hyperactive squirrel. "No. What did I miss?"

"He wasn't wearing his wedding ring."

Shane gaped at David, who punched his arm lightly. "You are so useless at observing. He definitely didn't have it on when he left."

Shane didn't quite know what to make of that.

Was this a long-term thing or was it just because Shane was here in his house? Would the ring go back on the moment he left?

"You knew Sam," he said to David. "What was he like?"

His friend regarded him compassionately. "He was warm, funny, a real Southern gentleman from Georgia. And Matthew adored him, just as Sam adored Matty. But Sam isn't here anymore. You are. And from what I can see, Matthew is adjusting.

He's never done this before. I think he might be getting ready to move on. With you. The man is crazy about you, anyone can see that. Except him."

Shane's heart skipped a beat and his body succumbed to a warm glow. "I'm falling crazy in love with the man," he murmured. "I just don't want to scare him off."

"You keep doing what you're doing, chipping away at him bit by bit. It seems to be working." David grinned wickedly. "And I'm sure all the kinky sex and blow jobs aren't hurting either." He leapt off the bed and went to the door. "I'm going to shower and get dressed. I need to try and find a way to get home and fetch some of my stuff. Maybe we can go over to my dad's house and face the music together."

His voice was hopeful. Shane shook his head. He needed to hold David back from doing anything until they'd had time to figure out what to do with what Matthew's father had left them.

"Hang on there. Matthew had an idea last night. He think he can sort things out but he'll need time to see what he can do. Just bear with him a while longer. He's hoping it will all come right." He hoped that was the plan anyway. To confront Walter with the video footage and get him to reinstate David's trust fund and allow him to get his personal possessions from the house. "Matty has a plan. Let him work it then we can decide where we go."

David looked relieved. "Okay. That sounds good to me." He smiled, seeming happier. "He's great at this stuff, isn't he? Sorting things out I mean." He disappeared out of the bedroom.

Shane clambered out of bed. He needed to get home to Bushwhacker and see what he could find on the woman called Mona/Manuel Casales. She might be just what Matthew needed to break this one and get that prick Walter by the short and curliest. Shane felt a sense of righteousness at being able to help his lover in this way. He knew Matthew might not always have an appreciation for his hacking talents, but he thought this might well be one time when he might need them. With a sense of rising excitement at the task ahead, he headed for the bathroom to shower. He'd be taking a taxi home. He wasn't in the mood for running this morning.

Making plans

Later that afternoon, Matthew called Shane. His lover answered, sounding pre-occupied.

"Shane Templar. Jeez, you bastard." The last words were muttered under his breath and Matthew smiled.

"Something giving you trouble, lover?"

"I just can't find my way around this bloody code I'm looking at. Every time I get close I find something else that looks hinky. It's driving me crazy."

"Hmm. Well, I can't help you with that I'm afraid."

Shane chuckled and Matthew's groin stirred at the sexy sound. "No, but I'm sure you can help me with another little problem I have later. I seem to have a stuffy disc that needs some attention." His snort of laughter echoed down the phone and Matthew grinned.

"Jesus, you have no shame. And that was a really bad joke by the way. Listen, we need to talk about this thing with Walter."

"I'm all ears, Matty. What's the plan?"

"I spoke to my boss, Bartholomew. He seems to think it will be a real battle to get David's trust fund released. It could take a while. A couple of years, in fact. Walter still has rights on the fund, and he's using them to best advantage." He heard Shane's indrawn breath on the other side. "So it looks like our little plan for leverage will have to be invoked."

Shane's voice was quiet. "Okay. What do you want to do?"

"I want to go and see Walter this weekend and tell him what we have and how we intend using it. But first we have to tell David and make sure he's okay with the plan."

"I can see that as being a wise move. When do you plan on doing that?"

"Tonight. My place around seven. I'd like you to be there. David might burst into tears or something and you're better at stuff like that than I am."

"Since when did I get to be the mother in this relationship? Are you saying I'm a softy?"

Matthew grinned at the distinct put-out tone in Shane's voice. "No, I'm saying I'm not good with weeping men, or seeing them tearing at their clothes in anguish. My clothes, actually. I'd like to avoid that if I can. And you are so good at bringing people off the ledge." His voice softened. "You've done it with me often enough."

"Huh. Well-saved, Langer. But just so you know I am one hundred percent man. I intend proving just how much of the man in me there is later tonight."

Matthew laughed loudly. This man of his was incorrigible. "Get your mind out of the bloody gutter, and I'll see you at my place later." He turned as Julia came into his office. "Babe, I have to go. See you around seven. Get a bloody taxi, my little roadrunner. Do it the civilised way for once."

He disconnected the call to Shane's snort of laughter and smiled at Julia.

"Shane has this habit of running around the city like a mythological suited crusader. He's so bloody fit, I wish I could do it."

Julia giggled. "I need to meet this masked man. He's done wonders for you. You're a different person to the one we first met."

The lawyer nodded. "He's pretty special. I'm lucky to have him in my life." He heard the words and realised that he meant every word without any pang of guilt or recrimination. Julia smiled. "Well, it's getting late. I'm off. Are we still on for drinks on Monday night?" He and Julia had been seeing quite a lot of each other after work and at lunchtimes. He liked the woman, with her warmth and her bright sense of humour. She was easy to talk to, didn't pressure him in any way and was always forthcoming with her advice. She also didn't put up with his moods and was refreshingly honest with her opinions. Julia laughingly called him her new BFF.

Matthew nodded. "Absolutely. Coolio's and a margarita await." She leaned in and gave him a gentle kiss on the cheek.

"I'm pleased to see you enjoying yourself. This man is really good for you."

"So everyone keeps telling me, including the man himself," he chuckled. "But I am starting to admit it's true." He glanced at the woman. "He spent the night at my place last night. He's the first man I've ever invited back to my home. That has to mean something."

He hadn't told her directly about Sam but she knew he'd had a tragedy in his past.

He looked at his watch. "I think I'm going to get off, too. It's six p.m. I have something I need to do tonight." He shut down his computer and started packing away all the files on his desk, locking them in his cupboard. Bartholomew Maxwell would have a heart attack if he found client files loitering on the desks.

"Enjoy the weekend and whatever is it you're doing with your man. I'll see you on Monday."

Julia left the office as Matthew picked up his jacket and made his own exit.

Shane got to Matthew's place about seven fifteen, his overnight bag and clean clothes slung over his shoulder. He'd got a taxi later than expected and hoped he hadn't missed anything. He knocked on the door to Matthew's place. When the door opened, his lover beckoned him in.

"Evening, baby. Come on in. DD's already been fortified with a couple of glasses of wine. I've had a whiskey or two myself." He looked his boyfriend up and down and raised an eyebrow, sending Shane's senses reeling.

"You look positively sinful. Are you anticipating getting lucky later?"

Shane hadn't actually given his outfit much thought at all, simply throwing on his stovepipe jeans and a tight-fitting white button-up linen shirt. He didn't think he looked particularly delicious but he was glad Matthew thought so anyway. "I always plan on getting lucky. So what are we doing with David then?"

Matthew led the way into the lounge. Shane noticed that a couple of the photos of Matthew and Sam that had been there before were no longer on show and Matthew still wasn't wearing his wedding ring. Shane felt like all his Christmases had come at once. His man was definitely getting attached whether he liked it or not.

"Shane! You look positively gorgeous." A rather tipsy David got up and weaved his way toward Shane to plant a sloppy kiss on his cheek, careful to avoid Shane's lips. Matthew grinned behind him as he poured Shane a large glass of red wine.

"You have some catching up to do," he murmured as he handed it to his lover." And I agree. I look forward to taking all of that off later and getting naked with you."

Shane's dick strained instantly against his trousers at the huskily whispered words. He sipped his drink as he sat down, trying to get comfortable. Matthew gave him a wicked smile as he sat down next to him and turned to face David.

"Right, DD. We have something fairly serious to talk to you about. You need to focus."

David's sat back, his face growing serious. "Is this about the trust fund?"

Matthew nodded. "I spoke to my boss today. He's told me it will be a helluva challenge breaking the hold your father has over your money. You dad is still a trustee, something I hadn't realised, and I don't think my father knew either. He's found some loophole in the setup where he was originally appointed. So if we did decide to fight this, it will take a long time to resolve it. It could possibly take years." He shrugged his shoulders. "I think your dad always knew this, but he kept it to himself as his 'ace.' Then if one day you got out of hand and started to fight back, this was his carrot to make sure you'd toe the line." He nodded at David.

David's face fell. "That's not good news. Did you manage to find those old papers you were looking for the other night? Is there anything in there that might help?"

Matthew nodded. "I found them, but they didn't help in the way you thought. They did confirm is that your father is within his rights to do what he's doing. So, all in all, not very useful." He took a deep breath. "But I found something else that might help us. But it means doing something that isn't legal and certainly won't make things better between you and your father. But it might get you your trust fund back so you can get out from under your father's control and do things for yourself."

His friend sat back, his face wary. He appeared to have sobered up a bit. "What sort of illegal thing, Matty?"

Matthew looked at Shane for support. He nodded and placed a warm hand on his, squeezing it in encouragement.

"When Shane and I were at the hospital, your father told me that the reason he'd put up with a homosexual lawyer for all those years was because he thought I had something on him, something left to me by my father." He laughed bitterly. "It turns out he has the same opinion of me as he has for his own son."

David's eyes glinted. "I know, and I'm sorry about that. Dad is a real prick." He frowned. "But what's this thing he thought you had on him?"

"I need to show you, DD. It's a bit upsetting, but you need to see it."

Matthew flicked the DVD player on and the video he'd set up already started to play. David leaned forward and Shane heard his hiss of breath as he realised what he was watching. His face paled as the video played, his hands clenching on his thighs.

Shane saw Matthew was on tenterhooks, ready to stop the video if things got too difficult for David.

David's face grew grimmer until finally the video went silent and the screen went blank. He looked at Matthew then Shane with eyes as hard as flint.

Matthew handed him his father's letter. "You need to read this too," he said quietly. "Then you'll understand."

David's face was like granite but he took the letter and started to read it. Finally he handed the letter back to Matthew and stood up, pacing like a caged animal around the lounge.

Shane watched him, his heart going out to him for what he must be feeling. Matthew went to his friend, laying a hand on his shoulder.

David turned with a ragged sigh and stared into Matthew's eyes. "I knew he was capable of violence, but that?" His voice cracked. "That's just sick. How could he do that to woman?"

"Mona wasn't a woman to your father," Shane said evenly. "She was an abomination in his eyes. A transsexual. The bottom line is this, David. Matthew and I think we should finish what his father started. Not to the extent of reporting this to the police, I think that ship has sailed, and we don't even know even if this woman is still around." Shane glanced at Matthew. He knew full well that Mona Casales had completed all her sexual gender reassignment treatments more than a year ago and was now living as a woman somewhere in Mexico. He'd managed to find out a lot about her in case Matthew needed it. But that was his ace in the hole. He wasn't admitting that now. He wasn't sure how Matthew would feel about it right now given his past reactions to things he'd done.

"What we can do is get you out from under his control, get your money back and then you can break free from him, something you should have done a long time ago, to be honest. You can start over on your own. Matty and I will always be there to help you, you know that."

"Blackmail my father with this video? Is that what you're suggesting?" David's eyes narrowed as he looked at the two men. Both Matthew and Shane kept quiet. Finally David gave a harsh laugh.

"He beat me to shit with that little tosser Roy helping him, and who knows who else he might decide to hurt one day. I say let's go for it. Tell the bastard if he doesn't give me back my money we'll hand a copy of this over to the newspapers and TV stations. I know enough people who'd be happy to take this on."

"We're hoping he doesn't call our bluff, DD." Matthew sighed. "We can't really make this public. Mona has a right to privacy and we have no idea whether she'd want to be plastered all over the news. So we only get one shot at this, and we have to be convincing."

He eyed Shane out. "Shay, what did you find out about this woman?"

Shane felt the world tilt. "Which woman?"

Matthew sighed. "I know you, lover. You probably raced home to that little buddy of yours and spent the whole afternoon surfing the net and doing what you do to find out more about her. I bet you know her shoe size, bra size and what she eats for breakfast already." He grinned. "See, now this is one time when I don't mind you weaving that magic you weave so well."

Shane's face flushed and once again his boyfriend raised that sexy eyebrow.

David was looking befuddled. "You've lost me, I'm afraid."

Shane glanced at Matthew. "It's my day job, David. I help companies with their security networks and test their systems to see where their vulnerabilities are. I have access to things normal people wouldn't, and I can find out stuff too."

David's expression was disbelieving. "You're a hacker, Shane?"

"Yes, my sexy stud here is a hacker, one of the best in the business if he's to be believed." Matthew chuckled. "I'm betting he has everything we need to know already."

"Christ, am I that predictable?" Shane growled in annoyance. He noticed David looking at him with a darkened expression.

"Shane, was it you who did that trick with Roy's phone and the gay porn?"

The breath left Shane's body and he stood up, moving over to David's side. Matthew watched them both. Shane laid a hand on David's arm. The man's body was rigid, the muscles taut.

"Yes. I've been meaning to apologise to you for that. I was going to do it yesterday then you distracted me by telling me about Matty not wearing his wedding ring." He glanced at Matthew and saw Matthew still at those words. Shane decided to gloss over them. "I never intended anything bad to happen to you; I'm so sorry. I wanted to teach Roy a lesson, so I hacked his phone."

He stopped as David moved away from him.

"He was very upset about that whole thing." David's mouth was tight. "He beat the shit out of me because he thought I had something to do with it. Then he threatened to shove his phone up my arse and for a minute I thought he was going to do it." His voice trembled. Matthew moved forward as if to comfort him.

Shane felt sick at the story. "I'm sorry," he whispered huskily. "I really am. If it makes you feel any better, you can tell him it was me and—"

Matthew strode forward. "No one's telling Roy anything. DD, Shane didn't know anything would happen to you. He was upset about it, but there's nothing we can do about it now. I know you got hurt, but I'm not having anyone come after Shane. That's just not going to happen. And Roy will if he knows it was him. He liked him a lot less than he did me and that's saying a lot."

Shane stared at him in amazement. Matthew's eyes glinted. The man was a veritable tiger protecting his mate. Shane felt a surge of love so deep it made him feel faint.

David nodded. "You're right. But I'd never have said anything to Roy anyway, Matty. We don't want anyone else getting hurt."

He turned to Shane. "Let's leave it at that." He smiled and chucked his friend on the chin lightly. "Roy definitely got the worst of it. He had people calling him night and day asking him for various unsavoury acts to be performed. All his friends thought it was hilarious. He took a lot of ribbing from them and from some of his ex-military friends. He definitely wasn't a happy bunny. I've never heard a man curse such a lot."

"So that's settled." Matthew exhaled, looking relieved. He looked at David. "Are we agreed then we're going to see your father tomorrow—Saturday?"

David nodded and picked up his wine glass, draining the contents.

"I'm going, too." There was no way Shane was being left out of this. Matthew opened his mouth to speak and Shane forestalled him. "Don't even try convince me otherwise, Matty. I'm not having you go on your own. David will be off getting his stuff hopefully, and there's no way I'm letting you be alone with Walter and Roy in that house. Not after what they've done."

Matthew regarded his lover with softened eyes. "Fine." He giggled.

Shane looked at him in astonishment. He'd never heard Matty giggle before. It made his knees weak and his groin stir even more. This man of his was a definite puzzle.

"We'll be the Gay Musketeers," Matthew said slyly. "All for one and one for all." He seemed to find this quite amusing for some reason as he snorted and laughed again. David shook his head with a knowing smile.

Shane went over to Matthew and patted his shoulder. "You're losing it, lover," he said kindly. "It's the strain. I think you need another glass of wine."

Matthew stopped chuckling at his own wit and caressed Shane's cheek. His eyes virtually undressed Shane, who felt his dick tug in his trousers and heat flood his body.

"All I need is you," Matthew said huskily.

Shane swallowed.

"Oh, Jesus. I'm going to bed if you two are going to fuck each other. Unless you want a threesome?" David said hopefully.

Both Shane and Matthew glared at him.

David shrugged. "Don't say I didn't offer." He grinned and disappeared down to the spare bedroom.

At the sound of a door closing, Matthew turned to Shane. "Do you think he really meant that?" Matthew looked flabbergasted.

Given the fact he'd never thought of David that way, Shane imagined Matthew's illusions about his friend had just been shattered.

He nodded, amused at the expression on his lover's face. "He did, yes. It wouldn't be the first time for him."

"I can't believe he actually asked that," Matthew muttered. "The man has no bloody shame. He's my friend for God's sake!" He scowled fiercely. "And as if I'd share you with him anyway. The man's a loony."

Shane chortled as he pulled Matthew into him, sliding his tongue in past the willing lips, feeling the heat and wetness of Matthew's mouth as he moaned and ground his groin against Shane's.

Shane wanted to get inside this man, possess him in every way possible. His dick was reaching skywards and searching for the light. He pulled Matthew's shirt out of his jeans, touching the man's hot skin and frantically lifting the shirt above his head. Matty reached up as his shirt was removed, and Shane lunged forward, his teeth fastening on his lover's nipple. Matthew winced in pain but pressed himself close into Shane's mouth.

"We can't bloody do this here," he gasped. "We need to go into the bedroom. David might come out and see us."

"He'd enjoy the show," murmured Shane as he feasted on his lover's other nipple, nibbling and teasing it with his tongue. Matthew was straining against him, his body tense and his breathing erratic.

"I'm not giving him a bloody floor show, Shay," he gasped. "Come on."

He took Shane's hand and dragged him through to the bedroom, tossing him onto the bed and closing the door behind him. Matthew unzipped his own trousers, pulling them down with urgency, together with his underwear. He sprung free and Shane licked his lips at the sight. Matthew climbed onto the bed and unzipped Shane's jeans.

"Lift yourself," he growled and Shane lifted his arse as Matthew ripped everything below his waist off his body. The younger man chuckled.

"God, you're bloody eager. Let me get my shirt off, you animal."

"No. Leave the shirt on. I like it." Matthew straddled Shane, sitting on his thighs. His erection jutted out toward Shane who just wanted to taste it. Shane grew even harder, like a periscope being launched. He moaned.

"God, Matty, you feel so good. Blow job first, then I want to feel myself inside you."

Matthew shook his head. "Not yet. Patience, honey." He reached over to his side of the bed and opened his side table.

Shane's eyes widened at what he pulled out. It was a pair of handcuffs. His dick gave yet another enormous surge upwards, and it felt as if his skin would burst with the pressure.

"Fuck, Matty, you are a surprise." He watched as his lover took one hand and cuffed it to the headboard, then took the other and did the same. Shane was now shackled to the metal frame, as Matthew slowly opened his shirt button by button. Both of them were breathing heavily, ready for the next play.

Shane watched his lover's face as their eyes met. Shane had never experienced anything as erotic as this moment. Of all the things he'd done with men in his lifetime not one of them came close to the satisfaction and desire he felt for this man sitting on his thighs, slowly torturing him with everything he had. Matthew leaned down and licked Shane's lips slowly, like a cat, and once again Shane knew why he always thought his lover had a feline air. The man was elegant, limber and at the moment, driving him crazy and out of control.

Matthew finished with the shirt and spread the two sides wide, his hands sliding over Shane's chest, his fingers teasing his nipples. He bent and bit Shane's stomach, drawing blood and leaving a bite mark. Shane yelped as his body bucked against the pain, and Matthew bent down and bit him again on the shoulder.

Shane hyperventilated, his breath coming so fast and shallow with the sheer sensations the other man was causing that he thought for a moment he was going to pass out.

"I didn't know you were a biter," he gasped.

Matthew's eyes were dark, his pupils blown. His breathing was heavy, his breath warm against Shane's skin. "Neither did I," he whispered. "But it feels good. Tell me if it hurts too much." He shifted back down Shane's legs, bent his mouth again and nipped Shane on his hip.

"You have to be the sexiest man I've ever bitten," Matthew murmured with a smile. "Actually, you're the only man I've ever bitten."

"I bring out the beast in you, obviously," Shane gasped again as Matthew moved toward his groin.

Matthew looked up. "You do, lover." His mouth enveloped Shane's dick as his hands cupped and squeezed his balls.

Shane cried out, not caring if David heard. He was beyond caring what anyone thought, simply living in the moment, feeling his lover's silky mouth sliding up and down him, teasing the tip with his tongue, tickling his slit until he thought he was going to erupt. He wanted to reach out and touch Matthew, feel the velvety smoothness of him in his hands, and the heat of his body, but he could do nothing but watch as his boyfriend's mouth bobbed up and down on his straining and extremely sensitive member.

"Christ, you're going to make me come. And I want to be inside you." Matthew gave one final swirl with his tongue, licking Shane from shaft to tip in one long stroke, then moved up over his body, holding him tightly and positioning himself over him, ready to take him inside. His breathing was harsh, his lips swollen and wet with Shane's fluids.

"Do you trust me, Shay? Enough to do this bareback when I say I'm clean? I want to feel you tonight."

Shane's heart skipped half a dozen beats at the thought of being inside Matthew with no barrier, just heat and silky skin. He nodded. "I trust you. And you know you can trust me, I'm good too. Do it, baby. Just like this."

Matthew groaned and reached for the lube. He reached down and coated his entrance, slightly inserting his finger as Shane watched. Matthew's eyes closed in pleasure at feeling his own digits inside himself.

Shane was in a state of total meltdown. Matthew put some lube in his hands and rubbed Shane's dick with it. He moved across and slid down onto it lightly, wincing as his muscles tightened around Shane.

Shane gasped at the sensation of feeling just Matthew. This was how making love was supposed to feel. Matthew slid up and down on Shane, each time taking him deeper inside.

Shane pulled his hands against the handcuffs binding him, his wrists feeling chafed and sore already with his frantic movements. The sight of this controlled man of his, always in charge, with his swollen lips, a total look of concentration on his face as he rode Shane and stroked his own dick, were causing havoc in his groin and his heart. Matthew's hands moved fiercely in cadence with his movements on Shane, moaning as he pleasured himself in two ways.

Shane pushed upward as Matthew came down, and soon the two of them developed a rhythm like a well-oiled machine, two people who knew well how to please each other.

Shane felt his climax building and he arched up on the bed. "Hell, Matty, just keep going." He moaned as Matthew sank deeper. Shane felt the heat in his groin and the prickle in his backside and the enormous pressure that was building in his stomach. He shuddered and ejaculated.

Matthew tightened around him, heightening the sensation.

Shane lay back, gasping on the bed, annihilated and feeling as if he'd been put on fast spin in a washing machine. His body ached, his wrists hurt and he felt as if there was nothing left inside him at all.

Matthew continued his frantic stroking movements of his dick and Shane felt his lover's body tauten and his buttocks clench against Shane's hips. Matty shouted out Shane's name as he came, thick ropes of come shooting onto Shane's chest as he jerked and spasmed above him and finally slumped in sheer abandon across Shane.

Once again the two men were sandwiched by semen. The sounds of their panting and moans echoed in the room.

"Christ, that was incredible. I—" He hiccupped a breath as Matthew looked up, staring at him with intense eyes.

He moved gently off Shane and lay beside his lover. Then slowly, he began cleaning Shane's chest with his tongue, licking the semen off with long, slow strokes that made Shane's dick twitch again and start a slow upward trend. Matthew purred as he performed his act of pure decadence. All Shane could do was watch.

"You are definitely part cat," Shane whispered when Matthew finished and came up to kiss him in a deep-tongued and tooth-clicking kiss that made his lips tender and sore.

"Could you take these handcuffs off me, please? I think my blood circulation has stopped." Shane pulled at the cuffs.

Matthew looked as if he was considering it. "I'm not sure I want to. I like you all wanton and slutty like this. I can do what I want with you and you can't stop me."

He pressed his body close to Shane's, his hips pressing into Shane's own, as his hands reached down between Shane's legs and cupped his balls, and slid down further to stroke his taint.

Shane's body left the bed. Matthew grinned and did it again. His pupils were dark, almost black, and he was starting to get turned on again if the hardness of his cock was anything to go by. Shane knew he'd be a gibbering wreck if he kept this up. But it felt so good.

Matthew contemplated Shane's body with lazy, hooded eyes. "I think I might just keep you like this for the night. That way, whenever I feel like it, I can take you, suck you and make love to you." He grinned as he murmured sultrily, *"Ich kann dich einfach gefangen halten."*

I can make you my prisoner.

Shane was hyperventilating now both at the German and at the thought of being used like that. It excited him. He was also seeing another part of his lover that was quite frankly a real turn-on and at the same time rather scary. The man was a born dominant, but he supposed being a control freak, that wasn't all that surprising.

He watched as Matthew considered him for a moment, then relented and reached for the handcuff key. He opened the cuffs.

Shane pulled his wrists free, wincing at the red livid lines on his skin.

Matthew's expression turned to horror. "Jesus, you're bleeding. God, I'm sorry."

Despite Shane's repeated entreaties that he was fine, Matthew bounded out of bed, all backside and bobbing bits and disappeared into the bathroom. He came out a minute later with a small medical aid kit.

"I need to clean those cuts and put some antiseptic on them." He opened the small bag as Shane sighed in exasperation

"I'm fine, honestly. It's just a scratch."

Matthew shook his head stubbornly. "I need to clean them." He poured some antiseptic fluid onto small swathes of cotton bandage and proceeded to wipe off the slight blood trails around Shane's wrists, before applying some ointment to them and rubbing it in gently.

"There, that should do you. You should have said they were hurting, Shay."

Shane pulled him in for a kiss. "I said it was okay. I enjoyed it, all of it. Even the biting. I hope I don't need a tetanus shot."

Matthew went rosy. "I've never done that before. You just drive me crazy." He took a clean swab and dabbed at the bites on Shane's body, his face tight as he saw the marks he'd left. When he'd finished, he kissed each bite one by one.

Shane kissed him back then pulled him down next to him as Matthew snuggled into his shoulder. The two men relaxed in silence for a while.

"Matty?"

"Hmm?" His lover sounded half asleep.

"We did this bareback. That must mean something, right?" Shane desperately wanted to tell Matthew that he loved him, but he didn't want to scare the man. He thought he'd test the waters first.

Matthew moved and sat up, his arms folded around his knees. "You said you were okay with it. Are you having second thoughts? It's a bit late—"

Shane placed a finger on Matthew's lips. "No, that's not what I meant. I wanted it, and I do trust you. I was clean when I met you and there's only ever been you since."

"Ditto," said Matthew softly.

"I just meant, doing it that way, it involves feelings, not just fuck buddies—doesn't it?"

There was silence. Shane waited, holding his breath. His heart was pounding. Then Matthew snuggled back down into Shane's arms, his head on his chest, his arm draped over his stomach.

"I took off my wedding ring, Shay. I didn't feel right sleeping with you here in this bed and wearing that. I thought I'd put it back on but when I went to do that this morning, I couldn't. I just didn't feel I needed it anymore. I took Sam's picture off the bedroom wall and hung it in my study. And tonight, yes, Shay, it involved feelings. You were never just my fuck buddy. I told you that." He kissed Shay's chest, his lips nibbling his nipples and causing sensations in his body that were not conducive to sleep. "Now can we go to sleep? I'm exhausted with all that activity and we have a pretty shit day ahead of us tomorrow."

Shay's face was creased in a huge grin in the darkness of the room. It might not have been an admission of love, but it meant something.

The Gay Musketeers Ride again

The following morning Matthew showered, dressed and wandered through to the kitchen to find David already seated with his hands around a steaming cup of tea. The man cocked an eyebrow at him.

"Remind me not to stay here ever again when Shane stays over. I got hardly any bloody sleep last night with the two of you shouting and screaming at the tops of your bloody voices." He scowled.

Matthew laughed. "You're just jealous because we didn't invite you." He looked around as Shane padded in clad in his jogging bottoms and nothing else. "Shay, DD said we made too much noise last night and could we please refrain from fucking each other's brains out with such vigour while he's trying to sleep."

Shane nodded. "Oh, yes, we'll certainly be looking into that. Not." He looked around for coffee and found the jar. He busied himself making two cups of coffee.

"I need to call Walter and tell him we're coming over." The lawyer looked unseeingly out of the window. He wasn't relishing that conversation. He sighed and picked up his mobile. It was nine a.m., but Walter was an early riser. No doubt he'd be up. He dialled Walter's mobile number and hoped he'd pick up. It rang four, five times then someone answered. Matthew's stomach clenched. Shane smiled reassuringly at him as David looked down into the bowels of his cup.

"Walter Debussy."

"I'm glad you don't have caller ID, Walter," Matthew said. "Or you might not have answered."

"Matthew? What the hell do you want?"

"I'm representing David. He wants to know whether you've reconsidered releasing his trust find back to him so he can carry on with his life and get out of yours."

Walter laughed harshly. "Tell that little queer he can go to hell. He's not getting that money. He'll have to become a rent boy to support himself."

"Are you sure about that? We're giving you a chance to do the decent thing here. It's your last chance."

"Fuck off. Now if you don't mind, I have more important things to do. Like take a crap."

"Walter, do you remember in the hospital when you mentioned something about why you'd put up with me for so long? And how I said I didn't know what you were talking about?" Matthew felt his anger slowly rising as his fingers clenched around his mobile, the knuckles white.

Walter was quiet, then said, "I remember." There was a slight undercurrent of something in Walter's voice.

Matthew felt a sense of satisfaction. He'd managed to rattle him with that comment. "Well, I lied." Matthew saw Shane smile and raise a thumb at him. "David and I are coming over after this call so he can collect his belongings and we can talk about how you will return his access to his trust fund."

There was a stunned silence on the other end of the phone, then Walter exploded. "You're intending blackmailing me, you little faggot? Do you know what you're doing?"

Matthew closed his eyes, knowing the risks he was taking for them all. He felt Shane's hand on his arm, giving him confidence. "I know exactly what I'm doing. Trying to right a wrong to your son. You're a judgemental son of a bitch. Now, name a time we can come and discuss this. Or I'm afraid I'll have no choice but to release the video and ask the woman you beat up to come forward and tell her story." He held his breath and waited for the reply.

When Walter spoke next his voice was choked with fury. "Come over to the house at midday. And Roy says don't bring that little pretty blond fag boy that was with you at the hospital with you or he might have to restrain himself." The phone was disconnected.

Matthew let out a huge breath. "Midday." He looked at Shane. "Walter says not to bring you with or things could get ugly with Roy. I think you should stay here, just let me and David go." He knew even as he said it his words were falling on deaf ears. Shane just looked at him.

Matthew sighed. "Shay, there's no point in causing grief if we don't have to. I don't want you getting hurt, babe."

"And who stops you getting hurt, Matty? Don't even let us have that conversation. I'm going with you and that's final." He stood up. "I'm going to shower and get dressed into a killer outfit. Perhaps the pink tutu. That could make things interesting." He grinned wickedly. Matthew watched as Shane's lean hips and tight backside disappeared into his bedroom. He sighed and David laughed.

"He's a real character, Shane is." His face shadowed. "But Roy really seems to have a bee in his bonnet about him."

Matthew nodded. "Shane gave him quite a mouthful at the hospital. He was really cocky with both of them and I think he made a couple of enemies there. I wish he'd stay here. But I know that's not going to happen."

He left David in the lounge and went in search of his boyfriend. He found him in the shower. Shane called out from behind the glass door.

"Are you coming in, Matty? I know how to relieve that tension you have."

"No. I'm coming to ask you to behave when we get to Walter's. I don't want you making Roy anymore anti-Shane than he is already is. Promise me you'll be good."

"Lover, I'm always good." The shower was turned off and the glass door opened. Matthew took a deep breath at the sight of his lover's lean body, the water dripping off him, making him want to lick it all up.

Shane grabbed a towel and wrapped it loosely around his waist, as he took another one and towelled his hair dry. "I'll be on my best behaviour. Unless either of those tossers make any move toward you. Then all bets are off." He discarded the towel on the rail carelessly and moved into the bedroom.

Matthew straightened the towel and followed him. He watched as Shane dressed, pulling on black chinos, a slim-fit grey, short-sleeved polo shirt that showed off his arms and a pair of black loafers. He looked incredibly sexy and for a moment, Matthew wished he could simply put the whole matter of David's trust fund behind him and crawl back to bed with this man.

Shane flashed him a dazzling smile. "Well? Do I pass muster as your body guard?"

Matthew nodded. "You look good in anything." He kissed Shane briefly on the lips. "I'm going to make sure I have everything I need to take through with me. I'll be in my study if you need me."

It was eleven fifteen a.m. when the three men got into Matthew's car and he drove to the Debussy residence in Knightsbridge. They were all fairly subdued. David sat in the back, Shane in the passenger seat as Matthew navigated the London streets.

It wasn't far, about four miles, but Matthew knew they were all nervous and would rather be in the car on the way to their destination than sitting back at Matthew's house, waiting. They made small talk and it was close to midday when they pulled up outside the gated mansion that was David's family home. The car idled at the huge wrought-iron gates as not one of them seemed predisposed to ring the buzzer for the intercom system that would let them into the stately grounds.

"The Gay Musketeers have arrived." Matthew sniggered. Shane looked at him perplexed as David grinned and chuckled.

"What is it with you and this whole Gay Musketeers thing that you find so funny?"

Matthew laughed. "It was a phrase my dad coined. When I was sixteen, me, David and another friend of ours went to a fancy dress party. We wanted to go as the Three Musketeers and we all sorted out our own costumes. My dad took one look at us just before we left and asked us quietly if we really wanted to go dressed like we were. Apparently we were less of the Three Musketeers and more of the Gay Musketeers. It appeared our costumes were fairly camp without really realising it, and he didn't want us to get beaten up. The only straight guy in the trio, Darryl, was mortified. He made us all tone down our outfits before we could be seen with him in public. The name stuck whenever the three of us were doing anything together, or got into trouble, which happened quite often. Even Darryl thought it was funny, but we didn't use it in public."

David chuckled. "I remember that well, Matty. I think at the time were trying to outdo each other and the costumes went somewhat haywire in our efforts to shock."

Shane shook his head in amusement. "That's a word I thought I'd never have thought would describe you, Mr. Langer: camp."

Matthew shrugged. "I was still coming out, learning the boundaries. Thank God I had my dad there to keep me on the straight and narrow. So to speak."

The three men chuckled and then went silent.

"So, shall we do this then?" Shane said as he observed the other two musketeers. "Matthew, it's on your side. You do the honours."

His boyfriend nodded and slid his window opened. He pressed the buzzer and waited. A man's voice echoed down the intercom.

"Yes?"

"It's Matthew Langer to see Walter Debussy." There was a momentary hiatus and then the large gates creaked as they swung open to admit the waiting vehicle.

Matthew put the car into first gear and drove up the long and winding driveway to the gravelled parking area before the house. It felt strange for him coming back here as a visitor instead of one of the family and resident lawyer. He was sure David felt even stranger having been kicked out of his family home. The men got out of the car and stood outside. Matthew laid a comforting hand on his friend's shoulder.

"Ready, DD?" Matthew asked quietly.

David nodded. "Let's get this over with."

Matthew gave a warning glance at his boyfriend. "Shay—"

Shane placed a warm finger on his lover's lips. "I know, Matty. Behave myself." He squeezed Matthew's arm and moved up the stairs, following David who was already striding up the wide stone steps to the front door. Matthew took a deep breath, centering himself, and walked up the grey slabs. The door was already opening, and a woman peered out. Her face broke into a warm and loving smile as she reached out her arms and drew David into them.

"David! What a lovely surprise. I had no idea you were coming. Come on in. Matthew? My goodness, this is lovely to see you both."

"Hello, Georgie," David said affectionately. He turned to Shane who was standing slightly apart from the other two men.

"Shane, this is Georgie Engel, our housekeeper. Georgie, this is my friend Shane Templar."

"It's good to meet you, Shane." The woman's eyes were warm as she appraised the newcomer. "My but you *are* a handsome devil. David is lucky to have a man like you at his side."

Matthew saw Shane fidget uncomfortably and assumed it was both at the compliment and the assumption he belonged to David.

"Errm, actually, Georgie, Shane is Matthew's boyfriend." David admitted.

Georgie looked at Matthew as he stepped forward, his smile fond. "Hallo, Georgie. How have you been?" He hugged the woman tightly. She hugged him back.

"It is good to see you, Matthew. And you actually have a boyfriend now. Wonders will never cease." Her face creased into a smile, which soon disappeared as she then spoke in quick German.

"Er ist in einer sehr schlechten Stimmung. Du must vorsichtig sein. Kümmer dich um David."

Matthew tensed and nodded.

"Danke für die Warnung, ich werde mich bemühen," he murmured softly, glancing at Shane and David who stared at them, each with a look of bemusement.

Georgie nodded and moved away into the adjoining dining room.

"Er, Matthew, was what all that about? I don't know whether to be turned on or worried. You have a funny expression on your face." Shane observed his lover's face closely.

"I heard my name mentioned," murmured David with a look of apprehension.

"I'll translate later, out of earshot of anyone else." Matthew said grimly. "Let's go get this over with."

As he moved away, Georgie called after him. "Matthew?" He turned to see her looking at him with a gentle expression. "I'm glad you found someone."

He smiled at her, cast an affectionate look at Shane and strode through to the open French doors into the lounge. Walter always received his visitors in there, his drawing room, and Matthew didn't think today would be any different.

Georgie had just told him Walter was in a very bad mood and to be careful and take care of David.

Walter Debussy stood by the long picture windows looking out into the large garden beyond. Roy Parsons stood by his side, a sneer on his face as he watched Matthew and David approach. When he saw Shane come in behind them, his face grew even uglier, and he stepped forward as Walter turned to face them.

Roy spat out his words venomously. "You brought that little slag with you? Didn't Mr. Debussy tell you to leave him at home?"

Matthew's temper rose with every step forward. He glanced at Shane whose face was white with the effort of holding his tongue as Matthew had asked him to do. But the lawyer wasn't letting that one pass.

"Roy, you prick, shut the hell up. I'm here to talk to Walter, not listen to your drivel. You're just the hired hand, after all." He saw Shane's bemused expression at the fact Matthew had ignored his own rules not to antagonise anyone. But calling his boyfriend a slag had really gotten his goat. Matthew turned to Walter, who was looking at him as if he was a particularly nasty specimen of bug that had just crawled out of a deep, dark hole.

David moved toward his father, his hands held up. "Dad, we really don't want to get nasty about this. Just give me back the trust fund Mum left me and we'll get out of your hair. You know you don't need the money." He looked around. "Is Lewis here? He should know what's going on."

Walter snarled. "Lewis is in the study. He's on the phone." Walter observed his son through narrowed eyes. "You had your chance, son. I wanted you to try and curb those bloody deviant desires you have and get happy with a woman and you couldn't even do that for me. Now you pay the consequences."

"Jesus, Dad, I've already told you being gay isn't something you can change!" David ran a hand through his hair in frustration. "I like men, not women. I can't change that any more than you can change from women to men."

Walter shivered in disgust.

David's comment led Matthew into the topic of conversation he wanted to pursue. "Talking of that, Walter," he said as he prowled around to Walter's side, "I seem to have possession of a certain piece of video footage—"

Roy stepped forward as he cut Matthew off. "You little cocksucker," he snarled. "You think you can come in here and threaten Mr. Debussy like this? You and your little fag friends? I ought to—"

"Roy, shut up." Walter's voice was hard. Roy stopped and looked at his boss.

Walter's voice was dangerous. "Tell me, Matthew. Doesn't this go against every ethical bone in your body to blackmail someone? I thought you had more integrity than this. I'd expect it from my son and probably your little fuck buddy, but you?"

"Hard times call for tough solutions, Walter." Matthew knew Walter was right about him and in an ideal world this would be the last thing he would ever have thought of doing. "But you left us with no choice. The bottom line is if you don't reinstate David's control of his own trust fund, I will give this over to the newspapers and we will ask Mona Casales, the woman you beat up, to make a statement. She's willing to come forward. You will be the laughingstock of the city. Is that what you want?"

Walter was trembling with rage, his face white, his lips pinched and his fists curled into balls at his side. "You dare call that thing in that hotel room a woman? She was a freak of nature. She made a bloody fool of me, you little bastard. And your father was going to report me to the police and convince her to make a statement. Nothing I could do would convince him otherwise." He smiled, his eyes deadened. "Then he up and died before he could do it and I thought, good riddance."

Matthew felt the world tilt at the fact another human being was getting pleasure out of his father's sudden death. His hands shook in impotent fury at his side and it took every ounce of self-control he had to stop himself from lunging Walter and beating him to a pulp.

He couldn't even speak as emotions overwhelmed him. Matthew saw David staring at his father in sheer horror, tinged with disgust. If he hadn't realised exactly what his father was before, he certainly did now. He felt an ache in his chest that his friend had to go through this.

A soft voice at his side said, "Matty, don't let him get to you, babe." Shane stood with his hand on Matthew's elbow, steadying him. He was looking at Walter with such an intense look of hate on his usually open face that he didn't even look like Shane.

Roy moved forward, his teeth bared and his face alight with what Matthew thought looked like a fiendish glee that he might do some harm to someone, his eyes focused on his Shane.

"You have two options, you bitter and twisted piece of shit." Shane's voice was calm, controlled. "You can put whatever you need to do in motion right now, to get that trust fund released. I'd suggest you sort it out really quickly before I get fed up and do something you regret."

David, pale but resolute, moved up beside Shane, the three men forming an alliance that felt unshakeable.

"And if I don't, you little queer? What will you do then?" Walter's words were tough but his bluster appeared to be lessening.

Shane smiled, and even Matthew's blood ran cold at the sheer menace in that sight. He reached into his jacket pocket and took out his mobile.

"Then in less time than it takes you to shoot your load into who or whatever you're currently fucking, which is probably less than two seconds, this little queer will click this little button on his phone and upload that video virally to every news and TV station in the country. Along with a written statement from Mona Casales about how you half beat *her* to death in a hotel room three years ago. Then we'll see how you feel about that." He finished with an air of finality and regarded Walter and then Roy with a fixed and cold stare.

The room was quiet.

The Gay Musketeers stared at the two men, in a lockdown staring competition that was Olympian in its grandeur. Walter was white, Roy tight with anger.

Matthew was gobstopped at Shane's tactic. He thought Shane had been magnificent and from the look of worship on DD's face, so did David. He wondered wryly whether he'd have to command a duel with David for his boyfriend's honour. He muffled a slight snort of laughter at the thought, despite the current tension in the air. But Matthew didn't like the look that Roy was giving his lover. It was a cold, calculating look of sheer malevolence.

Shane finally cocked an eyebrow to break the stand down. "So, gentlemen, what's it going to be? Trust fund released or me clicking this little itty bitty metaphorical switch and making you one of the most talked-about men in the city? And not in a good way."

Matthew saw the flicker in Walter's eyes and felt a surge of relief. He'd seen that before when Walter had backed down from something. Although it was a rare occurrence, it was a tell he recognised. "Get the hell out of my house, you bunch of perverted little faggots. That includes you, David, if you're going to side with these two pieces of filth. You'll get your trust fund back and then I never want to bloody see you again."

David swallowed and Shane took his arm firmly as he swayed slightly. "That's fine, Dad," he said huskily. "If that's the way you want to play it. I'm sorry you feel that way, of course, but I'm not going to be something I can't. I'll go upstairs and get my stuff."

He walked unsteadily over to the large winding staircase that led to the next level and walked slowly up the stairs. Matthew's heart was full of pain for the man who'd just been disowned by his father. He looked across at Shane who winked at him. In spite of the playful gesture, Shane's eyes were darkened and his face drawn. Matthew knew he was probably remembering the time he too had been asked to leave by his father. Matthew wanted to pull his lover close, kiss him, tell he loved him—

Christ, where did that bloody come from? He couldn't think about that now. Hell, he wasn't even sure he could think about it later.

The four men continued standing, still and intent. The atmosphere in the room was tense, thick with testosterone and dark emotions.

Matthew wanted nothing more than to leave this room and go outside where the air was more breathable, but he didn't trust Walter or Roy not to do something to David when he finally came down for picking up his belongings.

Walter turned to Roy. "I'm late for another appointment. I need to go. Stay here and make sure these people leave my home. And that includes my bloody son." Roy nodded as he regarded both

Matthew and Shane with narrowed eyes. Walter turned and strode out the room. As he walked out, Shane called out to him.

"Walter, by the way, you do know the correct use of the word 'faggots' is more in a culinary sense, don't you? Those delicious meatball things made of pork and stuff that you eat. I just wanted to clear that up in case you didn't know."

Matthew groaned as he saw Walter's back tighten.

Christ, lover, you just had to have the last bloody word, didn't you?

David's father didn't turn around, just kept walking out of the room.

Hopefully to reunite David with his trust fund, Matthew thought.

David came walking down the stairs dragging a suitcase. He looked defeated, and Matthew's heart went out to him. It looked as if he'd been crying. David tried not to look at Roy, probably not wanting to give him the satisfaction of seeing his red-rimmed eyes. He nodded at Matthew.

"I'm done, Matty."

Matthew reached out and touched his friend's cheek softly and the other man's eyes closed. But when he opened them, his gaze was fierce.

"Let's get out of this shit hole." He wheeled his bag out of the lounge. Matthew turned to follow him, Shane close behind.

"You want to watch your back, pretty boy. I know what you did to me. I'll get you back for that and just for being the fag boy you are." The words addressed to Shane came out of Roy but they sounded like the venomous hiss of a snake rather than something human. Matthew felt a cold shiver down his spine.

Please don't say anything, Shane. Please just walk away. I don't like this situation one little bit.

He heard Shane stop behind him and Matthew turned to him, silently willing his lover simply to carry on. Shane must have read the pleading look on his face and whatever he'd been about to say he swallowed. He ignored Roy's last comment as he followed Matthew out of the room.

They walked silently to the car and joined David who was standing smoking outside.

Shane gazed at him. "I thought you gave that up?"

David shook his head jerkily. "I had. But I really needed a fag. No pun intended." He finished his smoke, threw it to the gravel and stomped on it.

David's brother Lewis came to the top of the stone staircase and called out. "David." Lewis Debussy stood awkwardly as his younger brother tensed and faced him.

"Lewis. Glad to see you at least came to say goodbye." David's vice was flat. He glanced up at his brother with a faint look of contempt.

Lewis walked halfway down the steps then stopped. "Look, DD, you know what Dad's like. He sees things in black and white, and nothing ever makes him change his mind. If you'd just done as he asked, tried to change—"

"Fuck you, Lewis. You sound like Dad. Being gay isn't a disease, you arsehole, it's just the way I am." David strode forward angrily to the stairs and stood at the foot as Lewis watched with an air of apprehension. He seemed ready to run if his younger sibling came any closer.

Matthew and Shane waited, not wanting to interfere but ready to leap in if needed.

"If you'd ever understood anything about who I am and what I've had to face for being gay in this family and out there," David swept a hand out into the air, "You'd understand it's not something we take lightly. It's who I am, Lewis. I like men. Not women. That doesn't make me any different to you inside."

"You should have just done what Dad wanted," Lewis insisted, his eyes narrowing. "Then you wouldn't be in this position with Matthew losing his job and you being kicked out. Why did you have to make things so bloody difficult for yourself?" His dark brown eyes were unrelenting. He stared at Matthew. "Matty, you too. Why couldn't the two of you just get over it, or hide it instead of brandishing it about like a caveman club? Then none of this would have happened."

Matthew stepped forward in anger. "Lewis, I'm not even going to qualify that inane remark with a response. You're an ignorant, intolerant arsehole. You always were. David, are you ready to leave this place? I, for one, think you'll be far better off on your own anyway than with this bunch of stupid gits."

David nodded as he moved back to stand with Matthew and Shane. "You watched them beat me up, Lewis," he said. "I saw you at the top of the stairs. You did nothing to help me even when Roy was beating the crap out of me. You're a coward, and I wish you a great life under Dad's thumb. You both deserve each other." He turned to Matthew.

"My suitcase is in the boot. Can we get going, please? I really want to get out of here." He walked over to the car, opened the door, got into the backseat and sat staring up at the house he was about to leave forever.

Shane clambered into the passenger seat and Matthew settled himself in and started the engine. They drove down the drive, stopping and waiting for the gates to open before heading out into the street. The car was silent. They'd been driving for about fifteen minutes without uttering a word when Matthew turned to Shane with a grin.

"Shay, babe, I thought you *didn't* like pork faggots? You extolled their virtues back there. Lover, you have been lying to me these past few months." The car was quiet and then the sounds of three men giggling started, escalating to full blown guffaws as they released the tension of the last hour.

"Jesus, Matty, I swear, you can be so bloody droll. You kill me." Shane gasped as he wiped tears from his eyes. David was chortling in the back seat as Matthew chuckled loudly at his own wit. Matthew was glad he'd managed to break the awful tension. The men got themselves under control and the atmosphere lightened.

"By the way, what did Georgie say to you?" Shane asked curiously.

"She just warned me Walter was in a very bad mood and to watch out for David. I don't know if she heard anything said by either of them but something rattled her. She obviously didn't want them to hear her, hence the German." He changed gear expertly. "That bluff you pulled back there was amazing, Shane," he said as he steered the car through the afternoon traffic. "It was a stroke of genius."

Shane looked at him in surprise. "It was no bluff, Matty. I really did have it all primed and ready to go."

The lawyer's mouth dropped open. He heard David's low chuckle in the back.

"How the hell did you set that all up so quickly?"

His boyfriend shrugged. "I burned the video footage from the DVD onto my phone, and then set it up from there. That was an easy job."

"And the letter from Mona? Was that real too?"

Shane shook his head. "That *was* a bluff. But Mona did say if we really needed her to give a statement, she would."

Matthew was staring at Shane as if he'd suddenly sprouted a third eye on his forehead. "You *spoke* to her?"

His boyfriend nodded. "I tracked her down and told her what had happened. She was great. She'd heard about your dad's death. Mona was scared of Walter and even more scared of Roy. Apparently Roy had contacted her just before your dad died and told her she'd better not do anything against Debussy. She was still going to go ahead anyway with an assault charge. She trusted your father. Then," his voice grew quieter, "your father died and she knew she couldn't do it on her own. She decided to go stay with friends in Mexico."

"Christ, Shay, is there anything you can't bloody do?" Matthew's voice was awed. "That's an incredible feat to manage." His eyes glanced at his lover. "Is she all right? Mona? Did she understand I didn't get the letter so I couldn't finish what my dad had started?"

Shane nodded. "Yes, I told her about you only finding the letter now. She understood but I got the impression she never expected you to take up the mantle, Matty. You didn't disappoint her or anything like that, so don't worry." He reached over and caressed Matthew's hand as it rested on the steering wheel.

"You guys are the best friends ever." David's quiet voice echoed in the back of the car. "You both put a lot at stake to help me and I really appreciate it. But Shane, Roy really hates you. Please promise me you'll be careful and not go looking for any more trouble with him."

Matthew frowned. "I agree. Those last words he spoke to you, Shay, didn't sound encouraging. I think he twigged that you were the person that put that gay porn on his phone. He might be an arsehole, but he's not stupid. He saw how you handled the whole phone thing with Walter and I think he put two and two together."

"I'll be careful. No more messing with Roy." Shane promised. "Now do you think we can go and get some food? I'm bloody starving."

Slow dancing and secrets

Shane sat back with a sigh, his eyes smarting from the latest project he was working on for a very large and prestigious customer. He'd just managed to find half a dozen flaws in their security network, and he had the feeling they'd be very pleased with the results. He was certainly earning his rather large fee on this one though. It had been a bit of a bitch.

Things had gotten back to normal in the last month. David had his trust fund back and was now living in an apartment of his own not too far from Shane's in St. James's. He was still living the jet-set lifestyle and working as a consultant on the stockbroking side. He seemed fairly content, and even had a new boyfriend, an older and rather dapper Italian man called Marco. Shane was happy for him. The man deserved some bit of happiness after what he'd been through and the ever-attentive and very self-assured Marco seemed to be doing him a lot of good.

But the best part was that things between Shane and Matthew were definitely good. The sex was still mind-blowing, the relationship even closer that it had been, and Matthew was definitely letting his guard down more. Something had changed between them since the showdown with Walter, although Shane couldn't quite pinpoint when and why. But his lover was definitely less reserved. Shane still hadn't told Matthew he loved him although it had been on the tip of his tongue to blurt out many a time. He was biding his time, waiting for the really right moment. He didn't want to spoil anything they had by moving too fast. It had only been just over three months, after all.

Shane stood up, stretched and picked up his jacket. It was time to get over to Matthew's house. They were meeting David and his new boyfriend Marco at a new gay supper club in the city and he didn't want to be late.

Almost an hour and a half later he sat with his lover in the dimly lit boudoir of a rather elegant nightclub. He looked around him as Matthew gazed out at the dance floor at David and Marco jazzing it up.

"Hell, Matty, this place is really something," Shane said in awe. "Very posh and so sophisticated. Not like the usual all-noise-and-lights places I go to."

Matthew nodded. "It is rather swanky, isn't it? I have to say I prefer this to the nightclubs. At least here you can have a conversation and people can hear you talk," he said wryly.

Shane poked his arm. "Listen to you," he said with a grin. "Better be careful, Mr. Langer, or I'll be booking you into an old-age home." He chuckled at the look at Matthew's face and looked out at the dance floor, his face wistful. "Look at those two," he said with a smile. David and Marco were definitely forces to be reckoned with on the dance floor, their routine looking polished and professional as the two men danced to the light jazz tunes echoing through the room.

"David seems to have picked himself a winner with Marco. He seems all right. And boy, can he dance," said Shane enviously. He glanced over at Matthew who was studiously ignoring his hints to dance with him. He'd been making them all night, but so far Matthew hadn't bitten.

"It's fine when I'm on a club dance floor surrounded by hundreds of people and I'm anonymous," he'd muttered. "No one can see me make a twit of myself. I'm not the greatest dancer. It's another thing altogether when the dance floor is fairly small, secluded and everyone can see you."

Shane sighed now and took a sip of his drink. David and Marco came back to the table, slightly sweaty, looking very pleased with themselves.

"You two were great out there," Shane said, smiling at the two dance partners. "You know how to move, Marco. I'm very impressed."

The tall, thin Italian man grinned, showing white teeth in a swarthy face. He was in his late thirties, smartly dressed and great company. "It is easy when you have a partner like David," he said, fondly looking at the other man. "He is so easy to dance with and he follows my lead." He looked at Shane. "If you like, I can take you onto the dance floor, show you a few moves?"

Shane saw Matthew shift beside him and he grinned. If Matthew wasn't going to dance with him, perhaps he should take Marco up on his offer. Matthew would have to put up with Marco "showing him a few moves."

"Maybe in a bit. Let me finish my drink." He was aware of Matthew's eyes appraising him coolly and he chuckled. "Babe, I like to dance and if you're not going to do it, I'll just have to find someone who will."

Matthew looked at him over his wine glass. "Shane, baby, carry on. I can get all hot and bothered sitting here watching you. I can have my very own floor show." He raised his glass to Marco and the older man smiled.

Shane felt put out at his boyfriend's reaction. He hadn't expected Matthew to take it so lightly, him possibly banging his crotch and hips against another man's while they gyrated to the music. It took the fun out of agreeing to go up there with Marco in the first place. He took a deep gulp of his drink, his face moody.

Matthew leaned over and his breath tickled Shane's ear as he whispered. "Trying to make me jealous?" His tongue slid lightly into Shane's ear, making him gasp. "Remember you go home with me at the end of the evening. You're mine, Templar. Every inch of you."

He moved away with a husky chuckle, leaving Shane in a state of turmoil at those whispered words. His dick was already straining against his black, tailored chinos, simply dying to come out and meet the contender for his affections. Matthew raised his glass at his lover with a lazy grin and Shane scowled.

David and Marco had been watching the exchange with amusement. David chuckled. "Matthew, you have to take Shane on the dance floor at least once tonight. Perhaps the next slow one? I know you like those." He cocked his head, his eyes alight with mischief as the next song started. "I happen to know this is one of your favourites, Matty. 'Smooth Operator' by Sade. You could never resist it. Take your man on the floor, you useless bugger, and show him a good time."

Shane raised an eyebrow at his boyfriend and Matthew sighed.

"Fine, if it will stop you all nagging, a slow one it is. I *do* like this song." He stood up and held out his hand to Shane who took it. They made their way onto the floor, and Matthew pulled Shane into him with a flourish. The other couples on the dance floor were also moving closer as the strains of Sade's soft, dulcet tones wafted across the room. Matthew held Shane's hips loosely as Shane slid his hands onto Matthew's waist. Matthew stared down at him, his eyes soft.

"I haven't done this in a while. It feels good." They swayed slowly together to the sounds of the music, hips nearly touching. Shane thought he had never felt anything so right as standing here with this man, the scent of his aftershave and the distinct smell of Matthew in his nostrils, the closeness of his body a complete turn-on. Matthew pulled him closer, his breath deepening as their groins touched, their mutual hardness making them both smile.

"I have a burning desire to take you home right now," Shane whispered as his lips kissed Matthew's cheek softly. "In fact, I think I might just kiss you right here, right now…"

His lips sought out his lover's, finding them with a soft sigh, as lips parted and tongues slid slowly, slick and wet. The music played, but neither man heard anything, so caught up with each other's mouths and bodies as they danced. Finally, they pulled apart, and Shane nestled his head into Matthew's shoulder.

"We should definitely do this more often, Matty. I love dancing with you like this."

"I agree," Matthew murmured softly as the final strains of the song faded and people began to move off the dance floor. "You feel good in my arms." He leaned down and whispered into Shane's ear, his breath warm, tickling Shane's skin. "*Ich liebe tanzen mit dir.*" He moved away, leaving Shane completely horny and wanting nothing more than to rip Matthew's clothes off and take him on the dance floor. He took a deep breath and had to grin as his boyfriend tried to hide his hard-on by pulling his shirt out of his trousers, letting it fall over his groin casually. Shane had one, too, but he didn't really care if anyone saw it. Let them see just how much he wanted this man. Let them be envious of who he'd danced with. They made their way back to the table, to a grinning Marco and David. David waved his hands around in excitement.

"God, you two looked sexy up there together. The cutest couple on the floor, apart from Marco and I of course."

Matthew glanced softly over at Shane. "Impossible, DD. No one could look as good as us on a dance floor. Look who I was partnered with." He leaned over and kissed Shane's chin softly. Shane's whole being resonated with pride at Matthew's words.

"You are too smooth, Langer. Honestly." He ruffled Matthew's hair. Marco smiled.

"He knows exactly what to say. David, you could take a branch out of his book."

"Leaf, Marco," chuckled Shane. "A leaf out of his book."

Marco shrugged his elegant shoulders. "I will never understand this English language." He smirked. "I prefer to speak Italian to David in *sensitive* situations anyway. It drives him crazy."

Matthew nodded. "I have to say I have the same thing with Shane and speaking German. It really turns him on." He looked at Shane with mischief in his eyes and waggled his eyebrows. Shane inclined his head.

"You have me there. I can't deny that one."

"Unsere Männer sind einfach anzutörnen." Marco said wickedly to Matthew, who laughed as he looked at Marco with surprise. *These men of ours are easy to arouse.*

"Ich wusste gar nicht, dass du Deutsch sprichst. Ja, es ist ganz einfach, Shane mit Deutsch sprechen anzutörnen." I didn't know you spoke German. Yes, it's easy to drive Shane wild just by speaking German.

"It's bloody rude, you two, to speak in a language not everyone understands," Shane said indignantly. "I heard my name mentioned; what the hell did you say?"

David was leaning in trying to listen to what was going on. Matthew and Marco laughed.

"Just that it's easy to get you going, Shay, babe, with a well-chosen German phrase. The words 'pocket rocket' spring immediately to mind."

Shane scowled. "You think you're so funny, Matthew." But he to admit he was definitely even more aroused than he'd been earlier dancing with his boyfriend. He moved on his seat, trying to get more comfortable. The rest of the evening passed in more conversation and drinks. Shane even managed to get Matthew back onto the dance floor for another slow round. It was just as good as the first time. By the time the soft tones of Lionel Ritchie's "Hello" had faded, his lips were bruised from Matthew's kisses and he wanted nothing more than to get home and make love to his man.

It was almost midnight when they finally got home but they decided to have one last drink before going to bed. Shane was sitting with Matthew at the dining room table, enjoying his glass of red wine. Jazz music drifted through the air, the lights were low, the room was warm in the cold, early-December build-up to the crazy Christmas season, and in Shane's eyes, everything was just perfect. Matthew sat across from him with a very come-hither look in his eyes which had been driving Shane crazy all evening, the dancing making it that much more intense.

"If you look at me like that for much longer, Matty, I am going to sweep everything off this table and fuck you over it."

Matthew raised a lazy eyebrow, contributing further to Shane's hardened cock. "Oh really?" His voice was teasing. "I'd like to see you try." He raised his glass with a grin as he took a sip. Shane eyed him out, wanting to rise to the challenge, which certainly wasn't a problem giving what had been going on below his waistline all night, but he had a great respect for Matthew's wiry strength and thought he might well be the one ending up being fucked. It didn't matter either way, really, but it was an ego thing.

He continued sipping his drink as Matthew watched him lazily. The air was positively reeking with sexual tension. Matthew's phone rang somewhere in the house, suddenly disturbing the silence.

"Shit, who can that be at this time? It had better not be David getting into more trouble." Matthew stood up, and Shane noticed with satisfaction that the bulge in his trousers was definitely very well developed. He watched his lover make his way to the small study and disappear. Ten minutes later Matthew still hadn't come back and Shane frowned. He was feeling rather unloved. He stood up and made his way to the study to see Matthew still talking on the phone and scrabbling through a myriad of papers on his desk.

"I have no bloody idea what I did with it, Rachel." It was his sister. "I've looked through all the papers I have but I can't seem to find it." He picked up paper after paper and Shane perched on the corner of the desk as Matthew ran a hand though his hair in exasperation. "What else did he say? I thought we'd manage to sort that all out already." He turned away and foraged amongst more papers on the sideboard, exclaiming in exasperation as he looked for whatever it was he was seeking.

Shane glanced idly at the desk and its pile of assorted documents, seeing a rather interesting picture of a baby on it clipped to a sheet of paper. He picked it up, glancing at it. His body went cold when he saw what it was. The paper was addressed to Mr. Matthew Langer and Mr. Sam Cartwright and was from a very prestigious child adoption agency called Madison Carlinson Associates. His quick eyes scanned over the document. His chest tightened as he realised what he was looking at. His hands trembled as he laid the paper back down on the desk and shovelled a few more pieces on top of it. He was just in time. Matthew gave a shout of satisfaction and waved a piece of paper in the air.

"Hah. Found it, Rach."

He mouthed silently at Shane. "I won't be a minute, Shay. I just need to sort my sister out. Her agent's giving her grief." He grinned wryly. "It's nine a.m. in Tokyo. She tends to forget the time difference."

Shane nodded numbly and lifted his backside from the desk. He felt ill. He walked out the room and back into the lounge. He sat down, staring into the darkness outside, feeling as if his whole world had suddenly changed for the worse.

The papers were a confirmation of an adoption for a little girl called Emily. Two months old. It had been dated 15 May 2010, just a few days before Matthew's husband had died. Matthew and Sam had been going to be parents. His mind swirled with thoughts.

Why wasn't this little girl in Matthew's life? What had happened to change things—Sam's death? Perhaps the agency wouldn't allow Matthew to be a single parent. Why the hell would Matthew not share something like this with him? How could he keep something like this from him, even Matthew with his repressive tendencies? Shane had thought they were getting closer than that. Christ, he'd spilled his guts about everything that was important to him, including his past stormy relationship with his father.

He knew more about Sam now than he had, as Matthew felt more comfortable speaking about him. But this was a shock he hadn't been expecting.

"Shane? Are you okay? You have a strange look on your face." Matthew sounded a little worried as he came back into the room.

Shane looked up into the anxious eyes of his lover. He nodded. "Yeah, I'm fine. Just have a really bad headache all of a sudden. Not feeling too well. I've been on Bushwhacker all day, probably caused some eye strain or something."

Matthew sat down beside him. "All that wine you drank tonight probably didn't help. Here, let me rub your temples. That normally works for me."

His warm hands reached over and took Shane's head as he gently massaged the two pressure points either side of his lover's forehead. Shane closed his eyes. Normally he loved this man's touch on him but all of a sudden he wanted to be left alone. He needed to sort out his thoughts. He reached up and pulled Matthew's hands away.

"Matty, I'm fine, babe, honestly. I've just overdone it. If you don't mind I'll turn in. Perhaps a dark room will help." He stood up and kissed Matthew softly on the forehead. Matthew looked fairly gobsmacked at being abandoned, but Shane couldn't think of any other way to quell the rising turmoil inside him. He reached the bedroom, undressed, turned out both bedside lights and climbed thankfully under the covers of Matthew's bed. He lay there, unable to sleep.

It was about an hour later when he heard his boyfriend come to the bedroom. He felt Matthew standing silently in the door, the light from the hallway softly illuminating the bedroom walls. Shane pretended to sleep, even to the extent of taking a few deep, relaxed breaths to make it more realistic. He couldn't face any conversation now.

Matthew sighed, a soft exhalation of breath, then came in and closed the door, plunging the bedroom into darkness once again. He undressed silently and slid into bed beside Shane. Shane felt a slight stir to his hair as Matty kissed him tenderly on his head then turned away. He swallowed. Perhaps a good night's sleep might take away this feeling of betrayal he felt at his lover's keeping secrets. But sleep took a long time to come, and he lay awake listening to the sound of Matthew's steady breathing beside him.

The following morning he rose early, got up, showered and left Matthew's house before he woke up. He left a note saying he had forgotten he'd promised his new customer a status report last night and wanted to get it done this morning and he'd call Matthew later.

Shane got back to his apartment and immediately powered up Bushwhacker. He was going to find out more about this adoption and see what had happened. His agile memory remembered the case number, the agency name and most of the details on the document he'd seen. It shouldn't be too hard to hack in and find what he was looking for, even if it was an adoption agency with a code of secrecy.

As he worked his mobile rang. It was Matthew. Shane felt a pang of guilt as he ignored it. Shane wasn't disappointed as he trawled through the system set up for the adoption agency. Their system was tough but he was better. It took him a few hours, but soon he had everything he needed to know on the proposed adoption of Emily Short by Matthew Langer and Sam Cartwright. Once again, he found a sad story of both love and loss.

The thing he couldn't see in the "Langer-Cartwright" file were any actual details of the adoption.

"Baby Emily" and her date of birth was the only reference made to the little girl in the adoption records, something Shane thought was strange. Normally records were more detailed than this but these almost seemed to be redacted, so sparse as to only give the barest facts. He probably could have found out more about it, but he'd found everything he wanted to know, and the baby's parents and background really weren't of interest to him.

Matthew had not been kidding when he'd said he'd gone off the rails after Sam's death. The adoption agency had put a private investigator firm on him after suspecting he was out of control. The stories and pictures they had collated were shocking. Shane knew Matthew had been in a lot of pain after losing his husband, but Matthew's self-destructive spiral surpassed even what he had been told or imagined. He winced as he sorted through the file they held. There were pictures of Matthew sucking some guy off in an alleyway. Video clips of him roaring drunk and yelling at whoever was filming him. Pictures of him passed out in bars, kissing men in corner booths and one final nail in his coffin—a grainy video of him fucking some guy over the bonnet of a car. Shane felt sick by the thought that his Matty had subjected himself to this kind of thing. Not even in his deepest darkest moments had Shane acted like this, but then he'd never lost a man he loved before to a violent and senseless tragedy.

There was a letter on file which Shane read with a heavy heart.

Dear Mr. Langer,

It is with great regret that we advise you that we are not able to proceed with your intended adoption of female child, Emily Short, DOB 12 March 2012. As we have discussed, we do not believe you are a suitable candidate for parency after what we have recently been advised regarding your behaviour. We do understand that you are in a dark place and that the death of your late husband has been a great shock. However our first and only interest is for the child and we cannot, in all honesty, place a child with you in your current emotional state. Rest assured that any evidence we have collected in our efforts to determine your suitability will be kept private and secure. We can categorically confirm that it will be destroyed after the relevant period of time in which we are required to keep such material.

I sincerely hope you are able to see your way forward out of your current situation and this agency wishes you all the best for your future plans.

Yours sincerely,

June Carlinson

CEO – Madison Carlinson Associates.

Shane read between the lines. Madison Carlinson had got wind of Matthew's meltdown somehow, employed someone to spy on him, got the proof they needed, told him he was no longer fit to be a parent *(was parency actually a word?)* and promised that the incriminating evidence would be destroyed when there was no longer a need to keep it, such as if Matthew had challenged their decision. Shane dreaded to think of these pictures coming out in public. For a moment he was tempted to delete them from their archive folder. His finger actually hovered over the delete button, itching to remove the evidence of his lover's breakdown. Finally he sighed. He was already taking a chance accessing this database. If he deleted these photos someone might think it had been Matthew trying to destroy any evidence of his past. He'd be the first one they looked to as a culprit. Shane had had enough of getting others into trouble by his well-meaning actions. He didn't want to cause any more. Regretfully he removed his finger and ran it across the screen of laptop, gently tracing the image of his Matthew lunging toward the photographer with crazy eyes, hair all mussed and a snarl on his face.

"My poor baby," he whispered softly. He could understand now why Matthew had kept this hidden. Not only had he lost his husband, he'd lost his child too, and in the process, these pictures of him were probably the lowest point of his life, etched forever in Matthew's memory. Knowing Matthew as he did now, Shane knew Matty would have been ashamed and mortified if he'd had ever known about this. It certainly explained his boyfriend's control issues. He'd lost control and lost everything that meant anything to him. Shane logged out, checking that he'd kept his tracks hidden and closed his laptop. He sat back thoughtfully. This would have to be his secret. He could certainly never let Matthew know he'd pried into the blackest part of his life. Matthew would never forgive him. It would be seen as a cardinal sin. The fact Shane knew about this whole sorry affair was already starting to eat away at his soul. Not for the first time, he wished he could have left well enough alone. His tendency to probe into other's people personal affairs was certainly his Achilles' heel and may even be his downfall one day. Shane picked up his phone and dialled Matthew's number. His boyfriend answered, sounding wary.

"Shane? Where the hell did you get to so early this morning?"

"I told you, babe. I forget to send my report over to my client. They needed it for an emergency board meeting today. On a bloody Saturday, can you believe it? I had to come home and get it done before they sat down at midday. I'm sorry I had to leave you all alone." The lies tripped off his tongue.

"How is your headache? Is it any better?" Matthew's tone sounded guarded.

"Yeah, sorry about last night. I *was* really going to sweep everything off the table and screw you senseless, so I owe you one. Maybe tonight?" He held his breath as he waited for his lover to answer.

"Hmm. Not sure. I have that work do tonight remember, dinner with the boss and Julia. So I doubt I'll be home too early."

Shane's face fell. "I'd forgotten you were going out with them. Do you want to come over to my place now anyway and we can have brunch? I can go down to the deli on the corner and pick up some of that cold meat and coleslaw and we can watch a movie or something."

There was silence. "Or something sounds like a better bet to me." Matthew's voice held the trace of a smile. "I still have a hard-on from last night, so I expect you to do something about it before I go out tonight. It wouldn't do to go out with my cock looking as if it's going to take flight and stab someone."

Shane closed his eyes in relief at the fact Matthew didn't seem too annoyed over his rapid departure. "I think I can manage that. Come on over when you're ready. I'll nip down to Donnie's now and get us something to eat."

Two hours later all thoughts of food and drink were forgotten as Shane took care of Matthew's hard-on issue. He knelt on his bed, his arse raised whilst Matthew gripped his hips and thrust in and out of him like a man possessed. His lover seemed particularly voracious this afternoon. He'd given Shane one of his best blow jobs to date, and that was saying something as Matty was very good at it, and then with hardly any foreplay, he'd turned Shane over, gripped his backside and started pounding away. Shane wasn't complaining. He loved it when Matthew got rough and tough. The man could be a veritable animal.

Matthew reached around and gripped Shane's already hardening dick as he moved his hand up and down his shaft, while keeping up his rhythm. The younger man gasped as he felt the familiar prickling in his groin, the pressure and the heat drifting up his body from his toes, over his legs and into his hips like a steady rising tide of sheer pleasure. Matthew gripped him harder, pushing deeper. After a while, Shane gave a loud cry as he climaxed, spurting his own contributions onto Matthew's hands and the bedcovers below. Matthew continued his thrusts and finally cried out as he came, his hands gripping Shane's hips, making him wince. It had been a short, intense lovemaking session and one that Matthew had obviously needed from the feel of him. Matthew slowly withdrew from his lover and lay back, gasping.

"God, I needed that. You left me really horny last night, you bastard, after all that dirty talk about fucking me over the table. I was waiting for you to start something."

Shane pulled Matthew over into his shoulder and kissed the top of his head. "I had every intention but then that headache started and—"

Matthew lifted his head and looked at his boyfriend, his eyes bright.

"Don't lie. You didn't have a headache. I've never known you to be sick in all the time I've known you. Something happened to you last night. I could see it. You flicked off like a light switch. God knows I've done that to you before so I wasn't going to push you. But I would like to know what made you so withdrawn last night."

Shane was quiet. Matthew snuggled back in, his hand caressing Shane's stomach. "You weren't even asleep when I came to bed. You were pretending. I know you too well." He sounded hurt.

Shane's chest tightened. He had no idea what to say but he needed to cover his exploration of the adoption somehow. It might be time to take the plunge he'd been thinking of taking. If the waters closed about his head and drowned him, so be it. He just hoped Matthew was there throwing him the lifeline he so desperately wanted.

"It was nothing. I just got scared, that's all."

Matthew shifted and looked at him. "About what? I've never known you to be bloody scared of anything. You're my little pit bull. You can rip throats out with your bare teeth."

Shane smiled despite his nervousness in what he was about to say. "Scared because of just how much I feel for you. How much I need you."

Matthew stilled beside him. His hand stopped stroking Shane's stomach and the younger man closed his eyes, trying to fight back the slight panic he felt.

"Exactly how do you feel about me?" The other man's voice was husky, almost a whisper.

Shane took a deep breath. "I love you, Matty. More than anyone I've ever loved before."

There. It was out. Consequences do your damnedest. There's no going back now.

Shane wasn't prepared for Matthew's reaction. Whatever he'd expected, regret, denial, scorn, sympathy, even acceptance, he certainly hadn't expected his lover to growl, pull him into a fierce embrace and take his mouth with a need so potent it made him reel with the sheer passion of it. Matthew's mouth ground against his in a frenzy of need, his hands pulling Shane close to his own body, as if trying to wear him like a glove. It was exhilarating, mind-blowing and frightening all at the same time. When he was finally released, Shane's mouth was bruised and his lip was cut where his lover had forced it against his teeth. Matthew pulled him over on top of him, holding him so tightly in his strong arms that he could hardly breathe. But he didn't want to let this moment pass, so Shane remained quiet, listening to the fierce beat of his lover's heart and simply feeling…loved.

Matthew's voice whispered against his ear, his breath warm. "You drive me crazy. You're bloody cheeky, you're a maverick, and you never bloody listen to anyone. You do what *you* think is best, all the time. You also care so much about people—it's what I love about you. But it's not the only thing I love about you. I love the way you smell, the way you look, the way you make me feel."

Shane's eyes were prickling with hot tears at hearing words like this being spoken by his normally controlled boyfriend. "I love the way you look at me, as if I'm the only man in the world, and I love making love to you. I guess what I'm trying to say, Shane Templar, is that I love you, too. Heart and bloody soul."

Shane knew what a momentous moment this was and for a second, he didn't know what to say. Then his natural instinct for levity kicked in.

"Christ, Matty, trust you go all one-upmanship on me. I just tell you I love you, but you, you have to make a bloody poem out of it. A truly beautiful poem but still—"

His words were cut off as Matthew once again kissed him with lips that told him exactly how he felt.

"You are so mine," he breathed into Shane's mouth. "Always."

"Always," agreed Shane as he kissed him back with a heart that was full to the brim with every good feeling he'd ever had in his life. "I'm yours, Matty."

Matthew hummed as he showered, getting ready for his dinner date with Bartholomew and Julia. He had never felt so relaxed and content since Sam's death.

His and Shane's declarations of love for each other earlier had seemed to seal whatever deal he and the other man had going on. Shane's heartfelt words had seared his soul, reaching deep down inside to that place he thought he'd hidden. The minute Shane had told him he loved him, he just known he needed to tell Shane exactly how he felt, too. He couldn't fight it any longer. This man meant the world to him. He couldn't deny he was scared. For two years he'd fought any emotional involvement for fear of getting hurt again. And now he'd just made an emotional commitment to another man.

Who wouldn't be paranoid?

"Matty, you're going to be late, babe!" Shane shouted from the bedroom. "Your taxi is due in ten minutes."

"Shit." Matthew hastily rubbed water in his hair, gave himself a wash down below with shower gel, turned off the water and stepped out, wrapping a towel around his waist. He bounded back into his bedroom, seeing Shane lying there in his bed, flicking through TV channels.

"Have you seen the shirt and trousers I took out for tonight? In all the excitement of the afternoon, I don't know what I did with them."

Shane waved the remote at the far corner. "I put them on the valet rack. I didn't want them to get all creased when we rolled around on the bed."

He chuckled as his lover frantically got dressed, pulling on boxers and clothes in a panic. "Matthew, relax. You can put your makeup on in the taxi."

Matthew threw a fierce glare his way. "Very funny. I don't want to be late. I know Maxwell is pretty relaxed, but he is my boss I'm meeting for dinner for the first time."

Shane sat up. "I'll just stay here, all alone and amuse myself. Unless you want me to go home?"

Matthew shook his head as he finished dressing and leaned in to kiss Shane a quick goodbye. "No, stay. I like finding you here when I come home. You have Bushwhacker to keep you company anyway." He cast a smile at the laptop case in the corner of the room. "Honestly, do you ever go anywhere without him?"

He stopped as he realised what he'd said and scowled as Shane laughed loudly. "That's the spirit. You've just acknowledged my laptop is a man."

Matthew shoved his wallet in his pocket. "I still say you're bloody crazy. See you later, baby."

He disappeared into the hallway, only to come back a second later.

"Love you." He winked and clattered down the hallway and out into the street. He slammed the front door behind him as he went to meet the taxi.

Dinner with Bartholomew and Julia was a welcome affair, taking place at the rather swanky Balls Brothers venue just off Fenchurch Street station. The conversation was good, the food excellent and the drink definitely welcome. Matthew was still feeling light-headed after his confession of love for Shane. It felt good knowing his man was waiting at home for him. The trio chatted about work, life and the business in general and Matthew thanked whatever good fortune was smiling down at him on the day he first got the interview with his new company. He wasn't a religious man, despite coming from a fairly Christian background. His mother and sister were still firm believers. Matthew preferred to reply on his own talents and abilities to get him where he needed to be. But his karma was definitely being good to him lately.

He and Julia were spending a lot of time together, both at and out of the office. It had become a thing to have a standing dinner date at the pub across the road from work. Julia was warm, mature, funny and great company. Matthew knew she had a few skeletons in her own closet, but she wasn't ready to talk to him about them yet. Shane had joked that he might have a fight on his hands for Matthew's attention.

His phone rang as he got in the taxi around eleven p.m. His heart lurched when he saw a number he recognised. It was a number from his past, a number he had thought he would never hear from again.

"Matthew Langer."

"Mr. Langer. This June Carlinson. Do you remember me?"

"Yes. I remember you."

Who wouldn't remember the woman who had torn his heart out of his chest?

"I hope you are keeping well. I'm sorry to call you so late, but there is some news I really needed to give you. It involves a rather unfortunate security breach to our database, I'm afraid."

"What does that have to do with me?" he asked, his heart beating rapidly.

"Mr. Langer, you know the detailed circumstances of the adoption you applied for. Little Emily." Matthew's chest tightened and he was having trouble breathing. "You were aware of the…sensitivity…of the whole situation around Emily's potential adoption at the time. It's why you had to sign a non-disclosure agreement for everything connected to the affair."

"I remember," he said mechanically.

"Well, someone hacked into our system yesterday and it was flagged up on our security database as a breach. You remember we had *very* special on-demand security around this whole case because of who Emily's mother was and how she was conceived. We wouldn't do this for all our cases. This was unique as you know."

Matthew closed his eyes. He was well aware of the circumstances around Emily's birth. It had been a dreadful, heartrending story and the reason he and Sam had decided they definitely wanted this specific little girl.

"Well, the agency running the security can't tell who it was that hacked the system but they do know that someone did. Whoever it was covered their tracks very well, they are obviously a professional. But it means they got access to your name, your files and all the photographic evidence and video we had in our files about our investigation of you. Of course, there was nothing else in our files about the baby's background or parentage or the events of her birth and potential adoption. That was always kept separate in another much more secure database than ours." Her voice was slightly dry.

Matthew felt like throwing up. The photos and footage in that file was something he'd long put behind him, and the thought of anyone else seeing who and what he'd been at the time made him feel physically ill.

The other thing that made him feel like hurling was his immediate thought that Shane might have something to do with this. It was perhaps unfair, but it just seemed too much of a coincidence.

"Please don't worry. They say nothing was copied, or downloaded, it was simply accessed. So the chances are there is nothing out there in the public domain that will cause you any harm. But I needed to let you know. My team is working on it, but they are not very hopeful they'll ever find who did it or why.

Would you have any idea who would or could do this, and why, Mr. Langer?"

Matthew felt cold, his hands freezing, his brain numb. "No," he finally managed. "I don't."

"Well, I'll let you know if I hear anything else. I am sorry about this, Mr. Langer. I'm going to text you the lawyer's name that we are using in case you have any questions. If you need to speak to anyone about this, please call her direct. I think you may be getting a call from Mr. Busby too shortly after mine. Expect it. Good night, Mr. Langer."

And with that dispensing of her responsibilities and a reminder that Matthew had signed an NDA that allowed for any eventualities and which he'd signed in sheer numbness at the time just to get the whole affair over, June Carlinson hung up.

Matthew put his phone back in his pocket with trembling hands. All the happiness he'd felt five minutes ago had suddenly descended into a nightmare. He sat numbly in the taxi, seeing nothing as he gazed out at the street and scenery outside. Five minutes later his phone rang again. This was a number he didn't recognise but he had a feeling he knew who it was. He answered with a sense of dread.

"Matthew Langer."

The quiet broad Norfolk tones of Neil Oswald Busby, well known Member of Parliament and close friend of the Prime Minister echoed like a bad memory in his ear.

"Good evening, Matthew. This is Neil. It's been a while, son."

Matthew's mouth was dry. "Evening, Neil. I know why you're calling. And I can assure you I know nothing about this whole thing. I would never jeopardise anything from that period of my life. I have too much to lose." He stared blindly out of the taxi at the passing lights and glitter of the city. Faint music played from the front of the taxi and the driver hummed along.

Neil sighed heavily. "I didn't think you would have. But I wanted to make sure. My people think it's a random hack, as nothing was really 'touched' just accessed. If anything had been deleted or an attempt to get into the more secure files had been made, I can assure you we'd be having this conversation face to face." His voice was mildly threatening. "At a police station."

"I had nothing to do with it." Matthew's voice was tight. "And I don't know who stands to gain from it either. I can't even shed any light on that." He hoped in his heart that he was wrong about suspecting Shane and that his boyfriend would put his mind at rest when he got home.

His gut told him that would be just too easy a solution.

"I believe you, son. You were always a good man, even if you went off the rails. How are you anyway, Matthew? Have you managed to move on?"

Matthew didn't want to answer that one. He really wasn't sure anymore. "I'm doing fine, Neil, thank you. How is Stephanie?"

"My daughter is doing as well as can be expected." Neil's voice was heavy, tinged with grief even after two years. "She's still undergoing regular counselling, for both the rape and the loss of the baby. But she's much better. Thank you for asking."

Matthew knew better than to ask after Emily. Neil would never tell him anything about the child.

Neil Busby spoke gently. "Well, I just wanted to speak to you myself and reassure myself that this wasn't your doing. I'm comfortable it wasn't if you tell me such. You never lied to me before, Matthew. That was one thing I always admired about you. Sam was a lucky man. You look after yourself, son."

The call was disconnected and Matthew stared at his phone blindly. His eyes flooded with tears at the emotions surging inside him, emotions he'd thought were done and dusted but were now welling up like sewerage from an overflowing pipe. He blinked back his tears fiercely and wiped his eyes with his sleeve as he said a silent prayer.

I can't believe this is bloody happening. Please, Shay, tell me this had nothing to do with you.

Fifteen minutes later he let himself into his house. The house was in darkness. The bedroom door was ajar and there was only the faint glow from a light in the hallway.

Matthew felt like it was an analogy for where he suddenly found himself. He was in darkness. The one person that showed him any light was in there and when the door shut he would be totally in the dark again. He wanted so badly to be wrong about his suspicions.

Matthew walked into the bedroom and saw Shane cuddled under the blankets, only the top of his blond head poking out of the duvet. Matthew stood for a while, trying to calm his beating heart. Then he sat down on the bed and ran a hand across his eyes. He heard Shane move and sit up.

"Hey, babe. How was your evening?" Warm arms reached out to hug him and Matthew couldn't respond, couldn't move. His body was rigid, unresponsive.

"Matty? What's wrong?" Shane's voice sounded panicked as he reached over and switched the bedside light on, flooding the room with warm light.

Matthew stood up, agitated as he stared at his lover. He needed to see Shane's face when he asked him the next question.

"Shay, I need to ask you something. Please be truthful and don't be mad if you had nothing to do with it. I'm sorry I even have to do this and I have no idea how it will impact our relationship. But I have to ask you this."

Shane sat up, the duvet falling to his waist. Matthew could see his boyfriend's face grow wary.

The lawyer's throat closed up and he wanted nothing more than to throw up. "Did you hack into an adoption agency site and find out about an adoption Sam and I were planning?"

The look on Shane's face told Matthew everything he needed to know. He stared in stark horror as Shane's face paled and his body went rigid. He stared back at Matthew, his face set. Matthew could see the guilt in his eyes.

Shane had always worn his emotions on his face. It was who he was. Matthew stepped back, reeling at the knowledge of what Shane had done.

"Christ, Shane, why?" Matthew's anguished whisper was like a knife to Shane's heart. He could feel the hurt emanating from every pore in his lover's body and he wanted to push back the clock and start again. Matthew's face was stark, his eyes like burning holes in his white face.

"I saw the papers on your desk yesterday." Shane said. His hands were cold and he linked them together to stop their trembling. "While you were looking for the stuff for Rachel. I saw the baby picture, and I was curious. Then I realised what it was. It threw me. That you could have such a huge secret and not tell me about it."

"So you decided to pry into my past and see what you could dig up?"

Shane had to be truthful on that one. "Yes. I wanted you to share things with me. But you don't. This was the only way I could find out." He climbed out of bed, pulling on his jeans and coming over to Matthew. Matthew moved away from him and Shane stood there, feeling lost.

"I'm sorry. I shouldn't have done it. But I thought we were supposed to be sharing things. I've poured out my guts to you about my past. I wanted you to trust me so you could do the same."

He raised his hands in exasperation. Matthew stood stock still in the middle of the room.

"Some things are not for everyone, Shane." Matthew's voice was flat, deadly. "Some things are meant to be private. If I don't tell you things, it's because I want to keep them that way. We've only known each other a few months. There was plenty of time to get to know each other, for me to tell you about things when I felt it was time. And now that's over."

What did he mean, over?

"Matty. For God's sake, don't over react." Shane felt a surge of panic. He sat back down on the side of the bed, his legs weak.

"Did you see everything?" Matthew's face was implacable, his voice tight. "All the footage of me when I went crazy, when I lost my child? Our daughter—mine and Sam's?" He moved around the room now like a caged tiger, his body taut with tension.

Shane watched his lover, his mouth dry with fear. "Yes. I saw it."

Matthew swung around, eyes blazing and strode forward, pushing Shane backward onto the bed with a violent shove. Shane fell back onto his elbows and lay there helplessly while Matthew towered over him.

"So you know what I was like. You saw me at my worst, Shane. Something I never wanted you to see or even know about it. I had a hard time reconciling what I was then myself. And for you to have to see that, it's an absolute abomination to me. I tainted Sam's memory with what I did."

Matthew stopped pacing, his breath ragged. He ran a hand through his already mussed hair.

Shane sat up and drew his legs up onto the bed, sitting cross-legged. He stuck his trembling hands under his thighs as he watched Matthew. His bare-chested upper body was cold and clammy, but he didn't want to enrage his lover any more by getting up just yet. He'd probably be knocked down flat.

Matthew sneered at him. "You want to know the full story? Fine, I'll tell you. The night Sam died, we were supposed to be meeting my mother and sister for dinner. We were going to announce that we'd signed adoption papers that morning. For Emily. A sweet little baby girl who'd been conceived in the most unimaginable circumstances." His voice was flat. "Her mother was a fifteen-year-old girl who was gang raped at a party. By four men. She fell pregnant. If that wasn't bad enough, her father is a very high-ranking public figure." He took a deep breath. "I can't tell you his name. I signed papers committing me to secrecy." His tone got bitter. "Although I'm sure you could find out who it was if you really wanted to."

Shane's heart clenched even tighter in his chest at the disgusted look on Matthew's face. He uncurled his legs and moved to sit back against the headboard, the pillows cool against his naked back.

Matthew carried on. "It was all Sam's doing really. He moved in the same circles as the father of the girl professionally, and my husband was very well thought of. He got wind of the whole thing and got us involved right from the start. He thought it would be what a baby needed—two loving people in her life after all that had happened. We wanted that baby more than anything before. But it was all very hush-hush and we had to sign our lives away to protect the mother and the story from leaking. The grandfather wanted nothing to do with the child and made his daughter give up the baby for adoption. We were the lucky ones, Sam and I."

Matthew stopped and Shane saw him swallow as his hands clenched and unclenched at his side. His lover moved over the bedroom window and stared out into the street. His muscles were tight, his back and shoulders tensed like steel. "We never got to meet the mother as her father thought that would be too traumatic. She was already undergoing counselling. When she gave birth, Emily was immediately taken into foster care. Sam and I visited her all the time, and we signed the final papers on the morning of the day he died. We were going to take custody of her in a week's time from her foster parents." His voice quietened. "We fell in love with that baby girl. She was the cutest little thing you'd ever seen, with big, brown eyes and a sweet smile." His face was bleak, his eyes hard. "Sam used to take her teddy bears from everywhere he'd travelled. Christ, at one stage I thought he was going to buy out Hamleys, he was there so often." Matthew's voice trembled. "I had a thing for dragons. I collected them whenever I saw them and we had a plan to do the nursery—my study—out in a fairy tale theme with all the stuff we'd bought."

Shane was horrified by the story. Matthew's face was white, haunted. Shane moved swiftly off the bed and stood facing Matthew.

"Matthew—" His boyfriend waved a hand and the look on his face shut Shane up.

"Don't say a word. You know what happened next. Sam died. I went off the rails. I got drunk and high all the time and screwed other men. Not even the thought of Emily made me feel better. I was selfish, and it cost me everything." His voice cracked. "I landed in jail one night for being drunk and disorderly." Matthew's voice was distant, his eyes blank. "The birth mother's father came to see me. He wasn't happy that all the plans we'd made to get her child adopted seemed to be falling apart. He didn't think I could be trusted to keep things quiet and not spill the beans about his daughter. So he showed me those photographs, Shane. The ones you saw. Disgusting, shaming photos taken by the investigator he'd hired to follow me when he saw I was out of control. He told me he was going to hold on to them for a while as an 'insurance policy' and that I needed to get my life back on track. God knows what he would have done with them if I had said anything. Used them to discredit me I imagine. The adoption was cancelled."

Shane made a move toward Matthew but he held up his hand, warning him off. Shane had never seen such a look of pain on Matthew's face.

"Don't, Shane. Don't bloody touch me or I swear…"

Shane stayed where he was. He had a feeling Matthew meant every word. The sense of anguish Shane was feeling at being the cause of his lover's distress was eating away inside him like acid. He kept quiet, his heart cracking apart.

Matthew spoke again. "In short, I was a mess. And now I don't even know where she is." Shane could hear the anguish in his lover's voice. "I lost control, and they took her away from me. It would have killed Sam to know that. His last living thought might have been that at least I'd have Emily, and I managed to fuck that up as well."

He closed his eyes in pain. Shane waited for him to open them again and Matthew took a shuddering breath. "My mother didn't know about that. She knew about my meltdown, the fact I was drinking and taking drugs. She threatened to have me committed to a clinic in Dresden if I didn't clean up my act. And my mother would have done exactly what she promised. She's like that. So I cleaned up my act. But I didn't ever have the courage to tell her my cock-up lost her a granddaughter, something she would have loved. So you see, my 'control freak tendency,'" he spat the words at Shane, "went out the window and I lost my child. And you wonder why I try and control my life, make sense of it all?" He fell quiet. "And then you came along."

Shane saw the look on his boyfriend's face and felt a sense of pure loss. "Matty, I said I'm sorry. I made a mistake—"

Matthew's voice was scathing. "You seem to make a real habit of that, don't you? First with taking Walter's money, hacking Roy's phone, now again with me. Your actions have consequences, Shane. When does it become enough? When do you stop fucking interfering in people's lives?"

Shane felt the heat of temper rise in his chest. He ignored Matthew's warnings to stay away and moved over to stand in front of him, not too close but close enough to reach out and touch him if he needed. If Matthew wanted to get physical, so be it.

"It was all right for you when you needed me to find Mona. It was fine with you when I told Walter I'd send his video viral if he didn't release the trust fund. Don't be such a bloody hypocrite, Matty. You counted on me doing that, didn't you?"

Matthew ignored his outburst. "Do you know what kills me? The fact that if this case hadn't been particularly security-conscious, with the father of the girl insisting that his security agency plant a flag or some shit like that on the file, to tell him if anything happened—I would never have known you'd done it. You wouldn't have told me, would you?"

Shane didn't know what to say. He'd already decided he *would* tell Matthew what he'd done. He'd made the decision tonight when Matthew was out. He'd thought about it; after they'd told each other they loved each other he didn't think he had a choice. He wanted no secrets between them. He would have lived with the consequences and hoped he could have convinced Matthew to trust him again. But his boyfriend would never believe him now. So he remained quiet.

Matthew took his silence as agreement. He snorted. "You'd better hope they never find out it was you, Shane. Because you don't want to mess with the father of the birthmother, the man who's already called me tonight to find out if I had anything to do with it. I lied to him, of course. I had a feeling I knew who'd been in the file, but I was hoping I was wrong. If he ever finds out it was you, you could go to prison, you bloody idiot." The room was silent as both men came to terms with what had just happened.

Shane very much feared this was the irrevocable breakdown of their relationship.

Matthew's ire seemed to have passed and he appeared to deflate before Shane's eyes. Shane's gut spasmed at the pain in Matthew's eyes and his next whispered words.

"How could you do that to me? I can't believe you thought you had the right to bloody interfere like that." His lips tightened. "And if that man ever manages to track you down, God, I don't even want to think about that. So now you bloody know everything about me, Shay."

Shane moved forward and laid a hand on Matthew's arm. Matthew looked at it. His lips tightened and he pushed it away and moved away to stand again by the window, gazing out into the darkness.

Shane swallowed, his sense of loss eating away his heart like acid. "Matthew, I'm sorry. I didn't realise it would cost you this much. Cost us this much. I wish I could take it all back, turn back time. But I can't."

Matthew spoke softly without turning around. "Everything I wanted to hide, you found out. How the hell can you ever look me in the face again and have any bloody respect for me? I desecrated my dead husband's memory and lost our child. How can anything ever work for us now? This is why I didn't want to lose control, Shay," he whispered in pain as he turned to face Shane. "It hurts too bloody much when I do that."

Shane heard the slight catch in Matthew's voice at the last statement.

"They won't find me, Matty. The flag was something I hadn't considered. It didn't strike me that there would be any special security. There certainly weren't any indicators on the adoption site. If this flag is what I think it is, it's just a warning that someone's tried to access or gained access to a file. It doesn't mean they know who it is. I think I'm safe. But thanks for your concern. I probably don't deserve it." He heard the slight catch in his own voice and closed his eyes. The room was silent.

"You need to leave." Matthew's voice was defeated, riddled with pain. "I want you to go."

Shane nodded. "I just need to get dressed and get my stuff." He walked around and picked up the clothes that were hung over the valet rack on his side of the bed, dressing quickly with shaking hands as Matthew watched him. Finally he looked around for Bushwhacker and slung his laptop bag over his shoulder. He knew the answer to his next question but he was going to ask it anyway. "Can I call you tomorrow, see if you've calmed down so we can talk more?"

"No. You don't need to call me. It's over, Shane. I can't trust you. There's no point in talking anymore. You made me bloody lie for you, and you dredged up memories I wanted to forget."

Shane nodded. "I see. You're running again. We come across a hurdle in our relationship and you run. It's always your way or the highway, isn't it? No middle ground, no negotiation. I know I was wrong to do what I did, Matthew. And I'm so sorry it caused you such grief. I never intended that to happen. But I love you. I just wanted to be able to share your life no matter how bad it was, or what you'd done. But I guess that was just a pipe dream. You'll always be rooted in the bloody past."

Matthew said nothing, just stared at him, his hands clenched at his sides.

Shane's heart was breaking but he was determined to have his say. "Despite what we said to each other yesterday about loving each other, Matty, you know what? I don't think you ever *stopped* running. Have a good life."

He walked out of the bedroom, his eyes stinging with tears. His throat closed up and his chest felt constricted and he ached like he never had before.

Shane reached his apartment forty minutes later. He was breathing heavily with the exertion of running all the way home and having Bushwhacker plastered to his back. There had been a taxi in the vicinity but he'd needed to get rid of the restless energy that flooded his body, quell the sense of loss he felt, and running made him forget. He let himself into his home, plonked his laptop down on the dining room table and went to stand at the picture window, staring blindly out into the night. His body was sweating, his face shining with moisture. His hair was plastered to his temples.

Christ what a fuck-up of a night. It had started out so well and ended up with Matthew ripping his heart out of his chest. Deservedly so. He had never imagined he could cause such pain to his lover. Then again, he could never have imagined such a heartrending story as the one Matty had just told him.

"I know I interfered, Matty," he said to himself as he leaned his forehead against the cool glass of the window. "I wish I hadn't, I wish I could undo it. God, what the hell have I done to us?" He heaved a shuddering breath. Hot water and bed were probably the best thing for him right now. He'd need to give Matthew some space, let him get over what he thought was a betrayal.

But first...

Shane sat down at the table and pulled Bushwhacker toward him. Five minutes later he watched as his folder on Matthew Langer winked and disappeared. He'd meant to get rid of that file ages ago but kept forgetting. Shane kept one picture, a picture he thought might in the future bring Matty peace. Now wasn't the time, but perhaps if they got together again. Shane swallowed. *When* they got together again, it might make more sense. He couldn't think of this as being an 'if' situation. That would be far too painful. He'd wait a while, see if Matthew relented or contacted him. If not, he'd have to force the issue the way Matthew had done the first time they'd argued. But for now, he'd have to be patient and let the tormented soul of his lover find its centre and calm down long enough for Shane to apologise and try and make his peace.

Aftermath and tragedy

Matthew sat in his office, busily working through a pile of documents when Julia walked in. He looked up and smiled.

"Hi there. What's up?"

"I need to talk to you." She closed the door and sat down in the visitor chair. Matthew looked at her with apprehension. "This looks serious. Is something wrong?"

"I'd bloody say, Matthew. Have you seen yourself lately?"

Matthew scowled. Now he knew where this was going. "If you're going to get on at me again, don't. I'm fine, Julia."

"No, you're not. Don't bloody lie to me." Julia's voice was fierce. "You look like shit, you're not eating and even Bartholomew is worried about you. Now I know this is something personal, you breaking up with Shane, but it's killing you."

Matthew glared at her. "I appreciate your concern but honestly, it's nothing to do with you. I don't mean to be rude—"

"Oh tosh, you're my friend. At least I think we are?" She flapped a hand. "You can be as rude as you like, you know it won't make any difference to me."

Matthew did indeed know that Julia was very thick-skinned and could take a lot of his fairly high-handed stubbornness without batting one of her long eyelashes.

"I know you had an argument with Shane, and while I only know the high-level detail, I do know it's making you into a moody little bitch."

Matthew's mouth gaped open. He'd never quite been described that way before.

"So you have to ask yourself. If it makes you some sort of drama queen diva, then did you make the right decision to kick Shane out of it?"

Matthew was still gawping at the words 'drama queen diva,' something else he'd not been called before. "Did you just come in here to insult me, or did you have a purpose in mind for this conversation?" he asked sullenly.

She chortled. "I came to give you a talking to. Bartholomew agrees with me."

Matthew felt a sudden panic. "Christ, Julia, he's my boss. I can't let him think my personal life is affecting my job. Has he said anything to you about my work, or that I'm not performing, or anything?"

Julia shook her head sorrowfully. "Matthew, you're here at six in the morning, you only leave at nine p.m., and you work harder that anyone I know. So no, Bartholomew is not worried about your work. He's worried about you."

She leaned over the desk, and he saw her breasts jiggling under her shirt, which always tended to be fairly low. He quickly brought his eyes back up to her face.

"He's really very fond of you. He thinks of you almost as a son. You know his son died in a boating accident about five years ago? He has no other children."

"No, I didn't know that." Matthew felt sad that someone as good and gentle as Bartholomew had no child. His boss was an incredible role model, and Matthew had found himself trying to emulate some of the man's better qualities.

"Well, he really likes you. But he doesn't want to interfere."

"That's why he sent you then," said Matthew, anticipating a response. He wasn't disappointed.

Julia stood up and walked over to him and cuffed him lightly on the back of the head. "Oi. Enough of that, you cheeky devil. Remember to be civil to your elders."

Despite himself, Matthew grinned.

Julia clapped her hands. "Now there's the Matthew we know we and love. The one who always had a smile on his face when he had Shane."

At the mention of Shane's name, Matthew's face darkened. His friend raised her hands in supplication and said quietly, "I don't know everything that went on. But you are not a happy man, my friend. You haven't been for the last week since the breakup. I just want to see you happy again. I see you looking at your phone all the time as if you want to call him. So you can't be that far gone, Matthew."

Matthew sighed. "It's just taking time to get over it. I'll be fine." He knew he was lying. No matter what he was telling Julia, it was never going to be all right. He missed Shane so much it felt like a gap in his heart, like a part of him had been ripped from his body and left a festering, putrid sore.

He'd had time to think over the past week. He could still see Shane's white and stricken face. Matthew thought he might have overreacted – justifiably – but perhaps a little OTT. What Shane had done was reprehensible, but he'd not done it to be malicious. He'd done it to find out more about what made Matthew tick, to get to know him, and it was his inbred curiosity about things that had led down the path he'd taken. Matthew had to acknowledge that he'd taken the man on knowing what he did and that he wasn't going to change much on that score.

But Shane knew too many things about Matthew now, too many terrible things. Shane had texted or tried to call him every day. Matthew still re-read the texts on his phone that he'd saved.

Matthew, we need to talk. I don't want to throw it all away because I did something stupid. I love you. S x

Matty, please pick up your bloody phone. Let's talk. S xx

Matty, please call me. I miss you, babe. S

You stubborn bastard, can you at least text me back, let me know you're okay? S

"Matthew?"

He looked up. Julia was regarding him with a sympathetic expression. "You're thinking about him, aren't you?"

He stood up and walked to the window, looking down into the busy street below. His voice was tight when he spoke. "I'm always thinking about him."

Julia came up behind him and he felt her arms encircle his waist as she pressed herself against his back. He closed his eyes at the feeling of another human being against him. It was nothing sexual, just pure comfort, and Julia knew exactly how to give it. He reached down and covered her hands with his own.

"Then call him, Matthew," she whispered in his ear. "Talk to him. Try and work it out, you stubborn, stubborn man."

"I'm not sure doing that will make things any better. I said some pretty nasty things to him."

"Remember the last time I told you to try, Matthew? I told you to just try. And that time worked out pretty well. That's all you can do." She let go of him, kissed him softly on the cheek and moved away.

"Think about it." Julia moved over to the door and left with one last smile.

Matthew stood for a few more minutes and finally, he heaved a great sigh and sat back down at his desk. He'd have to think about things. He knew he wanted Shane still, more than anyone in his life, but he wasn't sure he could fully forgive what he'd done. Tonight he was going out with David for a few drinks, as the man had nagged him incessantly to be more sociable and he'd finally caved in. But maybe tomorrow he'd think more about it.

Shane was drunk. He snorted with laughter as Timmy gyrated on the dance floor with his current dancing partner, a huge man in tight jeans and a billowing white shirt. Timmy had a wonderful sense of balance and a dancing style par excellence. Shane knew firsthand just how the man felt when he swung those lean hips of his and rubbed his groin against his own. The other man was an absolute non-runner. He had no sense of dance, simply rolling his hips around and losing his rhythm every time the music changed beat. Shane found the whole thing extremely funny. He had a pretty good sense of rhythm himself and he thought he might go up and give the man a run for his money.

Timmy had convinced him to come out tonight, even though he really hadn't felt like it. But now he'd had almost a quarter bottle of tequila, things were definitely looking up. He needed to pee, so he stood up and waved at his friend, waving his hand vaguely in the direction of the bathroom. Timmy nodded

Timmy had been Shane's rock since he'd broken up with Matthew. There was no sex involved, simply a friend, as Shane just wasn't in a place yet to even contemplate another man in his life, not even for pure sex.

Timmy's biggest job seemed to be keeping Shane on the straight and narrow. He watched him like a hawk, curbing the drinking that had seemed to become a regular occurrence for Shane at the nightclubs in the past week.

Shane now knew what Matthew must have felt like when Sam died and how he'd spiralled down into the path of self-destruction. He told himself he was simply enjoying his newfound single status—without the sex.

Shane missed Matthew so much, and it still hurt every minute of every day. He'd tried to reach out and make contact, hoping something might give and they could talk. He'd taken the first step as usual, texting Matthew, calling him. But Matthew, control freak extraordinaire, hadn't responded.

Shane could wait no longer. He planned on calling him tomorrow, and if he refused to answer he'd be going around to his house. He'd do anything to make physical contact with the man. He'd beg if he had to. Where Matthew was concerned he wasn't too proud, and this last week had been pure hell.

He reached the bathroom, passing two men busy humping in the corridor, squeezed past them and staggered into the urinal. He unzipped his tight, ass-hugging jeans and heaved a sigh of relief as he pissed. Finally satiated, he turned and made his way out of the bathroom where the two men were still going at it.

"Jesus, chaps, get a room," he giggled as he passed them. Shane weaved drunkenly and decided he needed some fresh air. He made his way to the main door and found himself out on the street, the fresh air assaulting his senses and making his head reel.

It was quiet, hardly anyone around apart from a few bundles of rags in shop doors. People tended not to come out on the street on their own as it could be a fairly risky prospect despite the bouncers on the door. But in his current state he'd not thought about that until now. He leaned against the wall, and closed his eyes, starting to feel sick. Glancing at the door, he wondered hazily where the bouncers were. He hadn't seen them on his way out. There was a noise beside him and Shane smiled, thinking Timmy had come to find him.

"Timmy, that guy was really into you. He can't dance for shit, but at least you'll get laid. I don't know what your boyfriend would make of all that, though."

"Hello, you little slag." The sibilant voice in his ear came first followed by a hard punch to his stomach, leaving him doubled over and gasping for breath. "I bet you didn't think you'd see me again, did you, you little queer?" The vicious tones of Roy Parsons resonated in the street. Shane tried to stand up but was hit again, another couple of heavy punches to his gut that left him retching. His evening's tequila mix threatened to rise up and meet the pavement as he retched over and over.

"Not so cocky now, are you?" Shane managed to look up to see the man in front, who had a balaclava over his head. But he knew it was Roy from the voice and the eyes.

"Especially without those two boyfriends of yours. You must like being the meat in the sandwich with them, you little pervert."

"Fuck off, Roy," Shane managed to get out in a strangled voice. He was doubled over with the pain of Roy's gut punches, his stomach feeling twisted and bruised. His throat was sore from retching. "Go and find someone else to bully, you bastard."

"Oh no, I want you, pretty boy. You made my life a misery with those disgusting pictures you put on my phone. I know it was you. No one else could have done that. That and your complete lack of respect for me and my boss. This is payback time. I've been planning this a while. I even paid the bouncers to look the other way while I took care of business. They're old friends, so they won't say anything."

Shane righted himself and finally was able to face his attacker. He didn't feel particularly strong, the drink and the three gut punches making him less than sharp, but he was damned if he was going to let this man beat him anymore. He intended to square up to Roy, and he clenched his fists at his side, ready to take a swing. He'd go down fighting if he had to.

What he wasn't prepared for was the sudden swing of a baseball bat that connected violently with the left side of head, causing him to jerk to the side, driving him to the ground. He heard a crack in his ears, felt his cheek smack the pavement as his head exploded. His vision blurred. The pain in his temple was agonising.

He vomited up everything he'd eaten and drunk as lay on the cold grey pavement. His left hand had twisted awkwardly beneath him and he'd felt something snap when he went down.

Pain resonated through his body as Roy kicked him in the stomach violently. "I found out your queer boyfriend gave you the boot, so that makes you fair game for me now. Mr. Debussy warned me to stay away from you and your boyfriend because he was scared that bloody video would get out. But now you're no longer fucking him that doesn't apply in my book. Besides, I don't intend you telling anybody about this. So no one will know it was me anyway. You'll be dead, little cocksucker."

Shane felt sheer helplessness at the man's words. His head was ringing and his vision was starting to go black. He thought of Matthew and felt a sense of despair that he hadn't had a chance to make things right with him yet. This wasn't how it was all supposed to have ended.

Roy swung the bat again, connecting with Shane's right arm, sending a jolt of agony up into his being as the bone snapped. He struggled to get to his feet but the pain in both his head and arm was too great, and he couldn't use his arm to prop himself up. He couldn't even focus. His eyes were filmed in red.

Roy sneered. "I've been following you, waiting for my chance. This is going to be such fun, putting you down. No one's going to worry about a little queer boy being found with his head bashed in. I'm probably doing the world a service." He chuckled. "And by the way, just so you know before you check out, I watched your boyfriend's father die. Rather painfully I might add. Stupid bugger had a heart attack right in front of me when I went around giving him a piece of my mind. Say hello to him when you see him."

Shane felt his consciousness fading, and he thought gratefully of Matty. He saw his face, the warm smile and the curve of his cheek, heard the lilt of his voice. He wanted to go out with memories that made him happy rather than those that took him into dark places. The bat hit him again in the ribs and he heard a distinct crack as they broke too. He wondered hazily how many more bones Roy was going to be able to smash before Shane actually passed out. His head flew back once again as Roy kicked him hard in the jaw. His consciousness faded. As the bat was raised once again, he fell into the pit with the thought of Matthew in his memory. He murmured his lover's name as the blackness claimed him.

Inside the club, Timmy frantically searched for his friend. He'd been gone far too long. Shane wasn't in the bathroom, and Timmy thought the only other place he could look was outside. He hoped Shane hadn't decided to go home with anyone. Shane would never forgive himself in the morning if that was the case.

The big man fought his way through the gyrating and sweating bodies, over the dance floor, out to the exit. He burst out the door, wondering where the bouncers were. He immediately saw the scene taking place outside. He recognised Shane's clothing and his blue silky shirt. His friend was on the ground as a large man in a balaclava lifted a baseball bat ready to bring down onto the supine figure on the pavement.

With all the agility of his body and the strength of his anger in seeing his friend being beaten, Timmy launched himself at the man with a loud cry. He grasped the bat and wrenched it out of the attacker's hands.

The man turned to face the six-foot-two warrior, his eyes widening at seeing the terrifying fury etched across Timmy's features. Timmy punched him hard in the jaw once, then again and kicked him backward with one strong, muscled leg as the second blow fell. Shane's attacker fell to the ground with the angry Zulu atop him, straddling him across his waist, his hands pushing the man's shoulders back against the ground.

"You bastard," he snarled at the dazed man. "What the hell have you done to my friend?"

By now people were milling around, having come outside to see what all the fracas was about. Timmy gazed in panic at the still form of Shane as he lay there, blood congealing around his head, his body twisted awkwardly and a face as white as a sheet of clean, pressed paper.

"Call 999," he yelled. "Get an ambulance. Don't just stand there, you stupid bastards, call them now!" He saw someone pull out a mobile and dial a number.

The attacker was still lying beneath him and Timmy looked down at him with a murderous expression.

"You had better hope he isn't too badly hurt," he snarled. "Or I will come after you myself." His eyes were riveted back to Shane's still and broken body and he felt a sense of despair assail his being that he had been too late.

Matthew and David were just finishing their coffees in the restaurant when Matthew's phone rang. He glanced at the number. He didn't know it. Matthew tended to ignore unknown numbers, preferring people to leave a message. It might be Shane trying to make contact and an unknown number could simply mean he'd changed phones.

Christ, he'd become such a needy bastard.

He answered it. "Matthew Langer."

"Matthew, this is Timmy. You remember me? I am Shane's friend. We met at his apartment."

Matthew did remember the tall black man, one of Shane's ex-lovers. "Yes, Timmy. I remember you. What can I do for you?"

"Shane has been hurt. He's at Chelsea and West. You need to get here quickly."

Matthew's body went cold. He saw David looking at him curiously. "How badly is he hurt? What the hell happened?"

There was a short silence. "It isn't good. He's pretty bad. You need to come now. I'll meet you at the A and E waiting room."

"I'll be there shortly," Matthew whispered. He put his phone on the table with trembling hands and passed a hand over his face.

"Matty, what's wrong?" David regarded him in concern.

Matthew shook his head blindly as he stood up. "Shane's in the hospital. That was his friend Timmy. Something's happened and it sounds really bad, DD." His voice cracked as he picked up his bomber jacket and shrugged his shoulders into it. "I need to go. Can you settle up the bill and meet me at Chelsea and West A and E when you're done?"

David motioned him away. "Go, Matty. I'll sort this out. Go to Shane. I'll follow."

Matthew nodded through the tears welling in his eyes and darted out of the restaurant. It was nearly midnight. He gave a shuddering sigh of relief as he saw a taxi right outside and clambered into it.

"Chelsea and West A and E, please. Make it fast. I have a friend in trouble."

The taxi driver nodded. "I'll get you there as soon as I can, mate, don't worry." He pulled away into the traffic.

Matthew sat back, his heart racing. *I haven't even spoken to Shane, responded to him. What if something happens? Oh God, what if he dies and I never get to tell him again that I love him?*

He thrust his trembling hands between his knees and gazed blindly out into the traffic as it whizzed past. To his credit, the taxi driver drove fast, weaving in and out of the London streets with expertise. Matthew felt hot tears of dread trickling down his face. He made no attempt to wipe them away, thinking he deserved them for being so stubborn. He saw the taxi driver gaze at him sympathetically in the rearview mirror a few times.

Finally Matthew saw the huge bulk of the hospital in front, and the driver drove him as close to the entrance as he could get. Matthew opened the door and reached for his wallet.

The taxi driver waved him on. "Get in there, mate. You look gutted. Don't worry about the fare. Go see your friend."

Matthew felt like hugging him for his small act of kindness but all he could do was nod numbly. "Thank you," he said huskily and then he was sprinting across the concourse to the A and E entrance. Timmy wasn't hard to spot. He was the only six-foot-two-inch statuesque black man pacing anxiously up and down the waiting room.

He saw Matthew come running in and moved to meet him. "Matthew, you made it. Good."

"Where's Shane? How is he? Can I see him?" Matthew panted, out of breath. He wasn't as fit as Shane.

Timmy's face clouded and Matthew felt his heart stop.

"Timmy, what's wrong? God, please don't tell me," His voice tailed off as he almost lost it and swayed on his feet.

Timmy caught him with two strong hands and led him to a seat. He pushed him down into it and sat down next to him. "Shane is in surgery. He is alive, Matthew. He was very badly beaten but they are doing everything they can."

"Beaten by whom? Who would do that?" Matthew was dazed.

Timmy looked at him in sympathy. "By a man called Roy Parsons. I came out of the club we were at and found him beating Shane. I managed to stop him and the police came. They have taken him away."

"Roy beat Shane?" Matthew felt cold. "Christ, I knew that man was bad news. How bad is it, Timmy?"

He saw the other man hesitate. Matthew panicked. "Jesus Christ, Timmy, please tell me how bad it is." His voice rose.

Timmy laid a placatory hand on his arm. "I heard the paramedics in the ambulance when we came in. He has internal injuries, some broken ribs and a broken right arm as well as a broken thumb on his other hand. He also sustained a bad head injury. Roy hit him with a baseball bat. He has a fractured skull and he is bleeding inside the brain. They are trying to stop it." The look on his face spoke volumes about the seriousness of Shane's injuries.

Matthew felt his whole world collapse. He shivered, his body suddenly wracked with pain. He couldn't help shedding more hot, salty tears. They fell down his cheeks. "Oh God, Shay," he sobbed. "I should have been there. I should have been there with you."

Timmy reached out and drew the devastated Matthew into his arms, holding him as he cried. "We can only wait and see, Matthew. Shane is strong and tough. He will fight."

David arrived in a panic about a half hour later. He sat down next to Matthew, his arm lightly around his friend's shoulders in support as they waited for news.

Timmy paced up and down the corridor, looking like a Nubian warrior on patrol in his kingdom.

Matthew looked up at Timmy. "Tell me exactly what happened." Matthew's voice was quiet, but he needed to take his mind off things. "I want to hear everything."

Timmy looked at him in sympathy. "We were at the club having a good time. Shane disappeared to pee, I think. He was gone too long, so I thought—" He hesitated. "I thought he might have gone outside with someone, round the corner. It's where people go to—you know. Get their rocks off. Shane had drunk a lot, and I knew he'd be very ashamed at doing that to himself."

Matthew's face whitened. "Go on," he said softly.

Timmy sighed. "I came outside. The bouncers were not there ,which I thought was strange. I saw a man getting ready to hit someone on the ground. I knew it was Shane being hurt. I recognised his blue shirt. I ran at the man, kicked him and tried to stop him hitting Shane. Then I sat on him until the police arrived." He grinned showing white teeth. "The little bastard was most put out at that."

Matthew stood up and walked over to Timmy. He laid his hands both sides of Timmy's ebony-skinned cheeks, and then Matthew laid his forehead against the other man's. Timmy placed a comforting hand on his shoulders. "Thank you," Matthew whispered. "For saving him. I don't know what I would do if he had died. At least now there seems to be a chance."

Timmy smiled softly and reached out, enfolding Matthew in a bear hug.

"He is my friend," he said simply. "My Shanester. I had no choice. And I am glad you are here for him now."

Matthew nodded and walked back to his chair. He sat there thinking that if he never felt anything again it would be a blessing. It was too hard thinking you might lose someone else dear to him.

He just wanted to lie down, close his eyes and never wake up. He thought numbly that bears had the right idea, crawling into a cave and not waking up until things were better outside.

It was two hours later when he heard a quiet voice say, "I'm looking for the party for Mr. Templar?"

Matthew looked up. A white-coated doctor stood there, looking tired and drawn. Matthew stood up anxiously. "How is he, Doctor?"

The doctor observed him, no doubt seeing the lines of strain and the tear tracks on his cheeks. "Who might you be?" he asked, tiredness of his own straining his voice. "I need to know the nature of your relationship before I can disclose anything to either of you."

Timmy gestured. "I am his friend, Timothy, this is David and this is Shane's boyfriend. His name is Matthew Langer."

The doctor looked relieved. "That's the name on the card we found in his wallet. He listed you as next of kin, Mr. Langer." He held out a hand. "Dr. Frederick Shapiro."

Matthew nodded numbly even though the words "next of kin" sent a sharp pain to his heart. He'd had no idea Shane had done that. "What can you tell me? How is he?"

Dr. Shapiro gave a heavy sigh. "He's not particularly good. We've stopped the bleeding from the head injury. We won't know too much more until the swelling goes down. He was beaten very badly, but in a way he was lucky. He has a very thick skull. The fracture is not as bad as I would have thought, given the blow he suffered."

Matthew thought numbly in another time and situation he may have found that comment about the thickness of his lover's skull amusing. But not now.

The doctor observed him in sympathy. "If he hadn't, we'd be having a very different conversation. We've managed to set the broken arm, the thumb, taken care of the broken ribs. I'm hoping the internal bleeding has been sorted as well. We're keeping a close eye on it. He was a very lucky man. If he hadn't got treatment in the ambulance when he did, I doubt he would have survived."

Matthew almost fell to his knees and it was only both the doctor's hand supporting his elbow and Timmy's hands on his waist that stopped him. David's face was white.

"Can I see him?" Matthew whispered.

Shapiro sighed. "He's been heavily sedated and I'm going to keep him that way for at least the next few days, maybe longer. It will be better for him to rest and let his body try and repair the damage that was done to it. So he won't be conscious. But yes. You can see him. He's in a private room. If you like, we can set up a cot for you in his room tonight and you can stay with him." He eyes shadowed. "That young man will need all the help and support he can get."

Matthew nodded. "Thank you. I do intend staying."

The doctor nodded. "Come along then. I can only really let one of you back there." He smiled at Timmy. "I understand you're the gentleman who saved that young man's life?"

"I was simply in the right place at the right time." Timmy shook his head. "If anyone sees Shane now, it should be this man. Go, Matthew."

Matthew nodded. Timmy kissed his cheek gently. "I'll call you tomorrow. I know you will not leave Shanester's side tonight. Now go see Shane. Give him a kiss from me." The man's eyes were wet.

Matthew nodded numbly.

David leaned forward and hugged him. "Give him a kiss from me as well, Matty," he said chokingly. "Tell him to please get through this. Tell him we love him."

Matthew followed Dr. Shapiro down the long corridor, his mind blank. He remembered another time he'd followed a white-coated man into a room. The time he'd had to identify his husband's mangled body. That had destroyed him and he couldn't believe he was about to go and see yet another man he loved lying broken. He was trying hard to hold onto his sanity but he honestly thought he was going to lose it. Matthew took a deep breath as they stopped outside a room.

Shapiro looked at him carefully. "I need to explain something to you. He was hit very hard on the head. I have him sedated, but I can't tell you when he will wake up."

Matthew could hear the unspoken "or if" in the man's careful tones.

The doctor continued, "In these sorts of things, we just have to wait. It's up to the patient most of the time. But I believe in the power of talking. Talk to him constantly. Let him know that you're there. If he hears the voice of someone he loves deep inside, it could help him to come back from the dark place he's in. I've seen it before. So that would be my advice to you. Let him know you're there. Give him a reason to fight to come back to you."

Matthew nodded. The doctor laid a gentle hand on his arm and guided him through the door. At the first sight of the man he loved lying broken and shattered in the hospital bed, Matthew sank down into the chair beside him as hot tears fell down his cheeks. The other man patted his shoulder and left them alone.

"Shay, baby. It's Matty. I'm here." Matthew reached out a hand and stroked the cold cheek, his chest aching.

Shane looked like a wax doll, his eyes closed, long lashes lying against stark white cheeks. His head was covered with bandages, and Matthew could see his hair had been shaved off on the left side. There was a huge bruise on his jaw that looked like a boot heel imprint on his lover's skin.

His broken right arm wasn't in a cast but instead under layers of gauze bandages. Matthew thought dully they must have repaired it internally, with pins perhaps. Shane's chest rose and fell evenly and Matthew looked around with gritty eyes at the myriad of tubes, drips and paraphernalia keeping Shane sedated, medicated and quite possibly even alive.

The overwhelming grief threatened to claim him, and he had to clench his fists tight to keep from screaming profanities at Roy Parsons and the world in general.

Matthew Langer wanted so badly to lose control, wanted to kick, punch and destroy everything in range. He struggled to calm the rage welling inside him. That would do Shane no good. He closed his eyes, taking a few deep breaths, then opened them again. He leaned forward and gently kissed Shane's forehead, finding clammy flesh instead of the warmth he was used to.

"I'm here and I'm not going anywhere. I'm so sorry I wasn't there with you. I should have been. I don't care what happened in the past. We were meant to be together, I know that. I'm just sorry it took something like this for me to be able to tell you that."

He kissed his lover's lips softly. "I love you, Shay. Come back to me, baby. I can't make it without you." His unstoppable tears fell on Shane's face and he wiped them away gently with his fingers.

Matthew was bone tired. He pulled his chair closer to the bed, and took Shane's hand in his as he laid his head on the bed covers. He wasn't going anywhere. He belonged here with his man.

Shane vaguely heard a voice in his head, but it was so far away he could barely make it out. He desperately wanted to listen but he just couldn't seem to find his way out of the warm and comfortable place he found himself in, the place where he didn't have to think or feel. When he tried to reach for the voice pain threaded through his body like the invasive tendrils of a jellyfish, caressing him with agonising, loving whispers of touch. He didn't want the pain. Shane thought he'd stay there a little longer, in the darkness. He let himself drift back down into the blackness that whispered its insidious message of comfort to him.

The next few days Matthew camped out at the hospital. A camp bed was set up in Shane's room so Matthew could sleep there when he needed to. He wanted constant access to the doctors and nurses who staffed Shane's care. He thought they were getting rather tired of his barrage of questions on what was happening and his probing discourses on Shane's prognosis, but overall they were happy to respond.

Matthew's phone had not stopped either and when he stepped outside into the small garden to check his messages, there were always more to be read and dealt with. His mother called or texted at least twice a day to check on her son's well-being and that of his boyfriend.

Matthew wished Shane had got the chance to meet her. He knew they'd get on well together and he'd decided that was one of the first things he was going to arrange when Shane was well. He was taking him to Dresden to meet his sister and mother.

His sister called him one afternoon and Matthew was glad to hear her voice. "Hi, Rachel." He went out into the visitor's room to talk and sat down in one of the plastic chairs.

"Hi, little brother. How's the patient?" Rachael's voice was concerned.

Matthew felt his eyes prick with tears. "He's doing okay. The swelling in his brain has gone down, and the bleeding in his stomach seems okay. He looks better, but he's still not conscious." Matthew's voice clogged up with emotion. "I don't know what else to do, Rach."

"Matt, you're doing everything you should be doing. Talking to him, caring for him, loving him. He just needs to know you're there." Her voice was soft. "How's work taking all this?"

"Bartholomew and Julia insisted I take some compassionate leave. Julia's been here a few times to sit with me. I also have my laptop with me. I sit in the canteen and try to stay caught up on the day job."

"Have you anyone else there to support you? You know I'd be there in a heartbeat if I could, but this shoot—" His sister's guilty voice tugged at Matthew's heart.

"Sweetie, I know. Please don't worry about not being here. I have David and Timmy." His voice was wry. "They drive me crazy, trying to cheer me up and sometimes I just want to be alone with Shay. But they've been incredibly supportive and I wouldn't be getting through this without them."

They'd talked for a while longer then Rachel had rung off, promising to call again.

"But you still won't wake up, will you, sweetheart?" Matthew murmured as he sat beside Shane one evening. "You can come back now, lover. They're not sedating you anymore and it's up to you now. You know what an impatient bastard I am. I need you back here with me." He took a deep breath.

"I talked to your father yesterday. I've been trying to get hold of him but he was out of the country. I had no idea where you lived, so I didn't know how to get hold of your mum. So I called your father's office and after facing some gorgon of a bloody secretary, I managed to get a message to him. I told him his son was critically ill in hospital, and if really cared, he'd at least call me back."

He leaned forward and kissed Shane's cheek, which was no longer as cold as it had been. "And he called back, Shay. He wants to bring your mother down to see you. I think it may be in a couple of days, I'm not sure. I'll just expect them when I see them. He doesn't sound so bad, babe. A little abrupt and very business-like, but not all that scary. He sounded really concerned. He's putting off a business trip to China to come and see you so I guess that means something. *You* mean something, baby."

Shane desperately wanted to break free of the darkness that burrowed into his mind and flooded his being with the heaviness of a fire blanket. Somewhere in his mind, in between the blackness that surrounded and claimed him, he could more clearly hear the comforting cadence of his lover's voice and make out some of the murmured words of love Matty was expressing.

He so desperately wanted to open his eyes and tell him it was okay. But the darkness wouldn't let him go. At first he'd welcomed it. It had become a friend to him when the pain in his body got too much and the emotions of not having Matthew and being beaten and left to die overwhelmed him. But now, no matter what he did, he couldn't seem to break through the barrier that held him back. He was starting to get truly scared. He had times when he could hear Matty clearly, and on other days it was like listening to an underwater opera where the tones of the voices around him rose and fell with regular monotony, yet he couldn't really hear what they were saying. Words made no sense but the underlying feeling was one of safety, of love.

He let go again as it was better to be in the dark place rather than struggle to break free in a frustrating journey of semi-awareness and the feeling that he might never get out of the place he was in.

Matthew let himself into the chilled, dark house and closed the door behind him. He'd only come home to get fresh clothes and have a proper shower and perhaps a couple of hours of sleep in a bed before he went back to sit with Shane again.

To his surprise, that afternoon, Bartholomew Maxwell had appeared at the door to Shane's hospital room. He'd insisted Matthew go home and get some rest in a proper bed. Of course Matthew had refused. He didn't want to leave Shane's side.

Bartholomew had regarded him thoughtfully. "Do you trust me, Matthew?"

Matthew had nodded mutely. His boss, and a man he really respected and had come to like a lot, was one of the most honourable men he knew.

"Then forgive me if I tell that you look like crap and you really need to take care of yourself in order to be able to take care of your young man. So this is what I want you to do. Go home, have a shower, get some sleep in a bed instead of that bloody cot bed or the chair. You know me, Matthew. I will take good care of your young man here and if anything happens or changes you know I will call you immediately. You can trust your loved one with me, son. Go home and take some "me time" before you burn out. Or you'll be no use to anyone."

Matthew had seen the sense in the suggestion and he nodded in gratitude. "Thank you, Bartholomew," he murmured as the man's kindness threatened to unravel him. He seemed to have done a lot of unravelling lately. His friend had hugged him tightly and sent him on his way.

Matthew now lay in bed, looking at the painting he'd hung on his bedroom wall, the one which had replaced the portrait he'd done of Sam. In truth, most of the photos of him and Sam that had been in the house had been removed a while ago, wrapped in tissue paper and placed lovingly in a box in his study. He'd thought it only fair to Shane once he'd started spending more time at Matthew's home.

Matthew had finished this new painting before they'd broken up and had intended giving it to Shane for Christmas, now only a week away.

It was a portrait of Shane, painted from one of Matthew's favourite photos of him sitting grinning on a beach in Devon on one of the few weekend getaways they'd taken. He looked carefree and happy and Matthew smiled , remembering the trip.

"Please come back to me, baby," he whispered at the photo as he fell into an uneasy sleep. "I miss you so much."

The journey back

Shane was determined this time he was going to make it. The journey to consciousness was taking all his strength but he was hell-bent that he was going to complete it. He'd heard Matthew's voice more clearly lately as he fought his way past the darkness and the comfort of oblivion, desperate to get back to that beloved voice.

The pain ebbed and waned and caused him to lose his way, but he fought against it. He needed to be back on the path that brought him to Matthew.

Fuck you, darkness, he gasped as he swam upstream like a salmon against the current that threatened to drive him back. *You are not going to fucking beat me on this one.*

Matthew leaned back in the hospital chair and ran a hand through his hair. It had gotten too long but he just hadn't had the time or the inclination to have it cut. It had seemed pointless. Christmas had come and gone, and now it was Boxing Day.

In all honesty, Matthew hadn't given a damn about Christmas. With Shane not being around, there were no festivities to celebrate. He *had* put a small token Christmas tree up in the room, with a few baubles just in case Shane woke up. Matthew really wasn't in the Christmas spirit. He'd been given a plate of turkey and stuffing by the hospital staff but it had tasted like cardboard. He'd refused all invitations to join family and friends, much to their frustration. He couldn't celebrate or enjoy himself when Shane was still lying in a hospital bed. His boyfriend had been in the hospital for two weeks now with no indication of when he would wake up.

Dr. Shapiro's face had been grave when he'd spoken to Matthew earlier. "There are no guarantees, Matthew," he'd said gently, when Matthew had asked the question about Shane's prognosis. "He's not strictly speaking in a coma, he's just not ready to wake up yet. There is no way of knowing when he will come out of it. His body is healing nicely, and I'm pleased with how he's doing physically. But his brain is something else."

He'd clasped the other man's arm gently. "You're doing everything you can for him. Just keep doing it. It's only been a couple of weeks. Give him time."

Matthew sighed, stood up and stretched. He gazed at his lover's pale face. His hair was growing back but it still looked lopsided, fuller on one side than the other. Matthew smiled softly. Shane would have a hissy fit if he could see what it looked like. His lips were redder than they had been, the colour coming back to his face.

"It's Boxing Day, Shay. Your dad said he'd be here before then. He hasn't come yet. I suppose he is still the tosser you said he was. I thought he'd have made the effort by now."

"I probably am a tosser, son." The quiet words spoken behind him made Matthew turn and take a step back. The man who stood in the doorway was an older version of Shane, his silver-blond hair almost the same style, his features definitely proving that Shane was his progeny. "But I'm afraid this tosser had some rather pressing family business to attend to before coming up here."

The man moved into the room, not taking his eyes off his son. "His mother got ill at hearing the news and we had to make sure she was fit to travel before we came down. " Matthew was still mute at the sight of this older, more mature Shane suddenly appearing in front of him.

"I've been contacting the hospital twice a day to get updates. They tell me you've been taking very good care of him. To your own detriment I believe." He held out a hand to Matthew. "Ray Templar. My wife will be in later. She's got an appointment with my son's doctor to find out all about what's been happening with Shane."

Matthew shook the man's hand. "Matthew Langer. It's good to meet you, sir." He gestured awkwardly. "I'm sorry about the tosser comment—"

The man shook his head in amusement. "Not to worry, Mr. Langer. I've been called worse, I can assure you. Most of them by my son. And most of them deserved." He smiled sadly as he walked over to the bed and stood quietly contemplating Shane. The smile faded and a hard look entered his eyes.

"The man that did this to my son, this Roy Parsons—did you know him?"

Matthew wasn't surprised that Ray Templar would already know everything he needed to about his son's attack. The man was a multimillionaire and probably had more contacts and influence than Matthew could ever hope to have.

"I do. He works for my ex-boss."

Ray laughed shortly. "Ah yes, the slimy Walter Debussy." He reached down and moved a strand of hair off his son's face. Matthew felt a sudden lurch in his chest at the tender gesture. He didn't seem like a man who had no feelings whatsoever for his child.

"Do you know Walter?"

"Not personally, thank God. But I make it a point to know what's going on in my son's life. So I know about you and ergo, I know about your boss."

Matthew's jaw dropped. "You investigated me?"

Christ, this whole interference and nosy parker trait definitely ran in the family.

The older man nodded absently as he sat down next to his son and took his hand, slowly stroking it. Matthew didn't know what else to say.

"Was it just a homophobic attack? What happened to Shane?" Ray's voice was soft.

Matthew shook his head. "It was part of it. But Roy and Shane had a bit of a history too. Roy took a real dislike to him and—" he heaved a shuddering sigh, "it led to this." He waved his hand at the bed.

"Tell me *exactly* why this happened." Ray Templar commanded.

Matthew took a deep breath and told him everything. David's attack by his father, the showdown at the hospital, the gay porn planted on Roy's phone and finally, the video footage, the threat of revealing it to the press and the circumstances leading up to where they were now. He also left out the bit about the breakup. Let the man think they were still together.

Ray Templar listened carefully, nodding occasionally but otherwise letting Matthew tell the story. When he finished the other man looked at him appraisingly. "You're quite the little action team together, aren't you?"

Matthew wanted to giggle and tell him they called themselves the Gay Musketeers but he didn't think was something Shane's father needed to know.

"Why weren't you with him when he was attacked? I understand he was out with…another friend?" Ray's voice was non-committal.

"We're not melded at the hip." Matthew winced as he realised how that might sound. "He's free to go off and see friends."

The older man nodded thoughtfully. "Ah. I thought it was because you two broke up?"

Matthew looked at him in stupefaction.

Ray grinned and Matthew could see where Shane got his ability to disconcert from. It seemed these two men just loved shocking people.

"I told you I knew a lot about you two. And of course there's the fact that this Parsons animal told the police it was why he felt he could go after my son. Apparently Debussy warned him off either of you because of the video tape you told me about. He thought you might release it if anything happened to either of you. But once you two were no longer an item, in his twisted little mind he thought that it made Shane 'fair game' in his words. I can't see the logic myself, but who knows how diseased people think." The disgust in the man's voice was evident.

All Matthew heard was that the fact he'd broken up with Shane had contributed to the terrible beating he'd taken. His throat dried up and spots whizzed before his eyes.

"He attacked Shane because we'd broken up?" His voice choked. "Christ that means this was my bloody fault. If I hadn't done that this might never have happened."

Ray regarded him with soft eyes. "Matthew, the reason Shane is in this hospital is because some sick man took it upon himself to transgress human boundaries and beat the shit out of another man. You were not responsible for this. So don't even go down that road. I can promise you that self-recrimination and guilt is not a worthwhile past time."

He looked down at his son's hand in his. "Believe me, I know."

Just then a woman's voice said softly from the door, "Ray, darling, how is he?"

A woman with deep blonde hair and an open, lovely face stood at the entrance, gazing in at the room. She walked in and over to her husband, putting a hand on his shoulder and leaning down to kiss Shane's forehead tenderly. Her eyes filled with tears.

"God, Ray, look at him. All these years and this is how you get to see him for the first time?"

She turned to Matthew, and he could see where Shane got his vivid blue eyes. "I'm Natalie Templar. Shane's mother as if you hadn't already guessed." She smiled wryly. Matthew thought she was a very beautiful woman. "You must be Matthew."

He nodded and she came over and gave him a hug, wrapping her arms around him. He was nonplussed at the gesture, but he hugged her back awkwardly.

"Thank you for taking such good care of my son," she whispered. "The nurses say you have been incredibly good to him."

She let go of Matthew and sat down in the chair on the opposite side of the bed, and then looked at her husband. "The bottom line is he's doing as well as can be expected. He just won't wake up yet. We'll have to make him."

Natalie leaned into Shane. "Darling, it's your mother. You're father and I are here and we love you. Please wake up soon, sweetheart. We have so much to talk about. Birthday cards and Skype calls just don't do enough for me, I'm afraid. Please come back to us, Shane. We miss you. And your boyfriend here is really missing you. Matthew needs you, Shane." She smiled at Matthew. "Your man looks exhausted. You need to get back here and be with him."

Matthew had a lump in his throat at her words. "I'll leave you two alone with him," he muttered as he walked out the door.

An hour later, Shane's mother and father were leaving to check into a nearby hotel.

"We'll be back later to see him," Natalie said.

Ray nodded. "Matthew, we need to talk as well. I'm sure there are a lot of questions you might have about why Shane left and what happened."

"He left because you threw him out for being gay." Matthew's voice was harsh, but he was tired and he wanted to be alone with Shane.

Ray's eyes clouded. "Yes. I can't deny that's true. And I regret it every day of my life and have been trying to make amends for it ever since. But my son wanted nothing more to do with me. He's stubborn and a law unto himself as you probably know. He at least kept in contact with his mother which is a blessing. And of course the money he stole was another thing." His voice was wry.

Matthew stared at him in amazement. "You knew that was him?"

Ray chuckled. "Of course. He was young and very good, but I had someone who was better. Of course, now the man I knew is calling *him* for advice. He's become a real force to be reckoned with, apparently." The man's voice held a trace of pride. "But I let him think he'd got away with it. It was the least I could do." He turned to his wife. "Come on, darling. Let's leave the love birds alone. I'm sure Matthew wants to be alone with our Shane."

He shook Matthew's hand again. "Thank you for being there for him," he said softly. "I'm glad he has someone like you at his side." The couple walked away.

Matthew stared after them then went back into the room. He sat down and picked up his Kindle. He'd started reading to Shane from one of his favourite books, Peter Straub's *Shadowlands*. He was already halfway through it.

He'd only been reading for about ten minutes, when he heard Shane make a noise. He stopped and looked at the man in the bed carefully. Shane's eyelids appeared to be moving more than they had been. As Matthew watched, holding his breath, Shane's eyes opened.

He shot up, his heart thudding, and leaned over. Shane's eyes were unfocused, unclear but still bright blue and as Matthew watched, they focused on him.

"Matty?" The hoarse whisper of his name coming from Shane's mouth was heaven to Matthew's ears.

Shane recognised him, knew who he was. That had to be a good sign.

"Shay, I'm here, baby." Matthew leaned over as Shane coughed, his face creasing in pain.

He went to the door and called over to the nurse's station. "Shane's awake, call the doctor."

Then he dashed back in, hoping it hadn't been an aberration or a hallucination and that Shane would still be awake. His lover was still laying there, his eyes following Matthew's every move. Matthew's eyes filled with tears as he leaned over and kissed Shane softly on the lips.

"Thirsty." Shane's lips were dry. Matthew had been putting lip balm on them so they weren't cracked.

"Hang on, babe, I'm not sure if I can give you anything to drink. Just wait for the nurse, honey."

"I did it, Matty." Shane's voice was tired but pleased.

Matthew frowned. "Did what, Shay?"

"I came back to you." His lover's words echoed in Matthew's ears. The tears were falling freely down Matthew's face now as he leaned over and got as close to Shane as he could given his injuries.

"Yes, you did. You made it, my Gay Musketeer."

Shane smiled, closed his eyes and drifted back into a normal sleep.

Back together again

Shane woke slowly. He reached out his left hand and gently touched Matthew's hair. He was snoring softly, and Shane smiled at seeing him so defenceless. He'd always loved watching Matthew sleep. He grimaced as his right arm twinged. Stiff and sore, he could hardly move it. His ribs hurt when he did anything strenuous, like simply breathing.

His body ached, his limbs feeling like dead weight. He had a constant headache too, a dull throb in his head that simply sat there like a suet pudding and refused to budge. He felt bilious.

The sight of Matthew's wonderful face leaning over him had made him feel that the long battle upward out of the darkness that had hold of him had been worth it. The salty tears in his mouth as Matthew cried in relief over him had tasted like good wine. Everything bad that had happened between them seemed to have dissipated as if it had never been there in the first place.

Matthew stirred but Shane kept hold of his hair. He didn't want to lose contact even for a moment. But he had to let go when Matthew sat up and looked at him blearily, before his face broke into a wide and joyous smile at the fact Shane had woken up again.

"Hey, you." Matthew leaned out of his chair and kissed Shane. Shane closed his eyes at the feel of his soft lips against his. He didn't care that their breath was probably stale and his lips were dry even though he did have a distinct minty taste in his mouth. He wondered whether Matthew had been brushing his teeth for him. The thought made him wince in embarrassment. What else had the man been doing when he was non compos mentis?

"Your hair has got longer. I like it." Shane's voice was husky from lack of use.

His boyfriend ran a hand through his dark locks. "Yeah. I was too busy taking care of a certain someone to worry about cutting it."

They smiled at each other. Matthew took Shane's hand.

"Let me get you more upright. It'll do you good to change position." He grinned wickedly. "The nurses and I have been moving you around, exercising your limbs and rubbing your butt and back to prevent bedsores. It was more of a pleasure for me than it was for them. Although some of them did comment on your tight arse. I told them it was mine."

Shane laughed tiredly. "I bet you did."

Well, he now knew what else Matthew had been doing for him. Preventing bloody bedsores by rubbing his arse and whatever else he had to.

Shane cringed at the thought. Matthew helped him sit up and Shane hissed through his teeth as his damaged ribs complained. The stiffness and pain in his right side was excruciating and by the time he was sitting only slightly up, the effort had caused him to break out in a sweat.

Matthew took a damp washcloth from the bathroom and wiped his face gently. "I'm glad you're back, Shay. I missed you. You need to know Roy is in prison and he's unlikely to be getting out any time soon. He can't hurt you anymore."

Shane shivered at the memory of his beating. "I thought I was going to die, Matty."

His lover swallowed. "You nearly did, babe. But you fought back. My little pit bull." His voice cracked. "We had no idea whether you were going to be all right or not after the hit you took from that bastard. There was a chance of brain damage when you woke up. The doctors came in earlier and said it looked like we'd been lucky. The fact you recognised me and could speak—that was a good sign."

"I heard your voice and all I wanted to do was see you. It was what kept me swimming through the darkness. It didn't want to let me go. I thought I wanted to stay there. It was safer." Shane's voice dwindled off. "But then I kept hearing you and I wanted to get out." He frowned. "I thought I heard other voices too. Was my mother here?"

Matthew nodded. "Yes, babe. She was here. Together with—"

Shane felt a sudden crease of pain stab him in the head. He gasped, his face paling and his hands clutching Matthew's tightly.

"God, Matty, my head hurts," he whispered. "I can hardly think straight." His eyes squinted shut in pain and he wanted to be ill. He could see Matthew's anxious eyes watching him as Shane relaxed back on the pillows, closing his eyes. He felt the darkness claim him again and despite the fact he'd hated the darkness before, now he gladly sank down into its depths. The pain was just too much.

Just a few minutes, he thought tiredly. *Then I'll be back, Matty. Wait for me.*

Matthew leaned down and kissed his forehead tenderly.

"Sleep, babe," he whispered. "I'll still be here when you wake up."

Shane woke up some time later to find Matthew standing staring out of the hospital window out into the blackness. The ward was quiet, muted lights glowing down the corridors.

"Matty?"

Matthew turned swiftly and the look of sheer relief on his face made Shane's heart swell. "Welcome back. How's the head? I got them to give you something while you were sleeping. I hope it helped."

Shane nodded slightly, still not liking the feeling of the ache in his head that just never seemed to dissipate.

"It feels better. Christ, I've never felt pain like that."

"The doctor said it would happen. He seems to think it will eventually disappear, but we'll have to be patient."

"I'm glad you're still here with me," Shane murmured. He felt exhausted.

"Where else would I be? I love you. I'm never letting you go again, no matter what. You're stuck with me."

Shane grinned faintly. "I can live with that." He frowned. "How long was I unconscious anyway?"

"Two weeks. It was Christmas Day yesterday." Matthew replied quietly. Shane stared at him, confusion on his face.

"Two fucking weeks?" He watched as Matthew's shoulders shook slowly and he realised his boyfriend was laughing.

"It's funny?" Shane didn't see what was so amusing about wasting two weeks of his life.

"No, babe." Matthew giggled. "It's just that I'm so glad that potty mouth of yours is back. God, Shay, I missed it."

"I was out for two weeks? You've been here the whole time?"

"He has, son. Matthew has been incredible during all this." Ray Templar walked into the room. Shane's face darkened as he looked up at Matthew.

"You bloody called *him*?"

Matthew looked exasperated. "Of course I did. Both of your parents deserved to know their only son was fighting for his life in hospital. No matter what happened before."

"Son, your mother is here too. She's just in the ladies room." Ray Templar moved over to his son's bedside. His voice was choked with emotion when he spoke. "God, I'm glad to see you woke up, Shane. Your mother and I got here this morning—"

"I've been here two weeks and you only got here this morning?" Shane's voice was flat when he interrupted his father in mid-speech. It seemed nothing had changed even when he was supposedly dying in hospital.

Matthew interjected quickly. "Shane, your mother fell ill when she heard what happened to you. Your dad had to help her through it. He'll explain when you're better, but for now, just accept they're both here. Please."

Shane heard the plea in Matthew's voice and he nodded. He was too exhausted to get bitchy anyway. He felt like his whole body was moving under water, the sensation lethargic and tiring. Seeing as his father was here, he might just go back to sleep and be damned. He closed his eyes and got comfortable, as much as he could anyway with the pain in his head and his ribcage.

Matthew leaned in and whispered in his ear. "Shay, stop it." Shane opened one eye to see Matthew looking at him in amusement.

"You've been sleeping enough. It's time to wake up now. Mend some bridges."

The love in Matthew's eyes made Shane quail. It was something he'd never thought he'd see again. He nodded and opened both eyes. His father looked at him quizzically.

"Wise man, your boyfriend. We've had a chance to get to know one another and I think you picked a winner here, son."

"I don't need your bloody approval." Shane's good hand tightened on the covers. Matthew sighed and looked at Ray Templar.

"Maybe you should do this later when he isn't being such a bitch."

Shane opened his mouth to say something smart then stopped as his mother walked into the room. She came over and wrapped her arms around him, smelling of soft perfume and cinnamon-scented hair. Her eyes were wet and red rimmed. Shane's heart broke at the sight of his mother looking like that.

"Shane, darling, thank God you're all right. I was so bloody worried about you. I'm so sorry we didn't get here sooner, but when I heard you'd been hurt, I'm afraid I had a little bit of a fit and the doctor didn't want me to travel too far for a while." She glanced at his father, and something passed between them, some secret that he wasn't privy to. He wondered vaguely what it was.

"Mum. How is the epilepsy? Are you okay now?" Shane reached up his good hand and took his mother's hand in his. She nodded.

"Yes, I'm fine now. Your father didn't want to leave me so we could only get down here today. I'm so glad we did." Her voice shook slightly. "I was so worried about you. I last saw you months ago and the thought of not seeing you again, well it was just too terrible to think of."

Ray Templar nodded. "Son, whatever our differences were, I'm glad you're all right. I'm talking to the police about that dreadful Roy Parsons man. They have him up for attempted murder, possession of a knife and possession of an unlicensed firearm. I have a feeling he'll be going to prison for a while. Your big friend Timmy gave a very clear statement and he's a very credible witness."

"He saved your life, Shay." Matthew perched himself on the bed next to his boyfriend. "He came out and stopped Roy hitting you with the bat again. He rugby-tackled him and sat on him until the police arrived." He grinned. "I don't know what mortified Roy more. Being stopped from killing you or being sat on by a big, gay, black man."

Shane's face creased in laughter and his face winced with pain. "Jesus, Matty, don't say things like that when I'm in this state, you bastard. My ribs hurt and now you make me laugh?" He tried to stop snorting with laughter at the thought of Timmy sitting on Roy but failed miserably. Instead he took deep gulps of air to try and lessen the mirth he felt at the picture. Matthew and he shared a look and his insides melted.

God, he loved this man. Finally he managed to stop squirming as Matthew was starting to look worried.

"Jesus, sweetheart, I'm sorry. I didn't really think of your ribs. Are you okay?"

Shane wasn't. He was in so much pain he wanted to curl up and pull the covers over his head, but he made light of it. He flapped his good hand. His parents were staring at them both as if they were crazy.

"I'm fine. Just give me a moment. And now might be a good time to get me some more pain tablets please, Mum. My head is killing me."

His mother disappeared to find a nurse as he'd known she would. His father stood watching him warily.

"You've got a long way to go to get out of here, son. So your mother and I are going to leave now that we know you're okay and leave you in Matthew's very capable hands. She needs to get back for a checkup and I don't want her going home alone. But when you're better you have to promise me we will talk. I nearly lost you, Shane. For the second time. I don't want it to happen again."

Shane's mouth dropped at his father's words, words he'd never expected to hear.

His father reached down and took his hand. "I know we've had our differences. But it's time to resolve them, be honest with each other. Maybe I can get to tell you more about why I said what I did the day you left. I hope we can do that when you're feeling better, down at the house. And bring Matthew with you. He seems to be able to keep you in check, something I never could do."

Shane scowled at those words. Matthew grinned.

His mother returned with a nurse and a very large hypodermic. Shane winced as he looked at it.

"I said tablets, Mum. Not a bloody great needle."

The nurse ignored his jibe as she motioned them all to move away out of the room. "He needs this in his backside," she said cheerfully. "So give us a minute."

Matthew had plenty of comments to give about pricks and backsides but this wasn't the time or the place. He imagined Shane was thinking much the same thing from the smirk on his face. They moved out into the hall while the injection was administered, hearing Shane's muttered "Shit. That hurt."

The nurse bustled past them. "It'll make him sleepy, so you'd better get in there quick, Matthew, if you fancy a kiss or anything else before he goes," she said wickedly.

Matthew chuckled. "Thanks for that, Amy." The nurse winked as she hurried off.

Ray Templar watched as his wife went over to Shane to say goodbye. He held out his hand to Matthew.

"You've taken good care of my son, Matthew. He obviously adores you; you can see it. And I can see you love him. I'm glad this worked out. Please convince him to come see me when he's up and about?"

"I'll try but I won't force him. It's his decision."

Ray smiled. "I'd expect nothing less from you. Thank you. You have my number. Keep in touch with how he's doing, please. His mother and I really want to know."

Matthew nodded. "I will."

Natalie came out and hugged Matthew. "Thank you," she said simply. "I appreciate what you've done. You brought him back to us. But you're the one he came back for. Anyone can see that. Look after yourself, Matthew and take care of my boy for me."

The couple waved and walked back down the corridor. Matthew went back into the room to find Shane almost asleep. He managed to peer at Matthew from between half-closed lids.

"Hey, babe." He giggled. "Have you come to give me another prick?" His voice was slurred.

Matthew grinned. Shane was definitely away with the fairies.

"No, I think we'll leave that for later, lover. For now, you get your sleep. We can look at the whole prick situation when you're up and about."

He placed a soft kiss on Shane's lips and his boyfriend's hand sneaked up and pulled him closer. For a man with a lot of drugs in him, he had some strength. Shane's tongue slowly slipped past Matthew's lips. Matthew felt the breath leave his body as he kissed Shane back.

God, how he'd missed tasting this man, kissing him, being close to him. It felt so good to have him back. He'd never have made it longer without him.

Shane finally let him go as he drifted into sleep. "Love you, Matty," he said drowsily.

"I love you too," was Matthew's whispered reply. "Merry Christmas, Shay."

Going home

Shane knew he'd been driving Matty crazy. He was a terrible patient. He was three-F: fractious, frustrated and fed up. He'd had to take things easy over the last week as he got used to being mobile. He'd had to do all the physical therapy crap they wanted him to do before they'd release him.

Shane scowled now as he tottered around his hospital room in his loose jogging bottoms and a tee shirt, his legs still weak. His broken arm was healing and the physiotherapy he was having made it more mobile but it still hurt like a bitch and did virtually nothing he wanted it to do. He was determined to get fully mobile and get out of this bloody place. The last week had been hell, wanting to go home but not trusting his body to support him as he got used to moving muscles that had weakened. Matthew came in. He saw Shane standing up and raised an eyebrow.

"Wow. You're being adventurous. Need a hand for anything?" Shane saw him waiting to see what the response would be. Moving across and trying to help him when he wasn't wanted was like a red flag to a bull and likely to make Shane growl in his present mood.

"No. I went to take a piss and then I was just exercising these legs of mine." Shane moved determinedly over to Matthew, slightly unsteady but pleased he was making it on his own. "I want to go home, Matty."

Matthew sighed. "Shay, the doctor will be around tomorrow and hopefully he'll say you're okay to be released. It's just another day, babe."

"Another fucking day in this place," muttered Shane sulkily. "I don't think I can do it."

Matthew sighed. "You've caused mayhem here. The nurses love you, but even they're starting to get a little annoyed." He grinned. "I saw one of them loitering with intent the other night when you were sleeping. She had a pillow in her hand. I managed to convince her to put the weapon away."

Shane scowled. "Very bloody funny. You try having someone helping you take a pee all the time, washing you and doing that god-awful physical therapy which hurts like a bitch. And I can't even work on my laptop because of the headaches." Bushwhacker had been relegated to Shane's study at home, so the temptation to spend hours on end on a computer screen was removed. The doctor had recommended he not spend time staring at a screen.

Matthew chuckled as he moved toward his disgruntled lover. "At least you got your hair evened out." He said the words tauntingly and Shane knew he was teasing. He still took the bait.

"My hair was the last straw, Matty. It was awful and I looked like some bloody Crusty the Clown caricature. Now all I have is these bloody curls all over my head."

Matthew had cut Shane's hair for him and now his scalp was covered with soft blond curls that were more or less one length.

"But you look bloody adorable," Matthew said, his eyes glinting. "Like an elf."

Shane's glower would have turned a gargoyle into a gibbering wreck. "I am *not* a fucking elf," he muttered between gritted teeth.

Christ, did he really look like some fairy-tale character?

Matthew chortled and reached out a hand to smooth away the frown on his boyfriend's face. "Lover, I'm joshing. You look sexy any which way. And I happen to have a real yen for elves anyway."

He kissed Shane's lips softly. Shane's dick leapt to instant attention as it had every day since he'd woken up and been near Matthew. They'd had very little time to be together in any intimate way, other than a couple of mutual blow jobs performed in the privacy of the room and once in the bathroom. It was difficult for Shane to do much as he was still in pain and his headache still debilitated him to the point of nausea. He huffed and waved toward his groin as Matthew released his mouth.

"And this doesn't help. I've had blue balls for days and I can't even jerk off. My hand is too sore and my bad arm gets tired. Matty, when a man can't jack off, it's a bloody bad state of affairs."

Matthew laughed, a deep-throated sound that made Shane smile despite his bad mood. His lover had such an infectious laugh.

"Lover, God, you are in a bad way, aren't you? My poor baby." Matthew turned around and closed the door, locking it. He turned to Shane and moved over closer to him, a small smile on his lips. He reached out his hands and drew his boyfriend closer to him, kissing his temple softly with warm lips. He smelt of coffee.

"I know you're fed up, lover," he whispered in Shane's ear, his breath hot and ghosting on Shane's ear. Shane groin tingled and his dick hardened even more. At least that *was* one thing that still seemed to work properly, he thought thankfully. He felt Matthew's grin against his cheek as his lover's lips trailed softly down to his jaw line, kissing it with little pouty goldfish movements. Shane's breathing got deeper and he closed his eyes, savouring Matthew's nearness, his scent, his warmth and his sheer sexiness. He thanked whatever deities there were that he was still here in the land of the living to appreciate his lover.

"I think I need to relieve some tension in you. I owe it to the nurses," Matthew whispered as he drew Shane over to the bed and made him lie down. He settled next to Shane, hoisting his firm, fully clad body next to him.

"Lift your backside up," he ordered and Shane did what he was told. Matthew pulled his trousers down to his thighs and Shane's dick reared up instantly. Matthew chuckled softly. He reached into his back jeans pocket and drew out a small tube of lube. Shane watched as he squeezed some into his hand.

"You're carrying lube in your pocket now? Wow, you're some Boy Scout."

"I had a feeling I might need it sooner rather than later," Matthew murmured against Shane's ear, his tongue licking the inside and causing havoc in his body. "Now lie back and enjoy." His warm, slippery hands found Shane as he grasped him and started a slow, steady up-and-down motion that made Shane weak. Matthew covered his mouth with his own, his tongue sliding into Shane's mouth and caressing the underside of his own. Shane groaned in sheer pleasure.

"God, Matty, I missed this," he murmured huskily. "You, your hands, your lips. I thought I've never feel or taste them again when you kicked me out." His body reared on the bed as he gasped, his groin aflame and his legs tensing on the bed. He had a feeling it would take no time at all to make him come. Matthew gazed into his eyes, his own darkened with guilt.

"I know and I'm so sorry. If I hadn't done that, Roy wouldn't have come after you—"

Shane kissed him fiercely. All he could feel was the turmoil in his groin at Matthew's expert strokes.

"Never say that. It wasn't your fault, baby. I—oh dear God."

He couldn't breathe or speak as his body reacted to Matthew's touch and he closed his eyes and gave into the overwhelming sensations he was feeling. He grasped the back of Matthew's head, his fingers grasping his lover's hair tightly. Matthew's lips licked and sucked as his fingers worked their magic on Shane's dick. He felt himself swell and pulse in Matthew's hands, the warm sensation of gratification coursing through his body and he thought for a minute it must be dark because he saw stars. He pressed his face into Matthew's warm neck as he came, heat spewing out of him as his body absorbed his lover's by pressing him close. Matthew's soft breath tickled his face. Finally he was spent, his body drained, a sense of well-being floating through his limbs.

"Fuck, I needed that," he whispered as his aching body relaxed after being tensed so tightly. "I don't think it's ever happened that quick before though. That was a bloody world record."

"I think we *all* needed that, lover," Matthew murmured wryly as he released Shane's now-flaccid member and reached over to wipe his hands with the tissues at the side of the bed. "You've been a real little prima donna. Of course, you'll need to return the favour for me at some time." He laughed. "At least I can relieve my tension myself. I imagine you've been battling a bit."

Shane nodded. "It got a bit much. I tried, but I got tired and my arm ached, then my hand…" His voice trailed off. "I think one time I even fell asleep while I was doing it." He scowled. "Not a very good macho thing to do."

Matthew laughed loudly as he kissed him, his mouth searching, his tongue probing his mouth again. Shane sighed. This was definitely better than a DIY job.

Matthew took Shane home, back to his apartment, two days later. The new year had just begun and in Matthew's eyes, it was the start of a new chapter of their lives. Shane was alive and well and back with him, and that was what counted.

They sat now cuddled together on the couch as Matthew gently stroked the softly growing curls of hair on Shane's head, taking care to avoid the nasty scar that ran down the left side. The scar was about an inch and a half in length, ridged and thick, but luckily it seemed that as Shane's hair grew back most of it would be covered. There may be a small bit that extended beyond, but Matthew had told his boyfriend teasingly that it made him look even sexier and added an air of mystique.

He leaned forward and kissed Shane gently on the side of the scar. Shane tensed.

"Don't do that," he said softly. Matthew frowned.

"Why, did I hurt you? Sorry."

"Yes, it still hurts but that's not why." His lover looked at him, his blue eyes shadowed. "It's ugly. I can't wait until my hair grows back."

"Shay, nothing about you could be ugly." Matthew sat up and pulled Shane closer. "It's a battle scar. It's nothing to be ashamed of."

"Still." Shane was unwavering. "Don't touch it, please."

Matthew was thrown. "Okay."

There was silence as the soft sounds of John Legend echoed through the lounge. The huge picture windows were open, the bright lights of London and the Thames twinkling from afar.

"It feels good to have you here," Shane murmured. "I like having you here all the time. Feel free to stay as long as you like."

Matthew grinned. "Is that an invitation to move in, Mr. Templar? I'd have thought you'd have enough of me by now."

"I can never have enough of you," was Shane's soft reply. "And moving in together doesn't sound like a bad idea to me." Shane looked at his lover. Matthew kissed his forehead.

"We can certainly talk about that when you're better, if that's what you want. I love your place, so it's no hardship living here. I like the thought of coming home to you every night."

"What about your house?" Shane shifted against him. "What would you do with that?"

Matthew shrugged. "I'd rent it out. It's a good investment so I'm loath to sell it right now. And I wouldn't want us to live there together. There are too many memories."

Shane nodded. "I wouldn't like that either. I suppose we need to think about the situation though."

Matthew kissed his lips gently. "Let's get you better before we make any big decisions like that. You've still got a long way to go what with the headaches and the healing. I know the doctors said they'd go away, but I still worry." He stroked his lover's back gently. "Are you doing all right with everything? After what you went through, I wasn't sure whether you wanted to talk about it yet. I wanted to leave it up to you to decide. I didn't want to push you."

Shane didn't answer, simply tensed slightly against Matthew.

"You know I'm here if you ever need to get anything off your chest. Not just about the assault but anything else." Matthew was trying in a roundabout way to begin the dialogue to get Shane to agree to see his father. Ray Templar was in constant touch with him about his son, despite being in what seemed like a different country each week. But Shane simply ignored him and would only speak to his mother.

Shane shifted, and when he spoke his voice was tight. "I'm fine, Matty. I got attacked, I'm getting over it and that's all we really need to know."

"And your father?" Matthew asked quietly, knowing he was pushing but unable to stop himself. He wanted Shane to be happy, to get his family back.

"Nothing's changed. Just because I nearly got killed by some homophobic bastard doesn't make what my dad did to me any better."

Matthew wasn't used to hearing bitterness in Shane's voice. It was the one emotion his lover had always seemed to lack, being the sort who lived on the bright side of the street unlike Matthew.

"Your father really cares about you. I could see it-"

"I don't want to talk about it, Matthew."

Calling him by his full name was a definite sign Shane was getting riled. Matthew sighed, remembering the last time he'd asked about Shane's father and they'd ended up arguing. He couldn't bear that to happen now.

"Okay. I'm sorry. I'll cease and desist." He settled back against the couch, leaning his head back and closing his eye, letting the music waft over him and the feel of his boyfriend in his arms comfort him.

Shane took a deep breath to stop the feeling of panic that had suddenly risen unbidden in his chest when Matty had mentioned the attack. The memory of being beaten, of seeing Roy Parson's crazy eyes staring out at him, the dull sound the bat had made as it connected with his head and the pain he'd felt as he was beaten was overwhelming. Coupled with the fact that his head still ached, never ceasing, and the scar was throbbing, he didn't want anything else to remind him any more of what had happened that night. He certainly didn't want Matty kissing that awful thing on his head, the constant reminder that he'd nearly died. He didn't want Matthew tainted with it.

Shane sat up suddenly and looked at Matthew, who looked surprised at his quick action. "It's people like my dad and Roy who make people like us suffer, Matty. And my dad might have mellowed since then, but I haven't." His voice was determined. "So forgive me if I can't believe he wants to make amends."

Matthew reached out and framed Shane's face in his hands. "He cares about you. He's been watching out for you. Your father knew it was you that took his money, Shay. He told me that day at the hospital. And he let you have it."

Shane looked at him in disbelief. "How could he have known that? I covered my tracks."

"He said he knew you were good but he found someone better than you. He told me now that guy is the one calling *you* for advice. Your father told me you deserved to keep the money after what he did to you. And you didn't see him when you were unconscious. He really cares for you. I could tell."

Shane felt shell-shocked at Matthew's words. Matthew was a good judge of character and people and he was usually right. There was something else as well. Talking about fathers had nudged something loose in Shane's brain, something Roy had said to him when he was lying bleeding on the pavement. He knew it was important, but he couldn't remember what it was. It was something to do with Matthew's father. He dug down deep inside to bring it forth but it was having none of it. Frustrated, he focused again on his lover's voice.

"I'm not going to push. But you might think about it, seeing your dad again. And that's the last I'm going to say. I have something else in mind for you now."

As Matthew reached over and drew Shane to him for a deep and tender kiss, Shane forgot about everything else and concentrated on the feel of his boyfriend's hands unzipping his jeans and reaching in to take him in warm hands. All of a sudden, remembering what Roy had said didn't seem so important.

Fatherly visits and more passing out

Three days later, Shane was sitting curled up on the couch, dressed in his favourite tracksuit, just enjoying slouching and reading a newspaper. The doorbell rang. He called out.

"Matty? Are you going to get that?" He was quite comfortable where he was and if there was any chance he didn't have to get up, he'd take it. There was no reply. Shane called out again but he could hear the water running and guessed Matthew was in the shower. They'd only got up about an hour ago after a fairly hectic and unplanned evening's activity in bed as he'd buried himself in Matthew's body. It had hurt as his ribs were still sensitive, but it had definitely been worth the exertion. He grinned at the memory, getting off the couch and making his way to the door. He really enjoyed having Matty here full time.

When he opened the door, he caught his breath. His father stood there, a set expression on his face, his hands held tightly by his sides. He looked nervous.

"What are you doing here?" Shane asked ungraciously, without inviting him in.

"You haven't been returning my calls or my text messages, Shane." Ray Templar observed his son through soft eyes. "So I thought I'd come over and see how you were doing in person."

Shane laughed. His head was really hurting again. "You've never bothered before, so why is this any different?" His tone was bitter. Ray Templar winced.

"Because I haven't seen my son nearly beaten to death before and almost lost him," Ray said. "Are you going to let me in?"

"Shay, was that someone at the door-" Matty came out, freshly showered and dressed and saw the two men facing each other down in the open doorway.

"Ray. I didn't know you were coming over." He sounded surprised.

"Yeah, right, of course you didn't," Shane said sarcastically as he moved away from the door and went into the kitchen. He needed coffee, preferably something stronger. He made black coffee, added a hefty shot of whiskey and ignored Matthew's slightly disapproving look at the fact he was taking alcohol while he was still on medication.

He was fairly irritated at the thought there'd been some conspiracy between his lover and his father to engineer a meeting. The pressure in his brain built and he felt nauseous.

"Shay, I had no idea your father even knew where you lived," Matthew said as Shane grunted in disbelief. He gestured to Ray to come in. The man stepped over the threshold and Matthew closed the door behind him.

"Matthew had nothing to do with this visit." Ray informed his son. "I've always known where you lived, son."

Shane cocked at eyebrow at him in query. "Really? I shall have to move now then, won't I?" He wanted to ask his father how he knew but his innate stubbornness wouldn't give his father that satisfaction of showing he was itching to know. He busied himself topping up his coffee, ignoring extending the invite to either his lover or his dad. Matthew sighed.

"Ignore the prima donna, Ray. Can I offer you something to drink?"

Ray shook his head. "No thank you. I just wanted to talk to my son."

"What do you want, Dad?" Shane voice was uncompromising. "Say what you have to say and then you can leave."

"Jesus, Shane!" Matthew exclaimed. "Have some common courtesy, won't you?"

Shane felt his temper prickle deeply in his chest. "Stay out of this, Matty. It's none of your fucking business." Even as he said the words, he wanted to take them back. The flicker in Matthew's eyes and the faint shadow on his face told Shane he'd just hurt his boyfriend. But his head was pounding, his mouth was dry, his chest tight with seeing the man he'd been avoiding for nearly eleven years. He was tired and he wanted to crawl into a dark space and sleep.

"It's all right, Matthew. Shane has every right to be upset." Ray Templar took a deep breath. "I can see I need to make this quick. I'll give you a quick summary, then, shall I?"

Shane stared at him. He didn't want to compromise. He wanted nothing more than to raise a hand to his temple and rub it, try and massage the pain away as he waited for his father to speak. But he wasn't going to show that weakness in front of his father. Instead he gripped the side of the kitchen island tightly, willing the pain away. He saw Matthew's eyes glance at his white knuckles.

"Do you need painkillers, baby? I can get you some."

"No, for God's sake, just stop fussing and leave me alone." His words were harsh, his tone curt. Matthew regarded him silently for a moment then compressed his lips and turned to the coffee machine as he poured himself some.

Ray spoke quietly. "Shane, I've been keeping tabs on you since you left home. I know you took that money from my offshore company account, I know what you do for a living, I've known where you live and quite a lot else about you. That day we argued—"

"You mean that day you hit me across a room and told me I was a worthless faggot and a queer and that you were disgusted? You mean that day?" Shane's voice was cold and the memory of that night came surging back like toxic waste seeping out of an oil drum. His father's eyes closed and Shane was taken aback to see a look of sheer shame on Ray Templar's face.

"Yes. The day I destroyed any relationship I had with my son and acted like a homophobic bastard. The day I am the most ashamed of in my whole life. The day I would give anything in my life to go and take back."

"You can't. It's too late for that." Shane moved away from the tabletop then clutched at the edge as dizziness overcame him. "So thanks for the sermon, but honestly, you should go."

"Christ, Shane, give the man a chance." Matthew's harsh tone cut through Shane's head like a red-hot knife. "Stop being so fucking stubborn and let the man have his say." It was a measure of just how much Matthew was mad with him that he actually swore in front of Ray Templar. "I'd give anything to have my father back. Here you have the chance to make amends with yours and you're throwing it away. I know he hurt you. He was an arsehole. But he's here now."

Shane felt a blackness descend on him. "You don't know anything, Matthew. How it feels to have your dad despise you. Your father loved you."

Ray Templar's face was white and drawn as he moved toward his son.

"I've always loved you, Shane. That day I said those things, I wasn't myself. I have no excuses but I'd just lost twenty million dollars in an investment that went wrong, I had stockholders wanting me to resign as a result, and the newspapers hadn't stopped hounding me all day. I was at a low ebb then the thing with you happened and I just lashed out." His voice was full of pain. "I wish I hadn't but I did. I just kept thinking, 'What if the Board found out my son was gay?' I knew they'd use everything against me that they could, to discredit me and that would mean discrediting you as well. I was scared, and I overreacted, God help me. I've spent my life trying to make it up. I left you with your money. I asked your mother to feedback everything about your conversations, any photos you had. I tried to contact you, but you ignored every effort I made. You made it quite clear you couldn't forgive me and finally, I stopped. I didn't have the strength anymore. I needed to focus on the business and get it back on an even keel."

He stopped, out of breath and Shane watched his father out of eyes that were getting blurrier. He was having trouble focusing.

"Then you nearly died, and I just knew there was no way I could let you go again. Not without telling you how sorry I was." He drew a deep breath." Your mother wasn't the only one that was ill when she heard what had happened to you. The other reason we only got down here late to see you was that I had a heart attack. It took me a while to recover. The doctor didn't want me travelling as he thought I was a candidate for another one. I told your mother not to mention it." Ray was slightly out of breath and Matthew moved over to him and laid a comforting hand on his shoulder.

"You need to sit down yourself. Come in here." He drew Ray gently into the lounge as Shane watched them go. At the words "heart attack" a sudden memory had just risen in his head. The memory of lying on a cold, damp pavement with his head split open and the taunting voice of Roy Parsons telling him how he'd watched Matthew's father die.

"Matty," he gasped as the kitchen floor rose up to meet up him. "I think Roy Parsons killed your dad."

Matthew heard the words his lover uttered and saw his body collapse as he felt boneless to the floor. He felt a sweep of panic as he bounded over to Shane's side. His boyfriend's face was pale, his lashes dark against the pallor of his cheeks. Not only had his last words been utterly horrifying, Shane was motionless. His chest rose and fell evenly. Matthew looked up at the stricken face of Ray Templar.

"Call 999, Ray. Get an ambulance here." Shane's father nodded as he pulled out his mobile, his eyes never leaving his son's face.

Matthew cradled Shane in his arms, willing him to wake him. His heart was pounding. *He couldn't lose him again. God, please, not again.* His boyfriend's last cryptic words were still swirling in his head but at this point, all he wanted was Shane well.

"Baby, wake up. Shay, it's Matty. Can you hear me?"

Shane groaned and Matthew felt a surge of relief as his eyes opened.

"Matty?" he croaked. Matthew pulled him closer, kissing his cheek, his eyes, anything else he could just to feel Shane.

"I'm here. You passed out. The ambulance is on its way."

Shane struggled to sit up. "Ambulance? I don't need an ambulance. I'm not going back to the hospital—"

Matthew could see the panic in Shane's eyes as he tried to calm him down. "Shay, we need to have you checked out. Let the paramedics take a look at you. I won't let them take you to the hospital unless it's vital. I promise."

"I don't want to go back there, Matty." Shane whispered. Hot tears fell from his eyes and Matthew's heart broke at seeing his normally confident, brash young man in such pain. "I might not come back next time."

"Oh, baby," Matthew hugged him closer. "I'll make sure you always come back to me."

Shane snuffled and burrowed deeper into Matthew's chest. Ray Templar watched with an unfathomable expression in his face.

"God, you two are incredible together," he whispered, his face pale. "How could I ever think this wasn't right?" Shane's eyes flicked toward his father and Matthew saw something in them that said perhaps the two men might meet halfway after all.

Ten minutes later the paramedics had come and gone, pronouncing Shane physically fit. They'd said gently it was simply a faint and that his headaches were debilitating him, making him weaker and the stress he'd had that morning hadn't helped. Ray looked guilty at contributing to his son's collapse.

But the paramedics had suggested a hospital checkup might not be amiss. Shane had point blank refused it at this time and as he had a checkup in a few days, Matthew didn't press him. He sat now, with Shane nestled across his legs, half asleep from the strong pain killers Matthew had forced down him. Ray Templar sat now and watched the two men. Shane lay stretched out with his head pillowed on a cushion on Matthew's thighs, Shane's hands curled possessively in his lover's.

"What did you think he meant about Roy Parsons having killed your father?" he asked Matthew. "What was the story there?"

Matthew quietly explained what had happened to his father, and his heart attack. Ray already knew most of the story about the events preceding his father's heart attack.

"I don't know why Shane would say something like that, what bearing it could have on anything. My dad had a heart attack. That was a given."

Ray reached out and softly stroked his son's cheek. Shane opened his eyes, his blue eyes gazing at his father then slowly closed them again. But Matthew could see a faint smile on his face at the gesture. He held a sudden hope that perhaps Shane and his dad might be reunited in some small way after all.

"I'll wait until he's feeling better and then ask him. I don't want to upset him again."

Matthew felt Shane stir in his arms, his warm body pushing closer to his. He smiled and kissed his forehead, wrapping protective arms more tightly around the man he held.

"You truly love my son." Ray looked at Matthew with a soft glance. Matthew nodded.

"He's my world." He hesitated. "I lost a man once, my husband. I was married to him for three years, but two years ago he was killed in a car accident."

"I'm so sorry, Matthew. That must have been dreadful. I can't imagine what that's like."

"I thought I'd never be able to find another person I could love again. And then along comes this one, all mouth and no manners." Matthew smiled as his hands caressed Shane's soft hair. "And then nearly losing him as well—I never want to go through that again."

"He adores you. I can tell. He always wore his heart on his sleeve, Shane. He was easy to read, even as a child. That night—" his voice choked and Matthew saw the wet sheen of tears in his eyes. "I destroyed him, took away any sense of decency or acceptance he might have felt about being different. I can never forgive myself for that. I was a different man then."

"I think you might have a chance of getting him back, but it won't be easy. He's as stubborn as hell."

"I have time." Ray stood up. "I'm going to leave you now. Please tell Shane when he wakes up that I hope we can continue where we left off. He picked up his jacket. "I'll let myself out so you don't disturb him." He leaned down and planted a gentle kiss on Shane's head. "Tell him I love him."

"I will." Matthew watched as Ray left. Once the door had swung shut he lay back against the couch and closed his eyes. Shane still slept, his breathing even and his hands now curled into Matthew's sweatshirt. Matthew smiled. There was nowhere he'd rather be.

Shane awoke some hours later, a little stiff, his body slightly chilled. He shivered as he sat up. He smiled as he saw Matthew snoring softly, his head at an awkward angle against the back of the couch. Shane looked at his watch. It was almost eleven p.m. He disentangled himself from the comfortable warmth of his lover's body and leaned over to tickle Matthew's nose. It twitched. He grinned and did it again, watching as Matthew's eyes opened blearily then focused on him. They cleared and Shane felt sudden warmth at the loving expression he saw there.

"You're awake. How do you feel?" Matthew reached up and pulled Shane close to him, his mouth searching for his.

"Better. My headache's more manageable."

Shane leaned in, meeting his boyfriend's mouth with his own, and they kissed, lips warm, starting out tender and turning into much more. Shane could feel Matthew's desperation in each swift dart of his tongue, each nip of his lip and with the ferocity that he ground their mouths together.

"Wow, someone's pretty needy," Shane whispered as he moved onto Matthew's lap, his knees either side of his lover's body, feeling the heat and hardness in Matthew's groin as he pulled Shane down on him. Shane's own dick was rock hard, pressing against Matthew's taut stomach.

"You scared me to death," Matthew whispered as his hands slid under Shane's tee shirt, finding the warm skin beneath and making Shane gasp. "You say strange things, then pass out and leave me to wonder what the hell happened." His mouth took Shane's again in a mouth-opening wet kiss, and Shane thought he was about to be swallowed. He relished the feel of his lover's tongue on his, the hands that were slowly caressing his hips and the insistent push of Matthew's hardness against his backside and his groin.

"I'm sorry," he gasped when he could speak. "Talking with my dad made me crazy." He frowned and leaned back, looking at Matthew's flushed face. "What did I say that was strange?"

Matthew's eyes darkened. "Don't worry about it. We'll talk about it later. I don't want you getting upset—"

"Matty, I'm not an invalid, for fuck's sake. Just tell me what I said. I don't remember."

Matthew hesitated. "You said you thought Roy Parsons killed my father."

At the reminder, Shane shivered, hearing once again the gloating words of the man who had almost beaten him to death. "Yes, I remember. Just before I passed out earlier, I remembered something Roy said to me." He gripped Matthew's shoulder. "He told me he went to see your father the day he died to give him a piece of his mind about what he was about to do to Walter." Shane swallowed. The next words would not be easy for Matthew to hear. "He said he watched your father die, that your dad had a heart attack right in front of him."

Matthew went still. His hands stopped their stroking of Shane's body and they fell to the couch beside his legs. When he spoke he sounded confused.

"I don't understand. Roy went to see my dad? Why, to convince him not to out Walter? I can see him doing something like that, but surely he would have tried to help him?"

"This is a man who nearly beat me to death, Matty. I doubt very much he would have been particularly disposed toward helping a man who was about to cause trouble for his boss. We all know how Roy feels about Walter. He worships the bastard." Shane looked at his boyfriend in sympathy. Matthew's eyes were tight with pain.

"You think Roy stood by and watched my father have a heart attack and die?"

"I think it's a distinct possibility."

Matthew gazed at Shane in horror. "How the hell can I find out what happened? Whether that's true?"

Shane sighed. He moved off Matthew and sat beside him. The lovemaking mood had definitely gone—for now.

"You could ask him, I suppose. Or ask Walter. Perhaps he knew about it. Shit, maybe he was the one who sent Roy around to 'talk' to your dad in the first place." He looked at Matthew quizzically. "Did your dad have a history of heart trouble?"

Matthew nodded. "He had a heart condition, bought on by rheumatic fever when he was a kid. He suffered with it all his life. It was why when he died so suddenly, no one was really surprised. The doctors said it was just his time." He passed a hand over his eyes. "I need to go and see Roy. I need to ask him what he knows about this."

Shane nodded. "We can call the police tomorrow, tell them about it." He laughed sharply. "It'll just be another thing to add to his rap sheet along with the attempted murder charge. But if you go and see Roy, I want to be there with you. I don't want you be on your own with him."

"Shay, the man almost killed you. Are you sure you want to see him again?" Matthew reached up and cupped Shane's face in his hands. Shane nodded although he felt ill with fear at actually seeing the man who had tried to kill him.

"We see him together. Maybe it's what I need, too. But I'm not having him tell you a possible story about how he might have contributed to your father's death without me being there to hold your hand." His voice was fierce, protective. Matthew smiled and reached over to draw him into his arms.

"Okay, pit bull. We do it together, if we can get in to see him. I'll call someone in the morning and see if I can set it up." He smiled and Shane's heart lifted at the relief in his eyes at not having to do it alone.

"Matty? We still have one thing to talk about. About the hacking thing, the things I saw of you."

He saw the look of dread on Matthew's face as he closed his eyes. It had been the elephant in the room for too long and now it needed to leave. He knew Matthew had a deep sense of self-loathing at what Shane had seen. Matthew's voice trembled when he spoke.

"Shay, I know it was disgusting and something I wish you'd never seen. It eats away at me inside that you know that about me—"

His words were cut off as Shane leaned forward and pressed his mouth against his boyfriend's, trying to send every bit of love and understanding he had in that kiss.

"We've been through too much in our short time together to judge each other," Shane whispered against Matthew's warm mouth. "I don't see that man here in front of me. I see my man, the one who let his guard down and let me in. The one who stood up for his friend and lost his job to do what was right. The one who brought me back from a bad place and then took care of me. I don't give a damn what you did all those years ago. I just know I love you and nothing you do will ever change that. I don't feel any disgust. I'm just so proud you made it and found me." He wrapped his arms around his lover and hugged him tightly. "Let it go. We can't move forward if you don't. And that would kill me."

His mouth found Matthew's again and Matthew kissed him back fiercely, his need evident in the way his lips ground against Shane's mouth, his body hard and demanding. Finally he released him and laid his forehead against Shane's, his voice quiet.

"I adore you, you know that. I'll do anything for you. If that's what you want, I'll try." Shane became very aware of his boyfriend's body pressed tightly against his and he grinned.

"And now we have that out of the way, I think you deserve a reward for looking after me when I hit the floor again."

He motioned to Matthew to lift his arms then pulled the man's tee shirt over his head and threw it behind the couch. He tugged his boyfriend's sweatpants off his hips, Matthew lifting his backside to help. Shane reached up and drew off his tracksuit top, watching Matthew's eyes devour the sight of his naked torso. He chuckled.

"I love the way you look at me," he whispered huskily. "Even looking like this, I can still make you hard." He slipped his pants down his legs. He crawled back onto Matthew's lap, his backside already pushing artfully against the front of Matthew's groin. He wriggled himself on top, heard his boyfriend's gasp, and felt him surge. He smiled in satisfaction as Matthew spoke in a strangled voice.

"Shay, you always look as hot as hell."

"Hmm. My hair's still growing back, I look like a bloody elf, I'm still a little bruised and you think I'm sexy?" Shane nibbled Matthew's bottom lip, then moved to his ear.

"You are beautiful, baby. Inside and out."

"Talking of inside and out...where were we?" he murmured softly as he bit at Matthew's neck, sucking the skin. "I seem to recall a certain someone feeling very needy—ah, there he is." His hands slid down, grasping his lover's warm and very rampant erection, wrapping his hands around it and squeezing. Matthew's breath ghosted against his neck, raising goose bumps on his skin.

Shane reached for the lube which had been hidden down the side of the couch after their last session. He rubbed some in his hands, and rubbed it slowly along Matthew's shaft, over his balls, reaching in and lathering it onto him. His lover's body tensed, his back straining against the back of the couch at the sensation. Shane's mouth found Matthew's and as his tongue slid into his boyfriend's mouth, he sank down onto Matthew, taking him inside delicious inch by inch. He simply wanted to feel his man inside him, no preamble needed. He'd just take it slowly. Matthew's hands reached out desperately to stroke him as Shane settled on top of him

"God, Shay. That feels good." Matthew's agonised and whispered moans incited Shane to sink deeper, taking Matthew in then out, driving his body deeper and deeper onto Matthew. His lover pushed upward with each stroke, his breath deep, his eyes wild as Shane moved atop him. The feeling of Matthew inside, all silk and heat, hearing his man's moans of pleasure as Shane made love to him, made Shane feel complete. Matthew's hand stroked Shane, fingers tightening and pressing against his sensitive flesh as Shane felt his lover pulse and throb inside him, inside that sensitive channel that gave such pleasure and made his groin burn with feeling. He drove himself deeper down onto the other man, and Matthew groaned loudly.

"You know how to work me, don't you, you brat…"

His voice trailed off as he heaved a deep breath and arched his back against the couch back as a hot jet stream of his semen shot into Shane, the smell of sex permeating the room. Matthew's shout of pleasure echoed in the room even as Shane muffled it with his mouth. He wasn't far himself, his own hardness swelling in Matthew's strong and experienced grip, as he tensed his body, pressing himself against Matthew's belly with a groan. His wet heat left his body and jetted across Matthew's naked stomach and chest. They both collapsed, satiated, Shane once again sandwiched against Matthew's sticky, wet chest. After a few seconds of getting their breath back to normal, Shane pulled away, hearing Matthew's murmur of protest at him leaving. He looked into his boyfriend's eyes, holding his gaze and then slowly, deliberately, Shane moved down Matthew's body, licking at the semen on his chest, performing the act that Matty normally did for him. It was the first time he'd done this, and he had to say, it felt good. Matthew's pupils dilated as Shane licked him clean and Shane could swear Matty was already getting hard again. He could feel it.

"Jesus Christ, Shay…" His lover's whisper was awestruck, disbelieving. He watched as Shane made his way down his chest, across the muscles of his stomach and down toward his groin. Shane's tongue slowly, lovingly licked the fluid off his lover and occasionally bit lightly, causing Matthew to strain and swear loudly at each nip. Finally he was done and he crawled back up to take Matthew's lips in a tender kiss. His boyfriend wrapped warm arms around him, responding with a passion and a need that make Shane breathless. Finally they were spent, and Shane pulled his bruised lips away to smile into his lover's eyes.

"I take it you liked that, then?"

Matthew's voice was choked when he replied. "No one's done that for me since—" Shane knew it had been Sam that had taught this act of love and that had probably been the last time this had happened to him.

"I'm glad I could oblige. I rather liked it. We *will* be doing that again." He grinned as Matthew swallowed. "Now, I am getting bloody frostbite in my nether regions sitting here, so I suggest a hot shower, maybe a blow job or two if we can manage it after this session, then bed."

Matthew needed no urging as Shane slid off him and made his way to the bathroom. He heard Matthew chuckle behind him as he followed.

"You're insatiable," were the words he heard as he started the wet room shower, and stepped inside. Matthew stood framed against the bathroom doorway, his smile infectious. "But I do like it." He stepped inside, under the cascading water and raised wet hands to cup Shane's face. "I love you, Shay. You're mine and I'm yours. That's never going to change, you know that, don't you? No matter how many arguments we might have, seeing as we are who we are."

Shane lost his breath as he gazed into the grey eyes of his soul mate.

"I feel the same, Matty," he whispered as he leaned in to kiss the other man. "Always."

Redemption and Release

The next morning after a fairly hectic bout of lovemaking, Shane lay nestled against Matthew, his blond hair spread out over Matthew's stomach. Matthew stroked it gently as he wondered how to word the request he had. He was uncomfortably certain that his lover was going to make a meal of it.

"Shay? Are you asleep?"

Shane shifted slightly under the duvet and nodded. "Uh- huh. Trying anyway." The movement of his lips against Matthew's stomach tickled. Shane reached out a lazy hand and drew it slowly down Matthew's hip. "Why do you ask anyway now that you've woken me up?"

"I was thinking." There was a deep chuckle against Matthew's still warm and sweating skin.

"Always a bad sign, Matty. Do I have to screw you again to stop you pondering whatever it is you're pondering?"

Matthew laughed. "I'll never refuse an offer like that one— hell, hang on, for God's sake!" Shane's hand had wandered down to his groin and grasped him in warm fingers. Matthew choked back a breath at the feel of them wrapped around his already-rising cock. "I didn't mean right now, you horny sod. I need to ask you something."

"So ask." Shane's hands stayed where they were, flicking the tip of him. Matthew shuddered in pleasure. "Shay, please. I'm trying to be serious."

His boyfriend gave a deep sigh and sat up. His hands moved off Matthew's groin, leaving him feeling a little bereft. The bedcovers fell to Shane's waist as he regarded Matthew with a frown. Matthew could see the love bites he'd made from their earlier session, marking Shane's honey-coloured skin like dark blemishes on a peach. He felt a sense of satisfaction at seeing his lover marked in such a way. Shane raised an eyebrow.

"So? I'm awake and you've told me off for playing with you. Spill it."

"I need your help in getting payback on Walter." Matthew said the words quickly and watched his lover's face. He wasn't disappointed. Shane's eyes gleamed with a sudden predatory light.

"You want to get that twat back for his part in all this crap?" He sat back against the headboard, a small smile growing on his face. "And how do you think we should do that, Matthew? How can I help you?"

"You know bloody well what I'm going to ask you to do," Matthew growled as Shane's smile grew wider. "So stop looking so damned smug."

Shane raised his palms outwards with a shrug, a look of obvious enjoyment at Matthew's discomfort on his face. "Matty, babe, I have no idea what you're talking about. You'd better spell it out for me." His boyfriend's satisfied grin made Matthew's toes curl. He scowled as he huffed.

"You know I didn't have anything to do with Walter's bank accounts or his finances other than the one in the Cayman Islands—the one that you stole money out of," he said bitingly, watching Shane's grin grow even bigger.

God, the man was insufferable. He was really *enjoying this.*

"It's actually the only legitimate offshore bank account Walter had, which is why I knew about it. But the man has a raft of lawyers and brokers sticking his money all over the place. Who knows how dodgy it all is? This is Walter after all."

Shane shifted and raised an enquiring eyebrow. "And this involves me how?" He sniggered as Matthew slapped his arm in frustration, leaving a mark. "Babe, violence never solved anything. Not unless you fancy slapping my arse. Now *that* I can deal with."

Matthew's cock twitched at that thought of slapping Shane's backside until it was pink and rosy. It certainly had its attractions. Shane glanced down at the tenting duvet cover where Matthew lay and caressed what was under it softly.

"You like that idea," he murmured with a leer. "I'll put it on the menu for later."

Matthew was slowly losing control of this conversation. "Shay," he growled again. He pushed his lover's hand away from his hardened member. "I want you to find some dirt on him that we can send to the authorities. Maybe that will land Walter in jail where he belongs."

Shane chuckled. "I was just teasing you. But there is something you need to consider." He leaned forward earnestly. "We can't do this to send Walter to prison."

Matthew stared at him in disbelief. "Why the hell not? "

Shane shook his head. "David. We can't be the ones responsible for sending his dad to jail. It would kill him and any relationship we have with him. And he'll never agree to us doing this. You know he won't."

Matthew felt his heart sink. Shane was right. David might have been able to deal with the blackmail situation but Matthew had seen the look of relief on David's face when his father had capitulated back at the Debussy house and returned his son's trust fund. He wasn't sure if David would have had the guts to take it the step further as they'd threatened.

"I hadn't thought of that, how bloody stupid of me. I was so gung ho to get him some justice I forgot about David. Shit." He ran a hand over his stubbled chin. "So what now then? We just leave the bastard to carry on living the life of Riley?" Matthew's voice grew fierce. "He doesn't deserve to get away scot-free, Shay. Not after what he did to you. Because no matter what he says, he played a part in Roy hurting you like he did. And my dad, I'm sure of it."

Shane nodded sadly. "I don't think we have a choice. I can't even send an anonymous tip to anyone. If David found out about it I'd be his number one suspect. And I don't want to lose him, Matty. He's one of the Gay Musketeers, too."

Matthew nodded and sighed. "I guess we need to forget the whole idea then."

Shane moved closer to Matthew, his eyes darkened. "I have to say I like this side to you," he murmured. "The whole 'Avenging Angel' thing is pretty hot." He leaned forward, pressing his naked body against Matthew's chest, and his lips took Matthew's. Matthew closed his eyes at the feel of his boyfriend's mouth on his, hungry and demanding. Shane tasted of sex, spice and pure lust. His tongue probed Matthew's mouth like a small fish trying to find a place to hide. Matthew moaned as Shane chuckled against his lips.

"Can I play with you now, Matty?" he whispered as his hands slid underneath the covers and once again Matthew felt a firm grip around his aching cock. Matthew could only gasp as Shane then slid down his body, pushing away the covers and took him in his mouth. He lay back, watching Shane's head bob up and down as he devoured Matthew with practised moves and very obvious enjoyment. Matthew closed his eyes and gave into the havoc his lover was wreaking upon his body. There was time for more talk later. Right now it was playtime.

A week later Shane and Matthew sat together in an Italian restaurant with a group of friends. Everyone who meant anything in Shane and Matthew's life was gathered around the table.

Timmy, David and Marco sat to one side, Julia and Bartholomew the other. Food smells wafted over the restaurant making Matthew's mouth water. They'd finished their starters and were about to tuck into their mains. David swallowed a mouthful of lasagne and waved his fork as he opened his mouth to speak, narrowly missing hitting Timmy in the eye. The big man shook his head in amusement.

"David, my friend, you and that fork are a dangerous combination. That is now the second time you have nearly poked my eye out."

David finished his mouthful as the rest of the diners chuckled. "Sorry, Timmy. I wanted to ask Matthew what happened when he went to see that prick Roy. I've been waiting for an update. I think we all have."

The table fell quiet as Matthew and Shane looked at each other.

Shane toyed with the stem of his wineglass. "When we met him in the prison to find out why he said what he'd said, he was a prick just as you'd expect."

Matthew clasped his lover's warm hand as it sat on top of the table. The meeting had not been easy for Shane. He'd been tough as nails the whole time he'd sat there in front of the man who had tried to kill him, but when he'd left the small room, he'd fallen apart. Matthew had to make him sit down as his panic attack had taken hold of him. Shane continued his story.

"When Matthew asked him about his dad's death the bastard actually laughed." He took a deep breath. Matthew's hand tightened on Shane's. This part of the conversation had been hard for him too. "I honestly thought Matty was going to deck him."

Matthew sighed. "I restrained myself because I didn't want to soil my hands with the likes of that animal." His eyes gazed at the tabletop, focused on the salt pot in the middle of the table. "Roy went to talk to my dad to convince him not to go to the police with

Walter's videotape. My dad said nothing he said could change his mind. So Roy told him he'd come after me." He paused then his voice quietened. "Well, you don't want to know what he intended doing to me."

Shane and he had sat sickened whilst Roy was spouting his disgusting profanities involving various blunt implements, Matthew's backside and a well-aimed baseball bat, obviously Roy's preferred weapon of choice.

"My dad got upset that he was threatening me. Then Roy shoved him against the wall and that was it. Dad had a heart attack." Matthew gazed down at the table as Shane's hand caressed his. "Roy just watched and waited for my dad to die. He knew that if that happened, Walter's problems were over. Of course, he never thought that my dad might have sent me a copy. That never crossed his mind. If it had, or if my dad had told him, things might have been different." He shrugged. "But it didn't happen. When dad was dead Roy just walked out. He didn't even call an ambulance or anything. He just fucking left my father lying there." His voice tightened. The thought of his father dying alone and in fear for his son was something he could never forgive or forget. He raised his eyes to Bartholomew who sat stock still. "Sorry, Shane's potty mouth is rubbing off on me."

David opened his mouth with a grin to say something, but Marco shook his head slightly at his boyfriend, his dark eyes soft. David's mouth closed. Bartholomew leaned over and touched Matthew's hand.

"Nothing I haven't heard before, Matthew. What happened then? What can the police do about all this?"

Matthew shrugged. "The police say there's not much they can do about it. My dad died a natural death; even though it was provoked and there's not much they can do about it. But his attempted murder trial is coming up, and with Shay and Timmy testifying, we're hoping he'll spend a long time in prison." His face twisted. "I hope someone makes him their boyfriend."

Timmy's face darkened. "I too felt the same way when I found you on the pavement. I have never wanted to hurt a man as badly as that night." He scowled.

Shane smiled at him. "My hero. I know I've said it before but thanks for that. If you hadn't come out when you did…" He shivered. "Things might be a little different."

Timmy grinned, white teeth in his dark face. "The Zulu people have a saying: 'Darkness conceals the hippopotamus.'"

There was stunned silence at this rather profound statement.

Shane was the first one to speak. "What the fuck does that mean?"

Matthew shook his head even as he tried to control his laughter at the confusion in Shane's voice and the bad language.

Timmy laughed loudly. "It means, Shanester, that he might have accomplished what he wanted to do. But I would never have rested until I had found him, and beaten the hippo out of the dark into the light. He could not hide forever." He smiled wolfishly. "Then I would have had my revenge."

The table was silent and Shane reached over and took Timmy's hand. "Thanks for that, Timmy." His voice sounded choked. "I'm glad I made it. The thought of you in London hunting a hippopotamus boggles the brain."

The table erupted into laughter. After it had died down, Matthew leaned forward.

"Walter of course denies all knowledge about the whole thing. He says he never told Roy to go see Dad."

Bartholomew nodded. "Did you all see Debussy on the TV a couple of days ago, when that reporter was interviewing him about his connection to Roy Parsons?"

Everyone nodded. They had indeed seen the footage of the unfortunate interviewer being given the full force of Walter's ire and looking as if he wanted to hit the young man.

David looked down at the table as he spoke, his fingers straightening an imaginary crease in the tablecloth. "He said he had no idea that Roy was capable of such violence and that he was a vicious little psychopath who belonged in prison." He gave a harsh laugh. "He's a consummate bloody liar, my dad. How could he say that after what he let Roy do to me?" His voice trembled.

Marco leaned over and covered his lover's hands with his. "David, he's out of your life. You have me now." The two men smiled at each other with affection.

Matthew regarded them both. "Of course, the only thing Walter *was* worried about was the video getting out as revenge for Roy's attack on Shane." Matthew's voice quietened. "While I'd love to make him pay for what he did, that's not how I operate. The bastard will never pay for that discretion or any others, as much as I wish I could see him behind bars." Matthew looked at David. "Sorry, David, I know he's your father."

"He's not my father." David said. His face was hard. "Any more than Lewis is my brother. But I'm glad you feel that way. It's time this whole sordid story was put to rest. I don't really want to see my dad go to prison. I just want to forget it all."

Matthew looked at Shane as they shared a secret glance, remembering their earlier conversation. Marco's face was wreathed in sympathy.

"Maybe one day things will be different, *mi amor*," he murmured softly.

David shook his head. "Never," he said grimly.

Shane shifted. He looked uncomfortable. "David, despite everything, maybe you shouldn't be like me and give up on him. My dad seems to have changed. At least we're talking now."

Matthew smiled softly. Shane and Ray were indeed "in dialogue" as Shane called it haughtily, and things seemed to be getting better each week. At least Shane had accepted that his father might be trying to make amends. He was still prickly about it, but Matthew knew he was at least now willing to try and speak to his father. It wouldn't be an easy task for Ray to mend the bridges with his son, but the future looked rosier than it had.

The other good news was that no one seemed to have connected Shane with the hack on the adoption centre. Matthew was quite sure if he'd been found out, he'd already have been questioned by the police—or worse, by Neil Busby and his team. It was small comfort but the longer it was quiet, the easier he breathed. There was nothing else he could do about that. Shane was confident they never would find him, and that was good enough for him.

David shook his head. "It's not going to happen. But I appreciate the sentiment. If I ever need to talk to anyone about it I know who to come to." He smiled gratefully at Shane.

Bartholomew leaned forward and touched Matthew's arm. "It's a terrible story, Matthew. But your father spoke to you from beyond the grave eventually, and Roy is now brought to justice."

"But if he hadn't tried to kill Shane, we'd never have known any of this." Matthew's voice was harsh. "I'd rather have never known anything about it than have Shane hurt like he was."

"But I'm fine now, Matty, and Roy is in custody." Shane kissed his boyfriend's cheek. "The headaches are getting better, my ribs are healed and I'm almost normal." He grinned. "At least as close to normal as I can get."

Julia had been sitting quietly spellbound at the tale unfolding at the table. She giggled now, alleviating some of the tenseness at the table. "That isn't a word I'd use to describe either of you. You are two infuriating, exasperating men. But I do love you both." She looked at Matthew. "When do you leave for Dresden, Matthew, for your holiday?"

Shane leaned forward, his eyes shining, interrupting Matthew as he was about to reply. "In a couple of weeks' time. We leave from London City and then it's time for two weeks of doing nothing. It's going to be great. I get to meet Matty's mom, and his sister is flying in from wherever she is to see us, too. We're going to take a boat down the Elbe. Matty promised me he'd take me to see the sunset in Saxon, Switzerland from the top of the mountains as well. Apparently that's quite something to see." He stopped aware everyone was looking at him.

"Thank you, oh Saxony tourist guide," Matthew said drily. He grinned at Julia and cocked a thumb in Shane's direction. "What he said. We're going to stay at the family home and then I can take this one sightseeing before he self-combusts with excitement." He leered. "Although, Shay, what's going to happen to you when you hear all that German being spoken around you, I dread to think. I think I might be in for a hard time."

The table roared with laughter and Shane grinned.

Two days later Shane was dressing to go out to dinner with Matthew as he watched the news on TV. He froze as he heard a familiar name being mentioned. On the TV screen was a static shot of the scowling visage of Walter Debussy outside his office building, flanked by two burly and official-looking men. Shane felt a shiver of disgust run down his spine at the sight of the man. He called out to Matthew who was still in the bathroom.

"Matty? You might want to see this. There's something going on with that wanker Debussy on telly."

He heard a clatter as Matthew finished whatever he was busy with. His boyfriend hurried out of the bathroom, a towel wrapped down his waist and the traces of shaving cream still on his face. He looked anxious.

"Why are they interviewing him? Have I missed anything?"

Shane shook his head. "It's just started. Listen."

He picked up the remote and turned up the volume. The young red-headed reporter was standing outside the Debussy offices as she delivered her news.

"Earlier this morning, Walter Debussy was arrested on alleged charges of tax evasion, money laundering and fraud. He has been taken into custody for questioning. It's not quite known how this has all come to light, but sources say that an ex-employee of Mr. Debussy's has come forward to give privileged information regarding Mr. Debussy's business affairs. It is not known for sure who this might be, but rumours are circulating that the person assisting police with their enquiries is Mr. Roy Parsons. Mr. Parsons is currently in custody awaiting trial for attempted murder and various other GBH-related offences. We haven't been given any other information at this time but as we get the news, you can be sure we will let you, the public, know. This is Morgan Wentworth reporting for UBN News."

Shane and Matthew gazed at each other in wonder.

"Unbelievable." Shane's voice was awed. "That arsehole Roy spilt the beans about Debussy? I didn't see that one coming." He looked at his lover who was standing stock still, his jaw still dropped open. Shane chuckled and moved to nudge it shut with his hand. He cleaned the shaving cream off Matthew's face with his finger.

"Earth to Matty. It seems like you got your wish, lover. Walter is going to prison. And I had nothing to do with it." He smirked. "Maybe there is justice in this world after all."

Matthew huffed as he tightened his towel which was threatening to fall off. Shane watched with interest. Matthew saw the direction of his eyes and grabbed the towel tighter. "Maybe Roy didn't like what Walter said about him on television. It might have pissed him off to see that after all he'd done for him, Walter didn't give a crap about him." He frowned. "I wonder what they promised Roy to get the information? Maybe he's going to get a reduced sentence or something. God, that means he might not spend all that much time behind bars." His face tightened. "What if he gets out soon and comes after you again? I couldn't bear anything happening to you—"

Shane leaned in and shut his lover up with a fierce kiss. When he pulled away he brushed Matthew's face gently with his fingers.

"You're overthinking things. We don't even know yet how long the man's going to prison for. The trial is still looming." He grimaced. "And I'm not looking forward to it. But let's see what happens before you start worrying."

He pulled Matthew to him for a hug, feeling his boyfriend relax into him, his breath tickling his neck as Shane kissed his cheek.

"David's going to be devastated about his dad. We'll go see him tomorrow. But I for one am glad that smarmy wanker has got his comeuppance. Now come on, babe. Dress that sexy arse of yours and let's go to dinner."

It was almost midnight when Shane and Matthew left the restaurant. Shane's flat wasn't far, so they'd decided to walk. It was still a crisp, January night and the air was frosty and cold. Matthew held Shane close as they walked together down the darkened street. They were comfortable in their silence, making the occasional comment but happy to simply enjoy each other's nearness. When they got into the flat, Shane shrugged off his trendy lambs-wool jacket, and turned to Matthew.

"Do you want a drink?" Matthew nodded his assent and Shane poured two large whiskies from the lounge mini bar. He handed one to Matthew, who had subsided gratefully onto the couch.

"That was a good evening. I like wining and dining you."

Shane grinned as he sat cross-legged next to the other man. "I like being a kept man. Feel free to continue."

Matthew chuckled. "That makes me sound like your sugar daddy." He saw the twinkle in Shane's eyes and him open his mouth to say something. Matthew laid a quick finger against his lover's lips. "Don't you dare call me 'Daddy.' That's one endearment I won't take to." He sipped his drink. He stood up suddenly as he remembered something.

"I have been meaning to give you something since you came out of hospital. Let me go get it."

"You've been giving me something quite regularly since I came out of hospital, Matty," Shane called after him. "I can hardly bloody sit down."

Matthew shook his head in amusement as he walked back into the room carrying an A4-sized brightly wrapped package. It was gold Christmas paper, with red and green reindeers emblazoned across it. Shane raised an eyebrow.

"Reindeers? What am I, ten? You couldn't find a nice, tasteful adult paper, like naked buff Santa Claus guys?"

"Open it." Matthew's voice sounded slightly unsure of itself and Shane glanced at him in surprise. He ripped the paper off and sat there, staring down at what he held in his hands. Matthew swallowed.

"Do you like it?" he asked. "I wasn't sure whether it was your sort of thing, but you liked the other ones I did, so I thought maybe one of your very own would be—umph."

His words were muffled by the sudden leap of his boyfriend into his arms, latching his mouth onto Matthew's with a fierceness that told Matthew that Shane did indeed like his belated Christmas present. He wrapped his arms around his lover as he was thoroughly kissed. When he finally let him go, gasping for breath, Shane's eyes were shining with tears.

"It's beautiful, Matty. I love it. When did you find the time to do this?" He reached over and picked up the watercolour-rendered picture of him and Matthew standing hand-in-hand on the South Bank, windswept hair, laughing at each other. An old lady had been asked to take the picture. She'd said they were the most beautifully romantic couple she'd ever seen.

Matthew shrugged. "I did the one of just you for my bedroom at home—" he stopped as he realised Shane hadn't been to his house yet since coming out of hospital. They'd been so comfortable at his apartment it hadn't seemed necessary. Shane's eyes were wide.

"Then I did this one. I was going to give you the other one for a Christmas present but I decided I wanted that for myself. So I did this one for you instead."

"It's stunning, Matty. I really love it. It's so...us." Shane caressed the picture. He looked uncomfortable. Matthew frowned.

"What's wrong, babe? You seem out of sorts."

Shane took a deep breath and scooted out of the room. Matthew heard him in the bedroom, the sound of drawers being opened and low muttering as Shane hunted for what he wanted. Matthew grinned. The man wasn't the neatest tool in the store. Finally he appeared, brandishing a small, silver-wrapped present, the size of an A5 picture frame.

"I did this for you for Christmas, before I ended up in hospital," he whispered softly. "I wasn't sure whether I should give it to you, if you'd be mad with me again. I didn't want to chance it, because I couldn't bear it if you were." He took a deep breath. "I'm still not sure I should give this to you."

Matthew could see his boyfriend's hands shaking. He reached over and took the gift.

"Shay, honey, I promise no matter what it is, I won't get mad. Those days of us being pissed off at each other are gone." He saw Shane's amused smile. "Okay, the days of *me* being pissed off with *you* are over." He unwrapped the present and when it was open, he took a deep breath. It was the picture of a little girl, about two years old, with dark eyes, a crop of beautiful brown hair and a smile that could have melted the heart of a stone queen.

Shane said quietly, "You said you never knew what happened to Emily. I could see that it tore you up inside. Well, she's fine, Matty. She's with a couple who love the hell out of her, who give her everything she needs, and she's happy, Matty. That smile tells you that. You needed closure on that chapter of your life. I thought maybe if you could see what she looks like and see how happy she is you might get that."

His voice tailed off. Matthew's shoulders were shaking and the steady drop of his tears onto the picture frame made small sounds as they fell. Matthew thought his heart would break. He thought wryly that it seemed to be becoming a regular thing. He'd wondered so long what had happened to the little baby he and Sam would have adopted. He'd wondered whether she was safe, whether she was with people who loved her as much as he and Sam would have loved her. He'd lain awake at night wondering what she looked like, whether she was happy. And now the proof of it sat in his hands. Proof given to him by a man who had delved deep into his soul and found out his most unanswered question. He didn't care how Shane had found this all out, only that he cared enough to have done so. He must have done it when he found out about the adoption, before Matthew had asked him to leave. It made Matthew's action all the more reprehensible and he wanted to beg Shane's forgiveness once more. But that ship had sailed, and he had to move on rather than rehash his past mistakes. He was learning.

Shane sat down next to him, his face anxious. "Christ, Matty, I didn't mean to upset you so much. I'm sorry, babe, I thought it might help."

Matthew looked up, his face streaked with tears, and gazed into the deep blue eyes that stared at him with such love and misery in equal part that he wanted to hold him and never let him go. Matthew ran one loving hand down the front of the frame, raised it to his lips and kissed it, then put it down on the table. The little girl stared out across the living room, that joyous smile never waning.

"Shay, you incorrigible, wonderful and loving man, if you don't take me to bed right now and let me thank you, I'm going to have to do it for you." His voice was husky and he saw the relief in Shane's eyes as he realised Matthew was fine with it. More than fine. "I have this overwhelming desire to get up close and personal and show you just how much I appreciate your Christmas present." He stood up and reached for Shane, pulling him into his arms and wrapping them around his lover tightly.

"*Ich liebe dich,*" he breathed into Shane's ear. He knew he didn't even have to translate the words for Shane. He saw the tenderness in his lover's eyes as the other man stood up and held out his hand. Matthew took it. His lover smiled as he led the way to the bedroom. Matthew turned back briefly to see the picture and the smile again. That chapter of his life was over. Sam and Emily were the past. The man who held his heart and everything else that was important, the man who was leading the way out of this last darkness—he was Matthew's future.

The End

Author's Notes

I really enjoyed the research for this book. Despite the fact that this is a romance novel, I still think authors have a responsibility to make sure what they write about has factual substance. I can assure you I know nothing about hacking; Shane certainly knows more than I do. But a mysterious presence on the other side of Twitter gave me a little background. As for the sex research, this was one of the more pleasurable parts of the job. A certain gentleman I know warned me I was in danger of going blind if I watched any more. So I hope I managed to make the sessions between Shane and Matthew realistic. *grins*

About the Author

Sue Mac Nicol was born in Leeds, Yorkshire, in the United Kingdom. At the age of eight, her family moved to Johannesburg, South Africa, where she stayed for nearly thirty years before arriving back in the UK in December 2000.

Sue works full time in the field of regulatory compliance for a company in the financial services industry in Cambridge, but she still finds time to work until the small hours of the night doing what she loves best: writing. Since her first novel, *Cassandra by Starlight,* was penned, introducing the debonair Bennett Saville and his lovely lady, Cassie Wallace, Sue has since written the other two books in her *Starlight* trilogy.

She currently has five further novels completed, and at various stages of publication, ranging from two rather sexy gay male romances, her current passion, plus a paranormal suspense series and an erotic crime thriller. She enjoys the element of gay male romance in her books and this thread runs many of them, including her *Starlight* series. Her passion is keeping herself busy creating worlds and characters for her readers to enjoy.

Sue is a member of Romance Writers of America and Romantic Novelists Association in the UK. She is also a member of a rather unique writing group called the Talliston Writers Circle, which in itself has a story all of its own to tell.

She lives in the rural village of Bocking, in Essex, with her family. Her plan is to keep writing as long as her muse sits upon her shoulder. Her dream is to one day be able to give up the day job and get that big old house in the English countryside overlooking a river, where she can write all day and continue to indulge her passion for telling stories.

Boroughs
Publishing Group

Did you enjoy this book? Drop us a line and say so! We love to hear from readers, and so do our authors. To connect, visit www.boroughspublishinggroup.com online, send comments directly to info@boroughspublishinggroup.com, or friend us on Facebook and Twitter. And be sure to check back regularly for contests and new releases in your favorite subgenres of romance!

Are you an aspiring writer? Check out www.boroughspublishinggroup.com/submit and see if we can help you make your dreams come true.

www.ingramcontent.com/pod-product-compliance
Lightning Source LLC
Chambersburg PA
CBHW062016170626
46813CB00001B/179